"Phil was horrified to l... large hole in the wing. Brad... the plane back to the airport."

"Suddenly he shoved the nose of the plane down and at the last minute before hitting the ground he pulled back hard on the control wheel, pulling the nose of the plane back up."

"What do you mean? —She won't take second place to his love of flying."

"Jim executed the play perfectly, but as Phil caught the ball, his attention was suddenly caught by something bright and golden to his right. He stopped and stared at the most beautiful girl he had ever seen."

"Phil covered his face with his hands trying to block the scene of the crash out of his mind. He thought of Sue. He knew they would be notifying her soon and she was by herself. She would be devastated."

"He looked down at her. The greenish blue eyes seemed to have a bewitching glint in them that fascinated him. She pulled him down on the sofa and kissed him passionately."

SECOND FIDDLE

by

Lester Mitchell

This is a work of fiction. Any resemblance of any of the characters
to persons living or dead is strictly coincidental.

FIRST EDITION

AEGINA PRESS, Inc.
59 Oak Lane, Spring Valley
Huntington, West Virginia 25704

Cover by Charles Persinger

Dedication

This novel is dedicated to my daughter, Lueann Duke, for her encouragement and assistance and also to my nephew, Greg Futrelle, for without his expertise in literary instruction and efforts in editing and redrafting SECOND FIDDLE, it would not be as complete as submitted.

Chapter One

A thin, reddish cloud of dust threatened to catch Philip Barkley as he raced his bicycle along the dirt road toward the town of Kenly where his buddies were waiting at Red Ballard's grocery store. The road was level and well maintained by the county road crews, so pedaling wasn't very difficult for a young man in good physical shape. Since the bicycle was gliding smoothly along, he had become deeply engrossed in thinking of the latest episodes of Buck Rogers' flying adventures in the Buck Rogers comic magazines that he had recently read. Phil had become greatly infatuated with flying since he had recently gone up in a small plane and read every airplane book and Buck Rogers magazine he could get his hands on.

He vaguely noticed the town limit sign on the side of the road slide by. Suddenly, his mind was jolted by the thought of possibly meeting a beautiful girl that he had seen the last time he was in town with his friends. With great anticipation, he urged the bicycle faster. Even though a bicycle was better than walking, it still annoyed Phil that he didn't have a car for dating. Of course, in the fall of 1939, not even many adults owned cars. But Phil had a plan, and if his friends agreed to pitch in, they would soon be riding around on wheels that didn't have to be pedaled. As he coasted past the two-story brick building that housed the bank and a lawyer's office, Phil could begin to make out the sound of music coming from the record machine at Cash Corner. Kenly was a peaceful village surrounded mostly by tobacco and cotton farms in eastern North Carolina. With a main street only five blocks long, a visitor might be surprised to find a post office, movie theater, a fish market, and a few general merchandise stores in such a small town. But even more surprising would be the number of local teenagers who spent the warm autumn weekend afternoons swinging and swaying on the outdoor dance floor behind Red Ballard's store which was located about one-half mile north of the edge of town. Red was one of those savvy merchants who made it through the depression by knowing what was currently popular and offering it to his customers. In one corner of his store was a pool table. A sandwich counter filled another space. And outside, he had a gasoline pump. To the teenagers however, the most important item at Red's was the record machine on the dance platform. Most kids called it a "nickelodeon" because you could play one song for a nickel. Some called it a piccolo. Red made sure the latest, most popular records were in the machine, and the kids made sure it never stayed quiet. The only thing that never changed at Red's place was his refusal to extend credit to anyone, even his own family. That's why it came to be called

5

Cash Corner.

When Phil turned his bike into the parking lot at Red's place, he spied his best friend, Roland Varnes, and Roland's younger brother George, standing next to Bert Smith's '38 Ford convertible. Bert's father was a doctor and could afford such luxuries as giving his son a car on his sixteenth birthday. As usual, the car was loaded with girls. Phil chuckled at the thought that in a few weeks the girls might be flocking around another car . . . one with him in the driver's seat instead of Bert.

"What's going on, gang?" Phil greeted the group as he skidded to a stop only inches from Bert's fender.

"Hey! Watch where you're kicking up dirt," Bert protested as a cloud of dust settled over the side of his car.

"Sorry, Bert. I'm just glad I could stop in time." Phil looked at Roland and winked. "I'd sure hate to dent the fender on this old jalopy."

Roland and George laughed. A couple of the girls said, "Hi, Phil," in unison and then giggled at each other. Another asked him for a hug. Bert rolled his eyes toward the sky as Phil obliged the young ladies. What he had to tell Roland and George could wait at least a few more moments.

Most of the girls around Kenly competed for Phil's attention. At just over six feet, he was taller than most boys his age. His dark and wavy brown hair framed a finely chiseled face that was highlighted by a pair of chocolate colored eyes. But his smile might have been Phil's best feature. Sometimes it was like a sunrise, slowly bathing a person with a warm sense of sincerity. Other times it was like a beacon, flashing a row of perfectly white teeth while the corner of his lips tilted a bit to reveal a hint of mischief. Phil's trim, athletic physique was kept in shape through hard work on his father's farm and playing every sport that Kenly High School offered. Having to ride a bicycle everywhere he went didn't hurt either. His good looks and charming personality had earned Phil a reputation as a ladies man, but all the girls knew that he was also a gentleman. Every young lady around the area had, at one time or another, written Barkley as her last name, just to see what it would look like when she and Phil were married.

"How about dancing with me, Phil?" asked one of the girls.

"That would be great, love," he replied. "But let me catch my breath first, okay? I need to talk to Roland and George for a few moments. But as soon as we're through, I'm coming right back to sweep you off your feet."

"More likely he'll sweep the floor with you," Bert muttered.

"Now, Bert," Phil mockingly scolded. "If you were a real gentleman, you'd offer to put some money in the nickelodeon for our dance. If I had your money, that's what I'd do."

Phil and Roland and George walked away chuckling as they

left Bert to contend with the young ladies who seemed to like Phil's idea.

"What's up, Phil?" Roland asked after they had walked a few yards.

"Wouldn't it be great if Bert wasn't the only boy in town with a car?" Phil answered.

"Sure, but who else can afford one?" George said.

"We can!"

"And who's going to drop six hundred dollars in your lap?" asked Roland.

"We don't need six hundred." Phil replied excitedly. "We don't even need one hundred. What would you say if I told you we can get a car for fifteen dollars?"

"I'd say you're dreaming again." Roland chuckled.

"What kind of car?" George asked.

"Mr. Best has a 1923 Model-T Ford touring car parked under a shed behind his house. I was helping him clean up some scrap iron to sell, when he said something about wanting to get rid of the car. I was joking when I asked him how much he'd take for it, but when he answered fifteen dollars, it wasn't a joke anymore. He said it was in good running condition when he put it under the shed three years ago. It has a cloth top which is rotten, but everything else on it looks okay. It needs some work, but between the three of us, there isn't anything wrong with it that we can't fix."

"But where are we going to get the money?" George asked.

"Mr. Best said scrap iron is selling for a penny per pound. The Japanese are buying up as much as they can get their hands on and there is a scrap dealer who comes around here every Saturday morning. Surely we can find enough scrap iron lying around to make fifteen dollars!"

"That's not a bad idea, Phil!" Roland was beginning to get excited about the prospect of having a car. "Can we go look at it before we say yes?"

"Sure. We can go over to his house tomorrow. If you boys like the idea after you've seen the car, we'll give Mr. Best five dollars to hold it for us until we can come up with the rest. So bring your money just in case you like the car. Does that sound okay?"

"You bet!" George exclaimed.

"Yeah," Roland chimed in, "It will be great having something besides a bike to get around with."

"You said it, pal," Phil concluded. "Well, I think we have some young ladies waiting for us to show them how to dance." He winked at the Varnes brothers and they were off to con Bert out of a few nickels for the record machine.

The evening passed slowly for Phil and he often looked around among the group of friends hoping to get a glimpse of the pretty girl again. When it was time for he and his two buddies to go home, he was very disappointed that she had never showed up.

The next morning, a chilly September morning breeze motivated phil to quickly wash his hands and face in the outside sink on the corner of the back porch at the Barkley house. Inside, his grandmother placed a pan of steaming hot biscuits on the kitchen table for breakfast. As the odor of freshly baked bread drifted out the back door and past his nose, Phil could hardly wait to poke a hole in one and fill it with molasses. He looked up from the basin of water at his father returning with a pail of milk in his right hand and a small basket of eggs in his left.

Phil was proud of all his father had done to keep their farm during the Great Depression. Many other farmers in the area had not been so fortunate. Banks had foreclosed on many families while the government had sold some lands right out from under the owners as payment for taxes they owed. Somehow, John Barkley had managed to scrimp together enough each year to keep the money hungry financial wolves at bay. Phil knew it had been doubly tough on his dad after losing his wife and his father three years before. But John Barkley wasn't a quitter and his character had held together his farm and family more than anything else. Granny Barkley had moved in with them when John consolidated his father's farm with his own.

Though some of the neighbors might have considered them rich, the Barkley family was not much better off than most of the people who lived around Kenly. They had a modest, two-story house built of wood that was whitewashed every other year along with the other small surrounding buildings that enclosed tools, equipment, and livestock. The wide porch, with its fancy balustrade and massive concrete steps leading to the front door, wrapped around the house on three sides of the first story, making the house seem larger than it really was. The Barkley home was linked to the dirt road leading into town by a path about one hundred yards long that was lined with crepe myrtle bushes whose red flowers bloomed profusely each year in late spring. John Barkley wasn't a rich man, but he had taken great pains to avoid appearing to be a poor man.

The children had all taken their father's lead. Each one had specific jobs to do around the house and farm. Somehow, they all understood that hanging on during hard times meant pitching in together and putting up with a few inconveniences. Phil worked at odd jobs for neighbors in order to make his spending money. His two younger brothers, the twins, had worn hand-me-downs as long as they could remember. His two sisters had shared a limited wardrobe. Granny promptly mended anything that was ripped or worn through. Phil's socks had so many darns in them that he wondered how much of the original cloth was left in any one pair.

"The important thing," his grandmother always reminded him, "is that you are clean, inside and out. The good Lord doesn't mind if you are poor, but since water is free, there ain't no excuse for being dirty." Phil chuckled to himself as he dried his face and put on a clean shirt before walking into the kitchen for breakfast.

"What do you have planned for today, son?" asked Phil's father as he came in the door a moment later.

"Oh, not much. George and Roland and I are going over to Mr. Best's house to look at an old car he wants to sell."

Mr. Barkley poured the milk from the pail into a large earthenware jar, straining the milk through a piece of finely meshed cloth. "Are you thinking of buying it?"

"Yes, sir. That is, if it doesn't need too much work to make it road worthy."

"Looking for something better to drive for Saturday night dates?" his father asked as he gently scooped cream from the piece of cloth.

"Yes, sir. I kind of like the old pickup truck, but the girls like automobiles better."

"I don't know what's gotten into these young girls today," Granny Barkley chimed in while placing a large jar of homemade strawberry jelly in the center of the table. "When I was a young lady, we weren't allowed to go out on dates. The boys had to come over to your house and about all we could do was sit on the front porch."

"Well, mama," Phil's dad interjected, "I don't imagine some of these town girls have very big front porches like you did." He turned to Phil, winked, and continued, "Where are you going to keep this car, that is, if you buy it?"

"If you don't mind, I thought we could use the shed on the side of your tobacco barn down the path toward the hog pen. We aren't using it for anything, now that all the tobacco has been sold. And we'll have the car fixed before next spring. Is that okay?"

"Sounds reasonable to me, son," Phil's father replied as he poured seven glasses of milk and placed them on the table. "I suppose you'll need to borrow some of my tools too."

"I promise I'll take care of them as if they were mine," Phil answered.

Granny Barkley placed a large dish of scrambled eggs on the table and thought aloud, "It might be nice having an extra way to get to town on Saturday afternoon."

"Now mama, let's not start driving Phil's car before he even gets it," Phil's father said with a smile. "But maybe you can double date with Phil some night, if you'll get old man Clark to ask you out." By that time, all the other children were gathered at the table and were laughing at their father's joke. Granny Barkley playfully hit Phil's father with a dish towel and laughed along with everyone else. When everyone had settled down, John Barkley offered a blessing for the food, and they dug in.

Chapter Two

The following Saturday afternoon, Phil leaned on the railing of the front porch and propped his arm against a chair so he could hold the Buck Rogers comic book in his left hand and munch on a big, red apple with his right. He was a little too old for all the Solar Scout toys and secret decoder rings and rocket pistols that fascinated his younger brothers. But Phil Barkley was still young enough to look forward to each new issue detailing the exploits of his hero from the twenty-fifth century. Each month, for a few hours, Phil imagined he was right beside Buck Rogers, manning the controls of the spaceship, chasing Killer Kane and Ardala through the galaxy, and occasionally getting a kiss from the voluptuous Wilma Deering. And each month, as he closed the comic book, Phil's "adventure" would always end by remembering the one real experience in which he soared above the earth.

Just over a year had passed since the day he flew in the open cockpit of a barnstormer who had passed through Kenly on his way to points south and west. The pilot had flown right over Phil's house one Saturday afternoon when everyone else had gone into town. Phil guessed the plane had landed in the cow pasture on Mr. Campbell's farm, not more than a mile away, and he rode his bike like the wind to see a real plane. George Varnes had already arrived when Phil rode up beside him. There were six pickup trucks parked in the shallow ditch that ran along the side of the road. Their drivers stood near the hood of one truck while wives and children looked on from the back of one truck.

"What's going on, George," Phil asked.

"I don't know, but I think he's trying to get some gas. I don't think he has enough money though."

"Why do you say that?"

"I heard him tell those men he would give anybody a ride for two dollars."

"Are you joking?" Phil exclaimed. His eyes never left the small cub plane as he spoke, taking in every detail of the flying machine.

"Hey George, you have any money with you?"

"Not much . . . why? Wait a minute. Are you thinking about getting in that thing?"

"Sure. Why not?"

After borrowing fifty cents from his buddy, Phil swaggered right up to the pilot and said, "How long can I ride for two dollars?"

The ride lasted almost twenty minutes, but as soon as they lifted off the ground, Phil knew it would never be long enough. As they flew over his father's farm, Phil marveled at how neatly

11

everything appeared when it was laid out below so he could see it all at one time. Then they climbed higher and higher toward the clouds. suddenly, the pilot turned the nose toward the ground and put the plane into a dive. Phil's head was pressed against the back of the firewall between him and the pilot. At first he wanted to scream, thinking of what George had said about running out of gas. But as the ground came closer, Phil could feel the plane's nose inching up so that when they finally pulled up, the plane had a swooping effect over everything below.

"Did you like that?" the pilot yelled over the roaring engine.

"Yeah!" Phil replied. "That was great!"

"Are you strapped in up there?"

"Yes, sir."

"Well hold on tight and we'll do a loop. If you start feeling sick, raise your hand. Okay?"

Phil replied, but knew he wouldn't be sick. The only thought in his mind kept repeating itself over and over . . . I want to do this for the rest of my life.

When they landed, Phil swore George not to ever tell a soul about his experience. He knew his father wouldn't approve, not because it was such a daring act, but because he would see it as a waste of money. At that point, George admired Phil so much he probably would have followed Phil over a cliff, so he promised not to tell.

"I swear, Phil. It will be our secret. But what was it like?"

"Little buddy, it is like nothing you have ever done in your whole life. The countryside looks like a big quilt with everyone's farms all stitched together. Everything looks so tiny from up there. But the best part was the acrobatics. You've just gotta do it someday, George. Your stomach floats around and every nerve in your body tingles when you do a loop. I can't wait to do it again."

From that day forward, Phil Barkley knew he wanted to be a pilot. For now, he could be content to read Buck Rogers comic books. But someday, he would find a way to fly a plane of his own.

As phil drew deeper into his comic book, he didn't hear Roland and George creeping up behind him. Suddenly, a loud "bang" on the porch beside him nearly scared him out of his skin.

"Ha, ha. Gotcha Phil," Roland howled as he held his stomach with one hand and pointed at Phil with his other.

"You should have seen how far you came up off that porch," George chimed in. "I thought you were going to hit the ceiling."

"I'll get you two for that," Phil said as he jumped off the porch and began chasing Roland.

The Varnes brothers lived on the farm that adjoined the

Barkley property. Phil and Roland had been inseparable friends since they were small boys. George was three years younger than his brother and the two older boys had never minded having him tag along anywhere they went. Roland Varnes was a few inches shorter than Phil, but had the same, muscular physique. His jet black hair rolled over his scalp in a series of waves like the ocean rolling onto a beach. Roland appeared to be more serious than Phil, but only because he lacked his friend's mischievous smile. When it came to having a good time, no one enjoyed himself more than Roland Varnes. George, on the other hand, was a skinny kid with sandy brown hair and bright, blue eyes. He was a good natured boy, and the only things that seemed to bother him was when someone mentioned the patches of freckles on either side of his nose, or when someone said something bad about his brother.

On the third time around the house, Phil caught Roland and they both fell to the ground laughing. George jumped on top and they all punched each other and giggled until they couldn't move. After a few moments of catching their breath between chuckles, they decided it was time to ride their bikes over to Mr. Best's house to look at the car they might buy. Both of the Varnes boys were mechanically inclined and that is why Phil never thought twice about their ability to get the old Model T Ford in running condition.

"Howdy, boys," Mr. Best greeted them as they rode up to his house. "Did y'all come to look at that old Model T under the shed?"

"Yes, sir," Phil replied. "We're thinking of going in together on it."

"Sounds like a good idea. Let me put away this rake and I'll take you down there to see it. I love these old oak trees in the summer 'cause they give such good shade. But when fall comes, I think they are going to work me to death from picking up their leaves." A few moments later, they reached the shed and had pulled the tarpaulin cover away from the car.

Mr. Best began describing the car as if it were an old friend. "She's a might dusty, but I think everything is still in working order. I drove her under this shed, so I know she still ran when I parked her."

"How long ago was that, Mr. Best?" Roland asked.

"About four years ago, son."

"This fold-up top is about shot," George observed. "and the rear seat looks as if it might be rotten."

"Well, boys, I never said she was in mint condition. But you'll never find another one as good for only fifteen dollars."

"I like it," Phil declared. "How about you, Roland?"

"I think it is worth fifteen dollars," Roland replied, trying not to give Mr. Best the idea that they were excited about

13

owning a car. "Can we give you five dollars to hold it for us, until we can get the rest of the money?"

"I reckon so, boys. How long do you think it will take?"

"We don't know. Tell us more about this scrap iron business with the Japanese," Phil replied.

"Well, I've been hearing on the radio that the Japanese are at war with the Chinese. It sounds as if they are trying to build up their navy, and since they don't have great reserves of iron and steel, they have to buy it from other countries. There is a scrap dealer over in Smithfield who comes around here every other Saturday and he pays one cent per pound." Mr. Best paused for a moment. "How long do you boys think it would take you to find fifteen hundred pounds of scrap?"

"We ought to be able to do that in a month, don't you think so, Roland?"

"Yeah. I know where there are some old piles of trash and there is sure to be a lot of scrap iron lying around in them."

After the boys had given Mr. Best five dollars, they pulled the tarpaulin back over the car and headed their bikes toward Kenly and the dance floor at Cash Corner. It was a beautiful Indian Summer afternoon in mid-October. Leaves were turning various shades of yellow, red, and brown and the air was brisk with the promise of winter. As they rode past an orchard, Phil suddenly stopped to pick a ripe, red apple from a tree.

"You had better leave those apples alone, Phil," warned George. "This is old man Edgerton's farm, remember? He shot at some boys last year just because they were walking through his orchard."

"Don't worry, pal. He's probably gone to Kenly like all the other old folks do on Saturday. Besides, he won't miss just one. They look so juicy and fat, don't they?"

At that moment, a shotgun blast boomed overhead and pellets rained down on the three boys. Roland and George were already pedaling furiously as Phil hopped on his bike and quickly caught up with them.

"What did I tell you," George said between gulps of air.

"That old man is crazy!" Phil exclaimed.

"I think they just don't like children," Roland interjected. "You know, they never had any of their own."

"That's not a good reason to shoot at someone," Phil said angrily.

Soon, they reached Kenly and had all but forgotten their scare at old man Edgerton's place. As they pedaled down main street, they saw some of their friends sitting on the curb in front of the theater. Bert's convertible was parked about a half block away. The girls sitting in his car waved and shouted at Phil. The three boys leaned against the wall near their friends and began recounting the incident with Mr. Edgerton when the clatter of

14

skipping feet was heard along the sidewalk. It was Red Ballard's daughter, Cleo and two of her friends. Cleo had turned thirteen only four months before, but since that day, she had tried to dress and act as if she were sixteen. And except for her height, she had the body to convince anyone who didn't know better. The older teenagers had nicknamed her "Little Bit" because of her size and her tendency to flirt with much older boys.

"Hey Phil," she began as she reached the group. "How about a hug, sugar?"

Everyone else laughed as Phil let Cleo wrap her arms around his shoulders.

"I missed you so much, honey. Why didn't you come sooner?"

"Your boyfriend is always getting in the way," Phil joked.

"Philip Barkley! You know I don't have a boyfriend," was her retort. Then she smiled at him and asked, "Can you loan me a quarter, Phil? I want to see this movie today. I'll pay you back next time I see you."

"But I don't have any money, Little Bit. Besides, what happened to the quarter I loaned you on the Fourth of July?"

Cleo snuggled up to Phil and wrapped her arms around his waist. "Loan me a quarter and I'll give you some nookie."

Everyone else laughed as Phil's mouth dropped open. "I'm afraid you're not big enough, darlin'," he finally said.

"But I'm bigger than your fist, ain't I?" she quickly retorted.

Phil grinned sheepishly as he reached into his pocket for the coin. He couldn't think of anything snappy to say to this brash little girl, so the next best thing was simply to get rid of her. Cleo gave him a little peck on the cheek and ran into the theater with her two giggling friends. As soon as the door closed, all Phil's friends laughed aloud, hooting and pointing at him. His face reddened a bit as he noticed that even Bert managed to grin at what the bawdy little girl had said.

"Hey buddy," Roland said a few moments later. "Let's go down to Cash Corner and see who is there."

"Good idea," Phil replied. "I'm kind of thirsty for one of those icy RC Colas Red keeps in the drink box."

They pedaled lazily down the street toward the sound of music coming from the record machine. As they rolled into the parking lot, Phil noticed a car full of girls leaving on the road toward the town of Princeton. In the back seat was a girl with the most beautiful, thick brown hair he had ever seen. As the car pulled away, she glanced over her shoulder at Phil. It was the girl he had seen before! Her hand came up beside her face for just a second, then she waved at him and flashed a tiny smile that went straight for his heart. Phil immediately forgot everything else that had happened to him that day. He knew he had to meet this girl.

15

Chapter Three

With the harvesting of tobacco and cotton on the Barkley farm drawing to a close, Phil and the Varnes brothers found more time to collect scrap iron. By late October they had almost redeemed enough of the metal to pay for the Model T Ford. However, now they were having to go farther from home in their weekly searches since they had looked in every nook and cranny close to their own houses. One chilly Saturday afternoon, they were driving their bikes along an unfamiliar road in a direction they hoped would take them home when George noticed a path going into the woods.

"Hey fellahs!" he shouted. "This looks like one of those paths where people dump trash. There might be some scrap iron down this way."

"You're not waiting on me," Roland veered in behind George. Phil had quickly pedaled ahead of George and led them down the crooked path which grew quite thick with vegetation at certain spots along the way. After a few moments, Phil suddenly veered his bicycle off the path and yelled, "Snake!" Roland and George snatched their handlebars in the opposite direction and slid their bikes into some bushes. Phil began to laugh and said, "Gotcha!"

As the Varnes brothers pulled themselves from the bushes, Phil could tell by the looks on their faces that they would try to get even with him later. "Sorry, fellahs. I saw the trash pile up here and had to think of a quick way to get you two to stop."

"Sure, Phil," Roland replied sarcastically. "We believe that, don't we George."

"We sure do," George played along. "I just hope we can return the favor some day old buddy."

After ten minutes, the boys had found a few pounds of scrap iron and decided to move further down the path in hopes of finding other trash piles. They hadn't gone far before it became evident that a clearing was up ahead. Upon nearing the edge of the clearing, they found a house and some farm buildings.

"I wonder who lives here?" George asked.

"I think I know," Roland suddenly began to chuckle. "I think this is Old Man Edgerton's house."

"I think you're right, Roland," said Phil.

"Do you think they're home?" George asked.

"I don't think so," Phil said. "They go to Kenly every Saturday afternoon, like clockwork. They come home just before sunset because Old Man Edgerton is afraid to drive after dark."

"Well, you would be too if you owned a '31 Model A Ford with no headlights," Roland said.

"Hey fellahs," George began. "How about us pulling a prank

on them while they're gone? You know, get even with him shooting at us last month."

Roland and Phil looked at each other and grinned. "You've got a real mean streak in you little brother," Roland said as he patted George on the back.

"What do you have in mind?" asked Phil.

"Let's give them the old smoke out trick. Since its getting chilly at night this time of year, its a cinch that Old Man Edgerton will light a fire in his stove as soon as he gets home."

"So what?" Roland asked.

"So we stuff a bale of straw down his chimney. Since the smoke won't come out at the top of the chimney, it will have to come back out inside the house."

"Isn't that dangerous?" asked Phil.

"Not really," George replied. "Their chimney is really tall. I don't think any flames from the stove could reach the straw in the top of the chimney so it shouldn't catch on fire."

"How do we get up there?"

"I think that's a ladder lying on the ground beside the shed over there."

"Halloween comes a bit early to the Edgerton house," Roland joked.

"George, you go to the road in front of the house and watch for the Edgertons to come back," Phil directed. "It's getting kind of late in the afternoon. Roland, you grab a bale of straw and meet me at the edge of the house. I'll get the ladder and climb onto the roof."

Just as Phil finished packing the chimney with the straw, George shouted as he whizzed down the driveway from the road.

"They're coming! They're coming! Head for the woods!"

Phil scurried down the roof and almost fell down the ladder. He laid the ladder beside the shed where they'd found it and just made it back to the edge of the woods when the Edgerton's car pulled around to the back door of the house.

"Whew!" Phil exclaimed. "That was too close for comfort."

"Sorry, Phil," said George. "There's a curve in the road about a quarter of a mile from here so I didn't have much warning when they came into sight."

Just as George had predicted, Old Man Edgerton went straight to the woodpile and then into the house. His wife gathered up two bags of supplies from the car and followed her husband inside. A few moments later the three boys saw a slight wisp of smoke curling from the top of the chimney.

"Phil, you didn't pack the straw tight enough!" Roland exclaimed.

About that time, the back door sprang open and out stumbled the old couple, fanning themselves with hats and rubbing their eyes and coughing. Smoke billowed out of the

17

doorway behind them. Old Man Edgerton began to curse loudly as he looked up at the chimney. Suddenly, he began to look around as if he knew the culprits were watching him.

"Let's get the heck out of here," George suggested.

"You're not waiting on me, little brother," Roland agreed.

Even Phil stopped giggling long enough to get on his bike and pedal back down the path at top speed with his buddies. It would have been dangerous to stay any longer. Besides, nothing else could have been funnier than seeing Old Man Edgerton hacking his lungs out and stumbling out that back door in a cloud of smoke.

On a sunny, mid-November Saturday morning a few weeks later, Phil sat at the small table in his room that served as his desk and poured out the contents of a coffee can he had pulled from the farthest corner of his clothes closet. Among other treasures, the can contained all the money Phil and his buddies had received from redeeming scrap iron. In a few moments, he determined they had sixteen dollars and twenty-seven cents. That was enough to buy the Model T Ford and get some gas and maybe even a few spare parts they might need to fix up the car. He decided to visit his pals and see if they were as ready to buy the car as he was.

Roland, George, and their father were sitting on their front porch as Phil rode up to their house on his bicycle.

"How's it going, fellahs?" Phil asked as he hopped off his bike.

"Well, Phil," replied Mr. Varnes. "I was just talking to Roland and George about this war in Europe. I don't think you boys should be disturbed yet, but President Roosevelt seems a bit worried lately."

"About what?"

"I think it is because Russia attacked Finland not long ago, and Congress has just passed the president's request for making the military larger."

"How come that worries Mr. Roosevelt?" Phil asked.

"Well, the newspaper accounts say that Congress has no desire to enter the war, but they will support the allies with materials and supplies. I think Mr. Roosevelt is worried that the allies will need more than supplies before this thing is over."

"Maybe they'll get it worked out soon," Phil offered.

"I hope you're right, Phil."

Roland jumped into the conversation. "Do we have enough money to get the car?"

"Yeah, and couple of dollars left over. We have seventeen dollars."

"Well, what are we waiting for?" George said excitedly. "Let's go pay the man right now!"

By the time the three boys reached Mr. Best's house, it was

late afternoon. Mr. Best had just returned from his weekly trip to town for supplies and was enjoying the unseasonably warm weather on his front porch.

"Did you boys come to get the Model T?" he asked as their bikes pulled up short of his flower bed and let the cloud of dust float on by.

"No, sir." Phil replied. "We've just come to pay for it."

"Well, I'm proud of you boys. It didn't take you long to earn that money. You must have worked very hard. Do you have any idea when you will be able to take it home?"

"I'll have to talk to Daddy Barkley about that," replied Phil. "He has already said we could put it under the shed of the tobacco barn. But I forgot to ask him if we could use his pickup to pull it back home."

"Besides," added Roland. "We'll have to pump up the tires anyway. That car isn't moving with four flat tires."

"Well, I'm sure I have an old air pump somewhere in the tool shed," Mr. Best offered. "I'll be glad to let you boys use it when you come to get the car."

Roland and George ambled out to the shed to take another look at the car. Phil paid Mr. Best the fifteen dollars and joined his pals. After they talked about their plans for the car another fifteen minutes, Roland suggested they go to Kenly to see which of their friends were hanging around cash corner. Phil jumped at the suggestion! He couldn't get the pretty, brown-haired girl out of his mind.

As they rode into town and down main street, they passed the movie theater where brassy little Cleo and some of her friends were waiting on the sidewalk.

"Hey Phil," shouted Cleo. "Stop! I want to talk to you."

"Sorry, darlin'," Phil replied over his shoulder. "I'm late for a date."

The boys chuckled when they heard Cleo say "Dammit!" aloud.

"You know something," Roland asked. "She's going to be some kind of woman in just another few rears."

"You're right about that, buddy," Phil replied. "She'll be too much for me to handle."

"Maybe I'll give it a try," George said. Roland and Phil looked at each other and laughed.

When they arrived at Cash Corner, they drove their bikes around the back of Red's store. Bert was there in his '39 convertible with the usual compliment of girls fawning over him, hoping to get a ride around town. The pretty girl he wanted to meet was sitting in the back seat. She hopped out of the car as soon as she saw Phil. Up on the dance floor, a boy and a girl were trying to teach each other how' to Jitterbug as the nickelodeon blared out a song. The girl sauntered up to where

Phil was standing.

"Hey, handsome. Aren't you Phil Barkley?"

Phil was a bit surprised that she knew his name. "Ah," he stammered, "I sure am. And you must be . . ."

"They call me Grace, Grace Langston. I guess you're wondering how I knew your name, huh?"

Phil grinned, regaining some of his composure. "It doesn't really matter. Just don't believe anything my friends tell you about me." Grace chuckled as Phil offered her his hand to shake "I am very pleased to meet you, Miss Grace."

"Same here, handsome," she said, grasping his hand. "And you can drop the Miss. Anyway, where have you been lately? I haven't seen you around much."

"Oh, around the world and back again," he joked. She laughed. He took her hand and led her to the edge of the dance platform where they sat and watched the other couple for a moment.

"How ya been?" asked Phil, groping for words to start a conversation.

"I've been just fine. But I haven't seen much of you lately."

"I've been pretty busy," Phil remarked. "But you don't want to hear about that boring stuff. How about we Jitterbug a little?"

"Okay," said Grace. "There's a new song out called 'Hold Tight, Hold Tight'. Let's see if they have it on the nickelodeon."

"Here it is!" Phil exclaimed after they had looked for a moment. "Its number twenty-one on the chart here." He put a nickel in the machine and pushed the button.

Properly done, the Jitterbug required a lot of quick, energetic moves. Both dance partners had to be able to swing each other about, kick up their feet, maintain contact through lots of hand movements, and do it all in time with fast paced music. Phil was very good at Jitterbugging and some of the other teenagers just watched him to learn new moves they might try at home in their own rooms. Roland and his girl friend, Pat, soon joined Phil and Grace on the dance floor. After that, the couples poured onto the floor. Cash Corner was officially in full swing for another Saturday night.

Darkness found Phil and Grace sitting in the back seat of a Model A that belonged to a friend. Since they had danced several times that afternoon, they had became tired and were smooching in the back seat of the car.

Phil said, "Love, I am hungry. Would you care for a hot dog and drink?"

"Sure would," Grace replied. "Thanks!"

"Hey, George!" Phil shouted to his pal who was standing near the rear door of the store. "How about bringing Grace and me two dogs and a couple of RC Colas?"

"I don't have but thirty cents," George replied.

20

"That's just enough," shouted Phil.

"Oh, alright." George turned and went into the store. He soon came out and handed the hot dogs and drinks to Phil and Grace.

"Thanks, buddy," Phil said as he produced thirty cents in repayment.

"You are a sweet guy, George." said Grace.

Not long after they'd finished their food, Phil and Grace became aware of a chill in the air and they snuggled closer in the back seat of their friend's car. A few minutes later, Roland came around, tapping on the window and saying that it was getting late. Phil and Grace shared one more kiss before he and his buddies pointed their bicycles toward home.

Chapter Four

The Barkleys had been working real hard to finish harvesting the crop of cotton and corn. The tobacco had already been harvested and sold so now only the usual farm chores were needed done. It was a time of year to rest and relax so Phil considered it a good time to ask Daddy Barkley for the use of the pickup truck to pull the Model T home. It was Saturday noon and Mr. Barkley had already been to town and had just returned.

"Daddy," Phil began. "Roland, George and I have bought that old Model T Ford car from Mr. Best. We have got to pull it home since it won't run."

"What are you going to do with that thing?" asked Mr. Barkley.

"Well, Roland is a good mechanic, and I know a little too, and with George helping we can fix it up so it will run! You know Daddy, we don't have anything to date on except the bicycles. Girls just don't want to go with boys on bicycles."

"What? Do you mean that girls won't ride on the handle bars?" He laughed when Phil didn't immediately catch on that he was kidding. "You know, son, I've realized that and things are beginning to look better for us. The tobacco sold good this year. Sure, you can use the pickup truck this afternoon if you want. By the way, where are you planning to work on it?"

Phil replied, "Could we use the shed on the tobacco barn down next to the cattle pasture?"

"Well, yes" said Daddy Barkley. "I won't be needing that until next summer." Daddy Barkley handed the keys of the pickup truck to Phil and said, "Good luck, son!"

Phil was very pleased as he got into the pickup. He headed around the circular drive that came up to the front of the Barkley home. As he entered the lane that led down to the main road, he noticed the white board fence that encircled their home and continued down the lane on either side toward the main road. It was beginning to need a coat of paint. Phil wondered if his father would be willing to postpone the painting until he and his friends finished the Model T.

Phil pulled up to the Varnes farm and blew the horn. Roland and George came from around the side of the house where they had been pitching horse shoes.

"Hey, lets go get the Model T!" shouted Phil. The boys came running. They were tickled that the time had finally come to go and get their car. The two boys crawled in the pickup with Phil.

"Boy, I can't wait," said Roland.

"Me too!" exclaimed George. "Let's get going!"

Phil headed the truck down the road toward Mr. Best's farm. Suddenly Phil slowed the truck.

"What's the matter?" Roland asked.

"We don't have a chain to pull the car with, do we?"

"Nope," replied Roland. "I forgot about that too."

Phil turned the truck around and headed back to the Varnes' farm for a chain.

In a few minutes, they pulled into Mr. Best's driveway. They saw him down near the shelter where the Model T was located, feeding his chickens.

"Mr. Best, we have come to get the Model T," said Roland as they climbed out of the truck.

"That's fine," Mr. Best replied. "I'll be glad to get it out of my way. I can use the extra shelter space since my tobacco allotment has been increased."

Phil borrowed a tire pump from the old man and they each took turns pumping up the two flat tires. When the tires had enough air, they pushed the car out into the sunlight. Phil backed the pickup up to the front of the Model T.

Roland said, "You know guys, if we don't put something in between the bumpers of these two vehicles, the Model T will be slamming into the rear of the pickup. I know this car doesn't have any brakes at the moment.

"Good thinking, Roland," replied Phil.

"Hey, I have an idea!" said George. "Why can't we use a few of those old used tires lying over there? We could hang them on the chain between the two bumpers. That might cushion the slack motion between the two vehicles."

"Yeah, that might work," said Phil.

A few moments later, they had everything secured and had pulled the car onto the dirt road in front of Mr. Best's house. Roland sat in the driver's seat of the Model T while Phil and George rode in the truck. Phil put the pickup into low gear and slowly pulled the Model T down the road towards home. It was late in the afternoon when the boys arrived back at the Barkley place.

Phil said, "I'll bet Daddy will want me to trim these crepe myrtle trees that are along side this lane pretty soon."

"Well maybe he'll wait until after Christmas," George offered. "But they were sure pretty while they were blooming."

Phil continued down the path behind his house. He stopped the Model T so that the rear of it was near the shed on the side of the tobacco barn. The three boys then pushed the car under the shed and stood admiring their prize for a few moments.

"I can hardly wait to get started," Phil said. "Hey, Roland, did you notice the work bench I built in the rear of the shed?"

"Yeah, that will come in handy," Roland replied.

"Well, guys," George sighed heavily. "I'm pretty tired. How about we call it a day?"

"Fine by me," answered Phil. "Let's meet here tomorrow

23

after lunch and we can make our plans for what to do on this old car."

"Good idea," said Roland. "I already have some ideas that I think you'll like."

The next day after lunch, Phil was sitting on a stool under the front edge of the shed near the Model T car looking at an airplane magazine that he had borrowed from his Uncle. He heard a noise and an airplane flew by overhead. He looked up at the plane and then looked down into the magazine in his hand. He was sure they were the same! It was the new P-47 Thunderbolt fighter that the Army Air Corps had just developed. Just then, George and Roland rode up on their bicycles.

"Hey! Did you see that plane?" asked Phil.

"Yep," replied Roland. "And boy was he sure moving on out."

"Gosh, I wonder what it would be like to fly on of those things?" Phil mused.

"I don't know," said Roland. "Looks to me like it would be mighty dangerous!"

"Enough of that," George interjected. "Let's get on with fixing this car. I don't want to be an old man before I drive this thing."

Phil and Roland shot each other a look of surprise at George's remark.

"Okay, little buddy," Phil replied. "Where do we start?"

"How about removing this old fold-down top. It's almost rotten anyway so we can't use it."

"Yeah," Phil agreed. "We can keep a piece of canvas under the rear seat in case it rains. We won't be driving much in bad weather anyway."

"The leather in the front seat looks pretty good," Roland said. "How does the back seat look?"

"Looks good back here too," said George. "Listen, what do you think of this? We take the fenders and running boards off and make this jalopy look like a real hot rod."

"That's not a bad idea, little brother," answered Roland. He had been staring at the wheels for a few moments. "I've got an even better idea," he continued. "Let's saw off all these wooden spokes in the wheel hubs."

"Are you crazy?!" Phil and George said in unison.

"Let me finish," Roland said. "We can pick up four wheels from a Model A Ford at the junk yard and fit them onto the hubs of our car. The smaller wheels with larger tires will ride better and make the old Model T look more like a racer. What do you think?"

"It just might work," Phil replied. "We could fasten them onto the Model T hubs with stud bolts. That should hold the Model A wheels on even on a tough dirt road."

24

"I have another idea," said Roland. "I think we should hop up this engine a little by filing down the block."

"Now you're talking," said George excitedly.

"What do you mean?" Phil asked.

"By filing down the head to a minimum clearance, you increase the compression in the cylinders. That makes the engine more powerful."

"Sounds okay," Phil replied. "And to top it off, I think we should paint the car with aluminum paint to give it a silver look. Besides, the aluminum paint will stay on better than other paint.

"Yeah!" said George. "And we can paint the wheels and wire spokes red! That will make it look really hot."

"We could even paint a little red stripe around the top of the body," Roland added.

"Hey, fellahs. What is this thing?" Phil asked as he stood near a lever on the side of their car.

"Press it and see," Roland offered.

OOOOO-gah, OOOOO-gah was the sound that pierced their ears as Phil pressed the lever.

"Wow!" said Roland. "I guess that's a horn."

"Let's get started, guys," said George as the ringing in their ears subsided.

"Let's wait, boys," Phil replied. "You know how daddy feels about working on Sunday. Maybe we should just wait until next Saturday."

"Okay," answered George. "We could go to our house and throw a few horseshoes."

As they start their bicycles down the path and pass the house, they see Phil's older sister, Leah standing on the front porch. Roland's older sister was standing beside her. The boys waved as they passed by.

"Where y'all going?" yelled Leah.

"We're going to our house," George cried out.

As the boys turned down the main road to the Varnes' farm, Phil said, "I hope this old bicycle doesn't break down anymore. You know I had to repair the shaft in the handle bar yesterday. The handle bar broke down in the shaft of the fork. I had to try to hold it together by using a piece of wooden hoe handle then drawing it tight with a bolt and nut."

"It might last awhile if you don't put a lot of pressure on it," said Roland.

"I certainly hope so," replied Phil.

They arrived at the Varnes' farm a few moments later. As they passed by the side of the house they rode under a large Magnolia tree close to where Mr. Varnes stood talking to Phil's father. The two men continued their conversation as the boys drove by.

As there were only enough horse shoes for two people to

play a game, George went into the house while Roland and Phil played the first game. A few moments later, he emerged.

"Who's winning," he asked upon returning.

"Right now I am," Phil replied.

Suddenly a loud bang sounded Phil's heels, causing him to jump forward about three feet.

"What in the hell was that?" Phil shouted. "Where did you get those things, George?"

"Oh, they won't hurt you. They are those little Chinese firecrackers that you can order by mail."

As Phil and Roland continued with their game, George wandered around the yard exploding the tiny bombs. After a few moments, he spied his father and Mr. Barkley talking under the magnolia tree and decided to have some fun. He walked up to the two men, lit a firecracker, and handed it to his father. Too deeply engrossed in his conversation to notice, Mr. Varnes simply takes the object his son has offered.

"Throw it! Throw it!" George screamed.

Too late. By the time Mr. Varnes realized what had been handed him, he couldn't rid himself of the thing quickly enough. Seconds after the sharp, loud explosion, George's father was rubbing his fingers and swearing through his teeth.

"You little idiot! What did you do that for?"

George quickly backed away from his father. "I told you to throw it, daddy."

"I'll get you boy, and when I do I'll dust off your britches!" Realizing just seconds later that he can't catch the boy, Mr. Varnes yells after George once more. "I'll catch you at supper, boy. You have to eat sometime!"

Meanwhile, Roland and Phil have almost finished their game when Roland spied their sisters out of the corner of his eyes. The two girls were stealing their bicycles!

"Stop you thieves!" Roland cried as he began to chase after the girls. Phil joined the chase immediately, but the girls were already too far ahead to be caught. The boys could only hear Leah laughing loudly as she pulled away from them. A moment later, they stood in the middle of the dirt road, watching their transportation fade into the sunset. Roland turned and began to walk back toward his house, angrily muttering threats of what he would do to his sister when she returned home.

"Don't go just yet, old buddy," Phil said to Roland. "Watch Leah when they reach that small hill up ahead."

When Leah stood on the pedals to get enough power to climb the small hill, she put extra pressure on the handle bar shaft where Phil had temporarily repaired it. Suddenly, the shaft broke apart releasing the handle bar. When the handle bar came over Leah's head she went towards one ditch while the bicycle went toward the other one. Luckily, she landed in soft sand along the side of the road and escaped harm with only a few scratches and a bit of dirt on her Sunday dress clothes.

Phil and Roland laughed so hard they held their sides. Leah quickly scrambled to her feet, realized what had happened, and became very angry at Phil.

"I'll get you, Phil Barkley!" she screamed as she began to run toward the boys. "You should have told me that bike was broken!"

"If you had asked before you took it, I might have had a chance to tell you," he replied as he retreated toward Roland's house.

Soon Leah decided that it has not worth further effort to chase Phil and returned to the place where Roland's sister was waiting. The two girls left the bicycles lying beside the road and walked toward the Barkley farm. A short while later, Roland and Phil came to retrieve their bikes. Roland returned to his house and Phil took what was left of his bike to the shed where they had parked the Model T. He could make repairs there without his father ever discovering there had been an accident. It was certain that Leah would not dare mention it because he would scold her for taking the bicycle without permission.

This has been an interesting day, Phil thought as he sat on a stool beside the two broken vehicles. As his grandmother yelled out the back door for Phil to come for supper, he wondered what punishment was in store for George. His little buddy would probably go to bed hungry that evening.

Chapter Five

It was a cold January in 1940 and already had snowed a little. Phil was practicing basketball in the gymnasium at Kenly High School. Principal Yount came into the gym and walked over to where Phil was shooting at the goal.

"I am glad that you have decided to play basketball this year Phil," he said. "But don't let your grades suffer."

"No sir," replied Phil. "I won't let that happen!"

Mr. Yount liked Phil and took a great interest in him. He spoke to Phil almost every day. Phil was the star center on the basketball team and also played running back on the football team. His pleasant personality and good natured pranks had won him many friends around the school and town.

The Principal walked out of the gym, leaving Phil to practice. Several of the team members came in the gym and began practicing with Phil. Soon he tired and walked over where several of the high school girls were seated on the benches.

"I'm just about pooped," said Phil. "I have to rest a bit."

"You were beautiful out there," said one girl.

"Great going there, honey," sighed another, trying to get his attention. "With you in the game we are sure going to win that game to night, aren't we Phil?" said another.

"Sure we are," Phil replied with a winning smile on his face. "But if I don't get a couple of hugs it might be close."

The girls pushed and shoved trying to reach him. While Phil enjoyed the attention, he noticed Coach Sherman entering the gym. The coach also saw Phil surrounded by the girls and said, "Alright Phil, let's quit the politicking and get back to practicing!"

"See you ladies tonight?" Phil asked as he pulled away.

"You bet, love," they all replied in unison.

As he walked toward his team mates, Phil could hear the girls giggling behind him. An hour later, he was back on the bench, but he was sitting with seven other young men who were all as sweaty as Phil. The coach paced back and forth in front of them.

"Do that well tonight boys," said Coach Sherman, "and we'll win for sure. I know how badly you want to beat Pine Level. And you deserve to win! So hit the showers, relax for the next few hours, and come back here at six o'clock ready to play your hearts out!"

"We'll stomp 'em!" shouted several of the players as they headed for the locker room.

Since the school busses left the school around four o'clock, Phil had arranged to spend the afternoon with Clyde Perkins, who lived a few blocks from the school. They left the gym and

28

headed toward Clyde's house, passing the stores and occasionally stopping in to warm themselves by potbellied stoves that hissed with wet wood and to hear the men talk about politics and the war.

"How are you going to get home tonight?" Clyde asked.

"Daddy is coming to the game tonight," replied Phil. "I'll ride home with him after we win." Clyde grinned at Phil's bravado.

Clyde's mother had supper on the table as the boys walked in the back door of Clyde's house. Phil's mouth began to water when he realized they were having fried chicken. He was really hungry after the strenuous practice and the walk from school in the cold air. Clyde jokingly reminded Phil not to eat too much so it wouldn't weigh him down during the game.

After eating, the boys went upstairs to Clyde's room and listened to the radio. His father worked at the Post Office and had been able to weather the Depression well enough. Their house wasn't as large as the Barkley home, but then Clyde was an only child and the Perkins didn't need much space. Clyde's room seemed very large to Phil.

Thirty minutes later, Clyde's father drove the boys to the gymnasium. Coach Sherman was already there, waiting for the rest of the team to arrive for a bit of early warming up. Phil put on his basketball uniform and ran onto the court. As he was making a lay up shot, he spied Roland and George Varnes entering the gym with their parents.

"Step it up a little," Roland yelled at Phil. "You'll never win moving that slow!"

Phil laughed and said, "Go easy on me, pal. The game hasn't even started. Besides, if we move much faster, the boys from Pine Level won't come back after half-time."

"I wouldn't be too sure about that," shouted George. "They might be tougher than you think."

George turned out to be right. As the game progressed, it was difficult for Kenly keep up with Pine Level. The score kept swinging back and forth. Finally, with just under thirty seconds left to play, the score was tied. Number forty-two for Pine Level had fouled and Kenly got the ball. Clyde threw the ball onto the court into Phil's hands. They worked it toward their goal under full court pressure from the visitors. Phil was having a hard time finding an opening for a shot. He passed the ball to Clyde who was standing to the left side of the foul line, and glanced at the clock. Five seconds left. He glanced back at Clyde only to see that his friend was being rushed by two of the Pine Level players. Phil made a waving gesture and Clyde bounced the ball on the floor right between the two opposing team members into Phil's hands. Two seconds left! Since Clyde had been double teamed, Phil was wide open for a jump shot. As he took aim at the goal, he saw a Pine Level jersey coming toward him from his right. The ball floated toward the basket in a high, looping arc. For a split second, Phil imagined the entire crowd was silent, with each person holding his breath as the game's outcome hinged upon this one shot. Suddenly, pandemonium shocked Phil back into reality. The ball had swished through the net just as the buzzer had sounded to end the game. Kenly had won!

From every side of the gym, team mates and fans alike were crowding around Phil, cheering and shouting about the great Kenly basketball team. Phil even heard someone loudly predict that they would be the state champions this year. When they arrived home, Phil went straight to bed, dog tired from the combination of a good physical workout and the cold air. It had been a big day. During that night, it snowed several inches. The next morning, the bus came and picked up the Barkley children to take them to school. It was a light fluffy snow so the school bus had no problem getting to school. At noon the school let out for the lunch period. Most of the children were out on the school grounds playing in the snow. The baseball diamond was located at the rear of the main building. Phil and some of his buddies were at home plate throwing snowballs and horsing around. A small boy from first grade had wandered over and was watching the larger boys play in the snow.

"Baby" Ray Faison was the largest boy in high school and had been nicknamed "Baby" because of his size. He had noticed Mr. Yount standing near the third base plate watching the small children playing in the snow. Suddenly "Baby Ray" grinned, and Phil noticed it.

"What are you thinking, Baby Ray?" asked Phil.

"Oh, nothing much. Just that, well, what if someone hit Mr. Yount with a snowball?"

"Don't you think it might shake him up a bit, maybe shock his modesty or something?" Phil said.

"Nah. I hear he's a pretty good sport."

"But who's going to throw the snowball?"

Baby Ray called the little boy over and showed him a nickel. "Son," he began. "How would you like to earn this nickel?"

The little boy's eyes grew wide looking at the nickel. "Boy, would I!" he replied excitedly. "That would buy me a great big ice cream cone or a Royal Crown cola."

"Well, I am going to give you the nickel," Baby Ray continued, "but if you want to keep it you have to take this snowball here and go over to third base and hit the big man standing there. Do you see him? The one in the long overcoat and big hat over there at the third base plate?"

"Yes, I see him," said the boy.

"Well, do you want the nickel Son?"

"Yes, sir! Give it to me."

30

Baby Ray rolled up a hard snow ball, gave it to the little boy and put the nickel in the boy's pocket. "Now, you have to hit the man in the face, or we won't let you keep the nickel."

The little boy walked right up to Mr. Yount and stopped in front of him. The principal looked down at the little boy and smiled. Suddenly, the boy threw the snowball, hitting Mr. Yount in the forehead, knocking off his hat. The principal calmly picked up his hat, wiped off the snow from his face and hat, looked down at the boy and planted a hand on his shoulder.

From the corner of the school building, Phil peeked just in time to see Mr. Yount kneel in front of the boy. A second later, the boy pointed his finger toward home plate. Mr. Young followed the boy's finger, only to find no one standing at home plate. Phil ducked back and turned around to see Baby Ray Faison holding his sides from laughing so hard.

"Best nickel I ever spent," Baby Ray gasped.

Phil peeked around the corner once more, only to see Mr. Yount and the boy moving toward them. "I think it's time we vacated the area, Baby Ray," he warned. They ran to the opposite side of the building and hid until lunch period was over. Phil knew the first grader could identify them all, even if he didn't know their names. Phil and Baby Ray took great pains to avoid little boys and Mr. Yount for the rest of the day.

By week's end, the snow had melted. On Saturday, Roland and George came over to the Barkley farm to help Phil work on their Model T car. They built a fire in the furnace under the shed since it was chilly outside, and worked on the car all morning.

After lunch, Phil had returned to the shed to await Roland and George. He leaned back in a chair next to the furnace with his feet propped on the bumper of the car. In a few moments, the warmth of the furnace and the food in his belly teamed up to make Phil drowsy. He was almost asleep when a loud humming noise overhead startled him. He walked into the open, looked up, and was an airplane with three motors. Phil had never seen a plane like this before, so he hurried back under the shed and picked up his airplane book. Searching frantically, he finally found a picture of a plane like the one overhead. It could only be the Ford Tri-Motor that he was seeing. It was the workhorse of the skies, being used more and more for mail and passenger service all over the country. Roland and George arrived just as the plane droned out of range.

Roland said, "Let's get this cylinder head off the block this afternoon so we can file it down."

"All right," said Phil. "George, hand me that socket wrench."

Later that afternoon, the boys grew tired of working on the Model T and began kicking around a football near the white board fence of the cattle pasture. Phil made a bad kick and the football landed inside the cattle pasture. Seeing no animals, he hopped over the fence and to get the ball. As he bent over to pick up the ball, he heard a snort and looked through his legs. Daddy Barkley's prize bull was coming around the corner of the barn. This bull had no respect for any human except for Daddy Barkley. Phil grabbed the football and raced toward the fence. He swore he could feel the bull's hot breath on his back as he broad jumped over the fence, just clearing the top board. Roland and George were laughing so hard that they could hardly speak.

"Hey, I think we should get Coach Sherman to sign up Phil and that bull on the Kenly track team," said George. "They would be sure to win the high jump and the hundred yard dash anywhere in the state."

"Go to hell, George!" Phil snorted as he rolled over in the grass where he had landed. Suddenly, Roland and George began to point at him and laugh even harder.

"What are you two nitwits laughing about now?"

Roland replied, howling with laughter, "Looks like there will be a bright moon tonight . . . if you don't get your britches sewed up in the rear."

It seems that the big leap over the fence by Phil had been too much on his pants and they had split in the seat. Phil grumbled a little as it wasn't very funny to him.

"I think I've had it for one day," Phil finally said. "Let's quit." He headed up the path to the back door of his house, knowing that Granny would be able to repair his pants, but only after his brothers and sisters teased him for a few hours.

Chapter Six

By late June of 1940, the war in Europe had grown worse. France had surrendered to the Nazis while Italy had sided with them. Russia became suspicious of Germany's intentions and seized some of the small countries along her borders, including parts of Poland. Hitler openly threatened to invade England.

Even though the war in Europe was getting worse, the economy in the United States continued to improve. A lot of men that had joined the government's C.C.C. program in order to support themselves and their families were joining the military. The government had begun expanding and building new military bases in the U.S. and that was providing jobs for many people that were out of work.

On this warm Saturday morning Phil was reclining on the front porch with his head propped against a post beside the steps. It was his favorite spot to relax while listening to the radio and reading his Buck Rogers comic books. He was also waiting for Roland and George to arrive. During the winter, the three of them had worked very hard to get the Model T in operating condition. When the other two boys arrived, they all headed for the shed where the Model T sat.

"Fellahs, I think she looks great!" Phil observed. "She almost looks like a racer too."

"Let's get started," said Roland. "I want us to drive her into Kenly this afternoon."

They had named her Silver Bullet, partly because of the silver paint that covered the body and partly because she had been "hopped" up to outrun any Model T around. They had removed all the fenders from the body, installed Model A Ford wheels and tires onto the old Model T hubs, and removed the entire top, with the exception of the windshield. Two headlamps had been attached on either side of the radiator at the front. Roland had trimmed the body with a red stripe around the top and had also painted the wire spoke wheels red. The final touch was to painted the words Silver Bullet on each side of the body near the rear end.

"Phil, when you finish putting on that distributor cap, I think we'll be ready to start her up," said George proudly. He had done most of the work on the engine, being naturally gifted as a mechanic.

Phil installed the cap and told Roland to get in the car and turn on the switch. He went to the front of the car and tried to turn the engine with the crank. He said "Sure wish this thing had a self-starter." He tried to turn the engine with the crank but it failed to budge. "Come and help me, George." George came over and they both try to turn the engine. It will not turn.

Phil commented, "Well, it looks like we are going to have to pull the car down the road to start it. Since we have overhauled the engine and filed down the cylinder head, its just too tight to start by hand cranking." "I'll go see if Daddy will loan me the pickup truck to pull it with."

"Good" said Roland, "George and I will push it out from under this shed so you can hook a chain to it."

Phil went up the lane to the house and soon came back with the pickup truck. They pulled the Model T down the lane in front of the house and into the main road. Roland was behind the steering wheel of the Silver Bullet and George was riding with Phil in the pickup truck. Phil started down the main road pulling the Model T behind him.

"George, when I say the word, yell to Roland to let out the clutch to start the Silver Bullet, but not yet, I have to get a little faster."

"Okay" replied George. Phil increased the speed of the pick up a little and then said "Now," George yelled at Roland. "Now, let out the clutch! Roland let out the clutch on the Model T. The rear wheels slid in the dirt but the engine failed to turn over. Roland pressed the clutch back in and yelled, "go a little faster Phil" Phil picked up a little more speed and said "now to George. George yelled back to Roland "Let out the clutch now."

Roland let out the clutch again. The rear wheels slid in the dirt and then started to slowly turn over. The engine turned over but failed to start. "Hold it," he shouted. "Something must be wrong."

Phil pulled the vehicles over to the side of the road and stopped. They got out of the vehicles and started searching under the hood of the Model T. Phil inspected the distributor and George looked under the dash, checking the magnetos. Roland checked the switch wires. Everything seemed to be in good working order.

After some long aggravating minutes, the boys were about to give up. Suddenly Roland shouted, "Who in the hell left the gas turned off?" See there, the valve on the firewall is in the off position." George, "Oh," I though Phil turned that back on!" "Yeah" and I thought you had turned it on!" replied Phil. "Well, no ones at fault." "We all just didn't think of it." stated Roland. "I've got it turned on now, so lets try it again."

They get into the vehicles and Phil starts down the road again, picks up speed and told George, "Now!"

"Let out the clutch, Roland," shouted George.

Roland popped the clutch and suddenly the engine of the Model T came to life, sputtering and spitting and back firing like a giant firecracker.

"Stop, stop!" yelled Roland. Phil stopped the vehicles on the side of the road. "We've got to adjust the timing on this thing."

34

said Roland. "Or we'll blow the muffler." Phil agreed and Roland turned off the ignition switch on the Model T and he adjusted the timing on the distributor. "Okay" said Roland "now, try to crank it." Phil tried to crank the engine by hand but could barely move it. "Come help me" he said to George. George came over and they both were able to pull the crank. The engine came to life and ran better. "That engine has a lot of compression!" said Roland.

"I'll bet it has a lot of power too," replied Phil. "I wonder how fast she'll run?"

They returned Mr. Barkley's pickup truck to Phil's house.

Phil and George hopped into the car with Roland. They went down the dirt road, kicking up a cloud of dust behind them. "Give her some more gas, Roland," said Phil. "I know she'll go faster!"

"I know," shouted Roland over the engine's roar. "I only have the lever at half throttle. When we get to that straight stretch of road ahead, I'll give her the gas and we'll see just how fast she will run."

The three boys were getting very excited about the speed and performance of the "silver Bullet." when they came to the straight stretch of the road, Roland pushed up on the gas lever. The Silver Bullet was soon doing almost 50 miles per hour. "Hey, shouted Phil, that's about fast enough. Is that all she's got?"

"Not quite," replied Roland.

"Boy, this thing will really run," shouted George who had been holding on in the rear seat.

Roland slowed the Silver Bullet as they approached Rains' Crossroads. There was a country store located at the intersection and the boys decided they would stop there and get a cold drink and something to eat. It was getting hot and was already past noon time.

The country store was a favorite place for the men and boys in the community to gather and talk about the economy and the war in Europe. The boys occasionally came there also. This Saturday was no exception since there was already several men and boys gathered at the store. Some were sitting on benches under the store shelter, on the outside of the store. Phil drove up to the store and parked near the gas tanks.

Roland said, "We need to get some gas if we're going to drive anywhere."

"Okay," replied Phil. "How about three gallons, or is that too hard on your pocket?"

"No," said George. "That'll only be $.22 each and I can afford that." "I'll go with that too," answered Roland.

Several of the group of boys came out to inspect the funny looking Model T. "What kind of car is that?" one said. "You have to push that up hills?" said another, trying to aggravate the

35

boys. Phil, "Well, this is the Silver Bullet boys. She's a cross between a Model A and a Model T; and man, will she run!"

"Heck," said one of the boys laughing, "that thing will do good to get over a hill much less keep up with my A model coupe. There ain't a Model A, much less a Model T, in the county that can even get close to my coupe."

"Want to bet?" said Phil, trying to quiet down the guy.

"Yeah," said the guy joined by three of his buddies. "We'll bet you that thing-a-ma-jig there won't come close to my Model A coupe."

"How much?" asked Phil.

The boys talk a minute and then say, "Ten dollars of ours to five dollars of yours that we'll beat you."

Roland, George, and Phil counted their money and Phil answered, "Okay, we'll do it, but there has to be the same number of people riding in each vehicle to be fair."

"Okay, how about two in each car," replied the guy.

"Okay, lets go to that straight stretch of road down there," said Phil.

Roland seemed skeptical about the deal and said to Phil "You and I can go in the Silver Bullet and George can stay here and hold the money. Since this was your idea to start with, you can drive.

"Well, said George reluctantly, I reckon since I'm the youngest I'll have to stay." He took the money and sat down on the bench very disgusted. To miss out on the exciting ride was very disappointing to him.

The two boys got into the Model A Ford coupe while Roland and Phil got into the Silver Bullet. Phil shouted over to the other driver, "Now, we don't start the race until we come to the straight stretch of road. We will then stop side by side in the road. Roland will raise his hand up and when he lets it down, we will start, if no one else is in sight. We will race down to the end of the straight stretch, where there is a path that enters the road, then turn right into the path and go around the old tree stump that's in the hay field there. You must go around this stump and then reenter the main road and go back to the store. The finish line is the gas pumps back at the store, okay?

"Okay, we understand," said the other driver.

The two vehicles entered the dirt road and soon arrived at the straight stretch where the race was to begin. The vehicles lined up side by side. There were no other vehicles in sight so Roland raised his hand. "Go" shouted Roland and dropped his hand. Both the vehicles surged forward at the same instant. They raced down the dirt road with a large cloud of dust boiling up behind them. The Silver Bullet was beginning to fall behind a little bit. "Give her a little more spark with that lever, Phil," shouted Roland. Phil moved the spark lever a little and the Silver

Bullet began to inch forward and was almost even with the front of the Model A coupe.

"Yeah, yeah," shouted Roland, shaking his hands at the boys in the other car. The Silver Bullet was running on the left side of the Model A and they were nearing the end of the straight stretch. The path that they had to turn into was on the right and Phil knew he could not get enough ahead to turn right without wrecking the both of them. He waited to see if the Model A coupe would slow down but it didn't. At the last moment Phil pushed back on the gas lever and slowed the car. The coupe turned into the path sliding sideways and nearly turning over. Phil felt the rear of the Silver Bullet slide a little. He touched the brake slightly and the car straightened out. He passed the Model A coupe as they went around the stump of the tree. They reentered the dirt road with the Silver Bullet just ahead of the Model 'A' coupe. When the two vehicles straightened out down the straight stretch of road, Phil pulled down the gas lever as far as it would go and gave the engine all the spark as it would take. The Silver Bullet gradually inched away from the Model A coupe. As the two cars neared the end of the straight stretch of road, Roland was waiving to the boys in the coupe as it slowly disappeared into the cloud of dust behind the Silver Bullet.

As the Silver Bullet neared the store, they could see George jumping up and down in front, motioning with his arms and hands for them to come on. Phil pulled the Silver Bullet in towards the store and slid to a stop in front of the gasoline pumps. As Phil and Roland jumped out, the Model A coupe came sliding up beside them.

George grabbed Phil and Roland and the three boys danced a circle jig in their moment of celebration.

"Gosh," said George. "We sure got that thing named right. I've never seen a Model T run like that!"

"Neither have I," added Roland. "I mean, this thing will really go! But when we were trying to start her this morning, I thought for awhile that we had filed down the cylinder heard on her too much, being as it was so hard to get the engine to turn over.

"No," said Phil, "We got that old engine fixed just right. I'm tickled."

The two boys in the Model A coupe got out of the coupe and came walking over. "You guys cheated!" shouted one of the boys. "We want our money back!" "Like hell we cheated." Phil shot back. "We won fair and square." "You've got a different engine in that car," said the boy, "and that's cheating."

"No we don't," said Roland and George at the same time.

"This Model T has the same engine in it that came in it from the factory," Roland finished.

"Well, prove it," said the boy.

Roland unhooked the side hood cover and lifts it up exposing the engine.

"I'll be damned," said the boy in amazement. "I still can't believe it. I never thought I'd see a Model T outrun a Model A."

"Well, you're a believer now, aren't you?" asked George, appearing a bit boastful as some of the group laughed.

The group of men and boys at the store had now gathered around the Silver Bullet, inspecting and asking various questions about it. As the three boys divided up their winnings, they gladly answered the questions from the group.

"Hey guys," said George. "Let's go to Kenly and ride around some. Maybe some of the gang is there."

"Great idea," Phil responded, thinking that Grace might be there.

"Okay," said Roland as he pressed that ooooga horn. This startled a couple of boys that were real close to the horn and they fell backwards knocking down a couple of men. Everyone laughed including Roland. Phil and George were bent over laughing so hard.

"Alright now, let's get going," said Roland. "I'll drive since I'm already behind the wheel. Phil, you and George go and crank this thing. As Phil and George started towards the front of the car, Roland switched on the ignition. The engine suddenly started, surprising everyone, including Phil and George. One of the boys said, "Hey, how in the hell did you do that Roland?"

"Easy," shouted Roland. "We got an automatic starter on this thing." He knew that it was just a coincidence and it could only happen when the engine stopped with one of the pistons near the top of the compression stroke and the engine was hot from the race. When the switch was turned on, it sent a sudden light flow of current to the magnetized flywheel which caused it to slightly move. This caused the piston to move enough for combustion and therefore started the engine.

"George, you and Phil get in," shouted Roland above the noise of the engine. The awed group of boys moved out of the way as Roland nudged the Silver Bullet out into the road and quickly disappeared in a cloud of dust. As the Silver Bullet went down the road, George looked back and saw that the group at the store had come out into the road to watch. He waved goodbye with both his hands. The three boys rode on towards Kenly singing and very happy with their Model T race car.

As usual, on a nice Saturday afternoon there was group of teenagers in front of the movie theater. There was Bert with a car full of girls. Grace was sitting on one of the front fenders talking to one of her girl friends.

As the Silver Bullet came down the street, the group stopped laughing and talking and started looking at it. Roland picked up a little speed and went by them, pressing the ooooga horn as

Roland sped by them they yelled at him to stop. Roland, Phil, and George laughed and waved back at them. Roland went on down to the end of the block, made a u-turn and came back to where the group was. He parked a short distance away from Bert's car knowing of Bert's feelings about he and Phil. When he parked the Silver Bullet, all the girls jumped out of Bert's car and came running down to the Silver Bullet.

"Hey, let me ride Roland," shouted one girl.

"I want to ride too," said another. Quickly the Silver Bullet was running over with giggling teenage girls. George got out since he was a little younger than most of the teenagers there. He spotted one of his girl friends up near the theater and went to talk to her.

Phil and Roland took turns riding the girls around town on the Silver Bullet. They yelled at Bert each time they passed by but Bert just sat and looked at them. He was not too happy with the sudden turn of events, since he was used to having the center of attention and having the girls drool over his car. The girls found it fun and exciting riding in the Silver Bullet. Phil pressed on the ooooga horn and the girls yelled and giggled and waved to anyone in sight as they rode around town.

As the darkness set in, Phil asked Grace if she would like to have a hamburger and cold drink. She accepted and so Phil asked Roland if he and his girlfriend would like to go to Cash Corner for hamburgers and drinks. Everyone agreed, but what about George? Roland saw George sitting on a bench near the theater and called him over to the Silver Bullet. "We're going to Cash Corner. Do you want to go with us?" asked Roland.

"I don't think so," replied George. "June and I have about decided to go to the movie. You can pick me up at the hot dog stand up here when you all get ready to go home."

"Okay," said Roland. "See you then."

Phil, Grace, Roland and his girlfriend rode the Silver Bullet on down the street to Cash Corner. Phil parked the car in the parking lot behind Red's store near the dance platform and jukebox. Phil and Roland got out of the Silver Bullet and went into the store to get some hamburgers, and drinks. While Red was making the hamburgers, he asked Phil, "What in hell is that thing you boys rode up on?" Phil laughed. "Well, it ain't a Model T and it ain't a Model A. It's a cross between the two. I guess you could call it a 'half-breed.' "

Roland added, "We call it the Silver Bullet because it's painted silver and it will go like a bullet."

"I'd like to see that," said Red.

"Well, if you don't believe it, ask those boys that just came up in that Model A coupe there. We outran them in a race this afternoon," said Roland.

Red gave the boys their hamburgers and drinks and they

returned to the Silver Bullet. When they reached the car, they found a group of boys and girls standing around it, inspecting it, and talking to Grace and Roland's girlfriend.

"What kind of car is this?" asked one of the boys.

"Its a racer," Phil said, almost growing weary of answering the same question. "Ain't you never seen a racer before?"

"Yeah," replied the boy, "but not a Model T racer."

"Press the lever on the horn, Grace," instructed Phil. Grace pushed down the lever and a loud "ooooga" noise erupted from the horn, scaring the youths standing nearest to it. Everyone else laughed at them for jumping at the sound of the horn.

"I think we need some music, don't we?" Phil asked Grace.

"Would be nice," she replied.

He got out of the Silver Bullet and went up on the platform where the jukebox was located. Phil selected a number on the jukebox, put in a nickel and returned to the car. As Phil got into the Silver Bullet and sat down beside Grace, the music started.

Grace said, "Why, that song is 'You Are My Sunshine.' "

Phil responded, "Love, to me that is exactly what you are, my sunshine." He gave her a quick, firm hug.

"Oh, Phil," Grace said as she cuddled closer to him. "You are a sweet boy."

As they finished their burgers, some of the teenagers began to dance on the platform. The jitterbug dance had become popular with the teenagers and a lot of them were learning the moves. Since the jitterbug dance required a lot of physical movement of the arms and feet, most of the girl wore loose fitting, knee length skirts with shoulder straps that went up over their blouses. It was also popular for them to wear bobby socks and saddle shoes.

Grace asked Phil if he would like to dance the jitterbug.

"Sure," he replied, "but, I'm not very good at it."

"Well, maybe I can teach you a little, if you want," Grace offered as they stepped on the stage.

To Phil, Grace looked prettier than usual. She had on a black skirt with a white blouse and white socks with white saddle shoes with a black strap. This seemed to compliment her dark hair and blue eyes.

As they started to dance, Phil said to her, "Love, you look lovely tonight."

She replied, "Why, Philip Barkley, that's so very sweet of you. You don't look bad yourself."

They completed the dance and returned to the Silver Bullet to rest and relax awhile. Roland and his girl were in the back seat. He told his girl that he couldn't dance very well and they stayed in the Silver Bullet, smooching and relaxing. Grace remarked to Phil that his dancing moves had improved a lot. This pleased Phil so he hugged her and said, "Love, you are a good teacher."

After they rested awhile and drank a Royal Crown Cola, Phil said, "Love, can you dance to 'The Beer Barrel Polka'?"

"Sure," she replied. "Can you?"

"Nothing like trying," replied Phil.

Phil and Grace got on the platform. Phil put a nickel in the jukebox and selected 'The Beer Barrel Polka.' Phil and Grace danced and swung each other around. They kicked their feet in and out. Suddenly Phil picked up Grace and spun her around. Most of the other dancers stopped dancing and watched Grace and Phil dance. By the end of the song, the two were nearly out of breath, but when they finished, they drew a round of applause from the rest of the group. Tired and perspiring, Grace and Phil returned to the Silver Bullet.

"Where are Roland and Pat?" asked Grace. "I don't see them in the car."

Roland raised his head up to clear the top of the rear seat and said, "Still here." Then he laughed. "We're just relaxing."

Phil got drinks for him and Grace. They talked awhile and suddenly Phil said, "Roland, we have to go boy. It's after midnight and that hot dog stand up town where George is waiting closes at midnight."

Roland added, "Yeah, I guess we had better take the girls home now or he'll be coming down here madder than hell."

They took grace and Pat their homes. Phil thanked Grace for a wonderful evening and she returned the compliment with a long kiss. Roland pressed lightly on the ooooga horn. Phil broke his embrace with Grace and returned to the Silver Bullet.

"We must go get George," said Roland as Phil got into the car.

"I know," said Phil. "But you didn't have to blow that horn."

"Well," replied Roland. "I was afraid that if I didn't you two would become frozen in that position." He drove off laughing.

When the two boys arrived at the hot dog stand uptown, they found George sitting on a bench in front of it.

"Where in the heck have you two been?" shouted George, trying to appear perturbed.

"Now, I wouldn't ask you that same question," replied Roland.

George got into the Silver Bullet and the three boys started on down the main street toward home. It had been a very exciting and successful day for the three boys so George soon forgot his anger and began to hum a tune. Phil started singing "You Are My Sunshine" as Roland and George joined in. They soon left the pavement in town and the Silver Bullet kicked up a cloud of dust in the moonlight as they headed for home.

41

Chapter Seven

In the following weeks of summer, the Barkleys and Varnes had to work very hard on their farms. Since prices had risen recently, Mr. Varnes and Daddy Barkley had increased the size of their tobacco and corn crops. Daddy Barkley had also increased the size of his cotton crop. Phil had worked late every Saturday. About the only time he had available for driving around in the Silver Bullet was on Sunday afternoons.

Phil and the boys loved to ride around on the Silver Bullet. This had been very limited lately because of the heavy work load on the farm and also the fact that their pocket money was very short. Finding scrap iron to sell was becoming more difficult. This made it hard for the boys to obtain enough money to buy gasoline and repair parts to keep the Silver Bullet running and also to be able to have enough to date with. Phil knew that he needed to find other ways to make money.

The day was a warm, sunny Saturday morning in August, 1940. The farm work had been caught up with so Roland, George and Mr. Varnes had come to the Barkley place to visit. Phil had joined Daddy Barkley on the front porch where he was sitting, talking to Mr. Varnes, discussing the war situation in Europe. The boys had stopped talking and were listening closely. Hitler and Nazi Germany were capturing every country they attacked. Hitler had occupied France and was threatening to invade England. Reports said that he had sent a message to his troops to be ready to invade England at any time. President Roosevelt and Congress had become greatly alarmed about the war in Europe. President Roosevelt asked Congress to speed up the shipment of war materials to the allies. This meant more jobs for the unemployed in the United States but it also meant there was greater danger of the United States having to enter the war. This could affect Phil, Roland and possibly George if it was to happen.

Soon the conversation turned to other things. Phil said to Roland, "I believe I'll go to Kenly and see Principal Yount about the assistant school bus driver job. Since we are at the end of the school bus route he might consider me."

Roland replied. "I don't think that will help much since you don't make any money unless the regular driver is absent."

Phil answered, "I don't know. But I've heard that the regular driver has obtained a part time job on the tobacco market and might lay off driving a day or two each week to work there."

"Maybe so," said Roland. "It couldn't hurt to try."

George, getting excited about the prospects of a ride on the Silver Bullet said, "Let's go Phil. Mr. Yount will probably be home and I'll put ten cents toward the gas. Okay?"

The boys jumped into the Silver Bullet and soon disappeared down the road in a cloud of dust. Upon arriving in Kenly it didn't take long to locate Mr. Yount's house. They found their principal in his front yard mowing the lawn. Phil had a lot of respect and admiration for Mr. Yount as did all the students and faculty of the school. He was fair but stern in dealing with everyone. Being a former wrestler in college and having a wrestler's physique commanded him utmost respect from even the roughest bullies in the school. Mr. Yount's method of punishment for the boys that got out of line would be to grab them by their shoulders and shake them so hard that their teeth would chatter and their eyes would roll. Once you were shaken by Mr. Yount, you did not want a repeat performance. Any girls that got out of line would usually have to do work on their lunch hours or stay after school for their punishment.

Mr. Yount appeared to be in a happy mood so Phil and the boys felt more relaxed. "Mr. Barkley, what kind of vehicle do you call this?" asked Mr. Yount as he approached the Silver Bullet.

"I guess you'd call it a 'half-breed'," replied Phil. "It's a little bit Model A Ford and a lot of Model T Ford."

"Its our transportation," said George, cutting to the heart of the matter. " . . . and it'll run too!" he added.

"You had better be careful," said Mr. Yount. "This thing looks fast enough to invite someone to challenge you to a race." Roland glanced at Phil and grinned. Word had evidently gotten around very quickly.

"We are careful not to go any faster than we have to," replied Phil, carefully choosing his words.

"What do you boys do when it rains?" asked Mr. Yount.

"We have a small tarpaulin under the rear seat that we attach to the top of the windshield and then cover ourselves with it," Phil replied.

Phil got out of the car and went around to where Mr. Yount is standing and said, "Mr. Yount, I've come to talk to you about something."

"Well son, what is it?" says Mr. Yount.

"I want to apply for the assistant school bus driver position for my route. Is it still open?"

"Yes, it is," replied Mr. Yount. "In fact, I had been wondering if you were interested."

"Yes, sir!"

"How's your driving record so far, son?"

"Great!" said Phil. "No accidents, no tickets. I try to drive very carefully."

"Well, there is another boy that's interested, and he has a good driving record too. But since your home is located near the end of the route, it will save some doubling back. I'll let you have the job."

"Thank you, sir," Phil responded excitedly. "You won't be disappointed."

"I had better not be. You must never forget that there are a lot of children that ride that bus, Phil. Their lives are in your hands."

"Oh, I will always remember that!" Phil said, shaking Mr. Yount's hand. "Thank you very much, sir."

Roland and George placed themselves into the front seat of the Silver bullet with Roland under the steering wheel. Phil got into the rear seat and said, "Drive, Roland." They waved to Mr. Yount as they left and Roland pressed on the ooooga horn lever. Mr. Yount waved, smiling at the sound of the horn.

The boys headed out of town. "Hey," said Phil. "Let's go home and get on some clean clothes and come back to Kenly. The town is showing free movies tonight. The Merchants' Bureau has started to show the free movies in order to draw more trade to the town. The movies are shown on the side of a building in a vacant lot inside town."

"We'd better hurry," shouted George over the noise of rushing wind. "It's getting late in the afternoon."

The Silver Bullet raised a cloud of dust as Roland urged it down the dirt road towards Kenly later that afternoon. A few miles further, they came around a curve and saw someone walking down the side of the road in front of them. They recognized him as Snooks Wells, one of their black friends that lived nearby. They yelled and blew the ooooga horn. Suddenly George yelled at Roland, "Turn here, turn here! That's my girlfriend's house."

Momentarily confused, Roland slammed on the brakes and turned the Silver Bullet towards the lane leading toward the house. The front wheels of the car crossed the little bridge over the ditch at the entrance but they were going too fast for the skidding rear wheels to follow. The rear wheels missed the bridge and struck the ditch hard, flipping the Silver Bullet over. It landed with its wheels up in the air spinning. Phil was thrown out of the rear seat and landed in the sand near the overturned vehicle. He picked himself up, and slightly dazed, he dusted himself off and found he was not hurt. Running back toward the overturned car, he heard Roland and George each yelling, "Get me out! Get me out!" They were still in the front seat, pinned under the vehicle. Phil was relieved to hear their voices.

"Give me a minute. I'll try to get you out," he reassured them. He took hold of the side of the vehicle and tried to raise it up but could barely move it.

Snooks, who had seen the whole thing, ran over to help. "Let me help, Mr. Phil."

Together, they were able to lift the side of the Silver Bullet

44

up high enough off the ground for Roland and George to crawl out. Luckily, the accident happened where the soil was very sandy and soft. As they checked themselves over, they found that they had survived the accident in pretty good shape, only Roland and George had a few scratches and a couple of bruises.

Snooks began to chuckle. "You boys sure are lucky," he said. "I was scared to death you all had broke your necks."

After they argued a few moments about whose fault the accident was, they decided to right the car and check the damage. With a resounding thud, the car landed on its wheels after the four young men turned it over. The only damage they found was that the windshield has been crushed flat beyond repair. They removed the broken windshield and threw it into the woods. They decided that if anyone around their homes asked about the windshield they would say they just decided to take it off. The three boys knew their parents would be very angry if they found out about the wreck. They climbed back into the car with Phil behind the driver's seat.

"I'd better drive," he offered. "You still look a little shook up, pal," he said to Roland. "Snooks, we appreciate your help. can we give you a lift into town?"

"Sure can," Snooks answered. "I'm going to see them free moving pictures everybody keeps talking about. But you sure this thing is okay to drive?"

"Oh, yeah," Phil reassured him. "This car is tougher than anything else on the road."

"Well, I've been wanting to ride in this thing anyway. I heard she'll go pretty fast. Is that right?"

"We don't know how fast she'll go," said George. "We don't have a speedometer. But it'll out run any Model A in the county."

"Now George," Roland chided. "You had better hold it down at bit. We ain't raced every Model A in the county."

"And we don't want to," Phil added.

Snooks got into the rear seat with George and the boys resumed their trip to Kenly. Phil felt inclined to show off the Silver Bullet a little to Snooks so he pulled down on the gas lever. Soon there was a big cloud of dust behind the car.

"Hey!" shouted Snooks, holding onto the sides of the car. "This thing will really go!" His eyes were wide open and he was greatly enjoying the speed. Suddenly, he began to sing, "I got them V8 blues, shake rattle and roll, I got them V8 blues."

Suddenly, Phil came upon a sharp curve in the road. The rear wheels skidded a little on the dirt as they went around the curve. "Hold on!," shouted Phil. "We'll make it. Never fear when I'm here," he laughed.

"Give 'er the gun, give 'er the gun!" shouted Snooks from the rear seat. He was laughing and enjoying the ride immensely.

It was almost sunset when the boys entered town. Phil found the empty lot where the free movie was to be shown. He parked the Silver Bullet in a good vantage spot near the middle of the parking lot. The projection crew was already setting up the projector. A lot of people both young and old were arriving to watch the free movie. A few of the people brought their automobiles but most were pedestrians. Several of the teenage boys gathered around the Silver Bullet. They were friends and buddies of the boys. They came to inspect the Silver Bullet and to talk to the boys. They begged Phil to let them ride in the Silver Bullet sometime. He assured them that he would, but that they would have to help out with buying some gasoline.

George suddenly pressed down on the ooooga horn lever. The loud blast startled some of the boys and everyone laughed. "Hey, I'll bet you can hear that thing all over town," said one of the boys.

"You may be right," retorted Roland. "Hey, Phil, that gives me an idea. You know, we might just need help sometime like fixing a flat tire or something like that. This horn could be used in town here to summon help from the boys. We could blow the ooooga horn three times and that would be a distress signal to any of our friends that hear it."

"Say, that's a great idea! Let's pass the word around to the gang," Phil replied.

"I'll help too, if I hears it," Snooks remarked as he got out of the Silver Bullet. "but I got to go now. Thanks for the ride. That sure is some car!"

"You're welcome, Snooks," Phil replied. "And we appreciate your help this afternoon."

It was dark by then and the movie was about to begin. "Hi, Phil. Hi, Roland," said Grace and Pat as they walked up to the car.

"Climb in, love," said Phil, delighted to see Grace. She got into the automobile and snuggled up beside Phil. Pat got in beside Roland. George got out and went off to search for his friends. Since the movie people didn't announce the title of the movie to be shown, the people who came to see it have to take what they get. Just then, the camera operator started the movie. It was a "western" starring Bob Steele and his friends. Bob Steele was a two-fisted, fighting cowboy that the crowd liked very much. They applauded as the show began.

Phil and Roland settled down in their seats with their girlfriends. Since a lot of the people had to stand up to see the show, the couples in the Silver Bullet had to slink down in their seats as far as they could in order to gain any privacy.

Grace looked at Phil. "Honey where have you been lately. I haven't seen you in weeks."

"Sorry, love," answered Phil. "We have all been working

46

hard the past weeks on the farm. We've had no time for anything else!" He put his arm around her and she snuggled up close to him. "But things are getting better now."

She gave him a kiss on the cheek and said, "You know, sweetie, I have missed you a lot."

"Same here," Phil cooed happily.

As the movie continued, Phil and Roland managed to get in a little smooching, between the fights and shooting scraps on the screen, that is. Suddenly, Roland muttered, "Hey, pal. I'm not sure, but what's moved in beside us in that '38 Chevrolet sedan might be trouble."

Phil glanced over and saw three young men in the car. They appeared to be roughnecks from some other town. Neither Phil nor Roland had ever seen them before. They were drinking, cursing, and making crude remarks to people around them.

Roland whispered, "Let's try to ignore them. Maybe they won't bother us."

"I hope you're right," replied Phil.

But their hopes soon vanished as the man in the driver's seat stuck his head out of his window and yelled at Phil. "Hey you, in the driver's seat! You got it going good, huh?" He and his two friends laughed. "Gettin' you some of that good sugar, ain't you?"

Phil ignored the other driver, but he couldn't hide the fact that he was becoming very agitated. The driver of the Chevy noticed Phil's anger and continued his taunting.

"Hey, sugar," he said to Grace. "That ain't no Clark Gable you got there. He might think he is, but he's just trying to fool you." The other two boys in the Chevy are howling with laughter.

Phil's temper was about to boil over. Grace tried to calm him. "Just ignore them, honey."

As the movie continued, the roughnecks kept up their agitation by ridiculing the Silver Bullet. This was about all Phil could take, but he continued to hold his temper with Grace's encouragement. A few minutes later, however, the roughneck driver returned his remarks toward Grace.

"Hey, honey. Ain't you about tired of old Clark Gable there? Don't you want to know what it's like being with a real man? You don't know what you're missing by not being over here with me and my boys."

Phil finally erupted. "I'll shut that damned fool's trap!" he said, rising out of his seat.

Roland placed his hand on Phil's shoulder and shoved him back into the seat. "Listen to me, pal. We don't need to sink to their level. Let's just go to Cash Corner if we can't watch this movie in peace."

"That's a good idea," Grace pleaded. "The show's almost

over anyway."

"Well, okay," Phil replied. The tips of his ears still burned with anger as Roland eased out of the car to turn the crank in front of the engine. When the engine fired, Roland quickly hopped back into the Silver Bullet and they headed toward their favorite dancing spot.

By the time they arrived at Cash Corner, Phil was feeling much better. Seeing several couples already on the platform dancing brightened his spirits even more. Phil parked the Silver gullet near the platform so they could relax in it between dances. As he turned off the engine, someone put a nickel in the jukebox and the song "Three Little Fishes" began to ring out. Roland immediately began to sing along. " . . . so they swam and they swam right over the dam."

"Hey, I didn't know we had a singer in the car," said Pat, laughing.

"I didn't either," Phil added, laughing at Roland. "And I still don't." "You just don't know good singing when you hear it," replied Roland. "Phil, sweetheart. Would you like to jitterbug?" asked Grace.

"Sure would," replied Phil. "I'll see if I can pick out a good tune." Phil went up on the dance platform and put a nickel in the jukebox. Grace joined him. The jukebox started to play Chattanooga Choo Choo.

"Ooh, I like that one," said Grace, as she and Phil started to dance. Roland and Pat came to the platform to dance also. The platform was soon filled with dancing teenagers having a good time. When the song was over, the dancers returned to their cars to relax.

Since jitterbugging was a very physical dance, Phil, Grace, Pat and Roland returned to the Silver Bullet to relax. They were sitting and talking when they noticed a car parked nearby.

"Don't look now," said Roland, "but our roughneck friends seem to have found us again."

"Let's not pay any attention to them," said Pat. "Maybe they'll leave us alone."

They continued talking and eating popcorn. After a little while, the roughneck driver of the Chevy looked over at Grace. After a moment, he hit the side of his car and shouted at Grace.

"Hey you, sweet lips! Why don't you ditch old Clark Gable there and come over here. Me and my boys will show you some real romance." He turned to his buddies and laughed loudly. "Won't we boys?" His friends laughed along with him.

Phil could feel his temper rising rapidly. He was not used to seeing someone show disrespect to women and especially to ones he cared for so much. He rose to get out of the Silver Bullet.

"Hold it, pal. Just hold it," Roland began, trying to pull Phil back into his seat. "This ain't' the time or place, buddy. There are three of them and only two of us. Besides, they're much bigger than we are. They'd beat us to a pulp!"

Phil realized Roland was right and settled back down into his seat. He was simultaneously angry at the situation and embarrassed at his seeming inability to do anything about it. If ignoring these guys is the smart thing to do, he wondered, why does it feel wrong?

It wasn't long before the three roughnecks were cursing and taunting the couples again. Most of the other teenagers have moved away. Some even left the parking lot. Soon, the roughnecks began to ridicule the Silver Bullet again. Phil's anger was growing hotter every minute. Suddenly, one of the roughnecks pitched a beer bottle over at Phil's car. It missed the car, but glanced off Phil's forehead! In a few seconds, a small knot was beginning to form where the bottle hit him.

Phil jumped out of the car before anyone could stop him. As he rounded the front of the Silver Bullet, the roughneck driver got out of the Chevy and began to taunting Phil, calling him "Little Clarkie." Amidst the sudden calamity, Roland reached over the driver's seat of the Silver Bullet and frantically pressed the lever on the ooooga horn three times. When he pressed it three times again, the roughnecks came over to the Silver Bullet. Phil moved back around to the driver's side of his car. He could smell the alcohol on the breath of the roughneck driver.

"What in hell kind of horn is that?" said one of the roughnecks. He tried to grab the horn.

"Keep your damned hands off that!" Phil shouted, slapping the boy's hand away from the horn. The boy backed away momentarily.

"Clarkie, you had better settle down, now," warned the roughneck driver. "My buddy wants to blow that crazy sounding horn on your car and you're going to let him . . . or else."

"Or else, what?" Phil responded hotly out of the corner of his eye, he could see the third roughneck clenching his fists. The driver of the Chevy was slowly moving closer. I guess this is where I get beaten to a pulp, Phil thought. Roland jumped out of the Silver Bullet and stood beside Phil.

Just as the three roughnecks began to grab Phil and Roland, everyone quickly became aware of what sounded like horses galloping up the street. Suddenly, a gang of about ten boys led by George Varnes rounded the corner of Red's store and quickly formed a circle around the roughnecks. "What's going on, Phil?" George panted. He and his buddies had run the three, long, city blocks from where they were to Cash Corner as soon as they had heard Roland's distress signal on the ooogah horn.

Immediately relieved to see reinforcements arrive, Phil responded confidently, "Oh, not much, little buddy. These three drunk skunks were just getting ready to leave."

49

As soon as the three roughnecks realized they were surrounded and outnumbered, they wasted no time jumping back into the '38 Chevy and locking the doors. As they started the Chevy to try and leave, George and his buddies lifted up the rear end of their car. With the rear wheels spinning, the driver of the Chevy began to beg George to let him leave.

"Listen, buster," George replied. "Those are my friends you were bothering."

"We just wanted to look at that funny Model T," the roughneck driver whined as he turned off the Chevy's engine.

"I'll just bet you were," George remarked sarcastically. His friends had put down the car and were beginning to rock it from side to side. It was all the occupants could do hang on inside. They were begging for the boys to stop rocking the car.

"What's it worth to you," asked George.

"We got no money," replied the roughneck driver.

"Too bad," retorted George. "Give it to 'em, boys." George's friends gleefully rocked the car harder, until the wheels raised off the ground with each back and forth motion.

"Okay, okay!" shouted the roughneck driver after a few moments.

George told his buddies to stop rocking the car. After the vehicle rested motionless, the roughneck driver rolled down his window and handed George several bills and some change. After counting it, George exclaimed, "Hey, fellahs! This is enough for each of us to get a hot dog and a Royal Crown Cola! How about it? Do we want to let these bums go?"

"Where else are we going to have some fun and get paid too," one of George's pals remarked. "Might as well enjoy the 'fruits' of all our hard work." The rest of George's group laughed loudly at the joke.

"Okay, you bums," said George to the roughnecks. "Get the hell out of here and don't come back."

The roughneck driver wasted no time firing up his engine. He stomped on the accelerator pedal and spun the wheels of the '38 Chevy all the way out of the parking lot onto the paved street. Couples all around the dance platform cheered loudly at how George and his buddies saved the day. Smiling and slapping each other on the back, the group of boys headed toward Red's grill for their well-earned hot dogs. Phil and Roland thanked their friends for coming to their aid and then got back into the Silver Bullet with Grace and Pat.

"I'm just glad Roland remembered to use that oooogah horn as a distress signal," said Grace, obviously relieved that the incident was over. "It was about to be a nasty situation."

"I'm just glad that George and his friends could hear it way up the street where they were," said Pat.

"Me too," Phil laughed. "I was getting ready to be beaten to a pulp."

Grace chimed in as she sidled up close to Phil, "I think you and Roland deserve some credit for handling those bullies until help came."

"Yeah," Pat added. "I thought for sure that you two were about to punch that big bully."

"I came awfully close," Phil replied, feeling a bit proud due to this sudden praise from the girls. His winsome smile had returned to his face. Just then, George and a few of his friends walked up to the Silver Bullet. "Man, you were about to get socked good, weren't you?" he said to Phil and Roland while he rubbed the oooogah horn.

"You bet, pal," replied Phil. "We were mighty glad to see you and your buddies come around that corner there."

"Well, I almost didn't hear this old thing," George remarked. "If I had been inside the hot dog stand uptown," instead of sitting on the bench outside, I would never have heard the signal."

"Pal," Phil said, "We appreciate you coming to help out, don't we gang?"

"You're darn tootin'!" Roland shouted from the rear seat, with Grace and Pat agreeing also.

"Glad I could help," George replied, feeling proud that he could was able to come to the aid of his older brother and Phil.

The night was getting late. Most of the group had left for home, or other, more secluded places. Someone had put a nickel in the jukebox and the song "San Antonio Rose" was playing. It was a smooth song, and relaxing to Phil so he and Grace leaned back in their seats to enjoy it.

George asked, "Are you guys going to be here much longer?"

"No," replied Phil. "We'll be taking the girls home soon as this song is over. You can wait here if you want and we'll come back to pick you up."

"Okay," said George. "I'll go shoot some pool and aggravate Red a little while."

When the song was finished Phil said, "It's getting late gang. I guess we had better call it a night. I'm awfully sorry about the trouble ladies."

"Oh, honey," Grace said as she squeezed Phil's arm. "Don't be sorry. It wasn't your fault. I think you handled the situation like a real gentleman." She gave Phil a long kiss that started his heart pounding.

"Hey, hey," said Roland from the rear seat. "You two had better hold that down. We won't ever get these girls home."

Phil and Grace giggled back at him. "Party pooper!" Phil said, laughing.

Phil got out of the car and went around to the front to crank the engine. The two boys took their girls home, then returned to Cash Corner to pick up George.

"Man, it's been an exciting day!" said George as they headed out of Kenly toward home.

"You can say that again!" Phil replied.

Chapter Eight

By mid-September of 1940, the war in Europe had worsened. The Italians had invaded Egypt and the dreaded Luftwaffe was involved in an all out aerial assault on London. The Royal Air Force was causing him trouble, but Hitler kept pounding the British island with everything he had. But what really concerned people in the United States was Hitler's decision to combine forces with the Italians and Japanese in order to increase the effectiveness of his master plan to rule Europe. Almost as soon as the Axis Pact was signed, the U.S. Congress enacted The Selective Service Act. This allowed them to draft into military service all "able bodied" men between the ages of twenty-one and thirty-six.

Some of these young men had voluntarily enlisted so they could choose the branch of the military in which they would serve. Phil's neighbor, Jack Balance, had entered the Army Air Corps by passing tests that would allow him to become an aircraft mechanic. Phil once overheard some older boys at Cash Corner debating among themselves which branch of the military they would choose. One said he thought the Navy would be good because sailors slept in a bunk every night and didn't have to cook their food over camp fires. Another young man wanted to be in the Army infantry because his father had been a decorated soldier in 1918 during The Great War, and he wanted to keep up the family tradition.

Twenty-one sounded so far in the future to Phil, he hadn't thought much about joining the military. A lot of people thought the war would be over in another year anyway. For the moment, he was engrossed in a book about airplanes he had borrowed from his Uncle Bill. It had pictures of all the latest aircraft being built for the military as well as planes used in civilian flying. As he was poring over a color photo of the Ford Tri-motor plane used by the U.S. Post Office, he heard a low humming noise overhead. With Seymour-Johnson Army Air Base just thirty miles away in Goldsboro, Phil had seen a lot of military planes flying overhead in the past six months. This one was so high up, it was hard to make out exactly what it could be, but Phil stared at it long enough to recognize the wing shape and the number of engines. Looking in his uncle's book, he quickly determined it must have been a B-17, otherwise known as "The Flying Fortress." As he studied the picture of the well-armed plane, he imagined what it must be like to fly such a huge machine. He suddenly shuddered at the feeling of excitement and adventure that tingled through his body. He had almost become lost in another flying daydream when Roland and George Varnes rode up on their bicycles.

"Hey, Phil. What are you doing?"

"Oh," Phil stammered as his imaginary adventure abruptly came to an end. "I was, ah, just looking through this book about planes," he replied.

"Where did that bus come from?" asked George.

The sudden change of subject threw Phil for a moment, until he realized George was asking about the school bus parked in his front yard.

"Oh, that. Well, the regular driver has to work on the tobacco market, so he wanted me to drive it for a week. I went to his house yesterday to get it."

"It looks as if you've been trying to wear a ditch in your daddy's driveway," remarked Roland.

"Yeah, I know." Phil answered. "I've circled around the house a few times. That thing is so darned long, I felt as if I needed practice making turns before I started my route tomorrow. I'd sure hate to turn over a school bus loaded with kids, wouldn't you?"

"I know what you mean," said Roland. "Hey, you want to go to Cash Corner later this afternoon?"

"I can't," Phil replied, turning his eyes back into the pages of the airplane book. "This morning at church, someone told Daddy about what happened there last night. He said he doesn't want me going back there for a week or so at least."

"Didn't you tell him those other guys started the trouble?"

"Yeah. I even told him they had been drinking because I thought it would make him understand that that's not what normally goes on at Red's Place. Boy, that sure backfired on me. When he heard that, he almost told me never to go back there."

"That's too bad," said George, shaking his head. "I hope he doesn't say anything about it to our dad."

"I wouldn't count on it," said Phil.

Roland looked at George and said, "We had better get going, little brother. If we don't, someone might decide that we can't go to Cash Corner either."

"You boys going to drive the Silver Bullet?" Phil asked.

"We were thinking about it, but now I'm not sure we should go back to the house," Roland replied. "Maybe we'd better just leave now."

"Say hello to Grace for me, will you?" Phil asked.

"Sure, buddy," George said as he turned his bike around. "See you in the funny pages."

Phil watched them lead a small cloud of dust down the driveway toward the road. In a few moments, he was daydreaming about flying again.

The next day, Phil drove the bus to school with no problems. After all the students had disembarked, he gathered up his books, closed the doors, and took the keys toward the main

54

office. As he was handing the school bus keys to Mrs. Johnston, the school secretary, Coach Sherman was coming out of Principal Yount's office. A tall, muscular, dark-haired boy was just behind him. "Phil Barkley! Just who I was going to look for," the coach exclaimed. "Phil, I want you to meet Jim Kelford." He continued talking as Phil shook the boy's hand. "Jim has transferred to Kenly from a school up near Raleigh. He was quarterback of their football team last year and I'm thinking of starting him as ours this year." Coach turned to Jim and continued. "Phil is our star running back. I've seen him carry a football through a solid line with two men hanging on his back. He hasn't had much practice with a passing strategy though, so you'll have to work with him every chance you get, Jim. Well, I'll see you boys on the field this afternoon. Phil, why don't you take Jim to his classes and show him around today?"

At first, Phil felt a bit strange being seen with this new boy. It seemed as if every girl in the school was staring at them both. Of course, they had a good reason. Even Phil's first impression of him was about how handsome this fellow was. Jim Kelford stood two inches taller than Phil. His hair was dark like an oak barrel gets when it becomes wet, but his eyes were almost bright blue. With just the slightest ruddy tinge in his cheeks, Jim looked as if he'd just come inside on a winter day. Besides all this, his teeth were almost perfectly straight and white. If it had not been for the small, brown mole on his forehead, Jim Kelford might have been perfect. Anyway, the combination of his features gave him the look of someone who was always very alert . . . and in demand by the girls.

As the morning passed, Phil realized that he and Jim might soon become the best of friends. Jim was easy going and very observant. He didn't hesitate when called upon in class, even when he wasn't exactly sure of his answer. He seemed to have a very positive attitude, at least from the comments he made about things he noticed as they toured the school between classes. He also seemed genuinely interested to meet other people as they passed in the halls. Phil introduced him to Roland and George Varnes and most of the boys who played sports. Even the teachers all seemed to like Jim as soon as they met him. By lunchtime, it had become such a warm day that most of the older students ate outside. After their food was gone, Phil and Jim decided to hold an informal practice by starting a game of tag football with some of the other guys on the team. As the game began, other students gathered along the sidelines to watch. Jim called for a pass play in which Phil would go through the line and run about ten yards before cutting back to the left. Jim executed the play perfectly, but as Phil caught the ball, his attention was suddenly caught by something very bright and golden to his right. He stopped and stared at the most beautiful girl he had ever seen in his life, and she just happened to be standing with his sister, Anita. As the two girls smiled at Phil, the opposing team caught up with him and pounded him on the back.

Jim came running toward Phil, yelling, "You had an open field, boy! Why did you stop?"

"I, uh, I slipped," Phil replied with the first excuse he could muster.

"But this ground is as dry as a bone," Jim protested. "Maybe you should take off those slick bottom shoes." He slapped Phil on the back and added, "Just try to be more careful on the next play."

Phil's mind was on the sidelines as they huddled near the ball for instructions. Jim told them to execute the same play again because the other team wouldn't be expecting that. As they lined up behind the ball, Phil searched the sidelines for a glimpse of his sister's beautiful friend. She had on a powder blue dress that almost looked as if it had been starched and pressed ten minutes ago. Since she stood beside Anita, he could tell she was about five feet and nine inches tall, and every inch was packed into a voluptuous figure that some older women would envy. Even from this distance, Phil could make out that her eyes were almost as blue as Jim Kelford's. But her hair was what held his attention like a moth drawn to a candle. It was thick and wavy, coming down almost. to her shoulders, and it was so blonde, it was almost white.

The center snapped the ball to Jim, and Phil broke through the opposing line as if he were tracing his previous steps by memory. Somehow, his eyes never left the girl on the sidelines. About three seconds later, the football hit him in the head and he went down like a bowling pin. Howls of laughter arose from around the field. After another player helped him up, Phil returned to the huddle. He glanced to the sideline just long enough to see his sister and the new girl walking away from the field.

"Maybe we'd better stick to a running play," Jim was saying as Phil joined his team. "Phil can't seem to keep his eyes on the ball."

"I'm not feeling very well," Phil offered his second lame excuse. "I think it might be something I ate."

"Maybe you should sit on the sidelines and rest a minute," said one of the other boys.

"Maybe he should go catch that girl in the blue dress before she gets away. At least he could say he caught something today," said Jim. Phil shot him a quick glance and found Jim grinning at him with an understanding twinkle in his eyes. "I just hope she doesn't come to the game on Friday night," Jim continued. "If she does, we may have to let Phil trade in his uniform for a cheer leading outfit." Phil laughed along with the other boys as Jim slapped him on the back and said, "See you at practice this afternoon, right?" "Right," Phil replied as he quickly retreated toward the building he'd seen his sister and her new friend enter. Ten minutes later, after a fruitless search, Phil gave up as the bell rang for everyone to return to classes. I guess I'll just have to ask Anita about her later.

That night, after supper, Phil knocked on the door to his sister's room. He cracked the door after a moment and found her totally absorbed in a textbook, as usual. Anita was the best student in their family and she often brought home nothing but A's on her report card.

"Oh, I'm sorry, Phil. I guess I didn't hear you knock. Come in." Then, realizing what he was there to ask her about, she smiled and teasingly asked, "Are you feeling better now than you were at lunch today? Didn't that football hurt when it hit you in the head?" She covered her mouth with her hand and giggled.

Phil grinned sheepishly. "I just took my eyes off the ball for one second. Anyway, you should have seen us at practice during sixth period. I caught every ball and even made two touchdowns."

"I guess it helps when you don't have any distractions," Anita continued to tease.

"Okay, so you know why I wasn't paying attention at the game after lunch. Who is she?" "Why, do you think she's cute?"

"I guess she's alright," Phil replied, trying to hide his excitement.

"Oh, you're just thinking about her boobs. Honestly Phil, I'm beginning to think all men are alike. Everywhere we went today, the boys stared at her chest."

"Well it might surprise you to know that I could easily describe every feature of her face," Phil quickly defended himself. "For example, her eyes are the color of robin's eggs, and her cheeks are rosy like ripe peaches, and . . ."

"Okay, okay. You've proved your point," Anita conceded.

"And she has nice boobs too," Phil said with a grin. "Who is she?"

"Her name is Linda Anne Hinton and she has just moved here from Smithfield. She has a boyfriend, Phil."

"Did he move here too?"

"No, dummy, he lives in Smithfield."

"That's too bad for him. Do you think she'd go out with me?"

"She did say that you were cute . . . and funny!"

"Will you introduce us tomorrow?"

"I guess so."

The next day at lunch, Phil and Jim quickly ate and went to the large yard outside the school lunchroom to practice a few pass plays. Phil had been anxious all morning, anticipating the meeting his sister had promised. Running around and catching the football had helped him relax a bit, but he was still glancing around after each pass.

"What are you looking for?" asked Jim finally.

Phil hesitated as he handed the ball back to his friend. "Well, you know that girl I saw yesterday?"

"Yeah, the one with the blue dress and the blonde hair?"

"She's the one. Anyway, my sister promised to introduce us today at lunch."

Just then, the two girls walked around the corner behind Phil's back. Jim quickly seized the opportunity to have some fun at the expense of his new buddy.

"She shook you up pretty good, huh?" Jim chuckled.

"Man, I've been waiting for this all morning long, and if I don't see her soon, I think I'm going to bust!"

"You think she's pretty, don't you?"

"She's the most beautiful girl I've ever seen in my life!"

"What will you say to her when you meet?" Jim asked as the girls came within earshot.

Phil shoved his hands into his pockets and thought for only a second before answering. "The first thing I'll do is tell her how pretty I think she is. Then, I might try to find out what things she likes to do. Who knows, I might even ask her out for a date."

"Or maybe you'll just start by saying, 'Hello,' " his sister Anita interrupted.

Phil whirled around, his cheeks instantly becoming red. He glanced back at Jim, who was not totally successful at concealing his amusement, and instantly knew that he had been set up in this slightly embarrassing situation. He felt a swelling sensation in his throat as his heart began to pound unmercifully.

"This is Linda Hinton," Anita began her introductions. "And Linda, this is my brother, Philip."

Phil extended his hand and managed to stammer, "I'm, I'm very glad to meet you, Linda." He glanced at her right hand as they touched. Up close, she was even more beautiful than he had imagined. Her complexion was smooth and creamy. She had long, slender fingers and a tiny wrist on which she wore a delicate bracelet with the letter E monogrammed into a small heart.

"Well aren't you going to introduce us to your friend, Phil?" Anita chided.

"Oh, oh yes." His voice was still a bit shaky. "Ladies, meet Jim Kelford. Jim, this is my younger sister, Anita. And this is Linda Hinton."

"I'm pleased to meet both of you," Jim replied. "I understand you are from Smithfield, Linda."

"Yes," Linda answered. "My father works for the bank. He was transferred here about two months ago and my mother and I

58

joined him last week after we sold our house."

"Maybe you know a girl named Anne Creech." Jim said. "She's my girlfriend. She goes by the nickname of 'Strawberry' because her hair is strawberry-blonde colored."

"Yes, I think I do," Linda replied. "She and I never had classes together, but I remember seeing her around school. She is a very pretty girl in my opinion."

"Thanks," Jim said, beaming with pride.

Even though his friend was hogging the conversation, Phil was thankful for the brief exchange between Jim and Linda as it gave him time to regain his composure.

"You didn't tell me you had a girlfriend," Phil interjected to Jim.

"There's so much to tell about me, I just couldn't fit it all into one day," Jim answered, half joking. "Besides, I have to get you trained for football. I mean, we can't have any more episodes like yesterday . . . especially on Friday night!" Jim winked at Anita and began to laugh aloud after the last comment. Anita giggled along with him.

Linda blushed a bit at the remark. Anita had obviously told her friend the real reason for Phil getting hit in the head with the football the previous day.

Phil's charm was like a sixth sense, and he went with the feeling that it was time to pour it on thick. "I couldn't help it. I was blinded by some beautiful woman who had blonde hair like corn silk and a powder blue dress."

Linda's cheeks turned a darker pink. She was looking at the ground, standing with her hands clasped behind her back and making a small arc in the grass with the toe of her oxfords. She glanced up for only a second, but when her eyes met Phil's, he thought he could tell that his charm was working. Just as he was about to continue, the bell rang to end their lunch period. Phil is disappointed at not having more time to talk, and especially at not getting a chance to ask Linda for a date.

"We'll see you boys later," said Anita. "Glad to meet you Jim. I hope you play well Friday night."

"Thanks, Anita," Jim replied.

As the girls turned to leave, Phil quickly said, "It was very good to meet you, Linda. See you again tomorrow?"

Linda glanced over her shoulder and smiled. "Maybe," she replied.

As the two boys watched them walk away, Jim chuckled. "Sorry about that, buddy. I just couldn't resist. I couldn't let her see you with that 'lovesick puppy' look on your face."

"Don't worry, pal," Phil replied, never taking his eyes off Linda's hair. "I'll get you back some day." He laughed and gave his new friend a friendly punch on the arm. "Now tell me about this girlfriend of yours. Hey, maybe we could go on a double date sometime! How about it?"

"Sure thing, Phil," Jim replied. "But who are you going to bring?"

"I sure hope its a certain young lady with blonde hair that we just met."

As he and Jim walked toward their next class, Phil wondered just what kind of impression he'd made on Linda. He wondered if she would accept his offer of a date sometime. Even more, he wondered what that "E" stood for on her bracelet.

Chapter Nine

As October passed, Phil and Jim Kelford became good friends. They became so well acquainted because they attended history and chemistry classes together. They also went out at lunch breaks to practice with a football and to play games with their friends when the weather permitted. Phil anxiously awaited that time of day since he hoped to see Linda again.

But as each day passed, he saw less and less of Linda and Anita. This bothered Phil greatly since he wanted to get to know Linda much better. As it was very unusual for girls to act coolly toward him, Phil became more anxious. He kept wondering whether or not he had said something she didn't like or if maybe his clothes weren't nice enough.

One night Phil couldn't get it off his mind so he decided to talk with Anita. She was the closest person to Linda that he knew so she might know something. He found her in her room studying for an exam. He knocked on her door and she told him to come in.

He says, "Sis, I have something to ask you. And I want you to tell me the truth."

"What is it?" she asked.

"Well, it's about Linda. She doesn't seem very friendly toward me lately. Have I said something wrong or done something he didn't like?"

"Oh no," Anita exclaimed. "I thought she acted friendly to you."

"Well, she hasn't said much to me lately and I thought she was a bit cool toward me."

"Philip Barkley! I do believe you are getting sweet on her," Anita teased.

Phil looked sheepishly at the floor. "She's the prettiest girl I've ever seen and she seems to be a sweet person."

"She's friendly too," said Anita. "But I think she already has a boyfriend. She told me something about a boy named Eddie who lives in Smithfield. Maybe that's it."

Phil thanked Anita and returned to his room where he lay across his bed and began to ponder the situation. He felt better about himself, but this guy in Smithfield presented an entirely different problem. He finally fell into a restless sleep.

Over the next few days, Phil didn't get a chance to speak with Linda. He occasionally spotted her walking across the playground with Anita and some other girls, but they never came close to where the boys practiced football. He finally decided the only way to reach her was to write a note.

Thursday evening Phil sat at his small desk, telling Linda on paper how much he admired her and that he looked forward to the time when he could talk to her again. After supper he gave the note to Anita to pass along the next day at school. He was a bit disappointed to discover Anita had no reply that afternoon when they returned home from school. By Sunday, Phil had become so impatient to see Linda that he cranked up the Silver Bullet and headed for town. The late October weather was cool and cloudy and Phil had to button up his sweater to keep warm. He wished the windshield was back on the Silver Bullet.

He arrived in town and finally found Linda's house. He pulled into the driveway and parked near the front porch. He rang the door buzzer and was relieved when Linda answered the door instead of one of her parents.

"Hi there, Linda!" he began. "I was just riding around and when I figured out that this was your house, I decided to stop in and say hello."

"Well, that's awfully nice of you, Phil," Linda replied. "Won't you come in?"

A warm sensation came over Phil, and he liked it. "I can't stay long. Hey, instead of me coming inside, why don't you come out and let me show you the famous Silver Bullet that you've heard so much about."

"Sure, Phil. I'd like that," Linda replied.

They walked around the car together and Phil pointed out the wire spoke wheels and large tires. He showed her the engine and explained how it was started. When they came to the drivers side of the car, Phil pressed on the ooooga horn lever. The sudden loud sound startled Linda slightly, and she laughed at herself for catching her breath.

Phil apologized. "Oh, I'm sorry! I didn't mean to scare you."

"That's alright, Phil," she said, touching his arm reassuringly. "I just didn't expect that kind of noise."

"Would you like to go for a ride?"

"Ah, maybe some other day," she replied. "It is cloudy and cool and you don't have a top, or a heater. Besides, I thought you said you couldn't stay long."

"Uh, that's right," Phil stammered. "Well, some day soon, when the weather is warmer and the skies are clear."

"Sure, Phil. I'd like to ride in your Silver Bullet." She turned to go up the steps of the porch. "Thanks for stopping by, Phil. See you around school." She waved at Phil and suddenly turned to go into her house.

As Phil climbed into his car, he couldn't help but smile because Linda had smiled so sweetly at him before she went inside. But a few moments later, it struck Phil as odd that she hadn't mentioned the note that he wrote.

When Phil returned home, Daddy Barkley noticed that Phil was very quiet and not his usual happy self. "Son, are you sick or did you just have girl trouble?" Anita was sitting close by and began to giggle. Daddy Barkley laughed. Phil managed a weak grin, but hurried off to his room. Opening the door, he found his two younger brothers playing with his football equipment.

"Get out of here!" he shouted. "Now!"

Startled by the ferocious tone of their older brother's voice, the twins scrambled over each other to get out of Phil's room. They were bewildered at Phil's behavior because he is usually so good to them.

On Monday, Phil could hardly wait for the lunch hour. He hoped Anita would bring a reply from Linda to the note he wrote last week. When lunch time arrived Phil hurried onto the playground to practice football with his buddies and teammates. As they ran different plays, he searched the playground, hoping to spot Linda or Anita. Just as the period was almost over, Anita sauntered up to him with a small, folded piece of paper in her hand.

"Is this what you've been waiting for?" she giggled.

Phil didn't care. He grabbed the paper, thanked his sister, and turned to read Linda's note. A few seconds later, he turned back toward Anita. "Hey, sis. Tell her I said hello, will you?" Anita giggled again when she saw the big grin on her brother's face and the sparkle that had returned to his eyes.

"I'll think about it," she teased.

"You had better," Phil retorted. "Or you and your friends won't ever ride in the Silver Bullet again."

Anita laughed aloud as she turned to rejoin Linda and her friends in the library. She knew Phil would never keep his threat because he was just too kind-hearted.

Phil trotted over to a bench and sat down to read Linda's reply. But as his eyes scanned each line, his facial muscles became more tense. The note was friendly in tone, but short and to the point. She thanked Phil for dropping by to see her on Sunday. Then she simply stated that she had a boyfriend named Eddie Hart who lived in Smithfield. He was very nice and her mother liked him too.

The smile vanished from Phil's face so quickly, it surprised even him. He glanced up to make sure no one was watching him read the note so eagerly. When his eyes returned to the page, his smile returned a few seconds later. Linda continued by saying that she thought he was a very nice young man and she would like it very much if they became friends. She also added that she really would like to go for a ride in the Silver Bullet on a warm, clear day.

He felt better after finishing the note, but the business about a boyfriend still bothered Phil. As he rejoined his friends, Jim Kelford noticed that something wasn't quite right.

"That's all for today," Jim shouted to the others. He walked over to where Phil was standing. "Say, pal," he said, slapping

63

Phil on the back. "You feeling okay? You look a little tired, or sick even."

"Cut it out," Phil replied.

"What do you mean, Phil? Tell me what's wrong."

"I just don't feel good," Phil replied. "That's all."

Jim knew better than to press the issue further. He put his arm on Phil's shoulder and they headed back to their classrooms.

During the following weeks, Phil occasionally wrote notes to Linda. He even asked her for a date in one of them. Her replies left him slightly bewildered. She never specifically said no, but she never said yes either. From the way she wrote, however, he did feel that she somehow wanted to say yes, but felt that she couldn't. Phil wondered if her mother was at the heart of the problem.

Roland and George even noticed the change in Phil when they came to visit. One warm, Friday afternoon in November Roland proposed that they go to Kenly. "Maybe the gang will all be there. The town is having free movies again. We could go to Cash Corner afterwards."

"Yeah!" exclaimed George. "It seems like years since we've been to Kenly to see our friends. what do you say, Phil?"

"Well, okay," Phil gave in. "If that's what you guys want."

On the way to town, George sat in the rear seat and tried to liven things up. He began to sing, "I've been working on the railroad . . ." Roland joined in, and soon, Phil was singing along in spite of himself.

It was dark by the time they arrived at the vacant lot where the movie was to be shown. As Roland parked the Silver Bullet, Phil noticed Bert's car parked nearby with three girls in the car. One looked like Grace Langston. In a moment, she got out of Bert's car and walked up to the Silver Bullet.

"Hi, Phil. What's cooking? Haven't seen you boys in a long time."

"Hi, Grace. Want to climb in?"

"Sure, love."

"What kind of movie are they showing tonight?" Phil asked.

"I think its a Western with Tom Mix," Grace replied.

A moment later, Roland left to see if he could find Pat. George told Phil that he would meet them at Cash Corner after the show and he left as well. Phil and Grace settled back into the large rear seat of the Silver Bullet to watch the movie. Roland soon returned with Pat and the two couples quietly watched the movie for a while.

After about an hour, Grace whispered to Phil, "What have you been up to lately, Phil? You haven't been to see me in a long time. Is anything wrong?"

"Oh, no love," Phil whispered back. "You know, the weather has been too cold for us to use the car, at least on the days we could come to town. George and Roland have had to pick cotton and I've been busy driving cotton to the gin for baling." He paused a moment, then asked, "Why would you think something's wrong?"

"Well, you've been fidgeting for the last half-hour and you never fidgeted before."

"I'm sorry," Phil whispered. "I just don't seem to be interested in this movie. Maybe things would be different if it was a Buck Rogers movie."

"Okay," Grace sighed. "If you say so. Anyway, I wanted you to know that I've been missing you."

Phil looked at her and smiled. "Me too," he said as he kissed her gently.

As soon as the movie is over Grace quickly suggested that they go to Cash Corner and jitterbug. They all agreed and Phil told Roland to drive, acting as if Roland was his chauffeur. When they arrived, Roland parked near the dance platform. Moments later, Bert pulled up nearby. He glanced over at Phil and Roland with a look of disdain on his face. The two girls in his car waved at Phil, who smiled and waved back. Bert rolled his eyes.

Phil got them all a cold drink and they relaxed in the car, watching other couples dance. After two songs had played, Grace decided she wanted to liven up things, so she went to the jukebox and put in a nickel. As she turned to cross the dance floor again, the large music box begins to blare out the "Beer Barrel Polka." She stopped right in the middle of the dance floor, pointed her finger at Phil and motioned for him to come up and dance. Then, to Phil's amazement, she began to sing along at the top of her lungs.

By the time the second verse began, Phil was beside her on the dance floor. They jitterbugged for the rest of the song. At the end, everyone applauded and laughed at the performance.

Phil suddenly noticed that he was hungry and realized that they hadn't eaten supper. After asking what everyone wanted, he went into Red's store and returned shortly with the food. While they were eating, Roland, Pat, and Grace carried on a brisk conversation, but Phil seldom joined them. He seemed to be content just relaxing and eating and watching other couples dance.

After they had eaten, Grace said, "Let's all go for a ride."

"Good idea," Pat chimed in.

"Okay," Roland said. "Where to, gang?"

"Drive on, old man," Phil teased Roland. "Did you know Roland was a Senior this year, Grace? He's practically ready for the old folks home."

"I may be older than you, but I'm prettier too," said Roland as he cranked the Model T and started down the road. Phil

65

laughed along with Grace and Pat.

"Hey, I know where we can go," Roland said after they had driven along country roads for fifteen or twenty minutes. "Hell's Half Acre is only a few miles from here."

"Carry on, old man," Phil replied.

"What is Hell's Half Acre?" Grace asked. Pat and Roland snickered.

"Wait and see, love," Phil replied ominously. He thought it would be fun to see if he could frighten Grace just a little.

"No, love," said Grace. "Tell me now."

"Hells' Half Acre is a spot down an old woods path where there used to be an old saw mill," Phil began. "About the only thing left now is an old saw dust pile and a pathway leading there from the main road."

"What happened?" Graced asked.

"They say a man went crazy one day and threw a bunch of people into the saw. Blood and guts and bones went everywhere." Phil waved his hands as he described the gory scene. "They say the place is haunted by ghosts with one-arm or no head or one leg."

"Stop, Phil. You're scaring me. I don't want to go there."

"Too late," Roland said as he turned the steering wheel. "We're already here."

As they drove down the dirt path, Grace cuddled closer to Phil and didn't hear Roland and Pat, who continued to snicker in the front seat. A moment later, they came to a large clearing. As the Silver Bullet's headlamps swung across the landscape, about a half-dozen cars flashed into sight. Grace slapped Phil's arm as she noticed what the occupants of those cars were doing.

"What do you mean, trying to scare me like that? Why, this is just a lover's lane, Philip Barkley."

Roland parked the car and switched off the engine. The night was clear and the sky was full of stars. The moon was just beginning to peek over the horizon. The couples settled into their seats for a romantic evening. They didn't even notice another car drive up behind them.

Suddenly, a spotlight blazes light into the clearing and onto the Silver Bullet. Fearing it might be the bullies in the '38 Chevy they had embarrassed a month or so before, Roland and Phil lowered themselves and the girls into the seats so their heads couldn't be seen. A moment later, the booming voice of someone speaking over a loudspeaker startled them.

"Attention, North Carolina license plate number 734539. You are trespassing. Leave this place immediately. Be at the courthouse in Smithfield at ten o'clock on Monday morning." Then, as suddenly as it had appeared, the strange vehicle turned and left the area. A few moments later, other vehicles were leaving. When it had grown quiet again, the two couples raised their heads above the seats and looked around. In the moonlight, they could tell they were the only ones left.

"I vote for getting the heck out of here, pal," Phil said to Roland.

"I agree, buddy," Roland replied. They quickly cranked the car and headed toward the main road. The two boys dropped off the girls at their homes. All four were a bit shaken by the turn of events. Then, the Silver Bullet headed toward Cash Corner where they picked up George and went home.

"What's up, guys?" George asked.

"Just tired, little buddy," Phil replied. He didn't want word to get out about what had happened and he didn't want to worry George needlessly. Phil knew that the police could get the address of a car owner from the license plate registration at the police department. As they got closer to home, Phil became more worried. If he didn't show up at ten o'clock on Monday morning, they might send a deputy out to his home. Daddy Barkley would be very upset if that happened. Phil knew he might lose his driving privileges. He might even be restricted to his room. Then he'd never see Linda, or Grace, again.

Phil worried almost all weekend until Sunday afternoon, when he realized that he simply couldn't do anything about the situation. He decided not to skip school on Monday, hoping that they just couldn't find his address . . . or that maybe the police had just warned them on Friday night. Maybe the owner of Hell's Half Acre really wouldn't prosecute him. Still, he dreaded returning home Monday after school. He felt sure that a deputy had been to his house. As he prepared to get off the school bus at the lane leading to his house, Roland joined him.

"Hey, George," Roland called to his brother. "I'm getting off here with Phil. Want to come too?"

"Sure," George replied. "What's up, guys?" he asked as they got off the bus a few moments later. The older boys didn't answer.

Phil's sisters went up the lane ahead of the three boys. Phil remarked to Roland, "Well, I don't see Daddy waiting anywhere, do you?"

"Nope."

They heard a tractor in the distance and looked over the white board fence along the lane to see Daddy Barkley baling hay nearby. He saw the boys and waved at them.

"Boy, do I feel better!" Phil gasped with relief.

"Whew," Roland added. "Me too."

"What is going on with you two?" asked George. "What's this all about?"

"Alright," replied Phil. "I'll tell you all about it. But you must promise not to say anything about it to anyone . . . ever! It may not be over yet."

"Okay, okay. I promise."

As Phil finished describing what had happened at Hell's Half Acre on Friday night, George began to laugh. Then the laughing grew into a howl.

"What in the hell is so funny?" shouted Roland.

"You two have been had," George said between gulps of air. "I just put things together."

"What do you mean?" asked Phil.

When George had composed himself, he said, "Do you remember when you all left Cash Corner Friday night? Well, I had just finished a game of pool and was standing in the doorway of Red's place, waiting for him to fix me a hamburger. About that time, I noticed Bert getting out of his convertible and leaving with two men in another car. He left the two girls in his car. He wasn't gone very long and when he returned he came back to the girls in his car like nothing had ever happened."

"What's so strange about that?" Roland asked.

"C'mon, Roland," George chided. "I can't believe you asked that. You know Bert never leaves his precious car for longer than it takes to go to the bathroom. But the real interesting thing was that the car with the two men in it had a spotlight on the side, like a police car! Last, but not least, when they returned from their little trip, I noticed Bert and the two men laughing a lot."

"Why that little son of a . . . ."

"Just wait until I get my hands on him," Phil interrupted Roland's derogatory description of Bert. "I have to admit, I never believed he had the nerve." Phil looked at Roland. Roland managed a sheepish grin. In a moment, all three boys were laughing hard and pointing at each other.

"I hope you two have learned your lesson," George said finally, "If you two had trusted little brother more and let me in on things, you could have saved yourself a lot of worry."

Chapter Ten

With the arrival of winter, the boys couldn't ride the Silver Bullet very much due to cold or wet weather. They stayed around home on the weekends, playing games, hunting or just listening to their fathers discuss world events.

In March of 1941 there was much to discuss. Congress had just passed the "Lend Lease" law to help the Allied Forces arm themselves to protect Europe. Japan was trying to negotiate a trade pact with America, but Congress was cool to the idea in the wake of Japan's alliance with the Axis powers. They had further alarmed Americans by landing troops in Indochina. But Ambassador Grew had warned Congress of a possible sneak attack by the Japanese if trade relations are broken, so Congress had not yet come down on one side of the fence.

At school one day, Mr. Yount called Phil into his office and told him that the Congress has established the National Recovery Administration Act. It was set up to regulate wages and working hours across the country and it had become very popular with the people. They established the motto, "We Do Our Part." Mr. Yount asked Phil if he would like to have a job within the NRA. It would involve working in the Principal's office a bit, cleaning out the school buses, and chores around the school.

He told Phil that he could work during recesses and in his spare time during school. The job would pay $4.50 per month.

Phil jumped at the opportunity and immediately accepted. He knew it would greatly improve his financial situation. He had been hard pressed lately for dating and gas money since he was not getting to substitute drive the school bus hardly any.

"Well, son, you'll have to fill out these papers and also have your father sign this form. Then bring them back to me and maybe I can start you next week."

"That'll be great," replied Phil as he gathered up the forms and returned to his home room where the students were having a study period.

Phil was glowing with happiness as he sat down at his desk which was beside Jim's. He knew that besides having his money problems relieved, he now had something to write about to Linda.

Phil told Jim about the job and then settled down to write a note to Linda. In the note he told her about the new NRA job and asked for a date. He gave the note to Anita to pass along to Linda.

That night Anita went to Phil's room and handed him a note. "I think Linda is beginning to like you more. She seemed glad to get your note today."

"Thanks, sis," Phil said as he sat on his bed to read the note.

Anita still stood in the doorway, trying to see the expression on Phil's face as he read. Phil noticed her, looked up and repeated himself. "Thanks, sis." Anita knew that he meant for her to leave, so she closed the door as Phil continued reading. As he finished, Phil felt somewhat disappointed. She had mostly teased him about having so many girl friends by saying that he couldn't possibly have time for any others. She did not refuse to date him but did not say she would either. She did tell him that she would like to talk to him at lunch break the next day. That was the one thing that made the note worthwhile and Phil could hardly wait for lunch time the next day.

When lunch time arrived the following day, Phil hurried out to the playground and joined his friends who were practicing baseball. Soon he noticed Anita and Linda coming over to their area and he went to meet them.

Linda noticed how happy and exuberant Phil was. She had already observed his friendliness and the way he treated all girls with great respect. She saw that he was not only handsome, but also above average in manners and respectability. She realized that she was beginning to like him a lot. The lunch bell sounded, ending the lunch hour. Phil was very happy as he returned to his home room.

On Sunday, Phil cranked the Silver Bullet and backed it out of the shed. He started the vehicle down the road towards the Varnes home. Recent rains had packed the dust down on the roads, making it easier to drive on them. Since it was a warm day, Phil had become restless and wanted to go somewhere. He decided to see if Roland or George would like to ride around a little, so he pulled up in front of the Varnes' home. He pressed the ooooga horn and Roland appeared at the door.

"Let's go for for a ride,"he yelled to Roland

"Okay," replied Roland. "Let me see if George wants to go."

Momentarily, Roland and George came out and got into the Silver Bullet. "Hey Phil. Where are we going?" George asked with excitement. He was three years younger and smaller in size but the two older boys treated him respectfully. He realized this and knew that when he got into the Silver Bullet, everyone usually had a good time.

Phil hesitated a second before answering and then said, "Well, how about riding to Kenly for a little while?" He thought he might see Linda.

"Okay, pal," replied Roland.

Phil headed for Kenly on the packed dirt road. He pulled down on the gas lever and urged the Silver Bullet faster, occasionally darting back and forth in the road to keep from hitting mud holes along the way. That action slung George in the rear seat from side to side. It tickled George and he yelled at Phil, "Ride'em Cowboy!" He grabbed the seat and hung on.

Roland and Phil laughed at him.

The boys soon came into Kenly. They were singing and having a good time. Phil headed the car towards the section of town where Linda lived. "Where are we going now?" asked George.

"I think I know," retorted Roland.

"Ask me no questions and I'll tell you no lies," said Phil as he smiled at his pals.

Phil turned the corner in the Silver Bullet and went past Linda's home. He saw an automobile parked in the driveway with two people in it. As he drove by, Phil pressed the ooooga horn. Linda was in the car with her boyfriend, Eddie. She stuck her hand out of the car and waved at Phil. The boys waved back and continued down the street.

Phil headed the Silver Bullet out of town as George started singing, "I've got me a girl in Kalamazoo." He looked at Phil as he sang and burst into laughter. Phil realized that George was kidding and threw George a wink and a slight grin.

Phil drove out of town but didn't join in with the singing and talking of his friends. The thought of Eddie in the car with Linda bothered him. He tried to get it out of his mind by swinging the car back and forth across the road. George loved it and held on. A few moments later, Phil turned the car around and headed for Cash Corner.

George shouted, "Now you're talking!" He was happy because he had found a little girlfriend that he was getting sweet on.

Soon, they came back to Kenly and continued on to Cash Corner. There was hardly anyone there so Phil went back uptown to the movie theater. As they arrived at the theater, they saw several of their gang standing around the theater entrance. Phil parked the Silver Bullet in front of the theater and noticed that Grace and Pat were among the group that was waiting to get in the movie. They saw Phil and came over to the car.

"Hi, hon," said Grace as she hugged Phil. "Where you been for so long?"

Phil grimaced. "No where much, love." replied Phil. "You know it's been awfully cold to get out in this fresh air taxi cab!"

"Well, how about going to the show with me? It will be comfy inside."

"Oh, I don't know," replied Phil displaying disinterest.

"Come on, you tightwad," Roland chided.

"It's a good show," Pat chimed in. " 'Love Finds Andy Hardy' with Mickey Rooney and Judy Garland."

"Yeah, Phil. And you don't need to worry about finances wither, not with that NRA job coming up," said Roland.

"What NRA job?" Grace asked.

"Uh, it's nothing much," replied Phil. "Just a little job that the Principle has offered me at school."

"Well, you can tell me about it inside the movie, okay?"

"Ah, sure. I guess so," Phil remarked half-heartedly.

They all got out of the Silver Bullet and entered the theater. During the movie, Phil didn't talk much. He was thinking of Linda and the boy in the car.

Grace noticed that Phil was not very interested in the movie so she tried to get him to shape up. "Honey," she urged him. "You haven't told me about the new job yet. How about it?"

"Oh, I'm sorry love. I didn't mean to ignore you. I just wasn't thinking," Phil replied.

"Well I'm glad you've come alive," Grace teased. "Now you can tell me about this new job."

"I'm excited about it," Phil began. "It may not be a very big job to some people but it will to me, and it pays $4.50 per month."

"Oh, Phil. I'm glad! I guess this means we can see more of each other now."

"Maybe," Phil replied, looking back at the screen. He didn't want to look at Grace for fear that she could tell he was thinking about another girl. And from the corner of his eye, he could tell from the way she slumped back into her seat that she was disappointed with his response. Damn! He hated the idea that he might be hurting Grace, but he couldn't get Linda out of his mind!

In a few seconds, Grace asked, "Well, are you going to tell me the rest of the story?"

"Oh, yeah. I'm sorry, hon." Wanting to reassure her, Phil held Grace's hand as he told her what the job would be about and how Mr. Yount offered it to him. It must have worked because in a few moments Grace put her arm around his neck and they settled down into their seats to watch the rest of the show. It was almost dark when they got out of the theater.

"Roland looked at the fading light and then at Phil. "Hey, pal. We had better be getting home! It's going to get lots colder when that sun goes down and neither of us has overcoats."

"You're right," Phil responded. "Do you think we have time to take the girls home first?"

"Just don't go too fast," Pat warned. "Riding in your car is cold even with overcoats on." They all laughed.

They waited for George to come out of the theater and then got into the Silver Bullet. As Phil and Grace stood at the front door of her house, he kissed her lightly on the lips. Before he could turn to go, she quickly placed her hand behind his neck and pull him close.

"Phil, honey, what was that?"

He looked at her and grinned, then gave her a long passionate kiss.

"That's more like it," she exclaimed as they ended their embrace.

As Phil walked to the car, he suddenly wondered what it would be like to lose Grace and still not get Linda.

Chapter Eleven

On a warm Saturday afternoon in late April 1941, Phil had completed all the chores his father had assigned him that morning before leaving for town in the pickup truck. Phil took his radio down to the shed where the Silver Bullet was Kept. He was planning to polish the car, but decided to rest instead. After all, that's what warm and lazy spring days are for, he thought. He plugged in the radio, sat it in the doorway of the barn and listened to the latest news reports of Hitler's capture of all the Balkan countries and invasion of Yugoslavia.

Phil turned the radio to another station that played music. He walked over to the big oak tree nearby and lay down on the bench that was under the tree. Soon, his thoughts drifted to school and then to Linda. In recent weeks she had been more friendly to him and had talked to him occasionally. He broke into a smile just thinking about their conversations. Suddenly, Roland and George came skidding to a halt on their bicycles, breaking Phil's train of thought.

"Wonder what he's thinking about?" George asked Roland.

"There's no telling, little brother. But I'd bet it has something to do with a young lady."

"I'll never tell," Phil grinned. "What are y'all up to?"

"We thought you might like to throw some horseshoes this afternoon," Roland replied.

"Okay by me. We can alternate and play the winner of each game," Phil offered.

In the middle of the third game, Roland suddenly stopped throwing and squinted his eyes in the direction of Phil's driveway. "Wonder who that could be?"

"I don't know," replied Phil. "I've never seen that car before."

"Me neither," George added. "Do you reckon it could be the Sheriff?"

Phil and Roland grimaced. "Have you been expecting the Sheriff to show up, George?" Phil asked.

"Heck no," George retorted. "It was just a guess."

The car continued up the lane and around the curve in front of the Barkley house. It slowed for a second, then continued down the path toward the barn where the boys were playing. As it came to a halt, Phil recognized his father behind the wheel.

"Daddy, who's car is that?" he exclaimed as his father opened the door. "Where did you get it?" All three boys ran to the car for a closer look.

"Well son, we had a good crop last year with all the hard work you boys did and I wound up with some extra cash. So, I've been looking around for a good automobile. This '39

Plymouth was a good bargain. You children are getting too big to ride to town in the back of that old pickup anyway." He paused, stepping back to admire the machine. "How do you like it?"

"Oh boy!" was all Phil could day. "It has two seats and four doors, and a sharp looking body. It looks almost new too! Where did you find it, daddy?"

"An old preacher who lives in Goldsboro had it out in front of his house a few weeks ago. I passed by and noticed the 'For Sale' sign and decided to stop and ask about it. He said he was retiring soon and was going to live with his daughter and her husband in Louisiana. When he told me nothing was wrong with it, I believed him. I gave him fifty dollars as a down payment told him I'd be back today to pay him the rest."

"The way that engine is purring it sounds like it has been well cared for," Roland said.

"I like the way this black paint shines!" exclaimed George.

"Can I try it out?" asked Phil.

Mr. Barkley held the door open and waved his hand for Phil to climb in behind the steering wheel. He closed the door, walked around to the passenger side and got it. "What are you two waiting for?" he asked Roland and George.

"Boy, these seats sure are soft," George said as he rubbed his hands across the material. "I wonder what kind of cloth it is?"

"Probably has some wool in it," Roland explained.

Phil looked over the instrument panel to familiarize himself with the dials and gauges. Then, he pressed in the clutch pedal and put his right hand on the gear shift lever.

"Now Phil, you will have to go easy on these gears," warned his father. "This is a bit different from the Silver Bullet!"

"Yes, sir," replied Phil. "They seem kind of like the gears on the school bus."

"That's almost right," said Mr. Barkley. "But in a bus , I believe the reverse gear is to the far right and down next to high gear. With this car, reverse is on the left and up next to first gear."

"I see," Phil said as he gingerly shifted into reverse. After turning around, Phil drove down the driveway and out onto the road in front of their house. They seemed to glide along the dirt road as they headed toward the small general store at Rains crossroad and back to the farm.

"This thing rides as smooth as a snake in the water," said Roland as they all climbed out.

"Thanks for letting me drive, daddy," said Phil.

"You're welcome, son. I can see you'll help me take good care of it." He slapped Phil on the back. "Who knows? Maybe one Saturday night this car will have nothing better to do than take you and some young lady to a picture show in Smithfield."

Phil's eyes grew wide. "Do you mean it?"

"We'll see," Mr. Barkley replied.

On Monday afternoon, Coach Sherman called a meeting of the baseball team. Phil was selected as catcher and Jim Kelford was made pitcher. The coach announced their first league game would be held the following Saturday. Phil had been writing notes to Linda, telling her about the '39 Plymouth and hoping that she would consent to a date if she knew they could take a nicer automobile than the Silver Bullet. He also figured the baseball game would be a good excuse for her to say yes and appealed to her school pride. His father had given him permission to drive the '39 Plymouth to the game. Now, Phil thought, all I have to do is get her to say yes. That night he finished a note to Linda and gave it to Anita. By lunch time, the next day, he began to grow anxious for a reply. He found Anita alone on the steps to the school's front entrance.

"Where's Linda?" he asked as he approached.

"She's in the ladies' room," Anita replied. "She'll be here any minute."

"Did you give her the note?"

"Yes."

Phil waited for her to say more, but she just looked at him blankly.

"Well?" he finally blurted.

Anita laughed at his impatience. "She really has you hooked, doesn't she?"

"Just tell me what she said."

Anita reached into her purse and held out a folded piece of paper. "Here's our precious answer, Philly-willy," she teased.

Phil grabbed the paper and ran away from the sound of his sister's laughter and around the corner of the building. He was so nervous that his fingers didn't seem to want to cooperate. After fumbling with the paper for a few seconds, he had it opened. Minutes later, he returned to the baseball diamond where his buddies were involved in a brief practice session before lunch period came to an end.

"Did you swallow a happy pill or something?" Jim asked after taking one look at Phil's expression.

"Better than that," Phil replied. "I've got a date for Saturday."

"Well how about that," Jim grinned. "She finally said 'Yes.' That's great, pal!" He slapped Phil on the back. "She really is a very pretty girl. Where are you going to take her?"

"Don't know yet," Phil replied. "I thought about taking her to Wilbur's barbecue and maybe to Herman Park in Goldsboro. What do you think?"

"That's a good idea." Jim looked thoughtful for a second. "Hey, I've got a great idea. Let's double date! You haven't met my girlfriend yet and she's dying to meet you. Besides, it will make things a lot easier on you and, ah, what's her name?"

"Linda. Linda Hinton."

"Yeah, Linda. Anyway, she'll feel much more relaxed with another girl along on the date. What do you say, pal?"

"That's a great idea, Jim! You know, I told them they were wrong when they said you didn't have brains." Phil laughed as Jim threw an imaginary punch to his stomach in return for the teasing remark.

Phil could hardly wait for Saturday to arrive. When it rained all day Friday, he began to worry about the game being called off. Boy, that would really mess up everything, he thought. But Saturday arrived with white, billowing clouds high in the war, sunny sky. Phil spent most of the morning trimming his hair, shaving his face and generally striving for perfection in his appearance. After lunch, he packed his duffel bag with a freshly pressed pair of white bermuda shorts, a red knit shirt, a pair of clean white tennis shoes, red socks and a small bottle of aftershave lotion. His sister, Leah walked by his door just then and couldn't pass up the chance to tease Phil.

"Hey, I didn't know baseball players wore that kind of uniform. Bermuda shorts . . . brother, you're going to shine today!"

"Get out of here," Phil growled after the sound of her laughing as she ran down the hall.

Just then, daddy Barkley stuck his head inside Phil's room. "Think you'll be needing these?" he asked, holding the keys to the '39 Plymouth in his hand.

"Thanks, daddy," Phil said as he took the keys.

"Be careful, son."

With a happy whistle Phil backed the car out of the double garage where it was parked beside the pickup. As he drove down the lane toward the road, Phil noticed that everything was mostly dry from the bright sunshine and light spring breeze they'd had that morning. The sweet, fresh smell of growing vegetation wafted into the rolled down windows as he turned onto the road. The tobacco was almost half grown and the corn was almost a foot tall. Granny's crepe myrtle trees that lined their driveway had full leaves and buds and soon they would be covered in beautiful red blossoms. Her yellow and white irises were already in bloom and dressed up the white fence that ran along the edge of their property beside the dirt road. It was such a beautiful day that Phil couldn't help but feel that he had the world by the tail.

He arrived at Kenly early and drove behind the school building toward the baseball field. He parked the car in the shade next to the building and out of danger from fowl balls. While climbing out of the car, he noticed dust had accumulated on the paint from driving on the dirt road. He opened the trunk, found a large towel and wiped off all the dust. Today, of all days, he wanted the car to shine.

In a few moments, some of the other players arrived. Not having seen Coach Sherman, Phil decided to organize a pregame warmup session. At his position as catcher, Phil had his back turned away from the crowd and never noticed Jim Kelford sneaking up behind him with a baseball bat. Suddenly, Phil felt the bat touch the inside of his thigh and he nearly jumped out of his skin. All the other players laughed loudly at the antics of their co-captains. As Phil turned, he almost blurted out a curse word at Jim, but quickly held his tongue as he noticed Linda and another girl standing next to the fence behind home plate. He playfully punched Jim in the stomach and walked over to where the girls were standing. Jim followed him, still laughing at the result of his prank on Phil.

"Hi," Phil said to Linda. "Mmmmm, you sure look pretty today."

"Thank you, Phil."

Jim cut into their greetings to introduce the other girl. "Phil, I want you to meet my girlfriend, Ann Creech."

Phil made a small waving motion to the petite redhead. "So this is the famous 'Strawberry' I've heard so much about. But you lied, Jim. You said she wasn't pretty. I thin she's beautiful."

Jim scowled. "Don't try to get me in trouble, pal. We both have a lot to worry about today."

"What do you mean?" asked Phil.

"While we're out here on the field these two beautiful women will be up on the stands with all the other guys staring at them."

Just then, Coach Sherman walked onto the field. "Hey! You fellahs quit yabbering with the women and get ready to play ball."

Phil quickly suggested, "Let's go to Goldsboro after the game. Wouldn't you girls like to eat some barbecue and go to the park this afternoon? I hear they have some monkeys at the park, so Jim might feel at home."

"That's a great idea!" Strawberry replied amid their laughter. "Can you come too, Linda?"

"I'll have to go home right after the game," she said. Phil's heart sank. "But I'm sure mother and daddy won't mind. You can pick me up at my house. Ann, you could go with me. You know, we might need to powder our noses."

"Sure," replied Ann. The two girls winked at each other and laughed.

Phil couldn't suppress the wide grin spreading across his face. "Great!" he said. "Now, you girls wish us luck at winning this game."

By the bottom of the eighth inning, it looked as if Kenly

might lose since they were behind by a score of three to one. As they took the field in the top of the ninth, Phil grabbed Jim's sleeve.

"How are you feeling, pal? Got any strikeouts left in that arm?"

"I don't know, Phil. But I'm going to give'em everything I've got."

"I've been noticing what these guys swing at," Phil said. "These next three guys will be easy. The first batter likes to swing at low, inside balls. The second will swing at your curve ball, I'm sure of it! and the third guy will swat at anything that's higher than his bellybutton, but pitch'em outside so he'll miss. Got it?"

"Anything you say, buddy."

Acting on Phil's advice Jim made quick work of striking out all three batters. As they came into the dugout, Jim thanked Phil for the tips and said, "Now, I've got some advice for you. Sam is up to bat next and he'll probably get on base. Since you bat after him, here's your chance to get the winning run. I've noticed that you rest your bat on your shoulder. I think it causes you to reach into your swing. Pick the bat up off your shoulder and just before you swing, lean back onto your right foot." He handed Phil a bat. "Practice it once or twice before you go out to the on-deck circle."

Jim was right. Sam easily took first base with a line drive between short stop and second base. Phil stepped into the batter's box. As he began to concentrate on the pitcher, he vaguely heard Strawberry yelling from behind the plate for him to "put it over the fence." The first pitch whizzed by his elbow, but the umpire still called it a strike. Phil's face slightly flushed with anger at the sloppy call. I'll show him, he thought. He concentrated harder on the pitcher's every move. Suddenly, everything seemed to be in slow motion. The ball appeared to lazily roll off the pitcher's fingers. He could see the seams rotating as it grew closer. His brain flashed a message to his arms, "Swing!" Phil shifted his weight to his right foot, then recoiled his hips toward his left foot as his arms came down in a level arc across the plate. Suddenly, the slow motion stopped and everything was at normal speed again. He could hear the crowd screaming and cheering as the ball rocketed toward the left field fence. Phil slowly dropped his bat and began trotting toward first base, watching the left fielder all the time. Suddenly, the ball dropped behind the fence and the crowd in the bleachers went wild. Moments later, Phil was jogging toward home plate and the mob of his teammates, shouting and jumping in the air. He glanced into the stands behind the plate and saw Linda's angelic face beaming with pride.

After the win, the boys quickly showered and dressed. Phil

took Jim to where the car was parked and proudly showed off the 1939 Plymouth. Jim remarked that it had a lot more room than his car, as he climbed in and headed across town toward Linda's house. When they arrived, the girls were sitting in the swing on Linda' front porch.

"We thought you'd never get here," Strawberry chided.

"Just like boys," Linda chimed in. "Always late."

"I had to sign a lot of autographs," Phil replied.

Jim howled with laughter and slapped Phil on the back. "That's telling 'em pal." He looked up at the girls and joked, "Phil's even agreed to let me be his manager when he makes the big leagues."

They piled into the car and moments later were driving toward Goldsboro, laughing, talking, and singing with the pleasant abandon of young people who haven't a care in the world. Once, Phil glanced at Linda only to be met with a smile that seemed to melt his insides. She's been staring at me, he thought. I wonder what she thinks of me so far.

It was late afternoon by the time they reached the park. As they walked around the small duck ponds and fountains, Linda stopped several times to smell the flowers that were in bloom. They passed a group of children playing on the large swing sets. They soon came to the monkey cages. Phil purchased a bag of peanuts and moved close to the cages to feed the monkeys. One monkey was bolder than the rest and seemed to always shove his way in front so he got the most peanuts. Phil began to tease him, offering a peanut and then pulling it away as the monkey reached out of the bars. It quickly tired of Phil's teasing and began to dance around the cage and scream each time Phil pulled away the peanut. A few moments later, a crowd had gathered to enjoy the show Phil was providing.

Phil turned momentarily to glance at Linda. Suddenly, of the larger monkeys moved swiftly toward the font of the cage. He reached out and snatched the half-empty bag of peanuts from Phil's hand. The monkey tried for a few seconds to pull the bag through the bars, but it wouldn't go. A stunned Phil could only stare with his mouth open when, seconds later, the aggravated monkey threw the bag and hit Phil square on the side of the jaw. The crowd of people roared with laughter as Phil's face turned the color of the setting sun. He quickly moved out of reach of the big monkey's arms.

They soon decided to leave the park and head toward the barbecue restaurant. After a large, satisfying meal, Jim noticed that the time was getting late and he had to have Strawberry home by ten o'clock. They piled into the '39 Plymouth and were soon on the highway headed back to Kenly. Jim and Strawberry grew very quiet in the back seat Phil noticed that Linda was sitting closer to him than when they had come to Goldsboro. He slipped his right arm over her shoulder and felt his heart pounding. When she didn't pull away, Phil experienced a warm, happy sensation all over.

After dropping off Jim and Strawberry at the school, where Jim had left his car, Phil continued to Linda's house. He opened her door and accompanied her to the front porch. Linda turned and looked into his eyes. Phil noticed that she seemed a bit nervous.

"Phil, I really had a good time today. I have to go inside now."

As she turned to go, he grabbed her hand and gently pulled her back. He looked at her sweet face and felt that warm sensation returning. "Linda, I had a great time today as well. And it's only because you made it that way. Do you think we can do this again soon?"

"Well, maybe," she replied.

Suddenly, something inside Phil told him to kiss her on the cheek. He bent over to do it, but happily missed her cheek and kissed her lightly on the lips. Linda looked into his eyes for a long second. Then she slipped her hand around his neck and pulled his face close to hers.

"Why are you so persistent?" she said. Then she kissed him full on the lips for what seem like an hour to Phil. She quickly turned to go into her house. As she opened the front door, she turned as if to say something else. But she only smiled at Phil and disappeared behind the large, oak door.

As he headed his car toward home, Phil felt on top of the world. What a day, he thought. I won the game *and* the girl! He rolled down his window to feel the nip of the cool, evening air on is face and began to sing his favorite song.

Most of the lights were out in the Barkley home as Phil quietly pulled into the driveway amid the soft glow of the moon on the fields and pine trees and the sweet smell of blossoming irises.

Chapter Twelve

Phil looked forward to each school day. Sometimes, during lunch period, he met Linda and they found time to sit on the grass and talk. Every day, Phil tried harder to convince her to go out with him again. For some reason unknown to him, she seemed very reluctant. But he couldn't help but feel that she was really happy when they were together. In his heart, he knew she wanted to go out with him again.

Roland and George went to Cash Corner almost every Saturday night, but Phil seldom accompanied them. Since his father had no problem loaning the '39 Plymouth to Phil, the Silver Bullet stayed at the Varnes house most of the time. Most Sunday afternoons, Phil drove the Plymouth to Kenly and rode around with his other friends or drove to Linda's house. Sometimes, he would see her walking on the sidewalk with a neighbor girl. A few times, he even saw her with Eddie. On those occasions, if she noticed Phil, she would quickly look away. Every so often, Phil would See her alone on the front porch, if he was lucky. On those days, she would ride around with him for a while.

It was on those short rides that he tried to impress her. The compliments and conversation flowed freely. He joked around to make her laugh. He went to a lot of trouble to display his manners everywhere they went. He could feel her warming up to him each time they were together, but he still couldn't seem to convince her to go out with him again.

In late spring, there is more than enough work to go around on a farm. The tobacco, corn and other crops grow very fast and need tilling very often. Phil, Roland and George had been working after school and on Saturdays to help keep the crops growing on both farms. The Varnes brothers remembered well that a healthy crop was what allowed Phil's father to buy the '39 Plymouth and they wanted their father to be able to do the same.

One Saturday afternoon, when Phil had finished his chores, he walked back to the large oak tree beside the shed where they had worked on the Silver Bullet. Lying on one of the benches beneath the huge tree, he soon drifted into thinking about how things had changed over the past year. He no longer saw the gang at Cash Corner very much and seemed to be spending a lot more time with Jim Kelford and Strawberry. Suddenly, he thought of Grace Langston. He liked her very much, but not in the same way he felt about Linda. Grace was always a lot of fun to be around, but she never gave him that warm all over feeling he had when Linda was near. Suddenly, a loud noise shook him out of his daydreams. It was Roland and George on the Silver

Bullet.

"Hey, pal!" Roland shouted above the engine noise. "Get up off your lazy bones and come with us to Cash Corner. You haven't been there in so long I'll have to introduce you to everybody all over again."

Phil chuckled. Why not, he thought. I don't have anything better to do tonight. He shouted back, "Give me a few minutes to get on some better looking clothes."

"Sure thing," George replied. "While you're at it, put on a better looking face."

"Very funny," Phil retorted, amid the brothers' howling laughter. Phil emerged from his house fifteen minutes later, dressed in a sharp looking, white, short sleeve shirt, tan pants, and white tennis shoes. Another fifteen minutes passed before they rolled into the Kenly city limits. As it was still early in the afternoon, hardly any of the gang was to be found. So they headed the Silver Bullet toward cash corner where they ate hamburgers, drank RC colas and watched a few other boys play games of pool.

As the sun began to set, the gang began to arrive and the jukebox came alive. A short while later, Bert's car pulled into the parking lot, but parked as far away from the Silver Bullet as possible. Phil noticed two girls in Bert's car. One of them was Grace, and she was sitting next to Bert! At first it bothered him, but then Phil thought to himself that Grace had rights too and that after all, he hadn't been around much lately. He decided to act as if he didn't notice her and continued talking to some other friends. Only a few moments later, however, she was suddenly standing by his side, acting almost as if she'd been there for hours.

"Hey stranger," she said to Phil when he finally looked over at her. "What have you been up to lately?"

"Well, hello love," Phil replied, giving her a hug and a peck on the cheek. "Hey, we haven't danced together in a longtime. How about a jitterbug?" He felt slightly embarrassed for evading her question. It was obvious that she wanted him to tell her why he hadn't come to see her in so long.

As they stepped onto the dance platform, the jukebox blared out a new song and Phil began singing along as they danced. "I'm the Boogie Woogie Bugle Boy from company B," he sang with the biggest grin he could muster. Grace laughed and seemed to relax.

When the song stopped, Grace suggested that they sit in the car and talk for a while. Pat had finally arrived and had dragged Roland onto the dance floor and George had walked a few blocks up the street in search of some of his friends. This meant they would be alone in the car. Phil could feel his apprehension growing as they walked toward the Silver Bullet. He didn't really feel like conversation, and he knew she would get around to asking him where he had been for so long.

He had forgotten what a good conversationalist Grace was. She talked for almost twenty minutes about things he liked . . . cars, planes, baseball and other sports. He began to relax a bit and enjoyed her company, but his mind was already drifting. He began to think of Linda and wonder what she might be doing at that moment. Suddenly, Pat and Roland appeared next to the car and Phil took the opportunity to get away for a moment.

"Who want's a hot dog?" he asked.

"Pat and I would love a hamburger and an RC Cola," Roland replied. "What would you like, Grace?"

"I'm not really hungry," she said with downcast eyes. "Just a soda for me."

Phil returned with the food and sodas in a few minutes. The two couples ate and talked briefly about a few other people they had seen. When Phil finished his hot dog, he asked Grace to dance again. In less than five minutes, they returned.

"Back so soon?" Roland asked.

"Yeah," Phil replied, looking at his wristwatch. "It's getting kind of late, pal. We had better take these ladies home before their parents come looking for them."

Roland looked at his own watch and glanced back at Phil. "Okay, pal. Guess you're right."

"Love, would you like for me to take you home?" Phil asked Grace.

"Only if you want to," she replied, still not looking directly at him.

As the town of Princeton wasn't far from the side of Kenly where Cash Corner was, they arrived at Grace's house in just a short while. Phil walked her to the front door where they said their "goodnights" very quickly. Five minutes later, Roland repeated the scene with Pat, but took a bit longer to part with his girlfriend. As his fanny hit the seat in the car, Roland asked, "What's the matter, buddy? You and I both know those girls could have stayed out at least another hour."

"I know," Phil said. "I just couldn't seem to get into the swing of it tonight."

"Does it have anything to do with that blonde I have seen you talking to at school? You know, ever since you started talking to her, you seem to have less and less time to spend with the old gang. What's the matter? Aren't we good enough for you anymore?"

Phil shot a hard glance at Roland. "You know that's not true!" he said. Inside, he was deeply hurt to think that his best friend thought of him that way.

"All I know is what I see," Roland continued. "Grace asked

me if you had been seeing someone else."

"What did you tell her?"

"I tried to tell her as little as possible. I thought that should be something for you to do." He paused, then added, "But I had to tell her something, so I made up this story about you spending a lot of time with the baseball team and studying hard on weekends."

"Thanks, pal. I was trying to get around to telling her about Linda, that's the blonde's name, but the truth is, I just don't know where I stand with her. I mean, Grace is not really my girl anyway. We've just always gotten together for dancing at Cash Corner. I know she likes me, and I like her too. But with Linda, it might be more than that. The truth is that there maybe nothing to tell Grace. Heck, for all I know, I might not ever get another date with Linda. Do you see what I mean?"

"I guess I understand, buddy. But I'll tell you this, you're right about Grace. She likes you. You just don't know how much."

Roland seemed satisfied with Phil's answers and they continued talking about girls for the rest of the short trip back to Kenly. As soon as they found George, near the theater with his friends, they headed back home.

The next Monday, Phil found Jim Kelford and asked if he and Strawberry would like to try another double date on Saturday night, on the condition that he could get Linda to go out with him.

"Sure," said Jim. "How about we go to Holt's Lake?"

"Where is that?"

"It's a little nightclub near Smithfield. Strawberry and I have been going there for a long time. They have a large dance pavilion, a snack bar, swimming and boating, and even a small bowling alley. Some weekends, they even have live bands."

"Sounds great!" Phil replied. "I'll let you know as soon as I can if Linda says yes."

He quickly wrote a note to Linda and gave it to Anita to deliver. That afternoon, as they climbed aboard the school bus to go home, Anita handed Phil a folded piece of paper. He quickly opened it and read for a few seconds before his face broke into a huge grin. Linda had agreed to a date! Anita began to tease him, but he didn't mind. In fact, he even liked it a little.

Phil could hardly wait until Saturday night. He worked hard all Saturday morning to finish his chores so he could clean and polish the '39 Plymouth until it sparkled. Meanwhile, he had talked Granny Barkley into cleaning and pressing his best sportswear outfit. When he finally came in to get cleaned up, his clothes were all laid out neatly on his bed. He shaved his face until it was as smooth as baby's skin, then put on plenty of aftershave lotion and cologne. As the late afternoon sun began to grow pink, Phil pulled the '39 Plymouth onto the road and headed toward Kenly.

As Phil pulled into the Hinton's driveway, Linda stood up from the front porch swing where she had been waiting for him to arrive. Phil could hardly take his eyes off her after glancing up from behind the wheel. He almost hit Mr. Hinton's car in the rear end, but slammed on his brake pedal at the last second. Linda put her hand to her mouth and chuckled as she made her way down the steps.

She wore a short sleeve white blouse with puffed shoulders and a rounded neckline trimmed in pink ribbon, a loose fitting pleated skirt in a pink and gray plaid pattern, short white bobbysocks, and black-on-white saddle oxfords. Most of the girls her age dressed this way, but what held Phil's attention was her wavy, shoulder length, blonde hair. It seemed to shine in the fading sunlight and it bounced gently as she made her way down the steps.

He opened the car door for her and remarked, "You look very beautiful tonight."

"Thank you," she replied with a smile that melted his heart.

They talked happily about the past week at school as they drove to pick up Jim and Strawberry. By the time they all arrived at Holt's Lake, the parking lot was almost full. As they entered the nightclub, Phil was amazed at all the activity. He was even more surprised that he had never heard of the place until Jim mentioned it on Monday. They went to the snack bar first and quickly finished off a hamburger and soda each. Then Jim wanted to bowl a few games, so they went to the bowling alley.

Midway through the third game, Linda turned to Phil and asked, "Do you like dancing?"

"Love it," he replied. "How about the Jitterbug?"

She moved closer to Phil. "That's my favorite," she said in a low voice.

Phil could hardly wait to get her to the pavilion. He grabbed her hand and said, "Well what are we waiting for?" He called back to Jim as they were leaving, "Hey you two, we're going to the pavilion. Finish our games for us, will you?"

"Okay," Jim replied. "We'll catch you later."

Phil fished a couple of nickels from his pocket as they walked toward the jukebox. "What song would you like, beautiful?"

"How about . . . this one," she said while punching the button for "Boogie Woogie Bugle Boy."

Phil led her onto the dance floor. He stretched out his arms and she held on tightly to his hands. They leaned back and danced around in a circle, gaining speed with the fast music. Then, Phil let go of her left hand, held her right above her head. She twirled around several times, tapping her feet as she went while Phil's feet matched her movements. Suddenly, they let go of each other and Linda did a cartwheel maneuver, hands and feet touching the floor in time to the music. Phil followed with the same move, then grabbed her hands and twirled her around again. They continued like that until the dance ended a few moments later. By that time, they noticed that Jim and Strawberry had come into the pavilion and were waiting for them at a nearby table.

"Hey, you two are really good!" said Jim.

"Where did you learn to dance like that, Linda?" asked Strawberry.

"Oh, I've been practicing at home," Linda said between gasps.

"Me too," Phil quipped.

"Yeah, I'll bet," Jim retorted. "I doubt if Granny Barkley would put up with all that racket!"

"Just kidding," Phil replied with a grin.

They spent the rest of the evening dancing to popular tunes, slow and fast tempo. Finally, the time came to leave.

"Man, I'm bushed!" Phil exclaimed. "How about you driving back Jim?"

"Okay by me." Phil and Linda piled into the back seat of the Plymouth. As Jim moved the car out of the parking lot, Linda slid closer to Phil and he responded by putting his arm around her neck. His heart seemed to skip a beat, but he felt on top of the world! Looking down into her smiling face, Phil suddenly thought of Linda as an angel because of the soft glow of moonlight on her face.

"You really are the most beautiful girl I've ever met," he said in a low voice.

She seemed to blush for a second, then smiled at him. "Why thank you, Phil."

"Your skin reminds me of peaches and cream, and I've always loved peaches and cream."

She giggled. "That's very sweet of you to say so, but I think you may need glasses."

"What are you two whispering about back there?" Jim asked.

"Phil told me I remind him of peaches and cream," Linda chuckled. "I told him he needs glasses." Jim and Strawberry laughed.

"Strawberry and Peaches," Jim began. "Sounds like we're running a fruit stand, buddy."

That remark brought loud laughter from both couples. Within a half hour, Phil and Linda were in the front seat, having dropped off Jim and Strawberry at their homes. Soon, Linda was snuggled down against Phil's shoulder again.

"I won't mind if you call me Peaches, Phil," she whispered.

87

Phil grinned.

The next thing he knew, they were standing on Linda's front porch, saying goodnight to each other.

"I really had a good time tonight, Phil. You are quite a dancer!" She looked up into his eyes. "And you're a very sweet guy. I'm sorry it's too late for you to come inside."

Before he could reply, Linda reached up and gave Phil a short, sweet kiss on the lips. Phil closed his eyes, hoping the kiss would linger as long as the last one she gave him.

"Goodnight," she suddenly said, then turned and went into her house.

"Goodnight, Peaches," he replied. As she closed the door, he could see her smiling at the use of her new nickname. On the way home, Phil couldn't get rid of the fluttering in his stomach. He couldn't get Linda off his mind, either. Maybe I'm in love, he thought.

Chapter Thirteen

In the following weeks of June, 1941, Phil tried even harder to get Linda to agree to another date. He missed seeing her every day, since school was out for the summer. She seemed content to see him on the occasional Sunday afternoon just to ride around in his car. Phil enjoyed those times together, because even though they weren't what he would call a date, he and Linda were getting to know each other better each time.

One Sunday afternoon, Phil drove the Silver Bullet to Kenly. He went by Linda's house to see if Eddie might be hanging around. When he didn't see Eddie's car, he pulled into the driveway. He climbed the steps and knocked on the front door. In a few moments, the door opened and there stood Linda.

"Hi, Peaches!" Phil greeted her.

She smiled. "Hello, Phil."

"I was just riding around and thought you might like to come with me."

"I'll have to ask mother. Wait here a moment."

Phil sat in the front porch swing and waited until she returned.

"I can go," she said, closing the door behind her. "But I have to be back by five o'clock." She laughed as he showed his delight by dancing a little two step as he escorted her to the Silver Bullet.

They went to the nearby service station where Phil stopped for a couple of sodas. "Let's go to the pine tree grove next to the school," he suggested as he climbed back in the car. "It will be cool there and we can relax and drink these sodas while we talk.

"Okay by me," she said.

One thing Phil had learned over the past few weeks was that Linda was a cautious type, so he drove a bit more slowly than usual. He smoothly pulled the car under the shade of the pine grove and stopped the car. They both leaned back and relaxed.

"Do you remember Roland Varnes?" he asked. "Oh, yes. He seems to be a very nice guy. Isn't he your neighbor?"

"Sure is," Phil replied. "He and his younger brother, George, have been my best buddies as long as I can remember."

"Well, what about Roland?" Linda asked.

"Well, he is talking about joining the Army Air Corps. He wants to be an airplane mechanic."

"Why does he want to do that?"

"He says that since Hitler attacked Russia, the U.S. is shipping war materials there. We've already been shipping materials to England, you know. Anyway, Roland thinks it won't be long before he's drafted. If he volunteers, at least that way he can pick what branch of service he goes into."

"I hate this war," Linda said with disgust. "I wish they would hurry and get it over with."

"Me too," Phil echoed. "But it seems to be getting worse than better. I'm not going until I have to." Linda looked at him with surprise.

"You're not?"

"Not since I've met you, Peaches!"

"Oh, Phil. What a sweet thing to say. But aren't you afraid they'll draft you?"

"Not yet. They only made the draft a law last September. And we're not even in the war. They've probably already got enough men for shipping supplies to Europe."

"What would you like to do in the military if you had to go?" Linda asked.

"Oh, I'd like to fly if I could, but they say you have to have two years in college to be eligible. That's leaves me out I guess I'd try to get in the Army Air Corp and be an airplane mechanic, like Roland wants to do."

"Well, I hope you don't become a pilot. That seems too dangerous to me."

"But I think it would be exciting and thrilling," replied Phil, chuckling at her apprehension.

"It might be for you, but not for me."

Suddenly, Phil sensed that he needed to change the subject. "What do you want to do after you graduate, Peaches?"

"Well, I plan to be a secretary. I'll probably go to a school in Raleigh." She paused. "What do you plan to do, that is, if you don't have to get into the war?"

"I'm not sure. I've always wanted to learn to fly and be a commercial airline pilot, but it's too expensive."

"Maybe you could get into aeronautical engineering," Linda offered. "I hear that State College in Raleigh has a fine engineering school."

"I've thought about that. Daddy said he'll try to pay for some of my college costs, but I would have to work part time to pay for the rest."

"Oh, I'm sure you could do that easily, Phil."

"I guess so," Phil said in a far away voice. His mind had suddenly turned to thinking about how to get another date with Linda. A moment later, he simply blurted out the question. "Peaches, how about going with me to Holt's Lake next Saturday night?"

She hesitated before answering. "I'd really like to, Phil," she began. "but I can't. I already promised Eddie I would go out with him."

Phil gave her his best look of dejection, even though inside he was thinking of punching Eddie in the face.

"I'd rather go with you," she added.

"Can't you break it?" he asked.

"Oh, no. I couldn't do that. Mother would be so angry with me. she likes Eddie very much because he is quiet and, she says, 'reliable'."

"He sounds exciting," Phil said sarcastically. "Didn't you tell me before that he plans to be a bank teller?"

"That's right."

"Not a bank president? Just a bank teller?"

"What are you getting at, Phil?"

"Oh, nothing." He suddenly changed tactics, thinking that if he said too many bad things about Eddie, it might hurt her feelings. "How about July Fourth? They are going to have a band there and a big celebration. Jim told me that he and Strawberry are going. They'll even have fireworks!"

"Okay," she blurted out. "That sounds great!"

Phil was so elated that he leaned over and hugged her. "I can hardly wait!" he exclaimed.

Linda glanced at her watch and told Phil she had to be getting home.

As the following Friday was July Fourth, Phil bargained with Daddy Barkley to have off that day and the Saturday after. He was up at daybreak, hoeing weeds from the cornfield until time for breakfast. After eating, he would join the hired field hands who were "topping" tobacco plants. Each plant produced a large blossom that had to be removed in order for the plant to grow taller and produce fuller leaves. The worst part of that job was the hour it took every evening to remove the black, gummy tobacco sap from his hands and face. It almost never came out of clothes, much to Granny Barkley's consternation.

Thursday morning, Phil and some of the hired hands were finishing up the tobacco field when he became aware of a distant buzzing noise overhead. Looking up into the clear, blue sky, Phil spied a dark speck high above and realized it was an airplane. His mind wandered back to the Buck Rogers comic book she used to read. For a few moments, he envisioned himself chasing Killer Kane through space, with Wilma Deering as co-pilot . . . or was it Linda flying beside him?

"Keep moving, son," his father's voice boomed across the tops of the shoulder high tobacco plants. Phil, startled out of his daydream, quickly resumed his work. "Don't fall behind," his father sternly reminded him of their deal.

"Yes, sir." Phil responded.

The next morning, Phil worked hard to get his few remaining chores finished in order to have time for cleaning up the Plymouth. He collected eggs, took them to Granny Barkley, then returned to clean out the chicken house. Then he fed the hogs in the big pen as well as the two sows in a special pen with their squealing newborn pigs. Next, he checked the cattle yard to make sure they had enough water and salt blocks. Then he milked a few cows so there would be enough milk for the weekend.

After lunch, Phil pulled the Plymouth under the large oak tree in the front yard and began to clean it from top to bottom until it shone like new money. When that was finished, he began the ritual of getting himself clean. As the sun began to set over the treetops, producing bright red, pink, and orange hues in the hot evening sky, Phil stepped out onto the front porch, finally ready for his most important date yet with Linda. He felt so good that he sang "You Are My Sunshine" almost all the way to Kenly.

Linda greeted Phil at her front door dressed in a white, mid-length sleeve blouse under the crossed shoulder straps of her pink skirt. Her white bobby socks had pink trim that she had turned down almost to the tops of her saddle oxford shoes. As always, she had a pink ribbon in her beautiful blonde hair. "Hi, Phil," she said in that low voice that melted his heart.

They soon arrived at Holt's Lake, after picking up Jim and Strawberry. As they reached the nightclub, the reflection off flickering Chinese lanterns surrounding the building seemed to dance across the lake. When Linda glanced at him and remarked about how beautiful the lights were, Phil sensed she was in a romantic mood.

They went immediately to the dance hall since there was a band there that was already playing. As they walked in the door, Phil noticed a sign on the wall and began to read.

"Hey, guys," he called out. "Take a look at this. It says they are having a Jitterbug contest tonight. First prize is ten dollars in cash. Second place is five dollars, and third place is two dollars."

"I wouldn't get my hopes up if I were you," Jim cautioned. "There are some pretty good dancers here tonight."

"There's no rule that says we can't try, pal. How about it, Peaches?"

"I'm game if you are," Linda replied.

"Let's get warmed up," Phil said as he led Linda onto the dance floor. They danced to a couple of slow tunes and were hoping the band would play something a bit faster when the club manager announced that the contest would begin in just a moment. Phil and Linda returned to their table and sipped on the RC Colas that Jim had bought while they were dancing. A moment later, the manager announced the beginning of the contest. Phil and Linda took the dance floor with several other couples as the manager explained the rules.

"Good luck, Peaches," Phil whispered. "Same to you," Linda replied.

Suddenly, the band began belting out "Flat Foot Floogee."

"Hey, that's a good one!" Phil shouted over the music.

"Let's show 'em how its done!" Linda yelled back.

Their timing was perfect from the start. Soon, they were swinging each other around, doing leap frog maneuvers and cartwheels and throwing in a "Lindy" kick for good measure. The crowd applauded several times, but Phil didn't know if it was for something they were doing, or if it was for another couple.

After the third dance, only four couples remained on the dance floor. There were brief rests in between the songs, but only enough time to get a sip of something to drink.

"Are you getting tired?" Phil asked.

"Not one bit," Linda replied. "Are you?"

Phil replied that he was ready to dance all night and Linda giggled as they took the dance floor again. During the next number, Linda suddenly surprised everyone by doing what was called "Posin." Phil followed her lead. "Posin" was a step that was very popular in the northern states and it required dancers to assume a semi-squatting position with knees spread wide while keeping time with the music using the feet only.

Just minutes after they began the new step, something strange happened. The other couples stopped dancing and began to watch. Soon the audience was applauding and this time, Phil knew who it was for. As soon as the music stopped, the club manager grabbed the microphone and spoke over the crowd's wild applause.

"We've got a winner, Ladies and Gentlemen. Couple number four! Let's hear it for them."

Phil and Linda bowed to the audience, both blushing at the sudden adoration of an entire club of dance fans. Linda squeezed Phil's hand, then hugged him tightly. The manager walked over and handed them each a five dollar bill and turned to the crowd.

"Should we have this lovely couple show us that dance one more time?" The audience shouted their approval. "How about it, kids?" the manager asked.

Phil looked at Linda and she nodded. "Have them play 'Flat Foot Floogee' again," Phil told the manager.

A few moments later, they were walking to their table amid more wild applause.

"Now that was what I call dancing, pal," Jim exclaimed as he slapped Phil on the back. "Where did you learn that?"

"My cousin from New York taught me," Linda replied. "I taught Phil one Sunday afternoon."

They sat at the table for a while, watching other couples try the new dance step. At ten o'clock, people began moving outside in large numbers.

"What's going on?" Phil asked. "I think they are about ready to set off the fireworks," Jim replied. "Let's go see."

After the spectacular display of fireworks over the lake,

Strawberry looked at her wristwatch. "It's getting kind of late, guys. I think we should be going."

"Strawberry is right," Linda added. "I have to be home before eleven o'clock."

Jim piped up. "I'll drive, good buddy. I know you two have to be tired after that exhibition of your dancing skills."

"Sold, American!" Phil retorted, using the popular expression from an advertisement of the American Tobacco Company. They all laughed at Phil's wit.

It was ten forty-five when Phil pulled the Plymouth into Linda's driveway. Linda leaned against Phil's shoulder as he switched off the car. He put his arm around her neck and they both relaxed. A moment later, Phil reached into his pocket and produced the five dollar bill he had won. He pressed it into Linda's hand. "I want you to have this."

"Oh no," she replied.

"That's yours. You earned it because you are such a good dancer."

"No, Peaches. I want you to keep it. You can spend the five dollars you won, but keep this one for sentimental reasons. It will always remind you of this night."

"Phil, you're so sweet." Linda wrapped her arms around his waist and hugged him tightly.

"I just want you to know that you mean a lot to me," Phil explained.

"Phil, what is your favorite girlfriend like?"

"Oh, she is about your height," he began. "And has black, stringy hair and red, bulging eyes. Oh, and her measurements are 34, 56, 29." Linda slapped him playfully on the arm.

"You're the only girl for me, Peaches," he continued.

"What about the girl at Cash Corner?"

Phil was momentarily taken aback.

"You didn't know that I knew about her, did you?" Linda teased.

"Oh, uh, she's just a good friend," Phil said, thinking of a quick way to get out of talking about Grace. "But she is nothing compared to you. I want you to be *my* girl. But that's kind of impossible as long as you have Eddie."

She shot a quick glance into Phil's gleaming eyes and smiled. "Eddie is nice, but he is just a good friend too. My mother thinks a lot of Eddie."

"What do *you* think of him?"

Linda smiled again, but didn't answer. She simply snuggled closer to Phil. A few moments passed before she reminded him that she had to be in her house by eleven. They walked toward the front door. At the top of the steps, Linda turned so her face was even with Phil's.

"I'll always remember tonight," she said as she entwined her arms around his waist.

He looked into her eyes for only a second before kissing her long and deeply. She finally pushed at him lightly and they separated.

"I have to go in now," she sighed. "Goodnight, sweet Peaches."

Phil hesitated before going down the steps. He felt that fluttering in his stomach again, but this time it was accompanied by a light feeling in his head. He was one happy young man because he felt sure that Linda was falling in love too.

Chapter Fourteen

By late August, most of the tobacco had been harvested and hung in barns to cure. The process involved applying heat through "flues" that went into the barn from a large fireplace on the outside of the barn. When all the sap was dried out of the leaves, it would be graded into different quality types and sold at an auction with the brightest leaves usually bringing the best price. These bright leaves would be crushed and cut and blended into material for making cigarettes.

Drying the stems of the leaves was the most dangerous part of curing tobacco. During the last few days of applying heat, the fires had to be kept extremely hot in order to remove the sap from the large, thick stem on each leaf. If everything went just right, a few days later the heat would stop and the doors would be opened so just a little moisture could return to the leaves to prevent them from crumbling before reaching the market. The danger of a barn catching fire was always present in those last few days of curing.

It was on one of those days that Phil was tending the fires at a barn that was almost finished. Noticing that the woodpile was getting low, he decided to take the pickup truck to their large wood supply and get more. As he drove the short distance down the path, Phil turned on the radio his father had installed in the old pickup in order to keep abreast of the war situation. As the tubes warmed up and the volume increased, Phil began to understand that the reporter was talking about German submarine activity in the Atlantic Ocean. British and U.S. ships were being sunk right and left! And some of them were pretty close to American shores!

As Phil was thinking about how much closer the nation was coming to entering the war, he suddenly noticed a large amount of smoke rising above the nearby treetops. It seemed to be coming from the direction of the Varnes' farm!

Within minutes, Phil had sped the truck down the path, onto the road, and arrived at his neighbor's farm. He only felt small relief at the discovery that it was not their home, but a tobacco barn that had caught fire. The truck skidded to a halt in front of the burning structure. Roland, George, and their father were running with buckets of water from a small, nearby pond. Phil grabbed a bucket too. They worked furiously, throwing water on the fire, but after ten minutes, Mr. Varnes called for them to stop.

"Its no use, boys," he yelled above the roaring of the flames. "The fire is too hot now." He sat on a tree stump nearby and buried his face in his hands.

"I'm very sorry, Mr. Varnes," Phil offered. "I wish I could

96

have been here sooner." He knew how much Mr. Varnes wanted to buy a better automobile for his family. The loss of one barn of cured tobacco might mean almost half of a farmer's income for the year. This loss would set the Varnes' back for a couple of years to come. Roland and George walk over and put their hands on their father's shoulder.

"No one could help this, daddy. It just happens sometimes," Roland offered.

"Yeah," George chimed in, "We'll just work that much harder next year."

Phil suddenly remembered his own responsibility and jumped back into the pickup. "I had better get back to my own barn, fellahs. I'm really sorry we lost this one."

"Thanks, Phil," Roland answered. Arriving back at his own tobacco barn, Phil discovered that, if anything, his fire was too low. He added the last few sticks of wood near the barn and drove down to the big woodpile for more.

The next day was Saturday and Phil had arranged for Jim and Strawberry to accompany Linda and he to the drive-in movie at Goldsboro. Linda had agreed to go since Eddie was visiting his relatives in Charlotte and would be gone the whole weekend.

Phil arrived early at Linda's house and was invited in by her mother. He realized it was a good opportunity to get to know Mrs. Hinton a little better and put on his best manners. He complimented her on how young she looked. Somehow, it felt awkward. With women his own age, Phil was always at ease and his compliments were always received with delight. Linda's mother thanked Phil for his compliment, but he sensed she knew that he was merely attempting to flatter her. She was very friendly and asked Phil about his school subjects and hobbies during the twenty minutes it took for Linda to finally emerge from her room. The three of them sat for another fifteen minutes and talked about the war situation, until the familiar sound of Jim's auto horn sounded in the driveway. Soon, to Phil's relief, they were zooming merrily down the highway toward Goldsboro. He knew he was going to have to work much harder in order to convince Linda's parents that he was a better choice for their daughter than Eddie.

They arrived at the drive-in theater just before dark. Jim found a good parking spot near the center of the lot, stopped the car, and rolled down the window in his door to get the speaker. As it was still warm at that time of day, they all rolled down their door windows before settling back into the seats to await the movie's beginning.

"Hey, this is going to be a funny show," Strawberr said."Bud Abbott, Lou Costello and Big Mouth Martl Ray . . . they always keep the jokes flying."

97

Phil shouted, "Hurray!"

Linda poked him in the ribs and laughed. "Settle down, mister fidgety."

It wasn't long before they all settled down, into each others' arms. But about twenty minutes after that, a loud "slap" was heard from the back seat. Then Linda giggled.

"Watch it!" she whispered to Phil.

"I'm, ah, sorry," Phil whispered back sheepishly. "My arm slipped." Jim chuckled. Phil glanced at Linda and grinned.

The end of the movie came much too soon for everyone in Jim's car. But, knowing they had to be home at a respectable hour, the happy foursome soon left Goldsboro for home. As Jim and Strawberry backed out of Linda's driveway, Phil and Linda reached the top step on the porch of her house.

"Peaches," he began. "Let's sit in the porch swing for a little while. What do you say?"

"Okay," she replied. "But only if you promise to behave. "They both laughed.

As they sat in the swing, Phil asked, "Are you angry with me?"

"What for?"

"Well, for what happened earlier tonight."

"No . . . not if your arm really did slip."

He looked mischievously into her eyes. "I promise," he said. "Hey, how about going with me to a movie in Smithfield tomorrow afternoon?"

"I might like that," she replied. "What's playing?"

"Its Bob Hope and Bing Crosby in 'Road to Singapore.' I love those two guys. In fact, I like them better than Abbott and Costello."

"You left out Dorothy Lamour. I'll just bet you don't like to see her!" Linda teased.

"Oh, she's okay." He laughed. "I just forgot that she was in the movie."

Linda rolled her eyes back and grinned. "Okay, Phil. Whatever you say."

They swung for a few minutes without saying anything, both enjoying the sheer pleasure of each other's company.

"Well," Linda finally broke the silence, "if we can go to the rly afternoon show, I believe mamma and daddy might say v. My mother always wants me back by six o'clock on Sunday ngs. That's when they get home from visiting."

Okay, Peaches. I'll pick you up about two-thirty and we'll three o'clock show. That will put us back here by five- ow does that sound?"

be ready," she said, rising from the swing to go inside. d goodnight and Phil danced down the steps, climbed Plymouth, and headed for home.

They both enjoyed the movie and laughed about various scenes the whole way from Smithfield back to Linda's house the next afternoon. They stood on the porch for a few minutes, then Linda said she had to go inside. Before sending Phil home, she gave him a long, deep kiss and told him what a wonderful weekend it had been. As Phil glided his car onto the street, he felt so exhilarated that he began singing.

Linda heard him just before closing the door and smiled. "He's such a sweet boy," she said to herself.

As Phil turned off Linda's street onto the road that lead toward his house, something made him glance into the rear view mirror. He smiled, recognizing Mr. Hinton's car coming down the street behind him. As it turned into the street he'd just left, something else caught his attention. But he shook his head and thought, Its just my imagination. The closer he got to home, however, the more it nagged at him. He could have sworn he saw Eddie's car following Mr. Hinton.

Chapter Fifteen

Saturday, August 30, 1941, Roland Varnes departed for boot camp at Fort Bragg, North Carolina. Along with George and the rest of the Varnes family, Phil waved at his buddy as the train pulled out of the Selma station. He had a funny feeling in his stomach, but shook it off as they turned to get in the back of Mr. Varnes' pickup truck for the ride home. He wondered how long it would be until he saw his buddy again.

Roland had wanted to enter the Army Air Corps as an aircraft mechanic. He had told Phil that the draft would have gotten him sooner or later, so it was better to go ahead and enlist. That way, he could more or less choose which type of service he would go into. But when he took the Air Corps examination, Roland flunked the academic portion. When the recruiters offered him a position as a regular maintenance mechanic, Roland decided to take it.

Phil was most sorry for George. The way his young buddy had been acting over the past few days, Phil knew George would almost be lost without Roland. All summer long, the two Varnes brothers had put a lot of mileage on that old Silver Bullet. They had burned a lot of nickels in the jukebox every Saturday night at Cash Corner. Roland had even deferred his entrance into the service until George got his drivers license. There was no doubt in Phil's mind that George would be the hardest hit by Roland's departure.

That afternoon, Daddy Barkley drove Phil to Mr. Yount's house to pick up a school bus. Phil had been selected as a bus driver since he was a rising senior at Kenly High. With the pay from his bus route, the N.R.A. job at school, and a little money from odd jobs, Phil would have a lot more money to spend on dates and clothes. At times, the N.R.A. job interfered with football practice, but Coach Sherman was very understanding, especially since it didn't seem to hamper Phil's performance on the field.

With his spare income from the N.R.A. job, Phil could afford to buy factory made cigarettes. He occasionally smoked them while cleaning out the school buses during his lunch period. A few weeks after school began, Phil began to have regular, lunch time visits from a young boy named Dick West who lived on his route. Phil had given Dick the nickname of "Squirt" because he smoked cigarettes and cursed like a sailor. The fact that Phil was buying factory made cigarettes hadn't escaped Dick West's attention. It was slightly annoying to Phil that Dick was always begging for a cigarette. Finally, Phil had an idea.

One Friday, as Phil was sweeping out a bus, Dick snuck on board and asked Phil the usual question.

"I'll tell you what, Squirt," Phil began. "You sweep out this bus and I'll give you the last half of this cigarette I'm smoking."

"That's a deal!" replied Dick, grabbing the broom from Phil.

Phil sat in one of the seats, lit a Camel, and slowly puffed on it while watching the boy sweep furiously. A few moments later, he suddenly noticed from the corner of his eyes someone rounding the back of the bus.

"Here, Squirt. You take this," Phil said, offering to trade the cigarette for the broom. Dick quickly obliged and sat down to enjoy his reward. Just then, Mr. Yount stuck his head in the door at the front of the bus.

"How's it going, Phil?"

"Just fine, Mr. Yount."

Dick jumped up as the principal climbed the steps into the bus. He cupped the cigarette butt in his hand and shoved it into his pocket. Mr. Yount looked at Dick, then at Phil, then back at the pocket of Dick's pants where wisps of smoke were beginning to swirl around his arm.

"Son, aren't you on fire?" he asked excitedly. Dick replied by shaking his head, his cheeks bulging with the puff of smoke he had just taken seconds before.

"What is your name, young man?" Mr. Yount continued.

As Dick opened his mouth to reply, smoke billowed out around his head. He slowly pulled the cigarette from his pocket and told the principal his name.

Mr. Yount looked at Phil. "I thought I told you there was to be no smoking in these school buses!"

"Yes, sir, Mr. Yount. I try, but you know how it is sometimes."

Mr. Yount grabbed Dick by the hand. "Put out that cigarette this minute and come with me, Mr. West!"

As Mr. Yount stormed off the bus with Dick in tow, Phil felt sorry for Dick. But, he thought, better him than me. I have a lot more to lose! Besides, Mr. Yount is a pretty decent fellow. He won't beat the boy, or anything like that. But what if Dick blabs and tells Mr. Yount where he got the cigarette?

As it turned out, Dick West didn't tell Mr. Yount where the cigarette came from because he knew Phil would never give him another one. His punishment was to sit in Mr. Yount's office each day during recess period. He also had to write 500 times on a blackboard, "I will not smoke cigarettes in school buses. "Nevertheless, Phil stayed clear of Mr. Young for the rest of the day. That evening, when the bus pulled to a stop in front of Dick's house, Phil stopped the boy just as he was stepping out the school bus door.

"Hey, Squirt. Thanks." Phil tossed a Camel through the open door. Dick caught it, looked up at Phil and grinned, and turned to walk down the path toward his house.

The next day, as Phil was cleaning the Plymouth in preparation for his date with Linda the next afternoon, George Varnes rumbled up the path on the Silver Bullet.

"Hey, Phil! How about going with me to Cash Corner tonight? You can see some of the old gang, well, the ones who haven't joined the military, that is."

"Ah, not tonight, George."

George was silent for a second. Suddenly, he blurted out, "Grace has been asking about you again."

"Well, ah, just tell her I said hello, will you? I'm sorry, George. Maybe next weekend, huh?"

"Yeah," George replied lowering his eyes. "Maybe next weekend." Looking a bit dejected, George turned the Silver Bullet around and headed back home. Phil stopped cleaning the Plymouth and hung his head. He felt bad for George, but he just wasn't ready to see Grace Langston again. And if it wasn't for that, he would have gone with his little buddy anywhere. George is really missing Roland these days, he thought. The least I could do is ride around with him in the Silver Bullet for a while. Phil shook his head and returned to cleaning the car.

On Sunday afternoon, Phil picked up Linda at around 3 pm. She had begun to enjoy bowling so much that Phil found it easier to get her to go out with him if he planned Sundays around a few games at the alley in Smithfield. As they pulled into the parking lot, they saw Jim and Strawberry going in the door.

"Hey, you two! Wait for us!" Phil shouted from the car.

"Sure!" Jim yelled back. "The more the merrier!"

It is almost dusk when they leave the bowling alley and head for a nearby restaurant to rest and eat supper.

"What do you say fellahs? How about seeing a movie?" Phil asked as their meals were being served.

"Sounds good to me," replied Strawberry. "What's playing?"

"I heard that 'The Wizard of Oz' is playing downtown," Linda answered. "It's supposed to be a wonderful movie!"

"Could we, Jim?" asked Strawberry. "I've been wanting to see that."

"Sure, honey. I don't see why not." He turned to Phil and winked. "How about that, Phil? These girls want to take us to see a movie."

Phil chuckled. "Isn't it great to be dating two rich girls?" Linda and Strawberry giggled. They knew the boys would not even dream of letting them pay for the movie tickets.

A few hours later, as the film credits were rolling across the screen and the theater lights were coming up, Linda quickly glanced at her watch.

"Phil, honey, it's getting late. We must hurry if I'm going to get home before ten o'clock."

102

"Okay, Peaches," Phil grinned from ear to ear.

"Why are you smiling like that?" she asked.

"Oh, I was just thinking about a funny part in the movie," he lied. What had really made him so happy was the fact that she called him "Honey."

Chapter Sixteen

By November, snow had already fallen once and the people around Kenly began to realize it was going to be a long, cold winter. Daddy Barkley spent most Saturday afternoons listening to the radio for news of the various war situations across the globe.

"A large Japanese naval force has been sighted just south of Formosa," the reporter's voice droned out of the large Motorola radio. "Government officials suspect them to be headed for Indochina. Now for some brighter news . . . U.S. lend lease aid is helping the Russians defeat the Germans at Moscow and Leningrad."

"Maybe that Hitler fellah will learn his lesson yet!" Daddy Barkley interrupted the reporter. Phil smiled at his father's enthusiasm.

Just then, they heard a knock at the door. Daddy Barkley turned down the volume on the Motorola while Phil answered the door. George Varnes burst in almost before Phil could get out of his way.

"We got a letter from Roland today!" George exclaimed. "He was sent to the Philippine Islands, and boy, does he hate it there! He says it is hotter there than the inside of a tobacco barn in August."

"Whoa, son," Daddy Barkley said. "Slow down a bit. We aren't going anywhere. Sit down over here and tell us every little detail."

"Well," George began as he took a seat next to the fireplace, "Roland says he gets to work on a lot of military vehicles but it is very hard to do good work because of a shortage of parts and supplies. They have to patch up things and make do with what they can find. Roland's boss told him that he is real good at that."

Phil smiled at the beaming expression of pride on George's face as he told them all the news Roland had sent from way off in the Pacific Ocean. He wondered when Roland would get around to writing him a letter.

"Roland said for me to tell you hello, Phil. He says he misses going to Cash Corner on Saturday nights with you and me."

"I miss him, too," Phil replied. "I'm glad you came over to tell us about how he's getting along."

The next morning, Phil awoke to find that more snow had fallen during the night. Daddy Barkley joined him at the kitchen window to survey the pure, white blanket with which nature had covered the earth.

"I think it might be okay to drive the bus today, son," he observed. "But you had better be very careful. Remember, you are responsible for the safety of all those children who ride with you."

"I know, daddy. I guess if it was too bad to drive in, the school would have notified the radio stations. But I listened to the Kenly station for a few minutes and they didn't say anything about school being canceled."

"Well, those busses are pretty heavy. I think you won't have any trouble keeping traction on the road. But I'd drive very slow if I were you. I don't think the school would mind if you got there a few minutes later, just as long as everyone is in one piece."

Of course, Daddy Barkley was right. Phil arrived at school with no trouble. During his lunch hour, Phil finished sweeping out the buses, then went to the auditorium on the second floor of the main building where he found Jim and a few other boys playing around on the stage. Phil walked over to the window to look down on the school yard.

"Hey, Jim! Come here," Phil called out.

When Jim arrived, Phil simply pointed down. They could just make out the hat on top of Mr. Yount's head. He was standing midway up the steps at the school's front entrance which was directly below them.

"Do you see what I see?" Phil asked.

"Nope."

"Look at the slab of snow on that little roof over the front door," Phil chuckled. "The sun has been out just long enough to make the bottom slick and mushy. If we give it a nudge, it will slide off onto 'you know who.' "

Jim laughed aloud. "When I walked over here, I knew you were thinking of pulling a prank on someone. You know, you get this little glint in your eye and the side of your mouth crinkles up. But this looks a little dangerous to me."

"Nothing to it," Phil grinned. "There's no way he'll catch us."

They quietly opened two windows beside each other. Together, they counted to three and then shoved the snow. Slowly at first, then picking up speed, the white slab slid right off the incline onto Mr. Yount, nearly knocking him down! The boys laughed heartily as they watched the principal pick up his hat, dust it off, and put it back on his head. Suddenly, he turned and looked up in their direction. Phil and the other boys ducked quickly. But through the open windows they could hear the sound of the school's front door quickly opening.

"Let's get out of here!" Phil exclaimed. "He's coming up stairs!"

"You're not waiting on me," Jim replied, already moving toward the door that led to the hallway.

Luckily, the room for their next class was two doors down

the hall. They quickly ducked into the class and took seats among the other students who were already there. Phil's fanny had barely hit the seat when Mr. Yount's footsteps could be heard just outside the door. When the principal peered into the room, Phil coolly glanced up from a book he had quickly opened. With a bland expression on his face, he smiled and made a slight waving motion at the Principal, then returned to looking at the book. Mr. Yount stood in the doorway for a second, then quietly moved down the hall.

As the sound of his footsteps began to fade, Phil and Jim looked at each other and burst into loud laughter.

"What's so funny?" asked a girl beside Phil.

Phil quickly told the other students about the prank and everyone laughed until the teacher arrived to begin class.

"Don't you all tell on us, okay?" Jim warned.

The next day, Phil hurried to sweep out the buses so he could visit the automobile service station that was located just off the school grounds. They had recently begun to sell ice cream, and Phil can hardly wait to buy a cone of his favorite flavor - peach!

While eating the treat, he overheard the station owner talking to someone about needing part-time help on Sundays.

"Hey," Phil interjected. "I could work a few hours on Sunday afternoons."

"Can you work from noon until 6 pm?" the station owner asked.

"Sure," replied Phil.

"Say, aren't you that Barkley kid?"

"Yes, sir."

"I thought so. You're the one who rebuilt that Model T Ford and outran a Model A over at Rains Crossroads, aren't you?"

"Yep," Phil grinned. "That's me."

"Okay, son. You got the job. Be here at twelve o'clock sharp this coming Sunday."

"Thanks!" Phil exclaimed as he shook the station owner's hand.

That afternoon, Phil found Linda in the library and told her about the job.

"That's great, Phil!" she exclaimed. "Maybe you can start saving some money for college."

Phil was thinking more about the immediate future, however. "How about we celebrate this Saturday night?" he asked. "We could go see that Jack Benny movie, 'Love Thy Neighbor' at the theater in Smithfield."

"Oh, I heard it is a very funny movie," said Linda.

"Then you'll go?" Phil asked excitedly.

"Shhhh! Keep quiet, Phil!" Linda whispered. "You'll disturb the whole library."

"But, will you go?" Phil persisted.

"Okay, okay. I'll go," she gave in. "Are you happy?"

"Ecstatic!" Phil replied in his loudest whisper.

That Saturday night, when they arrived back at Linda's house after the movie, Phil reached for the door handle to get out. Linda pulled him back inside the car.

"I have something for you," she said, using that low voice that always made Phil tingle. "Guess what it is," she said.

"An airplane?" he joked.

"Don't be silly, Phil.

He wiggled his eyebrows up and down. "A kiss?"

"No. Well, not yet that is."

"I give up, Peaches."

Linda reached inside her purse and pulled out a small box covered in striped wrapping paper. "Happy Birthday, Phil."

He opened the box and pulled out a new, leather wallet.

"I didn't know if we'd be together on your birthday, and I knew it was coming up in the next week or two. I hope you don't mind that I gave it to you tonight."

"No, this is great, Peaches! Just what I needed, too. You've probably been noticing my antique, here." Phil reached into his pocket and pulled out his tattered, old billfold. He laid both of them on the dashboard above the steering wheel. "Thanks, Linda. You're so sweet."

Phil pulled her close and they shared a long, deep kiss until Linda gently nudged him away.

"Good night, Phil," she said and quickly left the car.

Phil jumped out as well and caught her at the front door. Linda turned, smiled, and kissed him again. He tried to hold her for a few seconds longer, but she gently freed herself and opened the front door.

"I'll see you next week, Phil. Good night."

Phil's heart beat wildly as he returned to his car. The entire way home, he heard a voice inside his head saying over and over, "She does love me. She does love me."

Chapter Seventeen

Phil had been working at the service station for a few weeks now and he liked it fine. He waited on customers at the pump island and acted as cashier. At times the mechanic swapped with him for awhile when there was an automobile repair that Phil could handle. Even though he missed going to Linda's on Sunday afternoons, he looked forward to working at the station. Sometimes, he got to see Linda just after work, when Eddie was not there.

The first Sunday in December was a cool, but bright winter day. Phil had gotten into the habit of arriving at the service station before the mechanic, hoping this would please his boss. Maybe he'd get a raise before too much longer. The mechanic was on time and opened the station. Phil got busy rolling out the oil display racks and tire racks. Almost immediately he had to start waiting on gas customers. The churches had let out and a rush was on. It was almost two o'clock that afternoon before Phil was able to catch up waiting on the customers. He went into the station, got a cold drink and sat down on a stool behind the cash register to rest a minute. He leaned back against the wall to relax a moment, and decided to turn on the radio for some music. As the tubes warm up and the volume increases, Phil hears a news reporter almost shouting out his report. Phil stopped fiddling with a pencil and listened intently.

"The Japanese have attacked Pearl Harbor!" screamed the voice. Phil wondered where he had heard that name before. Seconds later, he remembered that it was a naval base in Hawaii. Roland had been stationed there briefly before being sent to the Philippine Islands.

"Hey Lacy," he yelled at the mechanic. "Come here! Quick. You have to hear this. The Japanese have attacked Pearl Harbor!"

Leaning close to the radio, listening intently for more news of the attack, Phil didn't notice that several customers had lined up at the gas pumps. It startled Phil when one fellow became impatient and blew his car horn. He jumped off the stool to run outside.

"Sorry, sir," he offered. "We were just listening to the news. It seems the Japanese have attacked Pearl Harbor."

"Are you serious, son?" the man asked. He didn't wait for Phil's reply, but ran into the station to listen alongside Lacy.

The rest of the afternoon, not much work was done around the service station. A crowd had gathered and everyone was listening to the radio. There were a couple of women that Phil noticed as they returned to sit in their automobiles. He saw tears in their eyes and wondered who they knew that might have been in Hawaii, a son or relative or even a neighbor. Phil's mind flashed to Roland, but he had been shipped to the Philippine Islands several weeks before. Still, if the Japs had attacked Hawaii, they might attack the Philippines too.

Each account that was reported over the radio was more grim than the previous. Reports estimated that five battleships were sunk, one hundred and forty planes were destroyed, and approximately 2,000 people were killed or missing. Phil looked at Lacy very solemnly. "This means war for sure, doesn't it?"

Lacy nodded with a grave look on his face. "Let's close up shop, Phil. We won't be doing much around here anymore today."

Phil left the station, but decided to go by Linda's house instead of heading straight home. He felt as if he needed to talk to her. All the talk about the way those sneaky Japs attacked at dawn on a Sunday morning had left him with an angry feeling in his mind and a slightly sick feeling in his stomach. When he arrived at her house, he noticed Linda sitting on a sofa through the window. There were half-finished Christmas decorations around a few of the windows.

Linda rushed to open the door when Phil knocked. She hesitated for a second, then grabbed him and hugged him tightly. "Oh, Phil. What's going to happen? Everything sounds so awful."

"I don't know, sweetness," he replied solemnly as he patted her lightly on the back." A moment later, she pulled slowly away and invited him in to sit with her on the sofa. She held his hand as they listened to more reports on the radio.

"Is Eddie coming tonight?" Phil asked after a few moments.

"No," she replied quietly. "But Mom and Dad will be back in an hour or so."

"Do you feel like talking?"

"Oh, Phil. I'd like to, but I'm just so tired for some reason. Could you come back tomorrow night?"

"You bet, sweet peaches. I'll be here, say, around seven."

They sat silently for a long time. As the sunlight faded and the room grew dark, Phil decided it was time to go home. He and Linda shared a lingering kiss and he departed for home. when he arrived, Daddy Barkley was still up, listening to the radio.

"Sounds bad, son," remarked Daddy Barkley as Phil entered the family room. "Those Japs have got a lot of nerve! But don't worry, son. Maybe they'll realize what a big mistake they've made."

"I don't think so, Dad," Phil replied. "I just don't think so." He suddenly couldn't bear to listen to any more reports of the carnage that had happened half a world away. Just the thought of people being killed while they slept or relaxed on a Sunday morning was enough to make one sick. Phil went to his room and climbed into bed, wondering what the future would bring.

The next day, Mr. Yount suddenly called for all the high school classes to meet in the auditorium. He announced that President Roosevelt had just declared war on Japan and Congress had overwhelmingly approved. Then he gave a short speech on what it meant to be at war. "Our future is now threatened and we must unite together. Our minds and energy must now be fully applied to winning this war against freedom and our way of life. There will be suffering and sorrow and lots of hard work before this war can be won. But I'm certain that if every citizen helps like the people in this community are going to help, we can do nothing but win!" The students applauded wildly at their principle's confident, rousing words.

That night Phil arrived at Linda's house right at seven o'clock. They talked mostly about the war situation until it came time for Phil to leave. They both knew that Phil would probably be drafted since young men aged nineteen were having to register. Phil thought of enlisting but he wanted to complete high school if it was possible. Also, he didn't want to leave Linda until he absolutely had to go. When the old clock on the mantel struck eleven, Phil knew it was time to go home. Linda walked him to the door.

"Phil, honey. Please don't worry. Maybe it won't be so bad."

He looked down into her deep blue eyes and found a glint of reassurance. He smiled. "Maybe you're right." Then he added, "You are so sweet, and so beautiful."

They hugged each other for a moment before Phil kissed her as passionately as he could. She responded a second later by letting her lips linger on his and pulling him closer in her arms. As Phil's heart begins to pound and he gently moves his lips down the nape of her neck, Linda pushed him back gently.

"Whoa, fellah," she whispered with a grin. "Let's not get carried away."

As they gazed into each other's eyes, Phil asked, "See you tomorrow at school?"

"Sure," she replied.

As he drove toward home, Phil realized the empty feeling in the pit of his stomach was gone. It had been replaced with a wonderful feeling in his heart. Suddenly it dawned on him that he hadn't thought of what to get Linda for Christmas.

"Hey, daddy. Can I come to town with you today?" Phil asked his father the next Saturday morning.

"Sure, son. I'd be glad to have some company. Are you going to get my Christmas present?" he teased.

On Saturday, Phil and his father left early to drive into the town of Goldsboro. On the way, they discussed the war situation. Hitler and Mussolini had declared war on the United States, who had declared war on Japan. The United States declared war on Germany and Italy in return. Phil had the car radio turned down low as they talked. Suddenly, a reporter broke into the music program and announced that the Japanese had invaded the Philippine Islands.

Daddy Barkley looked at Phil. "Isn't that where Roland is?"

"It sure is," replied Phil anxiously. "I sure hope he is okay."

"Well," Daddy Barkley offered. "Since he is a mechanic, maybe he won't be in too much danger."

They rode in silence for a while. Phil tried to get his mind off Roland's plight by returning his thoughts to what to get Linda for Christmas.

"Daddy, can you help me with some good ideas of what I could get for Linda's Christmas present?"

After a few moments of thought, Daddy Barkley replied, "How about a necklace with a locket? She could put a small picture inside. I think girls like to do that kind of thing."

"Yeah, that's a great idea," Phil responded. "Why didn't I think of that?"

"Comes with years of experience," his father said with a wink.

The next week, Phil talked to Linda at school and asked her for a date. She agreed to date him on Saturday night but told him she could not see him on Sunday night as Eddie was coming over. Her Mother had invited him for supper. Phil was elated because he preferred Saturday night anyway. He saw Jim nearby and said to Linda, "Could we invite Jim and Strawberry along too?"

"Sure," she replied. "They are lots of fun to be with."

He went over to where Jim was talking to some friends Phil told Jim about the free movie that the merchants were sponsoring on Saturday night at the Kenly Theater. It was a kind of Christmas present from the merchants to the community for supporting them through all the hard times in the past years. Jim accepted the invitation to join Phil and Linda and the two boys agreed to meet at the theater.

"I'm sure Strawberry will come," Jim quipped. "You know how crazy she is about the movies and movie stars. By the way, what's going to be playing?"

"I'm not sure," Phil said. "Probably a western or something like that. They have to show something the whole town can enjoy."

"Well, it doesn't matter anyway," Jim laughed. "It's free, isn't it?"

"Yeah," Phil chuckled. "The best kind. That reminds me, we'd better get there early so we can find four seats together."

Phil picked Linda up early before the show was to start on Saturday night. When they arrived at the theater, Jim and Strawberry were already waiting for them in Jim's car. Phil and Linda came up and parked beside Jim and Strawberry.

Jim got out of the car and yelled at Phil. "Okay you slow poke. Let's get going. The seats are filling up fast."

They entered the theater and picked up some popcorn and cold drinks at the food counter. They found some seats about midway down the theater and settled down to eat and drink and enjoy the show. A few moments later, the crowd roared with delight as the lights dimmed and the movie began.

"Oh, good," said Jim. "It's a Bob Steele Western. This should be good."

"Yeah, if you like Westerns," Phil remarked.

"And if you like lots of fighting," Strawberry chimed in.

"I don't particularly care for westerns," Linda said. "But since it's free, you can't turn it down." They all laughed.

After they had finished eating, Phil put his arm around Linda and pulled her closer to him. He thought he noticed a slight resistance, but she smiled at him and it vanished from his mind. A sudden explosion of gunfire on the screen startled them back to reality. Phil took her hand in his and they both felt better.

After the show, Jim and Strawberry said goodbye and headed for Smithfield. Phil took Linda home and together they sat in the car parked in the driveway for awhile. Phil turned on the radio, but quickly found out that the only thing on was war news, so he turned it off.

He looked at Linda and said, "Sweet Peaches, it's almost Christmas and I don't think I'll get to see you again until after Santa comes."

"Yes, Phil," she replied. "I know."

"Well, I have something for you." He reached into his pocket and brought out a small package, wrapped neatly in red paper with a green Christmas ribbon around it. "Merry Christmas, Peaches."

"Oh, Phil," she exclaimed with delight. "You shouldn't have done this."

She gingerly opened the wrapping and pulled the necklace out of the box. "This is beautiful," she gasped. "It's just wonderful." She grabbed Phil and pulled him close. "Thank you, Phil," she whispered. They embraced tightly and shared a very passionate kiss for what seemed like hours to both of them. Phil could almost swear he was floating and pulled Linda closer. She relaxed in his arms for a moment before remembering to be cautious and gently pushing Phil away.

"Merry Christmas to you, too," she smiled. She held Phil's head between her hands and kissed him again, but not as passionately. "See you after the holidays, okay?"

"You bet," Phil replied.

Chapter Eighteen

The next couple of months were very cold and wintry. It was a dreary time for Phil. He found that the service station work was rather dreary and dirty at times, but since Linda still would not date him regularly, he stuck to it. The money came in very handy anyway.

Since the Japanese invaded the Philippines, there were reports of heavy fighting there. Phil found himself listening to the news reports almost every chance he had. He worried a lot about Roland being so close to the fighting. One day, the news told of all the heavy fighting in Europe and that there were 26 nations that had just formed a group called the United Nations. They declared their intent to defeat the Axis Partners which, by then, included Japan.

Phil came home from school one day and there was finally a letter from Roland in the mail. He quickly opened it. Roland apologized for not writing sooner. He went on to say that he had been real busy because help and supplies were very short there. The fighting was getting very bad there and reports stated that the Japanese were very vicious fighters. Word was getting around that they were mistreating American prisoners.

The next day at school, Principal Yount sent for Phil to come to his office. Phil was anxious and wondered if he had done something wrong.

"Have a seat, Phil," said Mr. Yount as Phil entered the office. "Phil, I called you in for a very important reason. I am sure that you are aware how serious the war situation is, what with the Japanese attacking everywhere in the south Pacific, and the spread of fighting in Europe, not to mention the German submarines that are attacking and sinking ships right off our coast here. Danger is getting closer everyday, and our government is going all out to protect us."

"Yes, sir," replied Phil. "I have been keeping up with the news lately, especially since one of my best friends is in the Philippines."

"Good for you, son. Anyway, I have been informed that all the nation's high schools are to set up small air raid warning stations on the school grounds. The war department is sending instructions and materials, such as airplane identification pamphlets for both the allied and enemy warplanes. I've heard that you have a keen interest in airplanes and already have experience at identifying some airplanes. Is that correct?"

"Yes, sir."

"I would like for you to head up and manage this project. You can do it within the guidelines of your NRA job, but you will probably also have to use some of your own time as well.

Pick out a few students who you think will make good assistants and train them to fill in for you when you can't be there. Can you handle this assignment, Phil?"

"Yes, sir!" Phil exclaimed. He felt an overwhelming sense of importance at being asked to take on this responsibility.

"Good," Mr. Yount responded. "But that's not all. The war department wants us to perform another project. They have asked that all students bring in all the tin cans, metal cans, and scrap iron they can find. The tin cans have to be crushed flat and packed in boxes so they can be picked up by a collector. The war department needs these items badly to help make ammunition and bombs. You and your helpers can mash the cans flat and take care of the collection at your air raid station. Can you handle both of these jobs and keep up with your studies too?"

"You bet, Mr. Yount! When do we start?"

"We'll have all the materials in a few days, so I won't know the specifics until then. They are even talking about everyone planting what will be called a 'Victory Garden.' Every household would plant a small vegetable garden anywhere they can on their property. I even heard a suggestion that window boxes could be used. Anyway, it would all be done to help provide an adequate supply of food for our nation and our boys in uniform. If this project also comes to us from the war department, I'll expect you to find a few more helpers. I'll let you know as soon as we get the information."

"Great!" said Phil. "I'll be glad to help, Mr. Yount. I feel honored that you asked me."

"Well, I think a lot of you, Phil. You have a positive attitude and that's what we're going to need to win this war. In the meantime, I think we can get started on the air raid warning station out in front of the school. There are a few pine trees on that small knoll on the left side of the building. I have an old tent at home that my son had when he was small. It is shaped like an Indian tepee and I think it would make a nice little office for your operation. Phil, the main purpose of this project will be to report sightings of airplanes. When you hear or see an airplane, take the binoculars that we'll provide you and identify the plane as either friendly or enemy. Then rush this information to my office. We'll handle it from there, okay?"

"Yes, sir."

"Well, that's all for now, son. Report back to me next Monday and we'll go over the details." Mr. Yount stood and shook Phil's hand. "Thanks for helping out, Phil. I'm sure you'll do a fine job."

Phil could hardly contain his exuberance as he walked back toward his class. I can't wait to see the look on Jim's face, he thought. He wanted Jim to be one of his helpers. But he also

114

wanted Linda to help, so he went in search for her. He found her with Anita in the library. When he told her about the job she acted very excited and happy for him. This made Phil feel extremely proud.

"Will you be one of my assistants?" he asked her.

"Well, sure," she stammered. Then she laughed. "But I'm afraid I don't know the first thing about airplanes. You'll have to teach me."

"Don't worry," he answered with a grin. "It'll be my pleasure." Anita laughed at her brother's sly facial expression. "Seriously," Phil continued, "Mr. Yount will provide some aircraft identification booklets and we'll study them together. It will be fun."

"Oh, Phil, I'm so proud of you. It sounds like a lot of responsibility."

"Thanks," he replied, blushing slightly at the extra attention. "Now, we will need to talk about this more very soon, like maybe Saturday night."

"Well, I don't know, Phil," she teased. "I kind of had plans."

"Aw, come on, Peaches. You know I asked first. We can go to Holt's Lake. Maybe Jim and Strawberry would meet us there! How about it?"

After a thoughtful pause, Linda accepted. Phil felt a little bit wicked for using Holt's Lake in his ploy. He knew Linda liked to dance, but he had also found out that Eddie didn't like to go to Holt's Lake. It was the advantage he needed over Eddie and he would use it every chance he got.

"Okay," she consented. "I'd love to go."

"Great!" he exclaimed. "You made my day, Peaches." Just then, Phil was surprised to feel the hand of the librarian on his shoulder. She leaned over and whispered to Phil.

"You'll have to be quiet, Mr. Barkley or I'll have to ask you to leave." Anita snickered, while Linda's eyes were riveted to her book.

"Yes, ma'am," Phil whispered sheepishly.

Phil quickly said his goodbyes to the girls and went to find Jim so he could tell him about the job. While they were talking, they agreed to meet at Holt's Lake on Saturday night for a double date.

It was late on Saturday afternoon when Phil completed his weekly chores. By the time he finished cleaning the car and getting dressed, Granny Barkley was calling him for supper. He finished eating quickly and checked his appearance at the large mirror in the hallway.

"Don't stand there too long, Phil. You might break that mirror," his sister Leah kidded him.

"Impossible," Phil calmly replied. "I saw you looking in it the other day. If it didn't break then, it's unbreakable." He winked at the twins who were looking up with admiration at their big brother's sharp outfit. They giggled at his remark while Leah stomped down the hallway, unable to come back with a snappy reply.

It was almost dark when he arrived at Linda's house so they hurried on to Smithfield and went straight to Holt's Lake. When they walked into the building, they found Jim and Strawberry had already arrived and were waiting at a table near the dance floor.

"Where have you two been?" Jim asked.

"Wouldn't you like to know?" Phil joked. Linda blushed and slapped Phil's arm.

"Don't listen to him," she said.

"We're here now," Phil quipped. "So be happy."

"I am," retorted Jim. "I am. But I could have been happier longer and sooner if you weren't so slow."

Before Phil could continue the happy banter, someone put a nickel in the jukebox and a new song rang out through the building. It was one of the new war-inspired popular songs titled, "Praise The Lord And Pass The Ammunition." Phil grabbed Linda's hand and began singing along with the record as he pulled her toward the dance floor.

Phil enjoyed having more space on the dance floor, though he knew it was less crowded only because so many young men had gone off to fight a war. To Phil, it seemed that those who remained behind were coping with the uncertainty and danger of war by enjoying life to its fullest. The only drawback to such enjoyment seemed to be that time passed much more quickly than it did just a few short years before. It seemed like they had just arrived when Phil looked at his watch and knew that it was time to take Linda home. He looked over at his beautiful blonde date and wondered how the war would affect their futures.

"Sweet Peaches," he suddenly said. "I have a song I want to play for you before we leave."

"What is it, Phil?"

"Just listen." He walked over to the jukebox, put in a nickel, pressed the selection button, and returned to his seat. As the song began, he looked into her eyes and took her hand. Then, he began to sing along with the music again.

He finished the rest of the song, even though it was the girl's part in response to the guy's part in the beginning of the song.

"Phil, that's sweet," Linda said when he was finished. "Would you do that?"

"Sure thing, Sweet Peaches. But only for you."

"Oh, I hope you and Jim don't have to go."

"Me too," Strawberry chimed in.

"Well," Jim butted in, "Strawberry and I have already talked

116

things over and decided that if things don't change by graduation time in June, I will go ahead and enlist. My birthday is in July and they'll probably draft me then. Since I want to get into the Air Corps as an aircraft mechanic, I'll have to beat the draft if I want to be able to choose."

"That's what I want to do," echoed Phil. "But I'm going to wait till the last possible minute. My birthday is not until November, and that's a long time away. Besides, I want to see Linda as much as I can before I have to go!" He put his arm around Linda and looked at her wistfully.

She smiled back at him reassuringly. "Phil, you know I'll be seeing you as much as I can, don't you?"

"I sure hope so, Peaches," he replied to her. To himself, he thought, I guess the old Barkley charm is beginning to work.

Chapter Nineteen

The winter months passed by and spring finally came. Linda had been dating Phil more often, but she still saw Eddie frequently as well. The war situation grew worse and worse with each passing day. Phil and Linda discussed it more and more on their dates. There had been some good news recently about Colonel Jimmy Doolittle's raid on Tokyo that boosted everyone's spirits for awhile. But it seemed that bad news was never far behind any good news. The British Army had been reported as defeated in North Africa by German forces under the command of Field Marshall Rommel. He had earned the nickname of "The Desert Fox." The British were in retreat and the United States was trying to rush forces to the area.

On May 6th Phil had been listening to the radio for about a half-hour when he heard the most shocking news yet. A news reporter suddenly broke into the program and announced that U.S. forces in the Philippine Islands had surrendered. Phil rushed into the family room where Daddy Barkley and the rest were seated.

"We heard it too, son. It sounds bad," Daddy Barkley said.

They all listened intently as the reporter went on to report that over 10,000 American soldiers had been taken captive by the Japanese.

"Do you think they have Roland?" asked Anita.

"Let's just hope he escaped with General MacArthur," replied Daddy Barkley. Phil was speechless as he listened to the remainder of the report. When it was over, he quietly got up and went back to his room.

The next day, Phil and Jim practiced on the baseball diamond during recess period at school. Since most of the experienced players were gone, the Coach had to recruit a lot of younger boys to play on the team. The practice session was not going so well for Jim and Phil due to the lack of experience of the younger boys. They both felt a bit despondent so they ended the session early and went back to their classrooms. Their classroom was located behind the stage in the front of the auditorium. The entrance door to the classroom was located at the rear.

Phil and Jim entered the classroom together. Jim's seat was located near the door at the rear of the classroom, so he sat down and proceeded to get some books to study. Phil went up to the front of the classroom where his seat was located. Jim was concentrating on his studies when suddenly a blackboard eraser hit the front of his desk showering him in a cloud of dust. It glanced off and landed in front of the entrance door beside his seat.

Jim looked up and saw Phil at the front laughing. He grabbed the eraser off the floor at the door and hurled it back at Phil. Phil ducked down and the eraser missed him. He pointed his finger at Jim and laughed, saying, "Ha, ha, ha. You missed, didn't you?" Then he grabbed up the eraser and hurled it back at Jim. Jim ducked down as the door opened. In stepped Mr. Wooten, the teacher, just in time for the eraser to catch him right on top of his forehead. A cloud of chalk dust blossomed out around his head. Momentarily dazed, Mr. Wooten gathered his composure, wiped the chalk dust away from his eyes and looked around. Jim was sitting in his seat and Phil was getting into his near the front of the classroom. Since there was no one else at the front of the room, it was evident that Phil had thrown the eraser.

"Mr. Barkley. What is the meaning of this?" he asked.

"Ah, I'm very sorry, Mr. Wooten." replied Phil. I was just letting off a little steam, I guess."

"Well, Mr. Barkley, I suppose it is high time we found a more proper way for you to let off steam." He walked to the blackboard and drew a small circle at about the height of Phil's face. "Mr. Barkley, you may stand with your nose touching the blackboard inside this circle for the next thirty minutes, or you can walk down to Mr. Yount's office right now. The choice is yours."

Phil walked to the board and placed his nose in the circle. He would have been ten times as embarrassed to see Mr. Yount about the incident than to have his classmates make fun of him for having to stand there like that for thirty minutes. But Phil found out that thirty minutes was a very long time when you have to stand at one spot for so long. His legs grew tired and he began to fidget. He tried standing on one foot for a while, and then on the other. Occasionally, a student would snicker at him, which reminded him of how embarrassed he'd be when Linda found out.

"That was pretty mean of Mr. Wooten," Jim remarked as they walked down the hall together after class was over.

"Let's not talk about it," Phil moaned. "Have I got all the chalk off my nose?"

"Yeah. Hey, how's it going between you and Linda?"

"Okay, I guess. I mean, she agrees to go out with me sometimes, but other times she won't. And I know she's still seeing that Eddie guy from Smithfield."

"Have you asked her out for this weekend?"

"Not yet. I thought I'd do that in a little while. Hey, would you and Strawberry like to double date again? We could go to Holt's Lake. Linda seems to like it there."

"Sure, pal. How about we take in an early movie, then go to Holt's Lake for dancing afterward?"

"Sounds great. I'll let you know tomorrow if Linda says yes."

Phil was pleased to find out that "Road To Morocco," starring Bob Hope, Bing Crosby, and Dorothy Lamour, was playing in Smithfield on Saturday night. He was glad to be able to take Linda to see a comedy instead of another western movie. When the show was over, the two couples immediately left for Holt's Lake Phil was surprised to hear Linda say she didn't feel much like dancing after they arrived. Instead, they ordered a couple of cold drinks and sat at their table, listening to songs being played on the jukebox. About a half-hour passed before someone played a popular, new tune called "Deep In The Heart Of Texas." Phil noticed Linda tapping her foot in time with the music.

"Hey, Peaches. Would you like to dance to this one?"

"Why, yes, Phil. I think I would."

When the dance was finished, they returned to the table where Jim and Strawberry were seated.

"Hey, you two," Jim said. "I have something to tell you."

"Sounds like a big announcement," Phil said, glancing at Linda.

"I went last week and applied to get in the Air corps. I'll be taking the test next week, on the fourth."

"Have you forgotten that it's the last week of school?" Phil exclaimed, totally surprised by the news.

"I know that," Jim answered. "Mr. Yount said I could take a day off. It won't make any difference in my grades. I'll still be able to graduate with you."

"Well, that's great!" said Phil. "Good luck, pal." He noticed that Strawberry's eyes were beginning to well up with tears.

"Well, you need not look so happy about it," said Jim sarcastically upon seeing the less-than-gleeful look on Phil's face.

"I'm sorry," Phil said. "I guess it's because I know that I'm going to have to make the same decision soon. I just wish we would win this war soon."

"Hey, play some music, Phil," said Linda, hoping to lighten things up a bit.

"Sure, thing, sweet Peaches." Phil went to the jukebox and looked over the selections. Suddenly, a broad smile comes over his face. He plops a nickel into the slot and punches a button. As he neared the table, the music began. He leaned over Linda, looked at her with a winsome smile and began to sing along.

When the song was over, Linda looked at Phil and slightly tilted her head. Her dreamy blue eyes glittered in the ballroom lights. With a sweet smile, she said, "Phil, honey, that was so sweet of you. Do you really mean it?"

"I do, I do, I do," he replied. He could hardly believe his own ears. She had called him 'honey'." Phil was sure his heart was melting. Even though Linda did not linger over their goodnight kiss, he was still a happy boy going home that night.

The next day, Phil and his family were seated in the family room listening to the radio after finishing off a big breakfast. General Douglas MacArthur had set up his headquarters in Australia and was fighting the war in the Pacific from there. After a few moments, Daddy Barkley switched off the radio and told everyone to get dressed for church.

It was just after lunch when a knock came on the door. Daddy Barkley opened it and George rushed in, sobbing uncontrollably.

"What's the matter, son?" asked Daddy Barkley.

Phil felt a sudden knot in the pit of his stomach. It could only be one thing.

"Roland is dead," George said between sobs. "The Japs killed him."

Phil threw his arms around George in anguish. Something inside wouldn't let him believe the news. "How do you know? Who told you?" Phil barked.

"They came a little while ago,"

"Who," Phil said, shaking his little buddy. "Who came, George?"

"Some men from the air base at Goldsboro, officers, I think."

Large tears seemed to jump from Phil's eyes. He hugged George tightly, the two of them wailing against the injustice of losing their lifelong friend and brother. Through his own sobs, Phil can hear his sisters quiet sobs. One of the twins asked what was wrong with Roland to anyone who might stop crying long enough to answer.

Daddy Barkley finally calmed both Phil and George long enough to get them out to the garage and into the '39 Plymouth. They drove back to George's house and went inside. George's father and mother were taking the news very hard and seemed to be in a state of shock. Phil stayed for a while to sit with them until he realized he was supposed to work at the service station that afternoon. Before they left, Daddy Barkley got a list of Roland's aunts and uncles so he could notify them and other relatives of the tragic news.

Phil was late getting to work, but when he explained things to Lacy, the mechanic told him to go back and stay with the Varnes. All afternoon, Phil sat with George in the Varnes' living room, silently remembering his friend and the good times they had. That night he couldn't sleep. He kept thinking about the war in the Pacific and those horrible little Japanese people. Oh, how he hated the Japanese.

Chapter Twenty

During the last week of school, each day seemed to drag by for Phil. He could not get the death of Roland off his mind and was very downhearted. At school, Linda did her best to comfort him, so they spent a lot of time together. Graduation was scheduled for Friday. When the day finally came, Phil felt despondent when he arrived at school. Besides feeling the loss of Roland, this was his last day of school, ever! He would not be seeing his friends and teacher anymore. It was the end of a way of life, and the beginning of another. He wondered what he would do after graduation. Then he thought of Jim. Almost at the same instant, Jim came up to him from behind.

"Hey, pal. Wait up!" Jim shouted excitedly. "I passed, I passed." He grabbed Phil's hand and shook it vigorously. "I did it, buddy. I'm in the Air Corps."

"That's great Jim. When do you leave?"

"I am supposed to report to Fort Bragg two weeks from next Monday," Jim replied.

"Boy, that's not far away," said Phil. "I'll miss you."

"I'll miss you too, Phil. But, hey, I'm not gone yet. We've got plenty of time for saying goodbye. Besides, I have some more important news."

"Oh yeah? What's that?"

Jim smiled and proudly announced, "Strawberry and I are getting married."

"Do you mean it?" Phil said. His spirits seemed to brighten with the news. "When did all this take place?"

"Last night," Jim replied. "She said 'Yes' last night. When I got home from Raleigh and told her that I passed the exam and would be leaving in two weeks, we began to realize that we wouldn't see each other for a long time. I figured that if we were married they might let us live together off base after boot camp. As long as I am in the states, that is. And, if they won't let us live together, she could rent a small apartment or room close by the base and we could be together when I am off duty. Anyway, we decided to get married! I have to admit. It was all my idea. She's such a great girl and the more I thought about it, the more I realized I couldn't bear to be without her."

"I think it's just great, Jim. Ah, when is the wedding?"

"Saturday afternoon."

"Tomorrow?" Phil exclaimed.

"No, next Saturday," Jim replied. "It'll be a small wedding in the chapel, with our parents and a few of our friends. I'd really like for you and Linda to be there if you could."

"Well, I wouldn't miss it, pal. And I'm sure Peaches will

want to come. In fact, this gives me an idea. How about if she and I throw you a little going away party right after the wedding. I hate to delay your honeymoon, but we might not be seeing you for a long time. What do you think?"

"I'm sure we can wait that long," Jim laughed.

Phil told Linda about Jim and Strawberry after school. She seemed very excited about the wedding and agreed with Phil about the party afterward. They agreed to discuss their plans the next night since they had a date then. Linda had begun dating Phil on Saturday nights and Eddie on Sunday nights. When Saturday night came, Phil and Linda stayed at her house, listening to the radio, playing records, and dancing a little.

As Phil and Linda danced, she could feel his strong arms hold her close. She felt more secure than she had ever felt with Eddie's timid arms about her.

"You really dance well, Phil," Linda remarked. "You've got such strong arms. I don't know why but I feel secure somehow when you hold me."

"Thanks, Peaches." Phil looked down at her and returned her affectionate gaze. He pulled her closer. "I like to practice every chance I get."

When the record ended they went out on the porch and settled in the swing. The warm, June evening was filled with a symphony of peeping, chirping and croaking of crickets and frogs. "Let's talk about the party," Phil said, putting his arm around Linda.

"Okay," she replied, snuggling closer.

"The wedding is at three o'clock next Saturday afternoon. I figure we can start the party at around six o'clock that evening. Maybe we can get the manager of Holt's Lake Club to let us have the dance hall until eight or eight-thirty. We'll invite some of our friends from Kenly and some of Jim and Strawberry's friends from around Smithfield. Most of them will be at the club anyway."

"Sounds good, Phil, but don't you think that will cost a lot?"

"Maybe not, Sweet Peaches, maybe not. I have a little money saved up, so I can afford a little extra. Anyway, I've become good friends with the manager. He buys his gas over at Lacy's service station, you know. I think he'll cut me a deal. Besides, I'll tell him that its the least he can do for one of our brave boys going into the Air Corps."

"You're a real charmer, aren't you?" Linda gave him an affectionate little slap on the chest.

"It worked on you, didn't it?"

"What will you do for music?" she asked, avoiding his question.

"Well, I know three guys that have a string band. It's kind of short notice, but I think I can get them for just their expense money."

"Great!" said Linda. "How about food?"

"I figure we won't be too hungry after the reception, so maybe we can set up a table with a few snacks. What do you think?"

"Sounds like you've got it all figured out." She sighed and snuggled even closer. "This is a really sweet thing you're doing for them, Phil."

"Maybe one day Jim can return the favor," Phil said, fishing for a reply. Linda was silent.

The following week, Phil was out in the tobacco field, breaking the tops out of the plants with his father and some hired field hands. Suddenly there was a loud noise and two single engine fighter planes appeared over the tree tops at the edge of the field. They seemed to be headed straight toward Phil like two bolts of lightning. He ducked down between the rows of tobacco, and in a flash they were gone. He stuck his head back up above the tops of the plants just in time to see them disappear over the trees at the other end of the field. He could have sworn that one of them clipped the top of a tree.

"Wow!" Phil shouted. "Those guys were really moving! I'd love to be in one of those babies."

"What were they?" asked one of the field hands.

"They were P-47 Thunderbolts from the air base at Goldsboro," Phil exclaimed. He was proud that he could identify the planes.

"Well, if they had flown any lower, they would have knocked the tops off this tobacco for us," said another field hand. "I could feel the breeze from them things!" The other field hands all laughed in agreement.

"That's what is called hedge-hopping," replied Phil. "It looks like fun too." As his imagination began to drift off to what it would be like in one of the planes, he was suddenly called back to reality by his father's booming voice.

"Back to work, everybody. The excitement is over."

Saturday eventually arrived and after a long morning of polishing the '39 Plymouth, polishing his shoes, and polishing off a couple of pieces of Granny Barkley's fried chicken, Phil headed down the road toward Linda's house shortly after noon. Linda was as excited about the wedding as Phil because she was waiting for him on her front porch.

The simple, but beautiful, ceremony was performed in a small church near Strawberry's home in Smithfield. Linda told Phil that she thought Jim and Strawberry looked more attractive and happier than she had ever seen them. After the reception, Phil announced to everyone that they were invited to the going away party at Holt's Lake Club. Then, he and Linda left to make sure everything was in place at the club.

It was almost six o'clock when Jim and Strawberry and others from the wedding party finally began to arrive. The manager told Phil that the dance hall was theirs at no charge until eight-thirty. It was his gift to Jim and Strawberry as a wedding and going away present in one. Everyone had such a wonderful time that it seemed like only a little while had passed when eight-thirty rolled around. Phil took the opportunity to have the band play one last special request. It was a new song, almost ready made for the new life Jim was about to begin. As the live music reverberated through the dance hall, Phil sang along.

"This is the Army Mr. Jones."

Everybody in the wedding party stopped dancing and crowded around Phil to help sing the song. When it was over, they all slapped Jim on the back and wished him and Strawberry the best of luck in the years to come. As Phil stood by watching Jim's friends wish him well, he noticed how moist the corner's of Jim's eyes were becoming. Strawberry was already sniffling back her tears and Linda was beginning to cry as well.

Finally, with all the others gone, Phil hugged his pal tightly.

"I'm going to miss you, buddy. We made a good team."

"We did, didn't we," Jim said with a slight choking sound in his voice.

By ten o'clock, Phil and Linda were sitting in her front porch swing, going over all the afternoon's highlights. Closer to midnight they were nestled close together against the cool, summer night air. Neither was saying much by then. Phil stroked Linda's long silky hair and Linda rested her head against the soft rise and fall of Phil's chest.

Suddenly, there was a bright flash of light and a loud boom, almost like thunder. The windows of Linda's house rattled loudly. One pane of glass on the side of the house actually broke. Seconds later, Mr. Hinton was standing on the front porch with them, dressed in his house robe.

"What in blazes was that?!" he asked in amazement.

"I don't know," Phil replied. "If it was thunder it's the loudest that I've ever heard, and I don't see a cloud in the sky anywhere."

"Maybe its time you came inside, Linda. It is getting kind of late."

"Okay, daddy," she replied. "In a minute."

Mr. Hinton closed the door behind him as he went inside while muttering, "Maybe it was someone playing with a stick of dynamite or some fireworks . . . but it isn't even close to Fourth of July yet."

As soon as the door closed, Phil pulled Linda close to him so quickly that a tiny gasp escaped her lips. "I love you, darling."

She took his face between her hands and pulled his lips to

hers. "I love you too, sweetheart!"

As their passionate kiss ended, Phil quickly remembered what he had been meaning to ask Linda all evening. "You know, sweet Peaches, I don't work at the service station on Sunday's anymore. How about if I come over to see you tomorrow afternoon?"

"I was wondering if you were going to ask," she replied. She kissed him again, almost hungrily.

"What about Eddie?" Phil asked when their lips finally parted.

"Oh, he has a cold," she quickly replied. "Anyway, I wouldn't date him anyway as long as I knew you were coming by."

Those words rang in his ears all the way back to his house. Phil was so happy he felt as if he might burst! It was all he had hoped for. She finally had chosen him over Eddie!

The next afternoon, as he was dressing to go to Linda's house, Phil was listening to the radio. A reporter was telling about an ammunition truck that had exploded at a small intersection not far from Kenly. No one could remember why they called the little community "Catch-me-eye", but it had almost been blown off the map the previous night. That must have been the noise we heard, Phil thought. Maybe Linda will want to drive over and see where it happened. When he arrived at Linda's he found that she had already heard about the explosion and was indeed curious about seeing the blast site.

Their imaginations never even came close to preparing them for what they saw upon arriving at the scene. Police were everywhere, keeping order and directing traffic among the huge crowd of sightseers. There was a huge hole in the highway at least eighteen feet deep. The four-story brick hotel that had stood nearby was merely a large pile of rubble. The large restaurant and many of the buildings within a two-block area were simply shells with charred roofs and broken glass.

"What happened?" Phil finally asked one of the policemen.

"Well, the best we can figure is that the rear brakes of the tractor-trailer caught fire. The driver stopped on the side of the highway here to try and put out the fire. When he figured out he wasn't going to put it out, he quickly told the people in the hotel to evacuate. They moved pretty fast, or a lot more people would have been killed. Anyway, the only two people that died were two men in an automobile that decided to try and pass the truck, even though they had been warned by the highway patrol to stop and take a detour. The last thing they said was that they were in a hurry and would take their chances. All that was left of their car was a piece of metal about the size of a barrel. It was found in that field over there behind the hotel. They found a few pieces of clothing in the twisted metal.

126

As the officer finished his story, Phil looked at Linda. It was obvious the account was making her sick, so Phil quickly thanked the officer and hurried her back to his car. The whole area was just too horrible to look at any longer.

They stopped at a roadside grill in a little community nearby and shared a hamburger and two sodas until Linda began to feel better. During the ride back to Linda's house, Phil was relieved when she brought up the subject of what they each might do in the near future.

"What are your plans, Phil?" she asked. "I mean, are you going to enlist like Jim did?"

"Not until I absolutely have to," he replied. "I don't want to leave you until they make me go." The corners of her mouth turned up and he smiled, thinking she must be feeling better.

"You're sweet, Phil. I don't want you to leave either, because I would miss you too."

"I've been thinking," he began. "I might be able to get a job in the shipyards at Newport News, Virginia. I've heard that if you work in the shipyard, you are exempt from the draft. That way I could get to see you at least once or twice each month."

"Yes, that would be nice, honey. But how about further in the future? What do you want to do then?"

"Oh, I see. Well you know how much I like aviation. I'd really like to be a pilot, maybe for one of those commercial airlines. If I couldn't do that, maybe I'd like to become an aeronautical engineer. But both of those jobs require college, and I don't think I can afford it anytime soon. If I could get that job at the shipyard, I might be able to save up enough money to go to college when the war is over."

"The engineering idea sounds great," Linda exclaimed. "But the pilot job is just too dangerous."

Phil was a bit surprised at how serious Linda sounded with her last remark. "Oh no," he retorted. "They undergo lots of training and they're really careful. They have to be in order for people to feel comfortable enough to fly on their airlines. I think it would be exciting!"

Linda looked him directly in the eyes. "I think it is too dangerous."

He smiled at her and pulled her close. "What about you, sweet Peaches? What are your plans?"

"I'd like to be a secretary, maybe an executive secretary. Daddy said he would pay for school so I guess I'll be entering Hardbarger's Secretarial School in Raleigh next fall."

"Hey, that's wonderful!" Phil exclaimed. "I'm sure you'll make someone a fine secretary. Maybe you could be my secretary when I get to be an executive." They both laughed.

"Maybe," she replied, and settled back into his arms.

The radio played a soft tune by Benny Goodman's orchestra.

127

Phil began to think back to the wedding. Jim and Strawberry seemed so happy together. Even though their futures were somewhat uncertain, they seemed to be ready to face that uncertainty together. They were so much in love. Phil wanted to feel the same way. He wanted to know that Linda would always be with him from that moment on. He squeezed her momentarily and blurted out, "Sweetheart, let's get married."

Linda suddenly pulled away from him, looking intently into his eyes, surveying his face to see whether or not he was serious. A second later, she wrapped her arms around him and hugged him tightly. "Oh, Phil. Those are the sweetest words I've ever heard." A second later she continued. "But you know we can't. How would we live? Neither of us has a job."

Phil was somewhat disappointed, but knew in his heart that she was right. "Oh, I don't mean right now, Peaches. But we could be engaged, couldn't we?" A sudden wave of desperation rushed over him. He felt that he couldn't let her get out of the car without hearing her say yes. His mind raced through all the possibilities. The worst one kept repeating itself. He would be drafted into the military while Eddie got to stay home. With him out of the way, Eddie might ask her the same question at just the right moment, and she might say yes to him!

"Phil, honey," she interrupted his thoughts. "You know I love you, but I just don't feel as if I can make a commitment like that right now. I want to finish my education. And I want things to settle down a bit more. This war is just awful. It's ruining everybody's lives. I don't want it to ruin ours. We can wait, can't we?"

"I guess so, love."

"Tell me, when are you going to Newport News?" she asked trying to change the conversation.

"As soon as I can," Phil replied. "One of my neighbors works up there and he is home this weekend. I think I'll go and see him after I leave your house. Maybe I can get a ride with him up to the shipyards."

"If you go, when would I see you again?"

"I'm not sure, sweetheart. I would have to come back when he comes back. Usually that's every two weeks."

"Good luck," she said.

"Thanks," he replied. As they drove the few remaining miles to her house, Phil couldn't seem to get rid of the feeling of rejection he had sensed in Linda's answer to his proposal. when they arrived at her home, he didn't stay long. She kissed him passionately at the front door, but somehow it still didn't ease the pain. All the way back to his home, he wondered just what his future did hold in store for him.

Chapter Twenty-one

Phil waited until the next day to see his neighbor that worked in the shipyards. The man agreed to let Phil ride back and forth with him in exchange for some gasoline money. He told Phil that they would come home once a month. Phil was disappointed about this because he wanted to come home more often to see Linda. His friend explained that they could not come home more often because of the gasoline situation. He had to save up on his gas in order to be able to get home and back.

On Wednesday, Phil and his friend left for Newport News, Virginia. As they rode along the highway, the car radio was on and Phil listened to news reports. They announced that the U.S. had begun bombing Germany with B-17 bombers.

"Say Phil, I hear that you know a lot about airplanes. What's a B-17 bomber?"

Phil was almost asleep but suddenly awoke when his neighbor asked the question. "Oh, that's what they call the Flying Fortress," he replied. "It has four engines and a tall rudder, or tail. It has a lot of machine guns to shoot fighter planes with. It has one in the nose, one on top behind the wing and a set of them under the belly. It can also carry a lot of bombs."

"That's good. I hope they get to blast Berlin off the map."

"Yeah, I hope so too," replied Phil.

"Say Phil, what are you going to do up here at Newport News?"

"I hope to get on at the shipyard, maybe as a welder."

"I don't want to dash your hopes, but there are a lot of guys trying to get on as welders. That's what I am. Do you have any experience?"

"Not much," replied Phil. I did some for Lacy over at the service station."

"Well, that gives you a slight advantage over some of the others. Last week I heard they are starting a welding school. maybe they'll train you."

"Great!" Phil exclaimed. "I sure hope so." He felt a bit more relieved.

At that moment a new song began to play on the car radio.

"I like that," said Phil's neighbor. "How about you?"

"Yeah, that's a real catchy tune," Phil replied.

Upon arriving in Newport News, Phil rented a room at the house where his neighbor was staying. He was happy that there would always be at least one person around that he would know. The next day he went to the shipyard. There was a long line of people waiting at the employment office so it was very late in the afternoon when Phil got in to be interviewed. The employment officer was not very encouraging. He told Phil that experienced people were being hired first, but that his application would be kept on file and he would be notified if his name came up.

Phil returned to the boarding house feeling dejected. One of the men noticed him and came over to him and introduced himself. He told Phil that he worked with a construction contractor over at Langley Air Base. Phil told the man that he was from North Carolina and was up there to try to get a job at the shipyard. His friend told him that his chances on getting a job at the shipyard anytime soon were very limited but for him not to give up, he might get on later.

"How would you like to work somewhere else?" the man continued. "At least until you hear from the shipyard."

"That would be great," Phil replied. "What kind of job is it?"

"We can use a carpenter's helper where I work. Can you use a hammer and saw?"

"Why, sure I can," Phil replied incredulously. "We use those tools nearly every day on the farm where I was raised."

"Hey, that's good," said the man. "You come with me tomorrow morning and I'll introduce you to my boss."

The next morning, Phil was a bit surprised to find that his new friend's company was constructing bomb sight vaults in the hangers at Langley Field. He couldn't have been more happy about the idea of being near planes. Working at the hangars would allow him to see all kinds of aircraft coming and going on the nearby runways. Even better, most of the planes were either twin engine bombers or fighters.

As the weeks passed, Phil was taken to the other side of the airfield to help work on a wind tunnel that the Federal Aviation Administration was building for use with experimental aircraft testing.

Early one morning, he had just begun work when he heard an engine skipping and sputtering as an airplane was trying to land. Looking out of the hangar, he saw a fighter plane coming in to land with a light trail of smoke coming from it's tail. It landed successfully and as it taxied down the tarmac, Phil noticed holes in the rudder and fuselage. He recognized the plane as a Navy TBF Avenger, a torpedo dive bomber.

That evening after supper, Phil told his friend about seeing the plane.

"It probably attacked a German submarine this morning," his friend replied. "Those were probably bullet holes in its tail."

"German subs?" Phil exclaimed.

"Sure. Don't tell me you didn't know we had German subs attacking our ships just off the coast. Heck, they've even tried putting off spies on our beaches."

"I never heard anything on the radio about it," Phil said. He was amazed that what his friend said was true, and in a second it hit him just how close the United States was to entering the war.

"Well, they wouldn't broadcast it over the radio because it would lower morale. Still, I can't believe you didn't hear the guys at the hangar talking about it."

In August, Phil and his neighbor made the long drive home. On the way, Phil kept the radio on and listened to news reports. He had become more concerned than ever about keeping up with the war. One report announced that the Russians had stopped the Germans at Stalingrad, thanks to the Lend Lease Air Supply program.

But even with all the war news, Phil could feel a growing excitement over the chance to see Linda again. Knowing he was coming home, Phil had written Linda a week before and asked for a date. Her return letter saying yes had arrived just the day before he left Newport News. As soon as he arrived home, Phil quickly washed the '39 Plymouth and began to get ready for his date.

"Aren't you tired from the long trip home?" Daddy Barkley asked as he watched Phil clean the car. "If I had been on the road for five hours, the last thing I'd want to do is wash a car. I'd probably take a nap on the front porch."

"Well, I am a little tired, daddy," Phil replied. "But since we have to return to Newport News tomorrow, I have to use every spare minute I have to be with Linda." He noticed the look on his father's face and threw in, " . . . and my family."

After the car was cleaned, Phil relaxed in the shade of the front porch with his father. They talked about the war and farming and what had been going on in the community during the month Phil had been gone. Later, as the sun began to dip below the treetops, Phil finished getting bathed and dressed for his date.

He arrived at Linda's just after dark. She was waiting on the porch but did not come down when Phil stopped in front of the house. He hurried up the steps and they hugged each other. She gave him a short kiss and Phil was overjoyed. He felt that she had missed him.

"I can hardly wait to hear all about what you've been doing," she said excitedly.

They sat in the porch swing and Phil told her all about Newport News, the guys at the boarding house, his job at the air base, and some of the things he's seen on the weekends. He told her about the plane with bullet holes and the wind tunnel.

"What's a wind tunnel?" Linda asked.

"It's where the F.A.A. tests airfoils for airplanes," he proudly replied. He had purchased a book about aircraft in which there had been a small section on wind tunnels. "It has a laboratory with a huge tube that exits one side and circles around and comes in the other side. There are giant, powerful fans in the tube that create air flows. The wind moves hundreds of miles per hour. Inside the lab, they install scale models of airplanes and airfoils. Then they turn on the wind and watch what happens to the models at different wind speeds."

"Sounds complicated to me," Linda said with a perplexed expression. "What's an airfoil?"

"Well, sweetheart, an airfoil is any surface such as a wing, aileron, or stabilizer, that's designed to make the airplane fly."

"Honey, you are so smart," Linda said with a smile. She hugged Phil and kissed him lightly on the cheek. He beamed with pleasure and talked a bit more about the different types of planes he had seen. Before they knew it, it was time for Phil to go home.

When Phil came home in November, Daddy Barkley greeted him at the door with a hug. As they stepped inside the house, he handed Phil a letter.

"This came for you yesterday, son."

Before he even opened it, Phil knew the letter was from the Selective Service Board. It was his first questionnaire.

"I'm sorry, son. You know it won't be long until the next one comes. Then you'll have to go."

"I know, dad," Phil replied, looking at the floor. "I guess its time to make a decision, huh? I sure was hoping the shipyard would call first."

"I was too, son." They sat in silence for a long couple of seconds. "Have you thought about what you are going to do?"

"I'm sure not going to wait for them to draft me," Phil replied. "I thought I'd take the exam for the Air Corps and try to be an aircraft mechanic like Jim Kelford."

"What if you fail?"

"Oh, I wouldn't worry about that," Phil smiled. "I always did better than Jim and he passed. But even if that did happen, I'm sure I could join the Army as an auto mechanic, like Roland."

"Well, good luck, son, whatever you do." Daddy Barkley patted Phil on the back.

That night, Phil told Linda of his plans. She was very quiet all evening and finally admitted that she was worried about him having to enlist. It made him feel warm inside.

"Oh, don't worry about me, sweet Peaches. I'll be alright," he said as he hugged her close to his chest.

She looked up into his eyes. "I hope so, honey. I do so hope you pass that aircraft mechanics test. I'd feel so much better with you there than in the infantry."

Phil made arrangements with his neighbor to tell his friends in Newport News that he wouldn't be coming back to work. The neighbor would check the boarding house for anything Phil might have left in his room and would return it the next month. Early on Monday morning, Phil arrived at the Post Office building in Raleigh, North Carolina. He went straight to the Air Corps recruiting office on the top floor. Already two lines were forming with young men waiting to take one kind of entrance exam or another. Phil stepped into place at the back of the shorter line. As he neared the entrance to the exam room, he noticed the letters "ACC" over the door. He was wondering what they meant when someone called "Next" and it was his turn to enter.

A recruiter filled out some papers and Phil signed them. "Go through that door and they'll give you the mental test in a few minutes," barked the recruiter.

"Yes, sir," Phil responded in a firm, crisp voice, trying to sound as if he knew something of military courtesy. The recruiter just smiled at him and nodded toward the door.

The mental exam lasted until eleven o'clock. Phil decided the test was really no different than his exams in high school. He went through it writing down only the answers of which he was sure. When he reached the last page, he went back to the front and began tackling the more difficult questions that he had skipped. And, just like in high school, he completed the exam about ten minutes ahead of everyone else.

When the other young men finished, the instructor told them all to return in thirty minutes and he would tell who passed. It was a long half-hour for Phil. He went for a drink of water. He considered going down the street to a cafeteria for a sandwich, but then decided to walk through the halls for a while. When thirty minutes had passed, Phil was sitting in the same seat in which he had taken the exam. A moment later, the instructor entered the room and began calling out grades. Finally he called out, "Philip E. Barkley . . . score eighty-six." A big grin broke over Phil's face. He was in the Air Corps! Well, almost . . . he still had the physical exam to take that afternoon.

As he left the room, he passed a group of young men talking about the exam. "What did you make?" one of them asked Phil.

"Ah, that fellow in there said I made eighty-six," Phil replied.

"Where do you go to college?" another boy asked.

"Well, I haven't been to college yet," Phil stammered. "I just graduated from high school this summer."

"Jesus, Ben," one of the boys said to another. "This old country boy aced the exam right out of high school. We've had two years of college and this is the third time we've failed. We'll never be pilots!"

Phil's ears perked up. "Hey fellahs," he asked. "What does

A.C.C. mean anyway?"

"You don't know?" one of them exclaimed.

"It means Aviation Cadet Candidate," answered another. "If you pass the test and the physical examination, you become a candidate for training to be a pilot, bombardier or a navigator."

"Wow!" Phil shouted. "You really mean it?" He didn't wait for their answer because he could tell from their faces they were telling the truth. They wanted it so badly and he had simply gotten in the wrong line. Now he was going to be a pilot and they might be his mechanics. It was almost too funny for him.

That afternoon, Phil passed the physical exam with high marks. Before he left the building he was given orders to report in four weeks to Miami Beach, Florida for boot camp. He could hardly wait to get home and tell everyone.

He stopped by Linda's before going home. He rushed up to the door and when she opened it, he grabbed her and swung her around on the porch. "I passed, I passed! Sweet Peaches, I made it into the Air Corps."

"Hold on, Phil. Wait a minute," she said. "I thought you would be happy, but not this happy."

"I'm so happy I can hardly stand it," he exclaimed.

"Well," she said, pushing him away gently and smoothing her dress. "I'm glad you'll be an airplane mechanic like you wanted."

"But sweetheart, I might become a pilot, or a bombardier or a navigator! I'll be flying them, not fixing them."

"What?" she exclaimed, quickly drawing away from him. "What do you mean?"

Something in the back of his mind registered the puzzled, almost horrified look on Linda's face, but Phil was so excited, he quickly forgot the feeling. "I took the A.C.C. test, and passed!" he replied. "It means 'Aviation Cadet Candidate.' I'm a candidate to be selected for training as a cadet to be trained as a pilot, bombardier, or navigator . . . that is, if I don't get washed out." He led her over to the porch swing as he talked. "First, they would train me in military courtesy. Then, they would give me a stepped up, two-year college program in about six months. If I get that far, they send me to a classification center to be tested and classified as either a pilot, bombardier or navigator."

Linda's face suddenly brightened. "That's great, Phil, I guess. Will it help you to become an aeronautical engineer?"

"I guess so, Peaches. That is, if I don't flunk out."

"Oh, Phil. You'll make it. I just know you will!" She flung her arms around his neck and hugged him tightly.

Phil could hardly wait to get home and tell Daddy Barkley his good news, so he kissed Linda, hugged her once more, and hopped in the Plymouth.

The next morning, Phil went to see the Varnes family to tell them his good news. Then he and George decided to take the Silver Bullet for a ride to Cash Corner so Phil could see some of his old friends. Phil was slightly disappointed that Grace hadn't been at cash corner, but when he and George drove past the front of the theater on their way home, he discovered why. She had been to see a movie and was just coming out the front door of the theater. He whipped the car into a parking space thirty feet down the street. Before he could get out of the Silver Bullet, Grace had run up beside them. A few moments later, Phil said goodbye to her and wiped a tear from her cheek.

It seemed as if the four weeks whizzed by and soon it was time for Phil's last date with Linda before leaving for boot camp. They decided to go to Holt's Lake on Sunday evening. It was after dark when they arrived. Not many people were there since most of the young mean had already enlisted or had been drafted. Linda and Phil danced to popular tunes by Benny Goodman and Tommy Dorsey. Phil was actually glad they hadn't come on Saturday night when the band played more jitterbug music. He wanted to hold Linda close on this last night together. As the evening wore on, Phil grew more pensive and less talkative. He realized this was the last night they would spend together for a long time. Suddenly he had begun to wonder if their love was strong enough to keep them together across the miles and through the lonesome months to come. And the question of where Eddie fit into the picture still haunted him.

Linda noticed that Phil had become quiet. "Honey, what's the matter? Is something wrong?"

He pulled back slightly and looked lovingly into her blue eyes. "Oh, I'm okay, sweetheart. Its just that I'm going to miss you."

She returned his gaze and squeezed him tightly. "I'll miss you too, Phil."

"Let's go home, sweet Peaches," he said.

When they arrived at her house, Linda turned on the radio in the living room and they snuggled close together on the sofa with the soothing sounds of Tommy Dorsey playing in the background. Phil pulled her close and they kissed. "Sweet Peaches, you know I love you, don't you?"

"Yes, Phil," she cooed. "I love you too."

He relaxed somewhat upon hearing her say it, but the question still nagged at his insides.

"More than Eddie?" he probed.

She glanced up at him. Her eyes betrayed a slight annoyance at his insecurity. "Oh, Phil. Eddie is a nice young man. I like him, my mother likes him, everybody I know likes him. But it's not the same. I love you, Phil. I don't love Eddie in the same way."

"Okay," he sighed. They settled back down for a moment,

135

but Phil still has one more question. "Did he get a draft notice? I thought he was a year older than me?"

"Only a couple of months older than you," she replied. "And yes, he did get a notice. But he flunked the physical exam because of flat feet and poor eyesight."

"Oh," said Phil. "I see." He was more worried than ever. Eddie could spend a lot of time with Linda while he was away at boot camp. He had already heard stories of some boys who stayed home stealing the girls from fellahs who were fighting half a world away. He held her close and kissed her as passionately as he possibly could. "Sweetheart, please say you'll wait for me," he whispered into her ear. "Don't let anyone come between us."

She looked lovingly into his chocolate eyes and reassuringly said, "I promise, Phil. I'll wait for you."

The next morning, Phil and his well-packed suitcase boarded the train at the station in the nearby town of Selma. He waved at his father through the window and noticed that snow was beginning to fall. Linda loved the snow. She'll have a white Christmas, he thought, and I won't be there to share it. But I'll bet Eddie will.

"Good bye, son!" Daddy Barkley shouted from the platform. "And good luck! Write to us," he continued as the train began pulling away.

Phil settled back into his seat, thinking of Linda. He hated so much to have to leave her. His heart already ached from the loneliness he knew he would soon feel every day.

Chapter Twenty-two

When Phil stepped off the train in Miami, he first thought of Rip Van Winkle. It felt as if he'd slept through the entire season of spring! Even though it was only ten o'clock, the temperature was at least eighty degrees. Closing his eyes, Phil basked his face in the warm, winter sunlight, smiled to himself, and wondered if there was still snow on the ground at home. But by the time he reached the front of the train station, he wasn't smiling anymore. He stopped near the curb, wiped the sweat from his brow, returned the damp handkerchief to his hip pocket, and rolled up his shirt sleeves. He looked around for a clue as to the direction of the training center.

"Where you headed, buddy?" asked a voice over his left shoulder. Phil turned to find the driver of a jitney cab standing not far away.

"Collins Avenue," Phil replied. "I'm supposed to report to the Air Corps Training Center."

"Boy, are you in luck," said the cabby. "I drive right past there on my way to Miami Beach. Throw your bag in here and I'll have you there in a jiffy."

Fifteen minutes later, Phil stood in front of the President Madison Hotel on Collins Avenue listening to waves crashing onto the beach behind the row of motel rooms that stretched a few hundred yards on either side of him. Palm trees swayed in the ocean breeze above well-kept lawns. He picked up his bag and headed through the front door of the motel office. A sign above the door read "U.S. Air Corps."

The officer seated at the front desk took one look at Phil and said, "Welcome, Mister. State your name and show your orders." As Phil pulled his papers from his shirt pocket, he wondered if the Air Corps would provide him a short sleeve shirt like the one this officer wore. After he'd filled out some forms, the officer gave him a room number, told him to stow his things and report back in ten minutes.

When he returned, the officer directed Phil to a softball field across the street from the motel. "Report to Sergeant Reese for drill instruction. From now on, you report to him for everything. Is that understood, soldier?"

"Yes, sir," Phil replied. He turned to go when suddenly he realized how warm his clothes would be while marching. Turning back to the desk officer, Phil asked, "Sir, what about uniforms?"

"Sorry, soldier. We don't have uniforms or supplies yet. You'll have to get by with what you have."

An hour later, Phil was miserable. He felt as if he'd sweated out a gallon of water. At least he wasn't alone. The other recruits appeared just as miserable. Between the sun and Sergeant Reese,

Phil wondered if they would live through the day!

"Fall in, soldier!" was the first thing Reese had said to him. Assuming that meant "get in line," Phil jumped in behind another cadet and tried to get the rhythm of marching. Two seconds later, Reese yelled, "About face!" The cadet in front of Phil suddenly turned and crashed into him. Phil hit the ground amid roaring laughter from the other cadets. The sergeant was immediately standing over him, yelling for everyone to shut up and stay in formation.

"What's your name, soldier?" the sergeant asked as he helped Phil stand.

"Barkley, Sir." Phil replied. "Philip Barkley."

"Not Barkley Sir," yelled Reese. "It's Cadet Candidate Barkley, Sir! Is that clear?" Sergeant Reese was right in Phil's face now.

"Yes, sir."

"Where are you from, Barkley?"

"North Carolina, sir."

"What do they say in North Carolina when they want you to turn around, Barkley?"

"Turn around, sir," Phil replied. A few cadets chuckled.

"Well, you're not in North Carolina anymore, son. You're in the Army Air Corps Cadet Candidate School! And here, when we want you to turn around, we say 'About face.' Is that clear?"

"Yes, sir."

Reese's nose was almost touching Phil's when he yelled, "Show me what you'll do the next time I say 'About face', soldier!"

Phil whirled around in his tracks, almost losing his balance. He stood with his back to Sergeant Reese. The sergeant walked around in front of him, got right in his face, and yelled again. "You been eating Mexican jumping beans, Barkley?"

"No, Sir."

"Is that how they turn around up in North Carolina?"

"No, Sir."

"Well, try it again!" Reese shouted. "And do it a little smoother this time."

This continued for twenty minutes. The other cadets stood motionless in the hot, midday sun, knowing better than to complain or groan. Phil practiced the maneuver until finally, Sergeant Reese was satisfied. Then, everyone resumed marching and that was what they did the rest of the afternoon.

At six o'clock the next morning, Phil and his fellow cadets were startled out of bed by loud trumpet music. So this is what reveille is like, Phil thought. They quickly dressed and ate breakfast before assembling in front of the motel office. By seven o'clock, Sergeant Reese was marching them down the middle of the street toward a golf course. By eight-thirty, Phil's

138

muscles were tight and burning with pain from an hour of rigorous exercise. During a break, Phil looked around at the other cadets, noticing all the different-colored civilian clothes everyone was wearing. What a ragged-looking bunch we are, he thought.

By Saturday afternoon, Sergeant Reese hardly yelled at anyone. The cadets were looking sharper at their drills. After Sunday morning calisthenics, Reese gathered them around him in front of the motel office and told them that the afternoon had been set aside for them to relax or go into town.

"If you go anywhere," the sergeant finished, "stay out of trouble and be back in your quarters by nine o'clock tonight. Is that clear?"

A chorus of cadet voices replied, "Yes, sir!" before he dismissed them.

Phil had two things on his mind as he strolled past the storefronts in Miami. Within an hour, he had purchased a cooler pair of trousers and some writing paper. Upon arriving back at his quarters, Phil began a letter to Linda.

January 17, 1943

Dear Sweet Peaches,

I began to miss you the moment I got off the train in Miami. It sure was a change going from the snow at home to the eighty degree weather down here. I'm staying at the President Madison Motel. There are palm trees everywhere and they even have some flowers in bloom around here at this time of year. The motel rooms are not far from the ocean. When I lie in bed at night I can listen to the waves pounding the beach while I think of how much I miss you. Even though it is pretty here, we don't have much fun. The officers won't let us cadets go down to the beach and there is no water in the swimming pool. I sure wish I could relax in the pool sometimes. My muscles are sore every day from the exercises and marching we do all day. Then, at night we have to sleep on springs because the Army is using our mattresses for some other defense purpose. I'm glad I brought my big overcoat now! I spread it over the springs and it gives me a little bit of cushion. These bunks are double deckers. My bunk mate is a fellow named Carmen Revaloe. His family lives here in Miami. Carmen got them to bring us over two bottles of rubbing alcohol so we can soothe our sore muscles at night. The second bottle is almost empty. I spent almost all of my money today on a pair of summer weight trousers. We don't have any uniforms yet and my wool pants were too hot to march in. I'll bet I've lost ten pounds from sweating! The officers tell us we should be getting uniforms and

139

supplies in the next two weeks. Well, that is all that I can think of to tell since all we do is exercise and march. I can hardly wait to begin pilot training, but I don't know when it will start. Some of the other cadets said they heard this is a rushed up program, so maybe we won't have eight weeks of boot camp like other Army soldiers. I'll write to you every Sunday since that is the only free time we have.

I miss you and am counting the days when I can see your sweet, beautiful face and kiss your soft lips again.

Tell your parents hello for me and tell Eddie not to hang around too much.

I love you,

Phil

Over the next two weeks, Sergeant Reeves slowed down a bit on drilling. Phil and his buddies were getting much better at parade maneuvers. They even began to attract small crowds of teenage boys and girls when they marched down the streets toward the golf course for their morning exercises. Some of the boys would fall in behind the soldiers and march in step with them. The girls mostly giggled and pointed at whichever soldier they thought was most handsome.

So his soldiers wouldn't be distracted by the children, Sergeant Reeves taught them the Army Air Corps song. Phil loved the sound of their shoes rhythmically tromping against the pavement while their deep, young voices sang out loudly;

A few of the nearby residents weren't so fond of their early morning singing. One man wrote a letter of complaint to the editor of the Miami Herald. The cadets stopped singing for a few days, until one morning when Sergeant Reeves addressed them in front of the Madison Motel.

"Men, I think you all know why we've kept quiet while marching for the last few days. One or two people in this neighborhood feel so well protected by us that they are in the habit of sleeping late. It seems we disturbed some of those sleepy heads. Well, today I want to read to you an alternate opinion.

"*Dear Editor*," the sergeant began. "*I have only one thing to say to the man who complained against our singing soldiers. Would he rather we have German soldiers singing while they march through the streets of Miami? Signed, The Mayor of Miami.*"

Phil let out a "yee-hah" before he realized what he was doing. The other soldiers looked at him for a second, then joined in, whooping and patting each other on the back. In another instant, Sergeant Reeves commanded, "Atten-shun!" and they began marching down the street. They hadn't gone ten yards when somebody behind Phil sang the first line of the Army Air Corps song and the rest of the soldiers joined in.

When reports came in of German submarines patrolling the coast, Phil's company was volunteered for guard duty at nearby motels and along the beaches. Late one afternoon, Phil and Carmen were on duty near the shore when they noticed something strange.

"Do you see those planes dipping down toward the water, Phil?"

"Yep. I wonder what they're after?"

"Hey, look. Aren't those two PT boats coming in off to the left there?"

"Sure are, Carmen. Something's up. I wonder if we should alert Sergeant Reese?"

"Nah. We can't do anything about it right now, anyway. Let's just watch for a few more minutes."

A few moments later, the PT boats were zigging and zagging among the freight ship convoy just offshore. Fifteen minutes after that, a large plume of water rose from the sea, followed shortly by a loud "whump" sound. Phil and Carmen looked at each other, both thinking the same thing . . . a German submarine.

The next morning, as the cadets marched toward the golf course, Phil saw a teenage boy running toward a group of his friends with something in his hand. As they passed by, he heard the boy exclaim, "I found it on the beach!" The boys were passing around a German sailor's cap. Suddenly, the war seemed a lot closer, a lot more real to the soldiers. No one sang that morning.

That evening, the solemnity of what had happened off shore was broken by a young, new recruit. Everyone had quietly climbed into bed after the command for "lights out" had been given. Windows were open wide to take advantage of passing breezes that might wander through the motel rooms. Suddenly, a loud voice called out from the darkness outside.

"Halt! Look who's here."

"What did you say, Mister?" commanded a second voice.

"Uh . . . ah . . . I mean, Halt, who goes there, sir?" the first voice timidly replied.

"Drop the sir, son . . . and say it like you are going to shoot me if I don't answer! Is that clear?"

"Yes sir! Halt! Who goes there!"

"Much better, soldier. Now say it ten times."

Phil and Carmen were laughing so hard they were gasping for air. They could hear other soldiers laughing in their rooms as well. The chuckling continued until the young guard had repeated his command ten times.

141

Suddenly, the second voice called out, "This is Lieutenant Jordan. The next sound I hear coming from these barracks will win someone a solid week of graveyard shift guard duty!" Everything became so suddenly quiet that even the crickets and birds hushed for a moment. Soon everyone was asleep.

The next day, Phil received a letter.

January 24, 1943

Dearest Phil,

I miss you too, darling. I miss your smiling eyes and the way you make me laugh. I miss dancing with you at Holt's Lake on Saturday nights. I wish this war would be over so you could come home.

I started accounting school in Raleigh last week. I'm staying with my Aunt Rose. That's why I took so long to write back. I only got your letter last night when I came home to get more clothes. Daddy says that if the Office of Price Administration keeps the price of gasoline high, he can't afford for me to come home every week.

School is exciting! I'm meeting lots of new people, mostly girls. Do you remember a girl from Pine Level named Grace Langston? She and I share a few classes. When I found out she was from Pine Level, I asked her to Aunt Rose's for supper this past Tuesday. We were sitting in my room, talking about people we knew from around Kenly, when she noticed your picture on my dresser. She said, "This looks like a guy I used to know." When I told her your name, she laughed and said, "So you're the girl who stole Phil's heart away from me." I was a bit scared, because I didn't know what she meant. But she told me all about how you two used to dance together down at Cash Corner. We had a good time talking about you that night. I'm really flattered too! If you picked me over her, I can only take that as a compliment, because she's very pretty.

Miami doesn't sound like much fun. I'm sorry they are working you so hard your muscles ache. But just think of how strong you'll be when you come home. I'll have to be careful dancing with you from now on, because you might just throw me through the ceiling! By the way, I did not tell Eddie what you said. Phil, that was a mean thing to say. You shouldn't pick on him. You know he wanted to join the Army just like all you other boys. And he isn't hanging around. He only comes to visit me on Saturday nights and we sit in the living room listening to the Hit Parade. And now that I'm in Raleigh, he won't even be able to do that but about once every two weeks.

See how much I miss you? I'm already getting cranky. Well,

142

mama is calling me for supper, and I have to pack more clothes after that. I'll write again soon. Oh, I almost forgot! I'm enclosing my Aunt Rose's address so you can write to me there. Write to me as often as you can. I love you and miss you lots!

Love,

Linda

Chapter Twenty-three

Dear Peaches:

It is dark outside and I am on a train heading north out of Florida, I think. My squadron was ordered to ship out earlier this afternoon. We quickly packed our duffle bags and they carried us to the train station in Miami. It was almost sunset when we left the station. They would not tell us where we were going and I still don't know.

I am trying to write this letter in an upper berth on the train, so I apologize if it is hard to read. I'm not sure I can stay awake long enough to finish it tonight.

Well Sweet, I am back again. I apologize or dropping off to sleep like that but I was real tired.

It is early in the morning now and still dark. My buddy in the lower bunk just said that we are somewhere in Alabama. He must be right because the air seems cooler.

I think I hear the Sergeant yelling out "all off" somewhere in the Pullman so I have to go. I sure miss you.

Love,

Phil

It was cold in the early March morning when Phil disembarked from the train. He looked across the tracks and saw a sign on the station that said Memphis, Tennessee. The dawn was beginning to break when his squadron was finally loaded onto buses. They rode through a business section and then through a large residential area. Phil thought, Memphis is a very big city.

Some time later, the buses entered an open area surrounded by large buildings. As they turned into a wide driveway, he saw a sign that said Southwestern College. So this is where we go to school, he thought. Just like the rumors had said.

The buses stopped in front of a building that looked like a dormitory. The soldiers were assembled in a large room just inside the entrance where they were given room assignments and told to report in one hour to the adjacent building where breakfast would be served.

After breakfast, the squadron reassembled in the dormitory entrance hall where the Sergeant gave orders to get settled in the rooms and to meet again the next afternoon at one o'clock.

Dear Peaches:

I am now at Southwestern College in Memphis, Tennessee. It is a pretty place with large oak trees covered in ivy all around the campus and even along the streets in town. The buildings here are beautiful. They are made of gray slate and remind me a lot of the buildings at Duke University at Durham.

The room where I sleep is on the top floor of our dormitory. It is large enough for four people in two bunk beds with a table for studying. It has a couple of closets to hang clothes. The squadron sergeant told us that we would be given a crash course in academics while here. He says it is like finishing two years of college in six months. We'll also study weather and get familiar with the Pratt & Whitney radial aircraft engine. We are also supposed to get some flight experience in small airplanes. I can't wait for that.

The Sergeant also advised us that we won't have much open post, maybe a little on Sunday afternoons. It seems we'll mostly be attending classes and studying, with some calisthenics and marching thrown in for good measure.

Peaches, I sure miss you and wish you were here with me but even if you were here, they wouldn't let me see you until Sunday afternoon. I met a guy from Wallace, North Carolina, and he is married. They won't even let him see his wife until Sunday. That's the way life is in the Army Air Corps.

Say hello to everyone back home for me. I miss you a lot!

> *Love,*
> *Phil*

A week later, Phil received his first letter at mail call.

Dear Phil,

I was so glad to get your letter. I was mighty worried not knowing where you were going. I am glad that you're in Memphis, Tennessee. I hope you like it there but it sounds as if you may not get to see much of it.

It's getting lonesome here. Most of the boys are in the service now. About the only boys left are the 4-F's and the teenagers. Eddie comes by occasionally and we go to a show or something. It's a lot different now than what it used to be.

I miss you too. Take care of yourself and study hard. And be careful around those airplanes!

> *Love,*
>
> *Linda*

In the following weeks Phil began to get used to the daily schedule. His squadron was up by six, finished with breakfast I seven, and into physical training by seven-thirty. The training included running an obstacle course called the "The Burma Trail." It was difficult for everyone and included running through woodlands, jumping creek banks, running up and down hills, and running along ravines and under culverts. After "P.T.", the soldiers were in classrooms by nine o'clock.

Classes were over at four o'clock military drill and parade review practice lasted until 5:30 pm. All the units in the detachment had to practice parade marching each day. This was done so they would be able to put on a real good parade review to the large crowds of civilians who showed up at five-thirty every Sunday afternoon.

Each night, the Sergeant would have mail call just before supper and also announce any news about the war. On the twelfth day of May, the Sergeant announced that the news was good. The Axis powers had just been defeated in North Africa. Phil and all the other soldiers exuberantly shouted their approval.

But bad news was soon to follow. The unit was called into the auditorium by the commanding officer and told that they would have to be restricted to the campus for an indefinite period. There would be no open post privileges and no one was to leave the campus under any circumstances. It seems that one of the regular students of the college had become ill with symptoms of the deadly disease, spinal meningitis. For Phil, the worst news was yet to come. A few days after the commanding officer's announcement, Phil discovered the infected soldier was his own friend, Chuck Erinhous.

Phil had met Chuck shortly after arriving in Memphis. Chuck was a Junior class student from Louisiana. Chuck had taken to Phil from the first week, when Phil had wandered into a recreation room and joined in with Chuck's group as they sang around the piano. Chuck was very talented, playing the piano by sound since he could not read music. Almost every evening, they would meet in the recreation room a little while after supper. Chuck would play the piano and Phil would sing and occasionally dance the jitterbug. Soon, there would be a crowd of young men gathered around them to help sing and unwind for awhile. One song that Phil and Chuck liked a lot was, "Coming In On A Wing And A Prayer." It was about a disabled B-17 Flying Fortress returning from a bombing mission. Everyone loved this song and had a good time singing it.

A month passed and the quarantine had not been lifted. The soldiers had to take sulfur pills and receive shots daily as precautionary measures. Morale quickly lowered to the point that an occasional fight broke out in the dorm. These altercations were normally settled quickly by the cadet corporals on each floor so no one got in trouble.

Phil had been promoted to cadet corporal and was in charge of the upper floor of his dormitory. He was proud of the promotion and carried out all his orders as quickly as possible. He seemed to have a knack for keeping peace and order on his floor and still keep the respect of the students.

The promotion also meant that Phil received rank insignia to wear on the shoulder epaulets of his uniform. These insignia were small, round brass pins for a Corporal rank. shortly before the quarantine had begun, Phil and a few buddies went downtown on sunday afternoon for a couple of hours. As they walked down main street, they occasionally met young army recruits that were in town. They each threw a snappy salute at Phil as he passed. He returned each salute and was enjoying the attention when one of his buddies remarked, "Phil, you had better not get caught with that cadet insignia on up here. You know, you're not supposed to wear them off the campus."

"Hey, you're right. I guess I forgot to take them off before we left campus," replied Phil. "I was wondering why they were all saluting me!"

One night Phil was awakened by loud noises on his floor. It sounded as if several people were laughing, giggling and running around up and down the hall outside his room. As Phil looked out of his doorway, he saw five soldiers dressed only in their shorts, running around chasing each other. As one of the boys passed by, Phil noticed he had an airplane tattooed on his chest with mercurochrome. He had his arms outstretched as if he was flying. Phil could smell the alcohol as the "human airplane" whizzed past.

One of the boys was from Georgia. He had a physique like a wrestler and had cut all his black hair off except a small tuft on top. He was running around in his shorts with his black hairy chest showing and acting like a gorilla. Phil found it hard to keep a straight face.

As Phil entered his end of the hall, the corporal of the guard came in at the other end. They quickly moved the boys back into their rooms and quieted the other boys in the hall. Phil and the other corporal spent most of the rest of the night investigating the incident. They found that one of the boys in the room next to Phil's had a good friend that lived in Memphis. He had arranged with his friend to have a girlfriend sneak a couple of half gallon jars of whiskey into the campus for him. He and the boys in the two rooms next to Phil's room proceeded to have a big drinking party.

The corporal of the guard and Phil had to report their findings to the commanding officer the next day. The commanding officer was lenient in his punishment to the boys.

The cadet that had smuggled in the whiskey was denied open post for the remainder of his stay at Southwestern. The other boys were given extra guard duty for two weeks.

At mail a few days later, the Sergeant announced that Chuck Erinhous had died. Phil and the other soldiers were very distressed. They knew that they would really miss their friend, especially in the evenings. There would be no one to play the piano and help entertain at their evening breaks after supper.

The quarantine was soon lifted. The detachment of cadets had been lucky, escaping from the spread of the disease for the most part. Only one other cadet had become afflicted, but recovered quickly due to the daily treatments they all received. Two weeks after Chuck died, the commanding officer ordered a medical discharge for the other afflicted cadet and declared open post on Sunday afternoon for everyone else.

One morning, a few days later, the Sergeant announced at breakfast that the squadron would begin flight familiarization at a local airport beginning the next day. Everyone happily shouted their approval, especially Phil. Most of the young men had never been up in an airplane and they could hardly wait for the day to be over.

It was a warm, bright, June day when Phil and his group were loaded onto a bus after lunch and taken to the local private airport at the edge of town. When they arrived, Phil noticed that the airport was a huge field and had dirt runways. It had a large building with offices and a large classroom inside. Part of the building was used for storage of airplanes. There were many small airplanes parked on the airport aprons as well. He observed that most of the planes were Taylorcraft or Piper cubs.

Phil and his group were taken inside the classroom and advised that they would first receive classroom instruction to teach them the basics of why airplanes are able to fly. Later, they would ride with civilian pilots for one-half hour at the time for a total of three hours. They would not actually fly the planes, but could follow the controls and maneuvers of their pilot while in the air. The primary purpose of the program was to find out whether or not any of the cadets would become afraid of flying, or prone to air sickness, or simply to discover if they disliked flying. Phil remembered the time he flew with the barnstormer in Kenly as a boy. He figured if he didn't get scared or sick then, there was no reason for him to get sick now. He could hardly wait for the classroom portion of this training to be finished.

Phil was surprised to learn that it is the top of the wing that lifts the plane into the air instead of the bottom. It somehow excited him to realize that he would not only begin to fulfill his life's dream of flying, but that he would actually become knowledgeable about aerodynamics.

Later that afternoon, Phil was introduced to a lady pilot named Jo Ann Somer, who led him to where a Taylorcraft plane was parked. She took him around the plane, pointed out the different parts of the aircraft, and told him why they inspected each item before takeoff. They checked the wings for damage, the aileron and elevators and rudder for freedom of movement, and the propeller for nicks or cracks. Then, they checked the gas tanks and engine oil for signs of water. Finally, they inspected the landing gear. Phil was impressed with Jo Ann's cautiousness and paid close attention to everything she said. But the bright blue and yellow paint stuck in his mind as the lasting impression he would have of this plane for the rest of his life. He would never forget this plane in what he hoped would be a lifelong career in flying. Phil eagerly anticipated each visit to the airport. After only two weeks, he felt that he and Jo Ann had become good friends. She also introduced Phil to other pilots who frequently came to the airport to fly. The most interesting of these people was a fellow named Brad Higgins.

Brad was the son of a wealthy lawyer in Memphis and he owned his own Piper cub. Brad had been rejected by the draft board for having flat feet and had been given 4-F status. Being about the same age, the two quickly became good friends. One day, Brad asked Phil if he wanted to go flying one Sunday afternoon.

"You bet your life I would," Phil quickly responded, thinking he might get to take over the controls for a short time while they were in the air.

"Tell you what, buddy," Brad proposed. "I'll pick you up at your dormitory Sunday about one o'clock. We'll come out here and have some fun, okay?"

"Sounds great! I can hardly wait," Phil said excitedly.

The following Sunday was another beautiful June day. Brad was on time and Phil climbed into his 1941 Ford convertible at exactly one o'clock.

"Guess you know I have to be back by 4:30 so I can stand in the retreat parade at 5:30," Phil remarked.

"No problem," Brad replied.

As soon as they arrived at the airport, Brad had the plane fueled and began his pre-flight inspection. Phil watched everything like a hawk, not wanting to miss one single aspect of what it takes to be a good pilot. Very soon, they were speeding down the dirt runway. As they lifted off the ground, Phil peered out of the window and saw the trees and houses rushing by underneath the plane. It was almost more excitement than he could stand.

Soon the Piper Cub was high in the air. They seemed to be floating along on the air currents with a steady hum of the engine. Occasionally, they passed through what looked like small puffs of white cotton. Phil remembered from his weather classes that these were cumulus clouds. A few moments later, they were over the highway that ran alongside the Mississippi River. Phil marveled at how the automobiles resembled ants marching along in a line.

A few moments later, Brad pulled back on the throttle and the plane started descending. Soon they were skimming along just over the tops of the fields and trees. Phil felt a twinge of excitement as he watched the trees and ground rushing under them so closely. A second later, Brad pushed the control stick and they began a steep turn to the right. The wing tips appeared to almost touch the ground. Excitement and fear crept into Phil's mind for the first time. The ground seemed awfully close for this type of flying.

Suddenly, Phil spied a group of cattle in front of the plane. They were scattering out and running in all directions. Brad laughed.

"I do this nearly every Sunday," he told Phil. "Some of these cows can really run. Hey! look at that old bull over there. He looks madder than hell, doesn't he? See how he slings his head and snorts and kicks up his heels?"

Suddenly, they reached a clump of trees along the creek bank at the pasture's edge. Brad brought up the nose of the Piper cub, just clearing the tree tops. In the next instant, the boys hear a loud bang. Almost immediately, the plane slows and Brad has to shove the throttle to full just to keep the plane in the air! Phil was horrified to look out the window and find a large hole in the wing. Brad saw it at the same time, then turned the plane back toward the airport. As they turned, Phil looked back to see a farmer standing in the edge of the woods, holding a shotgun in his hand and shaking his fist in the air.

The trip back to the airport was quiet. Phil realized what had been going on after thinking about it for a moment. Evidently, Brad had been doing this for many weeks and the farmer had become fed up. He had waited for the plane this Sunday afternoon.

After a somewhat difficult flight, Brad successfully landed the plane at the airport and quickly parked it in a hangar so it could be repaired.

As Phil got out of Brad's car, back at the dormitory, Brad apologized. "I'm sorry about that, Phil. It won't happen again."

In the weeks that followed, the examinations grew more difficult. Everyone studied longer and harder to make good grades. Phil's own performance seemed to be slightly above average. He didn't mind if he was not at the top of the class. After all, he thought, I only graduated from high school a year ago. And I've never been to college before, like some of the other guys.

150

In late July, the Sergeant reported that Mussolini had been overthrown and that some guy called Marshall Bagdolio had taken over as Premier of Italy. It seems that the Italian people were very upset and tired of losing to the Allied powers. He also reported to the squadron that there was heavy fighting in New Guinea and the Solomon Islands in the Pacific. The last bit of news bothered Phil the most, however. There were reports coming out of the Pacific that the Japanese were committing brutal atrocities on American prisoners of war. Phil immediately thought of Roland Varnes. And the more he thought about this disturbing news, the more angry and bitter he became. As Phil lay in his bunk that evening, he felt a profound hatred for these Japanese that he'd never seen. If only this schooling would end so he and the other boys could get into the war. Then those Japs would find out what bad treatment was all about!

The next morning, just after breakfast, the Sergeant called for Phil's squadron to assemble in front of their dormitory. He announced that they were shipping out, but wouldn't say where they were going. He told them to be ready by eleven o'clock that morning. Of course, everyone buzzed with excitement, wondering where they would be transferred, but no one could find out. By the time they assembled at eleven, all Phil knew was that they were headed for a classification center somewhere within the United States.

Chapter Twenty-four

August 2, 1943

Dear Peaches:

Here I am just a few miles outside of San Antonio Texas at a place called San Antonio Aviation cadet classification center. This place is built on what looks like an old cattle ranch. The land is flat has a lot of mesquite bushes and cactus plants, and boy, is it dry and hot here!

The barracks are built out of wooden boards and are long one story buildings. The highest building around is the base movie theater and the Post Exchange, or P. building.

My barracks is located on the side of the block next to the street. Across the street is a large grassy field with a baseball diamond in the corner. At the far edge of the field is a fence and mesquite bushes as far as you can see.

This morning I awoke early and looked out across the field. I saw what I thought were large billy goats jumping and playing around next to the fence. Then I realized that they were Texas jackrabbits playing in the field. These are the biggest rabbits I've ever seen!

When we arrived yesterday, I noticed that the highway runs through the middle of this place. On one side of the road there was a sign that read, "San Antonio Aviation Cadet Classification Center" and on the other side it read, "San Antonio Aviation Cadet Pre-Flight Center."

I am in the Cadet Classification Center. This is where they send the cadet candidates through rugged physical and mental tests. When these tests are completed, they evaluate you as a pilot, bombardier, or navigator, that is, if you pass. If you don't pass, they send you to the walking infantry. I hope I pass.

If you graduate here, they send you across the road to the pre-flight center. If I make it there, I'll have three more months of academic training. Seems like you just about have to be a genius to become a pilot in this Army.

I miss you a lot, Sweet Peaches. You are always in my dreams. I can hardly wait to see you again.

Love,

Phil

After their physical training session the next morning, Phil and his squadron were assembled and marched down the street to the physical examination buildings. Along the way they passed by some barracks with men hanging out of the windows and yelling, "You'll be sorry, you'll be sorry," and laughing. Upon finding out that they were passing the "reject" barracks, Phil became a bit concerned when he thought about how many men he saw there. It seemed to him that there were a lot of men that wouldn't become pilots.

In the following weeks, Phil was kept busy by taking physical tests and examinations in the mornings and mental examinations in the afternoons. The other time was taken up by physical training, drilling and standing retreat parades.

Phil hoped that he was passing all of the examinations. He was most uncertain after the psychiatric examination. After he had been interviewed by the psychiatrist, he was told to wait in the ready room. This was unusual since the other men were sent on for other tests. He began to worry and wonder what he had done wrong.

After waiting for forty minutes, he was ordered to report to another room at the end of the building. Phil entered and saluted the Major sitting behind the desk. He was the top officer in the psychiatric unit.

"Aviation Cadet Candidate Barkley, reporting as ordered, Sir."

"Sit down, mister," replied the Major. "There are a few questions that I would like you to answer for me, Mister Barkley."

Phil's knees began to shake. He concentrated on keeping them steady.

"First, where, in your opinion, would be the best location for the Allied Forces to invade Europe?"

Phil thought for a couple of seconds. "Sir," he responded, "I think that somewhere along the northern coast of France might be a good spot."

"Why not Italy? Are you aware that we have defeated the Axis in Africa and have a lot of men and equipment there?"

"Yes, sir," Phil said in a firm voice. "but I feel that it would be a lot more difficult to launch an invasion through those mountains between Italy and Germany. I believe there would be a heavy loss of life and equipment. The terrain between France and Germany, however, is much flatter. And, since we did a lot of reconnaissance there in the last big war over there, we probably know that terrain better than any in Italy. We also seem to have a lot of men and equipment in England and the channel is only 14 miles wide at some points. Last, but not least, I think the French underground would be a lot more help than the Italians when it comes to spying and activities like that."

"It seems as if you have thought a lot about the subject, Mr. Barkley."

"I'm very interested in the war, sir. I mean, how we are

153

doing and all that."

"Very commendable, son. Now, let's see if you've thought much about my second question." The Major paused, looked Phil straight in the eyes, and said, "Let's imagine that you are a fighter pilot who has just shot down a Japanese airplane. You see him bail out of his craft and his parachute opens. Would you fly back around and shoot him?"

Phil suddenly began to worry! In a flash his mind raced over a dozen explanations for why the Major had asked him the same two questions that had been part of his first psychiatric exam. Did I flunk the first exam? Are they giving me a second chance, to change my answers? Or are they simply making sure I'll answer the same way I did the first time? What if I'm already washed out and they're just confirming that I'm not pilot material?

Suddenly, a mental picture of Roland Varnes being beaten by a Japanese soldier flashed through Phil's mind. He didn't hesitate to answer the Major's question. "Yes, sir."

"Why, isn't that a bit inhumane, Mister Barkley?"

Phil's expression was flat as he explained his answer. "Well, sir, it might seem inhumane and I might worry about it a bit later, but I think that if the same situation were reversed, he would shoot me. Besides, if he lives, there is a good chance that he would be back in the sky later in another airplane. Then he might have the chance to shoot at one of my buddies." Phil paused for a second, wondering if he should speak freely. Then he continued, "Another thing that bothers me is those reports about Japanese soldiers mistreating their American prisoners of war. One of my best friends from school died in the Philippines. I often wonder if he had to go through some kind of hideous torture before he died."

"Well, Mr. Barkley, this has been very interesting and I thank you. You may return to your unit now." The Major stood behind his desk. Phil stood, saluted, and thanked the Major before leaving.

He returned to his squadron and worried for the next several days about whether or not he might have flunked the psychiatric exam. Every afternoon, after being dismissed from duty, he went to the squadron office to see if his name was on the reject list posted daily on the bulletin board there. After a few days of not seeing his name, Phil stopped worrying and decided that the Major must have passed him despite the questionable answers he gave.

Later, the exams ceased. The cadets mostly played softball when they were not doing short order drilling or physical training. They were only told that when the exams were evaluated, the results would be posted on the bulletin board. Phil could hardly contain his excitement. Of course, everyone wanted to be a pilot, and Phil was no exception. But he always felt unsure of whether or not he would be classified as one. He always kept in the back of his mind the thought that many of his fellow cadets had completed one or two years of college and were probably a lot smarter than he was. There was also a bit of fear in his anxiety. Phil couldn't stand the thought of being rejected and ending up in the infantry.

Late one afternoon, one of the boys came running through the barracks shouting, "The lists are up! The lists are up!" Phil jumped off his bunk, ran outside, and down the street toward the growing crowd of cadets searching for their names on the bulletin boards. Some of the young men were shouting happily. Others were walking away shaking their heads or shrugging their shoulders. The happy ones had, of course, been selected as pilots. Phil guessed that the others had been assigned as bombardiers or navigators. A few other young men were leaving the area cursing. A few others were even crying. In a few weeks, they would be learning how to clean a rifle in the dark and crawl on their bellies under whizzing bullets. Hoping he was not soon to join these rejects, Phil pushed and edged his way through the group of boys until he could finally see a few of the lists.

The bombardier lists were the first he saw. A few moments later, he jostled his way over to the navigator lists. His name was not on either list. He began to get the nagging feeling that he might be rejected. Finally, he shoved his way down to the pilot lists. He nervously scanned the list. Suddenly, there was his name; Barkley, Philip E. He was a pilot!

Phil leapt off the ground, nearly knocking down the cadet standing next to him. He shouted, "Yay! Yay!" at the top of his lungs almost the whole time it took to run back to his barracks. When he ran through the door, he found some of his buddies celebrating as well. They were slapping each other on the backs, shaking hands, and grinning like a bunch of schoolgirls who had just gotten their first date. Phil began loudly singing the Army Air Corps song. The other boys whirled around, then joined in upon seeing Phil's smiling face. When the song ended, they all shouted, "Hurrah!"

After congratulating his friends, Phil suddenly couldn't wait to tell Linda and Jim of his good news. Feeling sure there would be long lines at the telephones on base, Phil decided to dash off two quick letters. After all, he didn't really have much else to tell them except that he had been classified as a pilot. While sitting on his bunk with pen and paper in hand, Phil noticed the few boys in his barracks that had been rejected. They were easy to pick out as they slowly and downheartedly packed their gear in preparation for transfer to the "Reject Barracks." As he finished the letters and left the barracks to mail them, Phil suddenly felt-t very thankful for whatever it was inside him that made his officers feel he had the potential to be a good pilot.

That evening, after the rejected cadets had left, Phil and his buddies celebrated until the sergeant called for lights out. Phil couldn't go to sleep. He lay in his bunk, wondering how soon his training would begin and what types of planes he would be allowed to fly. As he rolled onto his side, he noticed that the guy in the cot to his right was also wide awake. Suddenly, this guy grinned at Phil and whispered, "Let's have some fun."

"What do you mean?" Phil asked.

"Let's get some bottles of mercurochrome and slip around to these sleeping drunks and paint airplanes on their foreheads."

Phil grinned. "Okay, sounds like fun!"

"Can you imagine the looks on their faces when they look in the mirror tomorrow morning?" the other guy giggled.

"I can hardly wait," Phil said with a smile.

Soon the two pranksters were finished with their mischief and were back in their cots. Just as Phil was about to drift off to sleep, the guy in the cot to his left began snoring loudly. The cadet who had helped Phil paint the others' foreheads spoke up after a few moments of the loud, sawing noise.

"Say Phil, do you want to stop that noise so we can get some sleep?"

"Sure," Phil replied. "But how?"

"Just help me pick up his cot. He's a very sound sleeper."

They eased the cot and sleeping cadet out the front door into the warm night air. Very gingerly, they carried him across the street onto the large parade field. In a few moments, they were back in their cots inside the barracks.

At daybreak Phil awoke to shouting noises. Some of the cadets had awakened and looked in the mirrors. "I'll get the idiot that painted my head!" one cadet angrily shouted. Some others found the prank funny and were laughing at each other. Phil and his buddy were laughing too. They had painted small airplanes on each other's foreheads to avoid suspicion.

Suddenly, there was a loud noise and someone cursing at the front door. It seemed that the boy who had slept in the middle of the parade ground had awakened. He entered the barracks, dragging his cot behind, and seemed very disturbed about what had happened. He swore he'd get even with the perpetrators.

After breakfast on the second day after the lists had been posted, Phil's squadron was notified that those men who had passed were now official Army Air Corps aviation cadets and they would be moved across the road to the pre-flight center the following day. They were to take the rest of the day to prepare for their move the next morning. Phil and his new friend finished their packing by lunchtime and decided to bowl a few games at the base bowling alley.

It was late afternoon when they left the bowling alley to

return to their barracks. When they came within sight of their barracks, they noticed two cots on the roof of their barracks. A duffle bag was perched on each cot.

Phil laughed as he slapped his buddy on the back. "That's even better than the pranks we pulled last night."

They entered the barracks to find most of their fellow cadets continuing the celebration from the night before. They were telling jokes, playing cards, and generally having a good time. Phil and his friend walked toward their cots, but upon arriving, found only empty floor space. No cots and no duffle bags! Suddenly, it dawned on Phil just whose cots he had seen on the roof. He knew someone must have figured out who painted airplanes on everyone. He looked at his buddy and winked. They played along with this prank by cursing and acting angry. The rest of the guys enjoyed seeing Phil rant and rave about their prank. Finally, some of the other boys offered to help Phil and his friend get the cots back into the barracks. By the time they came back inside, some of the other boys had begun singing popular tunes. At that moment, they were singing "Mairzy Doats."

The song ended suddenly when a Sergeant entered the room and a corporal shouted, "Ten-shun!"

"At ease, girls," the Sergeant began. He held up a clipboard and began reading. "All classified cadets in this barracks will fall out tomorrow at oh-six-fifteen hours. Be in full gear and prepared to move yourself and all your belongings across the road to the pre-flight training center." He looked up and finished with, "Is that understood?"

"Yes, sir!" the cadets shouted in unison.

On the second day in his new surroundings, Phil received a reply from Linda.

August 20, 1943

Dearest Phil,

Congratulations! I could tell from your letter that you were very excited about being classified as a pilot. I am very happy for you. But do be careful, darling. You know how heights scare me and I'm always afraid something might happen to you.

I have told all your friends here in Kenly. They are also excited and wish you the best.

When do you think you might be able to come home? I miss you a lot. I love you a lot, too. Remember, be careful.

Love,

Linda

He wasted no time writing back to her.

August 23, 1943

Dear Peaches,

Thanks for your sweet letter. Yes, I am very excited about becoming a pilot. Tell all my friends I said thanks for their good wishes.

Sorry about you still being scared of heights. We'll have to work on that some later.

I am now across the road in the San Antonio Aviation Cadet pre-plight Center. There are a lot of two-story barracks and classroom buildings over here. It's much nicer and I think I'll like it here.

They issued us our Air Corps Cadet uniforms as soon as we arrived. They look very nice with the insignia on them, especially the O.D. winter uniforms. The cap is shaped like a pilot's dress cap but has a large propeller in front over the brim.

I had some pictures taken and am enclosing one with this letter. I am also sending some to my family and George Varnes. Sweetheart, I received a letter from Jim the same day yours arrived. He is also very excited. It seems that he has passed the Air Corps Officers Candidate School exam and has been selected to go to OCS. If he passes there, he'll be what's known as a "ninety-day wonder" because he'll become a Second Lieutenant. I guess they call it that because it is a "wonder" if you survive the course in ninety days. Anyway, I hope he makes it and I wish him the best.

I don't know when I'll be finished here, but will probably get to come home for a short leave as soon as that happens. I miss you so much, I can hardly wait to graduate just so I can come home!

Tell your mom and pop I said hello.

Love,

Phil

In the weeks that followed, the cadets spent most of their time going to classes. They studied airplane and warship identification a lot. Phil had no trouble with aircraft since he had studied them so much when he was the air raid warden at Kenly High School. The warships were a different story, however. Phil spent every spare moment reviewing the pictures in preparation for the exams.

Phil's pre-flight training included shooting and disassembling an M-I rifle and a .45 caliber automatic pistol. Of course, there were the regular activities in calisthenics, drilling and chemical warfare training. The best thing about all of it was that the training schedule grew more lenient at the end of the week and on weekends the cadets were allowed more time for open post. They were allowed off the base premises from one o'clock until eleven o'clock Saturday afternoon and evening. Then, on Sunday, they could be off from nine in the morning until ten in the evening. After settling into training for a few weeks, Phil took one Sunday afternoon to visit San Antonio and see Fort Sam Houston and the Alamo. He realized he had always been interested in history during high school, but it was so much more exciting to see these historic sites firsthand.

As the pre-flight training drew near to an end, the cadets became more relaxed with themselves and each other. It became normal for small parties to spring up in any barracks on any given evening. One evening, Phil heard a lot of loud laughing at the other end of his barracks and decided to check it out. He found a large group gathered around the guy everyone knew as the barracks cut-up. What everyone found so funny this evening was the sight of this cadet burning farts. Phil had never seen such a thing before. This guy was lying on the top bunk, bent over on his knees with his rear end sticking up in the air. He would strike a match and hold it near his anus, then let go a fart. Each time he did this, a flash of flame shot into the air. It really was a comical sight.

One of the other cadets told the cutup that it would be a better show if he pulled off his underwear. The cutup thought this was a good idea and followed the suggestion. Then he waited for a moment until he could feel another fart coming. He stuck up his nude rear end, lit the match and held it close, and let go his gas. Suddenly, there was a huge flash of fire and the cutup yelling, "Yeeowch!" He jumped off the bunk, fanning his rear end and running toward the showers. Without his underwear on, the cadet had singed off all the hair from his rear end. Everyone was doubled over with laughter. That ended the fart burning show.

Chapter Twenty-five

November 11, 1943

Dear Peaches:

I am now in Bonham, Texas. It's a small town about the size of Smithfield. It has a courthouse square in the center of town and the street goes all the way around it.

Our air base is a small privately owned airport that the government leases from the owner to provide primary flight training for teaching cadets to fly. The owner is a former Army pilot who flew with Captain Eddie Rickenbacker. Listening to his stories of aerial combat in World War One is very interesting. They sure had it a lot rougher in those days than we do now.

Our flight instructors here are civilian pilots who have been issued flight instructors licenses by the Federal Aviation Administration. My instructor is Mr. Jeff Bram. He is single and has an easy going personality off the job. Boy he sure is strict on the job though. He makes us stay on the ball every second. I have already been up with him a couple of times. Flying is so exciting here!

The planes we are flying in are PT-19 low wing monoplanes. I like them better than the high wing Piper cubs that we used in Memphis. The PT-19 looks more like the real fighter planes they are using in the war, except for the open cockpits.

Sweetheart, thanks so much for that beautiful birthday card. It arrived right on time—today. You couldn't have timed it better. I miss you more each day. I'm sorry I didn't get to come home on leave after leaving San Antonio. We really are on a rushed training program because the military needs more pilots. I'm sure I'll get to come home after graduating from here. I'll save all my kisses for you until then.

Love,

Phil

On November 18th, Mr. Bram informed Phil it was his turn to take up a PT-19 that afternoon at one o'clock. Phil was one of five students under Mr. Bram's tutelage and some of the others had gone up that morning.

At quarter past one, Phil and Mr. Bram climbed the trainer plane into the clear, blue Texas sky. Phil followed through on Bram's movement of the controls by lightly holding his hand on the stick in his area of the cockpit. He imagined himself flying the plane all alone. As the plane leveled off at cruising altitude,

Bram called Phil on the intercom and told him they would go to a nearby auxiliary landing field where they would practice taking off and landing. Phil's excitement grew since he knew they would be doing a lot more than simply flying straight and level. The more twists and turns they did, the more Phil liked flying.

They soon entered the traffic pattern of the auxiliary field. Phil looked down to see that the field was a large pasture with a hard dirt strip down the middle. He saw several other planes parked near the wind sock with cadets and instructors standing around them. There were also several PT-19s scattered throughout the field further down the landing strip. Some of them had wings torn off, some had crushed landing gear, and some even had their wings "flopped." They reminded Phil of how a mother hen spreads her wings low to protect her chicks.

Phil called Bram and pointed his finger down. "What happened here?"

"Looks as if someone tried to solo and didn't make it," he replied.

Bram shot three landings and take offs before finally settling down the plane and cutting back on the throttle. He taxied over to the wind sock where the others were waiting. As the plane stopped, Bram hopped out of the rear cockpit. I'll bet he is going to take a break and shoot the breeze with the other instructors, Phil thought. Suddenly, Bram was standing beside the front cockpit where Phil was seated.

"Okay, Phil. Let's see you do your stuff. Take her up."

Phil couldn't believe what he was hearing. He was almost in shock. "But, sir," he stammered. "I've never landed a plane by myself before. I've never taken off by myself either."

"Oh, yes you have. You just didn't realize it. Phil, there has to be a first time for everything. Now get going!"

"But I only have six hours of flying time in, sir," Phil offered as an excuse. He didn't really understand why he felt this way. He had always wanted to fly, but this was such a surprise! Something inside made him want to put it off as long as he could.

"Mister Barkley," Bram continued. "These other gentlemen have been waiting for us to arrive so they may also perform their solo flights. You want to be an Army Air Corps pilot don't you?"

"Yes, sir." Phil replied, suddenly remembering that he could be washed out of the program at any moment. He realized this was his moment of truth and he was faced with a choice. Either he could fly the plane alone right then, or start packing for the infantry.

"Well, Mr. Barkley," Bram finished. "I suggest you get going."

"Yes, sir!" Phil barked in reply. Suddenly, he felt a surge of self confidence. I can do this, he convinced himself. I've followed the controls enough to know how it feels. It will be easy . . . I hope.

He pushed in the throttle and the engine responded with a roar. He taxied down to the end of the runway and quickly performed his pre-flight check. Then, he sat there for a moment to collect his wits.

He took a pack of chewing gum from his pocket and stuck it all in his mouth. Chewing the gum furiously and gritting his teeth, Phil placed his left hand on the throttle and his right hand on the stick. A second later, he shoved the throttle in as far as it would go.

The plane lurched forward and began to sway to the left. Phil kicked his right rudder and corrected his alignment with the runway. He remembered to keep just a little back pressure on the control stick while he built up speed on the strip. As he passed the others standing next to the wind sock, he smoothly pulled back on the control stick and felt the sudden loss of the ground tugging at his wheels. He was airborne!

While beginning his ascent, Phil glanced out to check the wings. He had to keep them level with the control stick. As he looked at the right wing tip, he noticed Bram waving at him. Was it a reassuring wave or was it a good-bye wave? Pushing the thought from his mind, Phil began working the controls. He adjusted the trim tabs and raised the one quarter flaps that he had used for take off. Then he decreased the throttle just slightly. He found that the plane was responding to the controls just like when Bram was flying.

Phil soon reached 300 feet of altitude and eased forward on the stick to level off the plane. He allowed the plane to pick up velocity until it reached cruising speed on the air speed indicator. He pushed the control stick a little to the right and at the same time he applied light pressure to the right rudder pedal. He gave the throttle a little more gas and pulled back on the stick a little to hold the plane's nose level with the horizon. The plane did what he wanted it to do, it was making a right turn. When the plane had turned 90 degrees he returned the controls back to the neutral position. The plane righted itself and began flying straight and level.

Phil continued on around the square traffic pattern and turned into the initial approach leg of the traffic pattern. He soon came to a spot that was at a forty-five degree angle to where he wanted to land on the runway. He had been taught to cut his engine at this spot and he would land close to this spot on the runway if he operated the plane correctly.

He cut the engine, lowered the flaps to one-half, and slightly lowered the nose to keep his velocity above stalling on the air speed indicator. Soon, he was almost even with the runway. This was the moment to turn the plane to the right. As he straightened the plane up on the final approach he noticed that he was a little to the left of the runway. He lowered the right wing and kicked a little right rudder. The runway came into straight alignment so he straightened the plane back up.

Phil looked straight ahead through the idling propeller. Seeing the ground come up so fast brought a lump to his throat. He chomped faster on the chewing gum and pulled back on the stick a little. The plane leveled off near the ground. As his speed slightly decreased, he eased back on the stick while looking out the side of the open cockpit. Then he pulled back hard on the stick. The plane bounced up in the air. Phil added a little throttle and leveled off again, then cut the throttle and pulled back on the stick. The plane bounced into the air again. Again, he added a bit of throttle to keep the plane from crashing and leveled off. Again he cut the throttle and pulled back on the stick. Again the plane bounced and would not stay on the ground. This continued for a fourth time.

Phil quickly realized he had to do something because the end of the runway was close at hand. He shoved full throttle to the plane and pulled back on the stick. He repeated everything he had done before; climbing to cruising height, making a series of slow right turns, lining up his approach, and coming in for the landing. He glanced into the rear view mirror only to be reminded that Bram wasn't with him this time. It was the most empty seat he had ever seen. Again, Phil entered the final approach. I must get down this time, he thought.

Once more, he leveled off the plane near the ground and eased back on the stick while glancing out of the cockpit to judge his height and speed. As his speed slackened at the right height he pulled back hard on the stick. The plane hit and bounced into the air again. Not again, he thought. Phil tried once more. Again the plane bounced off the runway back into the air. He gritted his teeth and leveled off again. This time, he cut the throttle and did not advance it. It worked! The plane bounced again, but not as high as before. He pulled back hard on the stick and felt the wheels strike the ground. They stuck to the runway! Quickly, Phil worked the rudders to maintain his alignment and taxied to where the others were waiting.

With a big sigh of relief, Phil realized that he was now a full fledged pilot. He had flown by himself and lived to tell. As he pulled the plane up to the waiting group, he flashed the biggest smile he could muster.

"Welcome back, Mr. Barkley," said Bram as the engine coughed to a stop. "For a moment there we thought you might be joining the grasshopper club."

"No one is more relieved than I am about finally setting it down, sir."

163

Bram laughed and slapped Phil on the back as he climbed out of the cockpit. "You just need to watch your airspeed more closely. You were trying to land too fast." As Phil's feet touched the ground, Bram held out his hand. "Congratulations, Phil. You're a pilot."

"Thank you, sir."

Suddenly, Phil realized his chewing gum was no longer in his mouth. He didn't remember spitting it out. I must have been so nervous that I swallowed that whole wad of gum, he thought. Oh well, the important thing was that I made the right choice and forced myself to see it through. I can hardly wait to get back to the barracks so I can write to Linda and Jim. What a day!

During the weeks that followed, Phil became quite proficient with the PT-19. He even began to experiment with aerobatics flying. Bram was a very good aerobatics instructor, but had rules that many cadets considered too rigid. The main rule was to fasten the safety belt as soon as you climbed into the cockpit. He had given demerits to each of his students on more than one occasion for violating this rule. They found they almost had to click the belt together before their fannies touched the seat in order to avoid demerits. Some of the cadets even began calling him "Baron von Safety Belt." Of course, they never said that when he was around.

One day, as Phil was taking acrobatics lessons, Bram instructed him to perform a loop. As they reached the top of the loop, Phil didn't have quite enough air speed. The plane stalled and began to fall over backwards. Phil quickly kicked the right rudder and recovered in level flight. Expecting a reprimand from Bram, he braced himself and glanced in the rear view mirror. The rear seat was empty! Phil quickly looked out of the cockpit and spied a parachute opening about a hundred feet below the plane. He laughed aloud when the realization hit him that Bram had not fastened his safety belt and had fallen out at the top of the loop.

Phil decided it best to quickly return to the airport. As they hadn't been far from the base, he was soon on the ground. After landing, Phil reported the incident to the Commanding Officer, as was his duty. The control tower reported seeing a parachute going down in a field several hundred yards away and sent a jeep out to pick up the man. Bram's face was beet red with embarrassment when Phil saw him in the training room that afternoon.

The next few weeks Phil had completed most of his dual training and was doing mostly solo training flights. On this day, he had been assigned to solo flight to do "Lazy Eight" maneuvers and "S" turns across a road. It was a balmy, sunny and clear day. Phil had completed all his assigned flight maneuvers and had returned to straight and level flights. He looked up into the clear, blue, Texas sky and thought how peaceful and serene it was up in the sky just flying along lazily. Feeling as if he was on top of the world, Phil began singing the popular song, "I've got spurs that jingle, jingle, jingle." It had a catchy tune and he loved singing it when he felt so good.

Suddenly, his tranquillity was jolted back to reality by a sputtering engine! Then it quit! Phil was horrified. Frantically he wondered what he should do next. Check the gas, he quickly thought. The gauge read empty!

Phil's next thought was to find a field to land in. He had been taught to always keep an emergency landing field on the ground picked out as you fly along. He had just passed over a large cotton field so he turned the gliding plane back towards it. He checked the wind direction by some smoke near the area. He calculated that he had plenty of altitude to reach the cotton field.

Nearing the field, he noticed that the cotton stalks had already been cut so it was a good field for an emergency landing. He let the plane glide on towards the spot on the field that he had picked out to land on. Suddenly he realized that he was too high to land on the spot. He pushed on the right rudder pedal and lowered the left wing. This caused the plane to go into a side slip, a maneuver used to quickly lose altitude in a short distance. Phil realized it was a dangerous maneuver to use so close to the ground, but he had practiced side slips a lot and was confident that it was the right thing to do at the moment. His execution was almost perfect and the plane landed only a few feet from the spot he had chosen. The plane rolled to a dead stop.

The first thing he did after climbing out of the cockpit was to check for any damage that might have occurred during landing. Luckily, he found none. Phil wondered what he should do next. He looked out across the field and saw a farm house about a mile away. He knew that if he didn't soon call the air base, they would miss him and begin a search. He ran all the way to the farm house and knocked on the front door, hoping someone was at home.

After what seemed an eternity, the door finally opened. "May I help you, young man?" asked the middle-aged farmer's wife.

"Yes, ma'am," Phil replied, still gasping for breath. "Do you have a phone? You see, I am an Air Corps cadet from the air base at Bonham. My plane ran out of gas and I had to make an emergency landing in that cotton field over there. I need to call my Commanding officer."

"My Lord, young man. Are you hurt?"

"No ma'am, I'm fine and so is my plane. But if I don't call in soon, the people back at the base will think something terrible might have happened to me. Do you have a phone?"

"I sure do," she replied while holding the door open for Phil to come inside. "It is one of those old crank types and I'm afraid that sometimes it doesn't work very well."

Fortunately, the phone was working at the moment. The operator connected him with Instructor Bram at the Bonham air base. A few moments later, Bram's voice crackled on the other end of the line.

"Hello? Who is this?"

"Cadet Barkley, sir."

"Where are you, Phil?"

Phil explained what had happened. Bram asked him to put the farmer's wife on the phone to give directions to her house. After that, he told Phil that a retrieval crew would be there within two hours. When he hung up the phone and thanked the farmer's wife, she offered him a glass of cool water an told him it would be alright if he sat on her front porch until the crew arrived. He thanked her and went outside to relax. As he leaned back in one of the chairs on the porch, something suddenly began to trouble Phil. It would be his fault that the gas ran out! He should have watched the gauge more closely. He was still worrying about whether or not they would wash him out of the Air Corps when a large truck and two automobiles drove up to the farm house. Phil hurried up to the automobile as Bram got out.

"Are you hurt, Phil?"

"No, sir. And neither is the plane . . . I've already inspected it."

"That's great. It looks pretty level from here. You did a good job of putting her down without cracking up. We may be able to fly it home."

"Yes, sir." Phil felt a bit better about the situation after Bram's praise for the good landing.

The base commander, an aircraft mechanic, Mr. Bram, and Phil got on the truck and went out to where the PIT-19 sat in the field. The mechanic took a can of gas and went up on the wing to pour it in. He looked back down at the commanding officer.

"Sir, the auxiliary gas tank is full of gas," he said.

"What?" exclaimed the commanding officer. "Then what was the problem?"

The mechanic peered into the cockpit. "It looks as if the switch isn't turned to the auxiliary tank, sir," he replied. Turning to Phil, the base commander said, "Well, well, Mr. Barkley. Can you explain that?"

"No sir," Phil stammered. "I, I didn't realize it had an auxiliary gas tank."

"You didn't think! You just didn't think, Mr. Barkley. You should have checked."

"Yes, sir." Phil felt a sudden dread come over him.

The mechanic said that he could fly the plane out of the field. Phil and the other two men climbed back into the truck. All the way back to the base, Phil grew more and more sure that he would be washed out of the program. The trip back to the base was very quiet. The commanding officer did tell Phil that there would be a hearing on the incident the next morning and he would be notified. That night Phil tossed and turned in his bunk bed until morning. He could not sleep from worrying about what the accident investigation panel would do to him the next day.

The next morning Phil reported to the flight training room for a course in air foil theory. At the beginning, he found it difficult to pay attention to what the instructor was saying. He felt sick to his stomach, still worrying about the investigation board. Suddenly, he became aware that the instructor was saying that the bottom of a wing did not lift the airplane into the air. Phil had heard this before, but now the instructor was explaining this crazy theory on the board with diagrams. He began listening very closely to the instructor.

"The wing surface is flat on the bottom," he began. "But is slightly round on the top side. The front top leading edge of the wing is round but trails down to the rear edge to a flat point. This makes the air pass smoothly under the wing, while air striking the front round edge of the wing is forced up and then comes back down towards the rear edge of the wing. This creates a vacuum on top of the wing which lifts the plane. The rate of lift of the plane into the air is caused by the forward speed of the plane and the angle that the wing is striking the air flow. This is called the angle of attack on an air foil and determines the amount of vacuum on the top of the wing or on an air foil."

Phil was so fascinated he failed to notice Bram enter the room. After a brief word with the class instructor, Bram motioned for Phil to come with him.

"Have a seat, Phil" he instructed as they entered Bram's office. He must have noticed the forlorn look on Phil's face because he quickly added, "It's okay, Phil. You won't have to go to the infantry."

Phil immediately sat up straight. A big smile filled his face and he let out a huge sigh of relief. "That's great, sir. Just great. Thank you very much, sir."

"The investigative panel wanted to wash you out, Phil. But I went to bat for you. I showed them your excellent academic record and your personnel folder. I also told them of your above average performance in flight training and that you possess a superior talent in flying ability and dedication. I was able to convinced them that it would be a great waste of talent to wash you out."

"Thanks again, sir. I really appreciate all you've done for

me."

"You didn't come out scott free. Your open post privileges have been revoked for two weeks. During that time, you will pull guard duty each weekend. You will also take a refresher course in PT-19 familiarization. Is that understood?"

"You bet! I mean, yes, sir! I'm just glad they listened to you, Mr. Bram. I was so afraid of being washed out."

"Let it be a lesson to you, Phil. Now, get back to class."

"Yes, sir!"

On the way back to the training room, Phil vowed that he would never again become placid while flying and that he would never fly one without knowing everything there was to know about it.

December 10, 1943

Dear Phil,

I was beginning to wonder if you were going to write me again. I know it's been three weeks since I've heard from you, but it seems like eternity. I love your letters so much.

Sweetheart, I know you must be enjoying your flight training there so much, for it shows in your letters. I also thought that it was funny about your instructor falling out of your plane. Even Eddie laughed about it.

But please Honey, be careful. I don't want you falling out of any planes. I miss you and I can't wait until you come home again.

Linda

A week later, it was time for Phil's final check flight. His primary training was at an end. Phil was pleased to learn that Lieutenant Bowen had been assigned to oversee his final flight. They had flown together a few times before and he had always given Phil high marks for performance. Bowen was young and single. Phil had discovered that Bowen loved a good time and was very "happy go lucky." Phil thought of him as a hot pilot type and admired him very much.

Lieutenant Bowen entered the flight training room and went to the water cooler. As he drank a large glass of cold water, he motioned for Phil to follow him to the flight line so they could begin the check flight. He didn't say much, and Phil noticed that Bowen didn't appear to feel well. Shortly after the ground check, they were climbing into the sky to begin Phil's tests.

Soon they had completed all of Phil's final flight checks and Bowen told Phil that he had passed each one.

Phil was so delighted that he shouted into the intercom,

"Thank you, sir!"

"Hold it, hold it," the lieutenant shouted back. "Not so loud, Phil. I have a terrific headache."

"I'm sorry, sir," replied Phil.

"It's okay. Listen, we can't go in this soon anyway, so why don't you just fly around a bit more. If you fly straight and level I can get a few winks. You don't mind, do you?"

"Not one bit," Phil almost whispered into the intercom.

They flew around the area until Phil decided they couldn't stay out any longer. He landed the plane and parked it in the hanger as Bowen had previously directed him. He noticed that Bowen was still asleep in the rear cockpit so he decided not to disturb him. Phil went to the training room and joined the rest of his Unit.

Later, when it was time for the unit to return to their barracks, the squadron leader had them all line up outside to march back in parade formation. As they began marching, the squadron leader noticed that the doors to the huge aircraft hanger, where Phil had parked his plane, were open on both ends. He decided to go through the center of the hanger with the unit since it was a shorter way to the barracks area. As the marching men neared the center of the aircraft hanger, Phil noticed that Bowen was still asleep in the rear of the plane. Just at that moment, the squad leader yelled for the unit to start counting cadence.

"Hup, two, three, four," they shouted in unison.

The sudden loud noise startled Lieutenant Bowen awake. He evidently realized that he was still in the plane, but not realizing what was going on, he dived out of the plane onto the concrete floor.

The squad leader saw him and quickly halted the unit. He ran over to try to help the lieutenant off the floor and to see if he was hurt. Bowen quickly stood, brushed himself off, picked up his flying goggles, and left the hangar in a huff. The men realized what had happened and started laughing. Bowen had been lucky. About the only damage he had suffered was a slightly skinned face and very bruised ego.

Chapter Twenty-six

Upon completion of primary training, Phil was sent to Greenville, Texas in January, 1944 for Basic Flight Training School. Greenville was farther north than San Antonio and the weather was much colder. The barracks were hastily built long, narrow, wooden structures that were one story tall. Near the center of each building was a large, coal burning, pot bellied stove that provided heat for the whole building. There were long rows of bunk beds down each side of the barracks with a wide aisle in the middle. The large bathroom was located at one end of each building. It was everyone's duty to help keep the place warm and clean. Phil was writing to Linda when a cadet came in and began moving his things to the bunk beside Phil's.

"Hey buddy, where are you from?" Phil asked.

"North Carolina," the fellow replied. "How about you?"

"I'm from North Carolina too!" Phil exclaimed.

"You ever heard of Rocky Mount?" the cadet asked.

"Sure," said Phil. "It's right up the road from where I live. You ever heard of Kenly?"

"Sure have! I used to go down there to a place called Cash Corner. Lot of dancing and spooning going on there." The cadet stopped unpacking his duffle bag and shoved his hand at Phil. "Shields is my name; Vic Shields."

"Glad to meet you, Vic," Phil said as they shook hands. "My name is Phil Barkley."

"Well, imagine that!" Vic grinned. "We're probably the only two Southern boys in the whole Army Air Corps. All I've ever met before now were Yankees and Texans."

The two young men sat on their foot lockers for a while, talking about home and the good times they each had in high school. Phil told Vic about Linda and how much he missed her. Vic told Phil that he used to have a girlfriend back at home, but she had found some other guy more interesting since he had joined the Army. Phil felt a bit sorry for Vic. After they talked a while longer, Phil began to wonder if Linda might find someone at home while he was away in the service. He remembered that Eddie still visited Linda a lot, even though she said they were just friends.

"Hey, Phil, I'm hungry," Vic said suddenly. "You want to go get a bite of supper?"

"Not right now," Phil replied. "I'm not very hungry. Besides, I want to finish this letter to the folks back home so I can get it in the mail tomorrow morning."

"Alright, buddy. I'll see you later."

As Phil tried to finish his letter to Linda, he found himself wondering whether or not he had been attentive enough to her.

She does tell me that she loves me in every letter, he thought. And she says she misses me more each day. But I wonder how much she misses me when Eddie takes her to a picture show?

He decided to fill his letter with less talk of flying and more about how she liked accounting school and how her parents were getting on with the war situation. He wrote about meeting Vic Shields and described the parts of Texas he'd seen while on his way to Greenville. He made sure this letter would tell her how much he loved her.

For basic flight training, the Army used the BT-13, a larger craft than the PT-19. It was low wing, single engine plane with a sliding canopy over two single cockpits. To Phil, it resembled a single engine fighter plane. The air corps had nicknamed it "The Vultee Vibrator" because it rattled a lot while on the ground. But Phil's biggest surprise about the plane came on his first day of training. As boon as he was seated in the cockpit, his instructor informed Phil that before he could fly the BT-13, he must learn to touch and describe each of the instruments and controls while blindfolded. At first, this frightened Phil because there were almost a hundred controls and instruments on the plane. Quickly, he remembered his vow. I'll just have to grit my teeth and study this plane very hard, he thought. I can do it! The concern on his face must have been very evident, because the instructor reassuringly patted him on the shoulder and said, "You can do it, Barkley."

Each day Phil attended a class before going to the flight line to fly. The instructor always began each day with a war progress report for about five minutes. Phil grew to like the reports, especially the ones about bombers and fighter pilots in action.

One day, the instructor said that the war news was not good. Reports had been received to the effect that Japanese soldiers had forced approximately 76,000 prisoners of war to march hundreds of miles across the Bataan Peninsula of the Philippine Islands in April of 1942. Around ten thousand Filipino and American prisoners died or were killed in this march. Another ten thousand were missing. Phil remembered that Roland Varnes had been reported killed in the Philippine Islands about that same time. He shuddered with horror and anger at the thought that Roland might have died in such a way. It made him all the more determined to do his best in flight training so he might get into the war quickly. Deep inside, he felt he had a score to settle with quite a few Japanese soldiers.

Phil remained on base for much of his open post time in order to study more. But occasionally he and Vic would go into town on Saturday afternoon to shop or see a movie. Soon, Phil was at the top of his class in both academics and performance. He began to spend more and more of his training time learning to fly aerobatics. However, Phil was soon to learn that there was more to being an Army Air Corps pilot than just knowing how to fly airplanes.

One Tuesday morning, a check pilot named Lieutenant Moore was assigned to accompany Phil and chart his progress in aerobatics flight. Moore was known as a perfectionist and a very stern instructor. Within thirty minutes after take off, Phil had completed all but the last maneuver in his check flight. He felt good about his performance so far, and began the "Lazy Eights," a looping, rolling, turning maneuver. Suddenly, at the top roll of the maneuver, Moore grabbed the control stick and slammed it back and forth between Phil's knees. He yelled through the intercom that Phil was not coordinating the rudders and ailerons properly. Twice more, each time Phil came to the top of the roll, Moore grabbed the stick and yelled at him on the intercom. Phil tried very hard to concentrate on following Moore's instructions to the letter, but it seemed that nothing he did was right. By the third attempt, Phil had a small bruise on his left knee. when the stick struck that knee at the top of the roll, he lost his composure. Phil gripped the stick with all his might and slammed it back and forth between Lieutenant Moore's knees. Then he felt Moore firmly, but smoothly, bring the stick back to a neutral position.

"I have the stick now, Mr. Barkley," he yelled over the intercom.

Phil quickly released his hold on the stick. Moore shot the plane into a steep right turn and they headed back to the base.

As they climbed out of the plane, Moore took off his parachute and shoved it into Phil's stomach. "Your job is to listen and obey, Mr. Barkley! For what you did up there you will now run five times the length of this runway with two parachutes on your back! Is that clear?"

"Yes, sir!" Phil snapped. He could still feel the anger in his blood and the bruises on his knees.

"Report back to me in the training center when you are finished."

By the end of the second lap, Phil had realized that he had lost his cool with Lieutenant Moore. He wondered if they would wash him out of the program for what he had done. He'd seen other cadets washed out for less. Technically speaking, he had struck an officer. That was cause for being thrown in the brig! By the end of the fifth lap, Phil could hardly walk. He stumbled into Moore's office and mustered enough strength to salute.

"At ease, Mr. Barkley," Moore said in his usual stern voice. He paused briefly before continuing, "You lost your temper up there, Mr. Barkley. When you remove your gear I want you to go into the training room and write two hundred times on the blackboard, 'I will never again lose my temper while flying.' Tomorrow morning you will report to your regular instructor. Is that understood?"

"Yes, sir," Phil replied meekly.

It was almost time for supper when Phil completed his task. He was so tired from running and writing that he decided to skip supper and went straight to his barracks. Moments after falling into his bunk, Phil was asleep.

He awoke the next morning very hungry. He roused Vic and together they went to breakfast. Along the way, he told Vic what had happened the day before and that he was worried about being washed out. Vic tried to reassure Phil by telling him that they probably wouldn't wash him out but Phil could not help from worrying. After breakfast, Phil reported to his instructor's office.

"Take a seat, Mr. Barkley."

"Yes, sir."

"It seems that you and Lt. Moore had an interesting flight yesterday."

Expecting bad news, Phil blurted out, "Sir, I'm really sorry about . . ."

"It says here," the instructor interrupted, "that you got the highest marks of any student yesterday for your check flight. Well done, Mr. Barkley."

Phil couldn't believe his ears! Moore had given him an excellent rating? After what happened? The instructor must have someone else's file here, he thought.

"But you must learn to control your temper, son. I hope you realize the consequences of losing your cool in a combat situation, especially when flying."

"Yes, sir. I won't forget," Phil replied.

The instructor noticed Phil's relief and flashed a small grin in the corner of his mouth. "That will be all, Mr. Barkley. You may carry on."

"Yes, sir! Thank you, sir." Phil saluted and quickly left the instructor's office.

A few days later, on a cold, damp, January afternoon, Phil was out practicing more aerobatics maneuvers like snap rolls, slow rolls, spins, side slips, and slip stalls. In the middle of a slip stall, he noticed that the sky was growing more hazy, almost murky. A second later, he realized that a very thin sheet of ice was forming on his windshield!

Phil immediately forced the BT-13 into a dive. Just a few hundred feet closer to the earth might mean the difference in freezing and one degree above freezing. Ice on the windshield meant ice on the wings and that was deadly to any pilot, no matter how good he was. once he reached a satisfactory altitude, Phil quickly entered the traffic pattern for landing at the base. The clouds had grown so thick he could barely see the runways. Upon beginning his right turn to enter the downwind leg of the traffic pattern, Phil noticed another BT-13 doing the same, a few hundred yards closer to the runway. Suddenly, it rolled over into a spin and disappeared! Phil dipped his right wing slightly, trying to catch another glimpse of the spinning plane. All he could see was a small plume of smoke rising through the clouds. He knew what had happened and the thought sickened him. The plane had accumulated too much ice on the wings and the right turn had been all it took to slip into a spin. Even though he hoped the pilot had been able to bail out in time, in his gut Phil knew that they were too close to the ground for that.

A lump suddenly climbed from his stomach into Phil's throat. Glancing at his own wings, he found them coated with ice. He only had one chance now. Ignore the traffic pattern and get to the runway as quickly as possible. He throttled up the BT-13 and nosed her down. The end of the runway was just off his right wing, so he swung the plane into a diving half circle and kept a sharp lookout for other planes. It worked! He was aligned with the runway and he had kept above stalling speed.

Phil brought the plane in so fast that after landing, he was almost at the end of the runway before it stopped rolling. Before he taxied to the hangar, Phil pulled off his flying cap and goggles. His face was dripping with sweat. only then did he realize how scared he'd been.

Upon reaching the flight operations room, he found that he was the last plane in, except for one. The local police had reported a crash near the airport and a fire crew was on its way to investigate. Phil and his unit were dismissed for the day and they all returned to their barracks. Just before supper, Phil began to wonder where Vic could be. He was usually back early enough to accompany Phil to supper.

Just then, the barracks door opened and in stepped an air police officer. He went straight to Vic's bunk and opened his foot locker. Quickly and silently, he began packing Vic's personal belongings into a box. Phil was suddenly and overwhelmingly struck with anguish at the realization that Vic had been the pilot who had crashed! The scene began to play over and over in his mind. The plane turned right and slipped into a spin. Then, there was smoke in the clouds.

Tears welled in Phil's eyes. To keep from sobbing in front of everyone there, he forced himself to get up and assist the officer with packing Vic's belongings. He thought clearly long enough to get Vic's home address so he could write a letter to his parents. He felt the very least he could do was to tell them what a fine son they had and how proud he had been to be Vic's friend.

By the end of March, the regimen of training had forced Phil to put aside his grief over the loss of his friend. He had completed all of his basic flight training and even had considerable experience in aerobatics flying. Besides Vic's death, the only disappointment Phil had experienced was the news that he would now be sent to twin engine advanced training school. He had really had his heart set on more single engine training, hoping that he would be able to get assigned to a fighter pilot school and get into the war before it was over. On the bright side, Phil had received a letter from Jim Kelford who had just been graduated from O.C.S. and had a temporary commission as a second Lieutenant in the Army Air Corps. Phil could identify with Jim's uncertain tone, since neither had yet been given orders. It seemed that no one knew where they would end up next.

Chapter Twenty-seven

April 2, 1944
Dearest Peaches,

I just arrived at Ellington Field in Houston, Texas. I am here to take advanced twin engine training here in the AT-10 airplane. If advanced here is anything like basic at Greenville, it will be interesting and exciting.

The air base here is nice. It has nice barracks to live in and also has Post Exchanges, movies, bowling, alleys, and lots of athletic fields. This is a real Army Air Corps Air Base.

They not only train twin engine cadets here but also train navigators. It is a huge air base with nice long runways.

Sweetheart, I am glad that Strawberry told you about Jim graduating from O.C.S. and getting his commission as a 2nd Lt. I think that is just great. I just hope that if I graduate here that they'll give me a commission and not appoint me as a warrant officer. They say that they have started giving out a lot of warrant officer positions here. In case you don't know, a warrant officer doesn't have a commission. He is about the same as a sergeant major.

Peaches, it was good to hear you are liking accounting school and making good grades. I always knew you could.

That was nice of George to visit you on Sunday when you were home. If he is taller than Roland was, he must be a good looking boy. Just wish I could see him, and you too!!

If George was driving the Old Silver Bullet when he came by, it must be tougher than I thought. That thing sure brings back old memories. I'm glad its still running for George.

Sweet Peaches, wish you wouldn't go to all the movies with Eddie. Just wait till I get there and I'll take you to a real good movie. I'll show you a real good time, okay?

I have to go now but remember, I love you! I love you! I love you!

All my love,

Phil

Later, Phil had almost completed flight training. He had completed night flying and had been on one night cross country flight with only another cadet as copilot.

This night he was sent on a triangle-shaped night cross country flight that would take him to Mid-County Airport and Navasota. Then he was to return to Ellington Field. One of his cadet friends had been sent along with him as copilot. Phil had flown over mid-county and Navasota. At each point he flashed his identification lights in morse code to the checker below and had received confirmation in morse code in return.

He was flying at 8,000 feet and had left Navasota far behind. He estimated he was over half way back to Ellington Field. The moon was shining brightly up in the heavens among millions of bright stars. It was a peaceful time Phil thought, listening to the melancholy drone of the two engines.

He looked over at his copilot friend. He appeared to be nodding. He tapped his friend on the shoulder. He jerked erect, looked at Phil and smiled.

As Phil looked out over the nose of the plane, he saw what looked like a blanket of snow down below and off in the distance. He suddenly sat erect, for he had never seen anything like this before while flying at night.

At this moment, he saw the lights of another plane ahead meeting him. As the plane passed under him, a voice came on the radio.

"Aircraft heading for Houston: are you a cadet from Ellington Field?" "Yes," replied Phil. "This is U.S. Air Corps 9831. I am Cadet Barkley. What's up? Over."

"Cadet Foggleman here. That is fog down there, Phil. I have just been in contact with the Ellington Field control tower. They say the field is closed down. Zero visibility. Fog over the whole area and heading west. They advise everyone within radio contact to immediately find a place to land as near as possible before the fog gets here."

"I read you, Foggleman," Phil shouted into the radio. "Let's head back to Navasota right now."

"Roger," replied the other cadet. "Lead the way."

As Navasota came within sight, Phil looked for the airport. He could just make out the runway in the darkness. It was a small private airport and did not have many lights to outline the runway.

Since Phil's plane was not on a commercial radio frequency he could not contact the control tower by radio so he decided to drag the runway once before attempting to land. As he came down the final approach, he noticed a red light in the control tower blinking frantically trying to stop him from landing. He was wondering why when his landing lights suddenly showed him the reason. The landing strip was a dirt runway and it had a lot of mud holes, evidently from a recent shower. He shoved the throttle forward and headed back up in the starlit sky.

"Where's the next nearest airport, Al?" he asked his copilot. "We can't land here, that's for sure."

"There are a couple of small towers nearby but I don't see an airport anywhere on the maps," Al replied with a worried look on his face.

"I remember seeing a place called Bryan on a map. I think it is nearby. Check it out." Phil noticed the sense of urgency in his own voice.

"Yeah, here it is." Al pointed out the location on the map to Phil. "But we don't have much gas left, Phil. I'm not sure we can make it."

Phil mentally began to work on the problem. It's about half as far from here as Houston. We only wasted a few moments on the diversion to Navasota. We can make it, I think.

"We're going to try it, Al. I think we can make it."

"I hope you're right." Phil detected the worry in Al's response. He suddenly thought of something to keep Al busy for a few moments.

"Give me a compass heading, will you?" Phil asked. "And then get on the radio to cadet Foggleman and tell him what we're doing. I'm going to keep looking for other options as we head that way."

"You got it, pal," replied the copilot, grateful for something to keep his mind off their trouble.

In a flash, Phil had his bearing and headed the plane toward Bryan. Ten minutes later, Foggleman was back on the radio.

"Calling Air Corps 9831. Calling Air Corps 9831. Barkley, do you read me? Over."

"Roger, Foggleman . . . I read you. Over."

"I'm almost out of fuel. I'll never make it to Bryan Field. I see the lights of a town off to my right and I'm going to try a landing near there somewhere. Over."

"I was hoping you could hang on for just a while longer, Foggleman. But you know your plane better than anyone else. Keep your landing lights on as you buzz the town and you might find a landing field. I'll report your situation when I land at Bryan. Good luck, buddy. Over."

"Thanks, Barkley. Good luck to you, too. Over."

Phil continued towards Bryan Field too busy to worry further about Foggleman. His gas gauge was reading almost empty. Now, even he was beginning to worry. Ever since Navasota, he had been trying to find fields in which to land, but it was just too dark to see anything clearly. Maybe if I get a bit closer to the ground, he thought, I could see a little better.

Just then, the flashing beacon from Bryan Field caught Phil's eye. He punched Al and pointed at the light. Al's face was beaming almost as brightly as the beacon. A quick glance at the gas gauge showed the needle bouncing against the empty mark. This is going to be close, he thought.

"We're going to make it, Al," he shouted, partly to reassure Al and partly to reassure himself.

As they neared the field, Phil was pleased to see that the runway lights were almost aligned with his approach. That would help a lot. Then, his heart sank. The wind sock indicated that he was about to make a down wind landing. But given the choice of which was more dangerous, Phil decided a down wind landing was preferable to a crash landing. Besides, a reassuring thought had flashed through his mind. From his weather courses in basic flight training, Phil remembered that where there is fog, there is almost never any wind along the ground. Since that is what made down wind landing so dangerous, the situation here wouldn't be that bad.

Phil headed his plane straight toward the runway lights and as soon as he saw that he could make the runway, he let down full flaps in order to slow his landing speed and runway run as much as possible. He did not want to take a chance on running off the end of the runway if he could.

As he approached the runway, he saw the control tower flashing a green light, telling him that it was okay to land. Phil could not contact the tower by radio since they were on another frequency than his plane.

As the wheels touched the pavement of the landing strip, Phil breathed a huge sigh of relief. Al was almost jumping up and down in his seat.

"We made it! We made it!" he said with the excitement of a child.

As they rolled down the taxi way, Phil noticed other AT-10's parked along the apron. He was glad that others had made it back safely like him. He turned his plane towards the parking area just as the engines sputtered and died.

"Whew," he said, looking at Al. "That was a bit too close for comfort."

Phil let the AT-10 roll to a stop. Then he hurriedly climbed out and ran to the operations office to check in with the commanding officer. He discovered that Ellington Field had called to alert other fields of the situation. Phil was told that he and Al were to spend the night at Bryan and return to Ellington the next day.

"Sir, do you have any information on an AT-10 landing or crash between here and Navasota? Cadet Foggleman was flying alongside me, but didn't have enough fuel to make it here."

"Oh yes," replied the C.O. "That must be the plane that the Sheriff near Shiro called in about. They reported that a plane had started circling the town real low with his landing lights on. The sheriff figured he must be in trouble and wanted to land, so he stopped several automobiles and they went to a large field just outside of town. They lined up all the automobiles and shone their headlamps on the field. The plane landed okay, but broke a wheel strut and knocked off a wing tip. Everyone aboard was okay."

"Thank you, sir. That's a relief."

179

Phil learned the next morning that all the planes had found places to land and were okay. Cadet Foggleman's plane was the only one that was damaged in landing. He later saw Cadet Foggleman who told Phil that he had received a letter of commendation for that night. It was not only for bringing the plane down safely but was also for notifying most of the other planes that night of the fog situation at Ellington Field. He had arrived ahead of the other planes to within radio contact of Ellington Field control tower and had immediately turned his plane back towards Navasota upon hearing about the fog and Ellington Field being closed. He called all the Cadet planes he could reach until he met Phil.

Several weeks passed and Phil completed most of his twin engine training. He felt that he had done well so far in the training and decided to relax a bit more on weekends by taking advantage of the open post. There was a lot to do in a town the size of Houston. Phil liked to keep things at a low key, so he mostly just accompanied friends into town for a beer or two on Saturday night. On Sundays, he liked to ride the busses around town and do a bit of sightseeing. On one bus ride, he discovered a place called "The Chinese Sunken Gardens." The next Sunday afternoon, he and some buddies decided to check it out. Phil was talking to his buddies at one of the sunken pools when he noticed girl standing next to him. She began describing the sunken pool and facts about the sunken gardens to him. He thought she was a very attractive dark haired girl.

"You must be from near here somewhere!" he said with a disarming smile.

"Yes, I'm a student at the Catholic school not far from here. I come here often to relax. It's such a beautiful place. Um, my name is Vicki, Vicki Fabriezio."

"Say, that's a pretty name. But my tongue would get twisted trying to say your last name."

She laughed along with Phil. "I know, that's why everybody just calls me Vicki. What's your name?"

Phil extended his hand. "Philip E. Barkley, Aviation Cadet, U.S. Army Air Corps."

They all strolled around the gardens for a while. Soon it was time for Phil and his friends to return to the base.

"We have to go now, Vicki. I really enjoyed meeting you!"

"Will you be back next Sunday?" Vicki asked. "I could show you some other sights near here."

"That would be great!"

"Then it's a date. I'll see you next Sunday at about two o'clock."

On the way home, Phil couldn't help but think that Vicki was not nearly as pretty as Linda, but she *was* nice and friendly. Upon returning to the barracks, Phil wrote a letter to Linda.

Then he stayed up late to study.

Monday morning, Phil heard the bugle blow reveille, but somehow he dozed back to sleep. A loud noise in front of the barracks woke him ten minutes later. He suddenly realized that everyone else was assembled outside for roll call and inspection! Thinking quickly, Phil grabbed his raincoat and headed out the door. If he was late for roll call, he would be given demerits.

The Lieutenant in charge of the unit was already inspecting the front row of men as Phil managed to slip into the rear row without attracting attention. Sometimes, he thought, if the Lieutenant is in a hurry, he won't inspect all the rows. I hope he is in a hurry this morning.

Of course, the Lieutenant was not in a hurry. When he reached Phil, he just stood there looking for a moment, saying nothing.

"I say, Mr. Barkley," he began, "is it raining where you are standing this morning?"

"No, sir," Phil blurted.

"Then why the raincoat?" A ripple of snickering passed through the men as they waited for Phil's answer.

"At ease!" the Lieutenant shouted. Silence followed.

"I reckon I dozed back to sleep after reveille, sir. I was studying very late last night," came Phil's embarrassed reply.

"Well, cadet Barkley, you can walk guard duty on your open post for the remainder of your stay here. There you can study very hard to find ways to stay awake. That's an order, soldier. Do you understand?"

"Yes, sir," Phil meekly replied.

The following Sunday, Phil realized he wouldn't be able to keep his date with Vicki. He didn't know her telephone number or if she even had a phone. Phil finally asked one of his buddies to get a message to her about what had happened. Soon, as he stood near the guard shack at the base entrance, Phil forgot about Vicki and began to recall the good times he and Linda had experienced at Holt's Lake find other places.

Finally, training was complete and a list of the graduates was posted on the bulletin board at the flight training center office. As Phil scanned the lists he saw many of his buddies being appointed as warrant officers, but his name wasn't on the list. That nagging worry about being washed out began to creep back into his mind. He scanned another list. On the third list, he spotted his name! Barkley, Philip E.: Pilot - Twin engine - Second Lieutenant.

Phil ran back to the barracks to celebrate with his buddies who had also been promoted. Only a few cadets had been washed out of the program. After a half hour of celebrating and congratulating others, Phil went to find a telephone and got in the long line of soldiers calling their families to tell them the good news. Finally his turn came for the phone.

"Hello?" the sweet voice echoed in Phil's ears for a few seconds.

"Hey, sweet Peaches," he said in a husky voice.

"Phil, is that you?"

"Sure is, darling. You are talking to Second Lieutenant Philip E. Barkley, twin engine pilot extraordinarre."

Linda laughed. Then Phil could hear her telling her mother, "Mama, it's Phil on the line."

"That's wonderful, Phil," she said, returning her attention to him. "I'm so happy for you."

"Well, if that makes you happy, this next bit of news will knock your sock off. I'm coming home next week."

"Oh Phil," she squealed, "that's wonderful! I've missed you so much. When will your train arrive?"

Phil sensed that Linda was about to cry from the shakiness in her voice. It touched his heart and he almost felt like crying too. "Sweetheart, I'll be graduating next Friday, May twenty-third. After that, we get a two-week leave to visit our homes and wait there for our next assignments. I already know that I'm going to Midland, Texas to train bombardiers and navigators, but the official procedure gives us an excuse to go home. I was hoping to train for overseas duty, but I guess they need me more here in the states."

"Oh, that's wonderful. It won't be as dangerous as going overseas."

"Maybe not, Peaches, but I would still rather be going overseas with some of my buddies."

Linda suddenly returned their conversation to Phil's leave. "I'll be out of school for two weeks on summer vacation beginning next week. Didn't that work out just great?"

"Hey, that *is* great!" Phil replied happily. "That means we can spend the whole time together. It will take me about three days to get home on the train and I'll have to get to Midland, Texas in time to get assigned quarters and get settled in. Maybe four days travel time for that so I will have seven days at home. Won't that be nice?"

"It sure will, Honey," she replied sweetly.

"I have to go now, Peaches. There are a lot of other fellahs waiting here in a long line. I'll call you later. I love you."

"I love you too, Phil. Hurry home."

I've got to go into town and get some officers uniforms—my pilots wings.

Graduation day finally arrived. Phil had been very busy the week before. He had to purchase an officer's uniform and his pilot's wings and all the insignia that came with being a Second Lieutenant. As he sat on the bunk tying his shoes, he paused and leaned back. He began to wonder what things were like back at home. He had been away for eighteen months! Phil began to reminisce about his life before the war. He remembered the day when he was lying on the front porch, at home, reading his Buck Rogers comic book, and dreaming of being a pilot. Now he finally was a pilot. He recalled the good times at Cash Corner, the dancing, the girls, the way a cold RC Cola felt as it slid down his throat on a hot, July day. He thought about how much work he and Roland and George put into bringing back to life the old Model T they named "The Silver Bullet." A lump grew in Phil's throat and he felt a tear trickle from the corner of his eye. Best of all, he remembered the day he first met Linda. That memory brought a grin to his face. She was the prettiest girl in the world.

A shout from a buddy brought Phil back to reality. "Hey, pal. Let's get going. It's almost time to graduate."

Phil quickly finished dressing and went out to where his squadron was assembling for their final march to the auditorium.

After a rather long speech by the commanding officer, the time came for each cadet to receive his commission and appointment as an officer in the Air Corps. Phil was so proud and excited as he started across the stage that he stumbled a bit at the top step. He regained his composure and stepped up to the C.O. to receive his papers and the government issue pilot's wings for his uniform. The C.O. congratulated Phil on his fine performance, then reached for the next set of papers. Phil returned to his seat with a huge feeling of exhilaration. He had done it. His dream was coming true! The only thing missing was someone from home to share this moment with him.

Suddenly, the last cadet marched across the stage and the band began to play "Off We Go Into The Wild Blue Yonder." All the cadets joined in singing the song at the tops of their lungs. When it was finished, the cadets threw their new officers' caps high in the air, following a tradition established many years before. Bedlam resulted as the new pilots celebrated and tried to find another cap that would fit their head.

Phil finally found a cap that would fit. He quickly reached inside and removed the wire ring that held the rigid shape of the top. By doing this the sides of the cap would flop down. The Air Corps pilots called it the hot pilot look and it distinguished pilots from ground officers. It was now a tradition of Air Corps pilots.

The next day, Phil hoisted his duffel bag onto the bus that was headed for the train station, and home.

Chapter Twenty-eight

It was a warm sunny day on May 26, 1944 as Phil's train pulled into the station at Selma, North Carolina. It had been a long and dirty train ride from Houston. The soot from the steam engine would blow in through the windows at times when the windows were open. Phil had tried to keep his windows closed as much as he could but at times it was too hot inside the cars so he had to open them.

As the train pulled into the station, Phil looked out to see if he could see anyone. He had called his father and Linda the day before and told them when he would be arriving at Selma. The station was nearly deserted, but just then he saw Daddy Barkley near the ticket office. And there was George! It looked as if he had grown a foot since Phil had seen him last!

Phil jumped down from the passenger car and hurried over to hug his father tightly.

"It's great to see you son!" his father exclaimed. "And congratulations. I know how happy you must feel. You've always wanted to fly and now you're a pilot."

"Hey," shouted George, trying to get a hug from Phil too. "Can you really do a loop-dee-loop Phil?"

Phil squeezed George tightly and laughed. "Sure I can, and a lot of other things as well. But I'll tell you about them later."

"You look good, Son," Daddy Barkley said as they walked toward the car. "You seem a bit taller, but thinner around the middle. I guess they've been feeding you well."

"Yeah," Phil chuckled. "They took off the fat and put on muscle."

Phil loaded his duffel bag into the 39 Plymouth. "Hey, the old Plymouth looks really good, dad."

"She still runs good too. I have to give George most of the credit. He washed and cleaned it this morning. He said it was your graduation present."

"Thanks pal," Phil said to George with a pat on the back. They all piled into the car with Phil behind the steering wheel. In almost no time, they were turning into the lane leading up to the Barkley's home.

"Boy this looks really good to me," Phil sighed. "I can't tell you how many times I thought about these pretty, red crepe myrtle trees beside the white irises. Who added those gorgeous yellow cannas?"

"Your Granny did that last fall," replied Daddy Barkley.

"It's just so beautiful. The house is mighty white. Has someone just painted it?"

"We painted it this spring," George replied. "And the fences too."

"I hired George to help so we could get it all done in one year," Daddy Barkley added.

As Phil pulled the '39 Plymouth up to the front of the house, he saw that his whole family was waiting on the front porch, smiling and waving. He had hardly stopped the car when he flung open the car door and bounded up the steps into their waiting arms.

"Tell us about flying, Phil!" shouted one of the twins.

"Well you go like this." He took his flat hand and made a quick circle around himself. "But I'll tell you all about it later when I have more time. Right now, I can't wait to get cleaned up."

"Yeah, you wouldn't want to go see Linda looking like that," teased Anita.

"Well, hurry and get washed up," Granny Barkley prodded. "I've made you a good lunch and there's no sense in letting it get cold."

"Oh, Anita. Would you press my gabardine officers suit a little. I can't put on these soiled khakis again."

"Sure thing, Phil," she replied, winking at him. "We can't have you going to see Linda with half the dirt of the country on your clothes."

It was late afternoon when Phil parked in front of Linda's house. She was sitting in the swing on the front porch. Phil jumped out of the car and started down the walkway, then stopped for a second. She had started down the steps to meet him. He looked at her and thought how much more beautiful she was than the last time he saw her. She was wearing a pale blue, knee-length summer dress that buttoned up the front. In her hair was a matching bow. Even her hair was different. It had light waves at the top, but she now had blonde curls that just covered her ears. He thought she looked thinner at the waist but her breasts somehow seemed larger. He was entranced by her beauty as she ran toward him. Halfway up the walk, their lips and arms met as the two kissed each other deep and longingly.

"Oh, Phil, I've missed you so," Linda exclaimed with tears of joy on her rosy cheeks.

"Darling," Phil replied, "You just don't know how much I've waited for this moment."

After a hug that seemed to last hours, they made their way up the walk and sat in the swing. A second later, Linda's parents came out the front door to greet and congratulate Phil.

"You really look nice in that uniform, Phil," beamed Mrs. Hinton. "Can you stay for supper?"

"Thanks very much, Mrs. Hinton. That will be very nice."

All through supper, Phil noticed that Mrs. Hinton seemed friendlier to him than she'd ever been before. He felt good about it and looked over at Linda. She smiled back at him.

By the time they finished supper it was almost dark outside. Phil and Linda left her parents and went riding around the countryside to Smithfield and some other places. He was hoping to see some of his old friendS, but found that they were mostly all in the military. Later, they rode out to Holt's Lake, but it was almost deserted since it was a week night. There were a few teenagers in the bowling alley but no one in the dance hall. Phil drove around the lake to a parking place on a knoll that overlooked the water. He and Jim had brought Linda and Strawberry there many times for relaxing, and necking. Just being there brought back a flood of fond memories for Phil. The night was dark, with only a few stars glittering in the sky and reflecting on the rippling waters of the lake. There were no other cars around. When Phil killed the engine, it quickly became very quiet, with only the leaves rustling in an occasional summer breeze. Linda snuggled up close and he held her tightly.

She looked up into his eyes. "I'm so proud of you, Phil. I feel so safe when I'm with you."

"I've missed you so much, darling. You are so beautiful and sweet and I love you so much," Phil cooed.

"Oh, I love you too," she replied, suddenly thrusting her lips upward to meet his.

They kissed hungrily, holding each other in an embrace that neither could break, even if they had wanted. soon Phil was caressing the soft nape of Linda's neck with his lips. Linda's breathing changed from quiet sighing to a series of tiny gasps. Her hands explored the firm muscles in his back and shoulders as she pulled him even closer. As his warm breath brushed her ear lobe, Phil felt Linda's hips nudge him slightly. His hands moved slowly and cautiously down the middle of her back until he reached her bottom. She moaned into his neck as he gently squeezed her buttocks. Phil began to lean his weight toward her, slowly easing them both into a more reclining position. The huge seat of the Plymouth gave them plenty of room and as they reclined, Linda slid her legs under Phil so they became stretched out beside each other with their hips pressing. With her back toward the seat, Phil could no longer massage Linda's firm bottom. As his lips moved further down her neck, Linda's breathing became shallow and more rapid. She seemed to alternate between sighing and gasping for air as Phil caressed her hair and face. He pressed his growing manhood more firmly into her hips only to have her reply with the same motion.

He gently began to unfasten the buttons on her dress. Moments later, as he gently pushed Linda's bra up and over her large, firm breasts, she arched her back toward his hot breath. He gently flicked his tongue across her nipple. A loud moan escaped her lips and her fingernails dug slightly into his back. She swung one leg over his hips and pulled his warm hardness

186

firmly into her longing thighs. As she did, Phil slipped his hand inside the top of her underpants and began slowly working them down over the hips that were beginning to grind against him in a slow, rhythmic motion. When he could move them no further, she lifted her weight and the panties almost slipped down to her thighs. Suddenly, she closed her legs and began to push Phil backwards.

"What's wrong, honey?" he asked, gasping for breath.

"Nothing, Phil," she hurriedly replied. Then, she covered her face with her hands and burst into tears.

Phil hugged her closely and tightly. "Don't worry, Peaches. It's okay."

"I'm sorry," she sobbed. "I want to, but I'm just not ready."

"It's okay," he repeated. "We don't have to do anything. I love you and that's what's important."

"Oh, Phil," she sobbed into his shoulder. "You're so sweet."

"Thanks," he whispered. "It's only because I love you so much."

They held each other for a long time. Finally, Phil gently pushed Linda back, holding her shoulders and looking deeply into her eyes. "Sweet Peaches, will you marry me?" he whispered.

She smiled and nodded her head. Wiping a tear away from her cheek, she laughed and said, "Yes, Phil, I will. I love you so much." They clung to each other tightly in the early summer starlight for an eternity.

It was past midnight when Phil kissed Linda goodnight on her front porch. They held their embrace for long moments, neither wanting the night to end. Phil felt so very happy as he drove home. He was engaged to the most wonderful and beautiful girl in the world! He could hardly wait until they were married. If there was only a way to get rid of the throbbing in his groin tonight!

He went to see her every night that week. They were so happy talking about their future together. One night he said to her, "Sweet Peaches, I can't leave you now. I'll miss you too much. Please come back with me to Midland. We can get married Sunday and leave Monday. Jim and Strawberry are at Wichita, Kansas and they live off base. We can do the same. How about it?"

"Phil, honey, you know how much I want to do that, but I just don't think we can right now. I want to finish school first. Then, I would be able to get a job and work. I would get awfully lonesome with you off flying every day. And what if you are sent overseas? I'd be left alone. I think we should wait awhile. Maybe we will know more about what's going to happen when I graduate from accounting school."

"But sweetheart, that's almost a year," he said anxiously.

"I know, Phil, but we had better wait." She patted his hand. "Listen," she said, changing the subject slightly. "Have you thought of what you want to do when the war is over and you get discharged?"

"Yep," Phil replied. "I would really like to be an airline pilot."

"Oh, Phil," Linda gasped. "That's too dangerous! I couldn't bear the thought of losing you in an accident."

"Don't worry, Peaches. "I'm really careful. It won't happen with me."

"I just don't want to even think about it," she replied. "Couldn't you go to college and get a degree in Engineering or something like that?"

"Well," Phil mused. "Maybe I could study aeronautical engineering. That way I could still work around planes."

"Oh, don't talk about planes, Phil. Every time you mention it, I just picture losing you in a crash!"

He could see that Linda was getting upset so he didn't mention to her that what he really wanted to do was stay in the Air Corps. After much discussion, Linda convinced Phil that they should wait to get married. She had said they could discuss it further when she finished school.

As the week drew to an end, Phil began to worry about something else. He had only been allowed a "B" gas ration coupon when he arrived home, and it was almost gone. He had taken Linda to Smithfield once and had used up most of the rest of the ration traveling back and forwards to her house all week. Since a "B" ration was only five gallons of gas, Phil knew he was taking a chance of running out of gas. But it was Saturday and he badly wanted to see Linda. He decided to take his chances. He could always walk home.

Phil and his father were sitting on the front porch after lunch, discussing the war and the government's rationing program.

"It's been pretty tough on us here at home, son," Daddy Barkley replied to Phil's question about how things had been around the farm. "You know about the gasoline. But they are also rationing coffee, sugar, tires, and meat. You even have to have a stamp to get shoes. I guess we are lucky compared to our city friends since we can raise our own meats. But it's the tires and gasoline that causes us the worst problems. Those tires on the old pickup truck are still fairly good but the tires on the Plymouth are about shot. I could get some tires on the black market, but I hate what those people are doing. I'd rather go without something than to buy it from them."

"Well, I'm proud of you, dad." Phil responded. "Every time someone buys something from the black market, they take away from the military and they reduce the chances we'll be successful against Hitler and the Japs."

"Have you had any flats yet, son?"

"Yeah, I've had three so far. That reminds me, thanks for putting those blowout shoes in the car. They sure came in nice to cover the holes in the tires when they go flat." Phil chuckled. "One of those tires on the Plymouth has enough blow out shoes in it to almost make two tires in one."

Daddy Barkley laughed. "Sorry about that, son. Listen, how is the gas holding out?"

"I have just about enough to go to see Linda tonight. I may run out on the way home though. I guess I'll have to ride the bike to see her tomorrow."

"Maybe not, son."

"What do you mean?"

"Well, I figured you might need an extra gallon or two while you were home, so I've saved up five gallons by scrimping where I can."

"Hey, dad, that's great! Thanks. But won't you run out?"

"No, son. It's alright because I've just received my "C" ration book for the pickup truck. I'll get by for the rest of the month. Don't you worry. Go on and see your girl."

"You bet," exclaimed Phil. They both laughed at his exuberance.

It didn't take Phil very long to clean up the 39 Plymouth and pour the five gallons of gasoline into its tank. He figured it would be enough to get t? Goldsboro that night, Holt's Lake the next night, and then to the train station and back on Monday.

He picked up Linda before dark and they went to Goldsboro. They ate southern style barbecue at Griffin's Restaurant and then went to a movie. It was late when they returned to Linda's house. They did not want to leave each other so they sat in the car for a long period of time holding each other close. Phil felt very warm and happy as Linda clung to him. He hugged her reassuringly.

"Sweet Peaches, would you like to go to Holt's Lake tomorrow night?" he whispered.

"Yes, honey. Would you?"

"You bet. I'd go anywhere with you," he replied.

Late the next afternoon, Phil said his goodbyes to Linda's parents since they would probably be in bed when he and Linda returned that evening. He would be on a train to Texas on Monday and wouldn't see them for a long time. He was a bit surprised that Mrs. Hinton had a tear in her eye as he and Linda left for Holt's Lake.

After a seafood dinner in Smithfield, they arrived at Holt's Lake and went straight to the bowling alley. After a few games, they wandered into the dance hall. There were not many people there so Linda and Phil had the floor practically to themselves.

He went to the jukebox and selected the song, "I couldn't sleep a wink last night." As they danced, Phil held Linda closer than he had all week. They began singing along with the song as they slowly swayed to and fro across the floor.

Linda looked up into Phil's eyes and smiled. "Oh really?"

"Yes, really," he softly chuckled. "How about you?"

"Oh sure, honey. I slept like a log." They both laughed.

When the song ended, someone else had selected a few of Guy Lombardo's records. As they danced to the soothing music, Phil could not help but gaze into Linda's lovely face. Neither said anything. They simply enjoyed being in each other's arms, dancing closely to the sultry music. They both knew it would be their last night together for a long time. Soon, a tear formed in each of Linda's eyes, then rolled down her cheeks.

"Don't worry, sweet peaches. We'll be alright," he whispered.

After awhile they tired of dancing. They climbed into the '39 Plymouth and Phil drove around the lake to their parking spot. It was a clear night with a new moon promising to peek over the tree tops at any minute. There wasn't a cloud in the sky. A million twinkling lights danced across the lake as starlight reflected on the mirrored surface of the water. Only the sadly sweet cry of the whippoorwill broke the dark, restful silence.

"Looks like diamonds in the water, doesn't it?" Phil whispered.

"Yes, darling. Its absolutely beautiful here."

"Its so peaceful too," he added.

Suddenly, Linda pulled his face to hers and kissed him hard. He closed his arms around her and eagerly returned her kiss. His lips continued down her neck and back up to her tender ear lobes. She began moaning and stroking her fingers through Phil's hair. He responded as he had their first night together overlooking the lake. Before long, her dress was unbuttoned again. Soon, Phil was tugging her panties against her hips again. This time, they slid around her knees. Linda responded by gently tugging at the top of Phil's pants. Seconds later, his knees were uncovered as well. As their lips met for a long, passionate kiss. She gasped for breath and opened her eyes. He gazed lovingly, but questioningly, into the moonlight that danced across her deep blue eyes. A tiny, loving smile was her silent reply. In another second, Phil discovered to his delight that Linda was a virgin. Moments later, their hot, shallow breathing turned to groans of ecstasy as Phil's love exploded inside her.

A short while later, as their embrace relaxed, Phil gazed lovingly into Linda's eyes. She smiled back at him and they pressed their lips together lightly. The moon had cleared the trees and now flooded the car with a pale, romantic glow. "I love you so much, Phil," she whispered.

It was after midnight when Phil pulled the car into Linda's

190

driveway. As Phil stopped at the front door, Linda held him tightly. "I don't want you to leave me, darling."

"I don't want to leave, honey. But you know I must."

"I know," she replied. "I won't forget tonight."

"I won't either," he cooed into her ear. "It's still not too late to come with me to Texas."

"Oh, Phil. Don't spoil the night with that. I mean, we've talked about it enough. Part of me wants to come with you, but we both know that its best if I stay here now."

"I know, sweetheart." They held each other tightly for a few more moments of silence. Finally, Phil kissed her and backed away, down the steps and onto the sidewalk.

He drove home slowly, thinking about what tonight had meant for both of them. It was surely the happiest night of his life. She had proved that she loved him more than anyone else in the world. But he still wanted her beside him as his wife though. A half-hour later, Phil crawled into bed, weary but not able to sleep. It only seemed like an hour later when Granny Barkley knocked on his door.

"Wake up, Phil. Get dressed and pack your bags. By the time you eat breakfast, it will be time to leave for the train station."

"Oh no!," Phil exclaimed as he jumped out of bed. "Not already."

Chapter Twenty-nine

It was June 5, 1944, by the time Phil arrived at Midland, Texas. He went to Headquarters to check in and get his orders. He was assigned a room in the Bachelor Officers Quarters and told to report each morning to the war orientation room. Then he was to go to the bomb sight training building and take a two week ground course in bombardier training. Early the next morning he reported to the war orientation room. As he entered the room, he noticed the officers were all excited. He asked one of the pilots what was going on.

"It's D-Day," exclaimed the young man. "The Allies had invaded Europe at Normandy."

"Hey, that's great," replied Phil excitedly. "How's it going?"

"Don't know for sure yet. They are reporting a lot of casualties, but they are on the beach and there is heavy fighting."

The Commanding officer called for attention. Okay fellahs, and especially you new guys here. I just want to remind you that the information you hear in this room is restricted. It is not to be repeated outside this room until the civilian news media has reported it. Carry on."

Later Phil left the war orientation room and reported for bombardier training. He was shown the Nordan and Sperry bomb sights and was given instruction on their operation. Inside the building they had built several tall metal framed tripods. On the top was a seat and a bomb sight. The bomb sight operated electric motors attached to wheels on the bottom of the legs of the tripod. A student sitting in the seat and operating the bombsight could move the tripod over small targets painted on the floor. This would simulate a plane on a bombing run.

Phil made good marks on the ground test and was checked out in the AT-11 Bombardier and Navigator training plane. Later Phil began flying missions with bombardier cadets. He found that it was not much fun to have to fly straight and level for prolonged periods. He had noticed a new looking single engine AT-6 advanced trainer plane parked in front of the operations office. It looked like it would be fun to fly and do aerobatics in so he decided to ask the operations officer about it. He told Phil that it was sent to the base so that pilots that were still on flying status and had been assigned ground duty, could maintain their four hours per month flying time. All pilots had to get a minimum of four hours flying time per month in order to get their flight pay. He said that the AT 6 could also be used to bone up on aerobatics.

"Say, how about me flying it?" asked Phil.

"Sure," replied the operations officer. "But I will have to

check you out in it first."

"When can we do that?" Phil asked, excitedly.

"Well Lieutenant, you will have to get in line. Just sign the register here."

Phil quickly signed the register and in a few days, the operations officer called him. Phil liked flying the AT-6. It was faster than anything he had flown and did aerobatics real well.

One morning later, Phil went to the war orientation room early. He had been keeping up with the war news and was encouraged since the invasion was successful. There was heavy fighting in France. This morning there came some shocking news. Hitler was now sending robot bombs to bomb England. They had evidently been able to develop rockets and were installing wings and tails on them and sending them to targets in England. They were doing a lot of damage and everyone was very concerned. Phil was warned again that this information was top secret and not to be discussed.

He stayed in the war orientation room until the war status about the Philippines was announced. It reported that the U.S. was now bombing Japan with B-29 Superfortress and that there was real heavy fighting in the Philippine Islands. It was reported that large casualties were being inflicted on both sides. The war news was about over when Phil started thinking about what to do Saturday. He decided that he would go with some of his new buddies to Odessa and have a few beers.

The Midland Air Base was located about half way between Midland and Odessa, Texas. They were both small rural towns. Most of the owners and oil field management personnel lived in Midland while most of the oil well workers and cowboys lived in Odessa. Phil liked to go to Odessa because there was more action there. There were more bars and dance places there than in Midland. But sometimes, the action grew a bit rough. one Saturday afternoon, he and a friend had just arrived in Odessa. They were walking across the railroad track that goes down the center of main street when suddenly gun shots rang out nearby. They ducked down in between a couple of parked cars and peeked around to see what was happening. Phil saw a cowboy hiding behind a light pole in front of a bar shooting at someone across the railroad tracks. Another cowboy was hiding behind a pickup truck shooting back at him. The two cowboys had fired several shots when two police cars came roaring up the street. The two cowboys stopped shooting and fled on foot. The police jumped out and gave chase. Phil did not stick around to find out if they were caught or not. He and his friend when back up to the main part of town where they felt safer.

The next day, Phil left the war orientation room with his friend and went towards the flight operations office. There he saw a friend, Ben Miller. "Say, Ben, since I don't have anything else scheduled for today, I think that I will check out the AT-6 and have some fun doing aerobatics. Won't you come with me?"

"Sure, would like to Phil but I've got a bombardier training flight to do today. Maybe next week. Hey, you busy tomorrow night?"

"Yeah, Ben. All filled up with go and nowhere to go," laughed Phil. "You know, this is about the deadest place I've been stationed yet. Except maybe Bonham, but I didn't have any time to mess around much there."

Ben looked at Phil and grinned. "I know what you mean Pal. I would be mighty bored if I didn't have Sue with me. Say, how about you come over and have dinner with us tomorrow night? Sue enjoys your visits. She says you are funny."

"Hey, thanks Ben, that's nice of you. Maybe a game of horseshoes tomorrow afternoon?" Phil loved to play horseshoes. He had become good at it when a teenager and it brought back memories playing with Roland and George.

"You bet. Come as early as you can," replied Ben.

The two friends shook hands and Phil continued on to the flight operations office. He signed out the AT 6 for local flying and soon took off down the runway. As soon as the plane left the runway, he lifted the wheels up switch and headed up into the clear blue sky. He liked the way the AT 6 handled. It was smoother and lots faster than the old Vultee vibrator BT-13.

He soon climbed to 10,000 feet of altitude and started doing aerobatics. He did snap rolls, slow rolls, lazy eights, tail spins, slip stalls, and high speed vertical turns. Once in a high speed turn, he exceeded the red line on the air speed indicator and felt the plane start into a high speed stall. He quickly pulled back on the throttle and recovered. This scared him an little but it taught him the feel of a pending high speed stall. It was exciting to him to see and feel the reaction of aircraft when flying at the maximum speed allowed.

It was when he was doing a loop that he noticed a thunderstorm building off to the west. He decided to see if the AT-6 could climb to the top of it so he pushed the throttle forward and started climbing. When he reached 16,000 feet he was still climbing but was not at the top of the thunderstorm. The top of the thunderstorm had a flat cap that looked kind of like a rooster comb. Flying under it gave him an eerie feeling. Suddenly, Phil noticed a tickling, itchy feeling in his knee caps. Then he noticed that his finger nails were turning purple. Uh oh, I'm not getting enough oxygen and this plane is not equipped with oxygen masks, he thought. I had better get down as quickly as I can. He put the AT-6 in a power dive and leveled off at 8,000 feet. Phil knew he had been lucky not to pass out. He was glad he had remembered the effects of low oxygen from his high altitude pressure chamber training at Ellington Field.

He looked out over the wing of his plane towards Midland Air Base. He noticed that there were thunderstorms everywhere and they were almost too close around the base. He knew that he had been taught not to fly in thunderstorms if he could help it so he headed for the air field as fast as the AT-6 could go. He landed the plane and hurried to the flight operations office as the storms closed in on the field. As he hurried up the steps to the Flight operations office, there came a bright flash of lightening and a huge clap of thunder.

Phil turned around and saw an AT-11 plane that was just about to land suddenly dive into the runway and explode in a huge fireball. The lightening bolt must have struck the plane! He ran inside the operations office yelling that a plane had crashed. The operations personnel already had heard and seen the plane crash. Ambulances and fire trucks were already rushing to the scene. Phil looked out the window at the wreckage. It looked as of the plane had been blown into small pieces. The largest part of the plane that he could see in the smoke and debris was the rudder. It was sitting upright on the side of the runway.

The operations officer said that the crash personnel had reported that there were no survivors. The pilot had previously reported that he had canceled the bombing training mission and was returning to the base on account of bad weather. He reported he still had eight of the 100 pound bombs left on board along with 4 bombardier cadets. Phil thought of his friend that was supposed to have flown a bombardier training mission that day.

"Do you know who the pilot was?" he asked the ops officer.

"Yes, it was a Lieutenant Ben Miller."

Phil's knees buckled under him. In shock and dismay, he sank down into a nearby chair.

"Did you know him?" asked the officer.

"Yes, we had become good friends. He has a wife in town. They had only been married a short time. Just this morning, he had invited me over for dinner tomorrow night." Tears came streaming out of Phil's eyes and he choked and quit talking. The operations officer patted him on the shoulder.

"I'm real sorry, Lieutenant."

Phil covered his face with is hands trying to block the scene of the crash out of his mind. He thought of Sue. He knew that they would be notifying her soon and she was by herself. She would be devastated. Someone needed to be there. Phil hurried to his barracks. He knew he must go help her if he could. He quickly dressed and called a taxi. This was no time to wait on a bus.

Ben and Sue had rented one side of a duplex apartment in Midland. As Phil's taxi pulled up in front of the apartment, he saw two Air Corps officers leaving. He knew they had just notified her about Ben. Phil hurried up to the door. Sue opened the door crying profusely. She saw Phil and grabbed him. He held her and let her cry on his shoulder for awhile. Finally, he was able to tell her about seeing the crash. He told her that it was not Ben's fault. The lightening bolt had just happened at the wrong instant.

After Sue calmed a little, he asked her what the officers had to say. She told him that they had said that the military would fly her with Ben's body back to Minneapolis on Monday, if she could be ready by that time. She had told them she could. Phil stayed with her until bedtime and came back on Saturday to help her pack and ship their belongings back home on the train.

The next few months Phil tried to get Ben's crash out of his mind. He flew every extra volunteer mission that he could. He spent a lot of his time on the firing range shooting the M-1 rifle, the 45 pistol and the Thompson machine gun. A lot of nights he wrote letters to Linda. He sure missed her badly. He told her about Ben's crash. In each of her return letters, she warned Phil to be careful. She was so scared that something would happen to him.

Later, Phil was doing the night bombing flights for the cadets. The night was dark with hardly any stars visible in the sky. He had climbed his plane with 10 one hundred pound bombs and four bombardier cadets to 10,000 feet altitude and had leveled off.

Suddenly there came a glowing bluish white light that lit up the whole cockpit. Phil turned his head and looked into the bombay compartment where there were ten, one-hundred pound practice bombs hanging. He saw that the top dome light in the bombay had shorted out and long streaks of fire was shooting down and touching one of the bombs. He yelled to the student cadet in the co-pilot's seat.

"Hey! Go back there and yank those loose wires from that light. See how they are exposed? Yank them loose with your hand! Hurry! Do it now!"

The cadet just sat there looking at the arcing light. He was frozen with fright. Phil shouted to the student cadet seated in the nose of the plane at the bomb sight. He was staring back up at Phil with his mouth open, his face was ashen. Phil yelled to the two students in the rear of the plane. They did not move either. He knew that bomb was growing warmer. Someone had to do something.

In a flash, he unbuckled his safety belt, slipped out of his bulky parachute harness and rushed through the narrow doors of the bomb bay compartment leaving the airplane controls unattended. He yanked at the wires. They would not come loose. He started twisting and yanking at the wires with both hands and all his weight. Sparks shot all around. Suddenly the wires came loose and the arcing fire ceased. He rushed back to his seat and grabbed the controls. The plane had gone into a steep spiral dive. Phil kicked hard right rudder and pulled back on the control wheel as hard as he could. The spinning lights on the ground slowed and stopped. He saw four red lights flash by just under the plane. He knew he had just missed hitting the air base radio control tower. He realized just how close he had just come to crashing his plane. Sweat popped out on his face as he leaned back in his seat breathing hard. He landed the plane as quickly as possible. He worried that something else would happen to it. As they sat on the runway, after the engines had died, Phil realized that both of his hands were burned and had blisters on them. He jumped out of his seat and began screaming at the cadets.

"Mister, the next time I tell you to move, you had better move or I'll have you washed out of this program! Do you understand?!"

After his tirade, Phil made his way to the hospital to get his hands treated. Then, he returned to the operations office to complete the accident report.

Phil was given a few days off duty to let his hands heal. While waiting around, his thoughts were about Linda more than ever. His heart ached for her nearness more than ever. Another letter came from her.

Dear Phil:

I received your letter today. It is night here in Raleigh and I am so lonesome. Honey, I miss you so very much that I can hardly stand it. I dream of our last night together. It was so wonderful.

Honey, I am so sorry about your friend, Ben. I know they meant a lot to you. It was nice for you to help Sue like you did. I love you because it's you.

I hope your hands heal fast too. I know how bad you want to get back to flying.

Phil, please be extra careful. Don't fly unless you have to. It's too dangerous and I'm scared for you. I will be lost if something would happen to you.

Love,

Linda

The weeks began to drag by for Phil. He had gotten used to flying bombardier and navigator cadets and it was repetitious. Now it was getting boring to him. Phil got to thinking about some of his friends that had graduated with him. Most of them were now overseas. He wished he was. Some of his buddies were now flying B-29 bombers attacking Japan. General MacArthur had returned to the Philippines and some of his friends were being sent there. He had been at Midland for almost four months when one day in September, he was reading notices on the bulletin board in the flight operations office. One of the notices caught his eye. It read, "Volunteers wanted for overseas training in B-26 aircraft!" He became excited and called to the flight operations officer.

"Sir, what about this? Why do they want volunteers for the B-26?"

"Well Lieutenant, in case you don't know, the B-26 is a twin engine low level attack bomber. It has a cigar shaped fuselage, short wing spans, and a couple of powerful 2,000 horsepower engines on it. It is called the Flying Prostitute. No visible signs of support, if you know what I mean. It is said that it takes off and lands at approximately 140 miles per hour and is hard to fly. It won't fly on one engine alone. You have to have both to stay in the air. Now my friend, are you still interested?"

"Don't know. I might be," replied Phil, thinking that flying there was dull. It might be interesting. He wanted to go overseas anyway.

"Why the call for volunteers, Sir?"

"Well, they've been testing her out on the coast of Europe and she is reported to have a very high mortality rate. You still interested?"

"Sure, anything to get out of this place. Ah, who do you have to see?"

"Well, it's your ass and not mine! You'll have to go to the personnel office. They'll fix you up."

Chapter Thirty

October 3, 1943

Dear Peaches,

> *Well, here I am in Dodge City, Kansas . . . the cowboy capital of the world! This is where I will complete my training for the B-26. The land out here is so flat, it's a wonder they don't have airplane training facilities all over the place!*
> *This is a very interesting place, with a lot of history about the old, "Wild West." Believe it or not, there are still a lot of people out here who dress like cowboys! I've enclosed some pictures I took over the weekend while visiting some of the sights around town.*
> *First, I went to the Atchison, Topeka and Santa Fe railroad station. They have a restored area with old restaurants where the waitresses, who are called "Harvey Girls," wear costumes like the dresses they used to wear fifty or sixty years ago. Then, I went to the famous Boot Hill cowboy cemetery. The pictures of tombstones were taken there. The next time I have a day off, I plan to visit old Fort Dodge.*
> *Guess who I got a letter from? Jim and Strawberry! They are stationed in Wichita, a town that is about 150 miles east of Dodge City. If I can catch a ride with someone, I'll go visit them soon.*
> *Well, it is almost time for "lights out" and I need to get a good night's sleep. Tomorrow, I actually get to climb into a B-26 and see what the controls are like.*
> *I love you, Peaches, and I can't wait to see you again.*

> *Phil*

Over the next two weeks, Phil worked hard on familiarizing himself with every aspect of the B-26. It was a hot plane with tight handling. Phil found that he liked the quick response of the controls and the feeling of pure power surging through the sturdily built aircraft when all its engines were revving at takeoff speed. Somehow, it reminded him of the feeling he used to have driving around in the Silver Bullet. But Phil also knew that this was an aircraft to be greatly respected. Besides having the nickname, "Flying Prostitute", the plane was also known as the "Widowmaker" because so many pilots had been killed while trying to learn to fly it.

Phil liked his instructor and the six other trainees in his group. They had all volunteered for this training and had similar personalities. So it wasn't long before they all became close friends. One of the guys had a car. His name was Tom Grogan and he was from Beaver Falls, Pennsylvania. When Phil proposed that they spend a weekend in Wichita, Tom and a few of the others readily agreed. The following Saturday morning, they set out around seven o'clock and arrived in Wichita just before eleven. Tom dropped Phil off in front of Jim Kelford's apartment building and arranged to be back Sunday afternoon.

Phil was greeted by strong hugs from his old high school friends, who both grinned from ear to ear.

"Phil, you look great!" said Strawberry.

"And you haven't changed a bit," Phil replied. "As beautiful as ever!"

"Stop making goo-goo eyes at my wife and come on in." said Jim as he slapped Phil on the back. "I see the Air Corps has been treating you well, old buddy."

"Yeah, I can't complain," said Phil. He backed away from Jim one step and patted his friend on the stomach. "And I see you haven't been missing any meals lately."

"Well, I can't help it if I'm married to the best cook in the whole state of Kansas, can I?" Jim gave Strawberry a reassuring hug and a little pat on her backside.

They all laughed together, then sat in the tiny living room recounting all they had been through in the past few months. By one o'clock, they had caught up on all the news each other had to share and even finished off the sandwiches Strawberry had made for lunch.

"I have an idea," Jim started. "Why don't we go out to a nice restaurant tonight, and maybe a nightclub afterwards? There's lots to do here, Phil, what with all the aircraft plant workers and Air Corps personnel in town. What do you say?"

"Sure, Jim. That's a great idea! I'm ready for some excitement after spending a few weeks in Dodge City."

"Phil, would you mind if we invite a friend?" Strawberry asked. "You know, just to make it a foursome."

"Why not?" Phil replied. "The more, the merrier, right?"

"You bet, pal." said Jim, slapping Phil on the knee.

"Anybody I know?" Phil asked.

"I guess that depends on how much you read the papers," Strawberry replied. "She was Miss Wichita and first runner-up in the Miss Kansas beauty contest last year."

"Wow," Phil responded.

"See, she lives down the hall, and she's really a good friend of mine. She lost her husband, who was a Navy pilot a couple of months ago. He was killed in the Philippines. It has almost devastated her life. She's so depressed lately. You have such a great personality, and when we heard you were coming, we thought you would be the perfect person to cheer her up some."

"Well, I'll do the best I can," Phil replied, wondering just what he was getting himself into. "You know I can't refuse you anything, Strawberry."

"Great!" said Jim. "You won't be sorry, old buddy." Jim winked at Phil and grinned.

Later that afternoon, when they were all ready to leave, a knock came at the door and Jim answered.

"Jean, this is one of my old high school buddies, Phil Barkley," Jim begins his introductions. "Phil, I'd like for you to meet Jean Collier."

As she stepped into the small apartment, Phil got his first glimpse of the prettiest girl he'd ever seen, besides Linda. Jean Collier had dark, wavy hair that hung in curls, just below her ears, and framed her sharply featured face. As he gazed into her sparkling, greenish-blue eyes, Phil realized that she was almost his height. Her cream-colored dress hugged the curves of her trim body in all the right places. When she smiled and extended her hand, Phil realized he'd been staring.

"Uh, nice to meet you," was all he could manage to say.

"She won't bite, Phil," Jim snickered.

They shared a nervous chuckle at Jim's remark. Phil suddenly felt guilty, realizing that he'd been comparing Linda to Jean. Linda has larger breasts, he thought, but this girl is much prettier. And what a shape! No wonder she was a beauty queen.

Around five o'clock, the foursome walked through the front doors of the J.C. Penney department store in downtown Wichita. It was a large, six-story building that took up almost an entire city block. Jim and Strawberry suggested that they split up for a while as he wasn't interested in women's clothing and she wasn't interested in hardware or sporting goods. Since the store had a well recommended restaurant, they all decided to meet there for supper at six-thirty.

"Isn't she a fine looking filly?" Jim asked Phil after the women were a few feet away.

"Sure is," Phil replied. "But I see what Strawberry means about her being depressed. I've been trying to talk to her since we left your apartment, and haven't gotten one good conversation off the ground yet."

"Oh, don't worry about her, buddy. She'll warm up to that old Barkley charm sooner or later."

"I guess you're right, pal. By the way, this isn't some kind of fix-up date is it?"

"Are you kidding? Strawberry knows you and Linda are still together. Hell, she and Linda write to each other about once a month. In fact, I wouldn't be surprised if Linda knew all about Jean. I mean, not about us going out this weekend, but about Jean being a beauty queen and losing her husband and all."

Phil felt a minor surge of panic sweep over him. What if Linda did know about Jean Collier? Would she suspect something if he didn't write about her in his next letter? How much should

201

he tell Linda about this weekend in Wichita? And, if Linda thought something was going on between him and Jean, would that give Eddie a chance to turn her away from him?

"Hey pal, relax. Strawberry and I are chaperoning the whole evening. You know we're not going to get you in trouble with your girl." He put his arm around Phil's shoulder and they walked off toward the sporting goods department. Phil wondered if Jim could read his mind, or if his worry simply showed that much on his face.

Later, as they sat together in the restaurant, Phil decided to just enjoy himself and not worry about Linda. He told himself nothing was going to happen that he would be ashamed to tell his sweet Peaches. He was just visiting friends in Wichita and doing them a favor by cheering up one of their other friends, who happened to be very pretty and who happened to be a woman.

"Jim, I'm kind of short on money," he began joking. "Could you loan me fifty dollars?"

"But I only have thirty dollars," Jim replied.

Phil delivered the punch line. "Well, give me the thirty and you can owe me twenty." They both laughed hardily. Phil looked at Jean, who got the joke and laughed a half-second later than Strawberry. He decided she had a pretty laugh, almost sexy. He would enjoy cheering up this ex-beauty queen.

Strawberry pitched in. "Say Phil, have you been doing much high flying lately?"

"Now, Strawberry, you know pilots aren't allowed to drink before they get behind the stick." Another laugh from the former Miss Wichita. Phil felt as if Jean was beginning to relax and enjoy herself.

Suddenly, Jean asked Phil what kind of work he did in the Army Air Corps. He told her all about the B-26 and how it reminded him of the Silver Bullet. Jim chimed in by poking good-natured fun at Phil's old automobile. Jean laughed when Jim revealed that the car had no top and how, on more than one occasion Phil was drenched in a spring rain while driving home from a baseball game. of course, Phil knew this was an exaggeration, but he played along because Jim was having some success at helping cheer up this young, beautiful widow. As his buddy was going on and on about the old jalopy, Phil found himself staring at every detail of Jean's face. She had a complexion most babies would be jealous of, and the straightest set of dazzlingly white teeth. He nervously glanced back at him the second time she caught him staring at her.

That evening, as Phil was making the sofa into his bed for the night, Strawberry came into the living room.

"Phil, I want to thank you for making such a fun evening. Jean told me she had a wonderful time."

Phil felt sort of embarrassed. "I was glad to help. She seems

202

like such a nice girl and it's such a pity that she has to be a widow at such a young age. I'm just glad she felt comfortable enough around me to laugh and enjoy herself."

"You're so sweet." Strawberry leaned over and kissed Phil on the cheek. "Goodnight, Phil."

As he lay on the sofa, trying to go to sleep, Phil tried to think of Linda, but the image of Jean's laughing face kept creeping into his mind.

Chapter Thirty-one

After Phil had completed his B-26 training, he was transferred to Frederick, Oklahoma to learn to fly the new A-26 attack bomber. He arrived at the base after lunch on January 2, 1945 and went directly to the commanding officer of the Air Base to report for duty.

The C.O. welcomed him to the base. He explained to Phil about the operations and that it was primarily a base to train French pilots to fly B-26 and B-25 airplanes and to train U.S. pilots to fly the new A-26 low level twin engine attack bomber. It also had a test flight maintenance unit which tested twin engine aircraft and a few single engine aircraft for the Air Corps.

He requested Phil's transfer orders so Phil handed them to him. After he read Phil's orders, he looked at Phil and said, "Lieutenant, it will be a good while before we can train you for overseas duty in the A-26 so I'll assign you to training these French students."

A look of surprise washed over Phil's face. "But, sir, I don't like instructing and besides, I have a letter from the Commanding General of Central Flying Training Command to train for overseas duty in the A-26." He had not expected this turn of events.

"Well Lieutenant, you will have to understand that I have Captains and Majors on that list and they also have letters from the Commanding General. You will have to await your turn. Any further questions?"

"Yes, sir, I understand sir." The look of dejection on Phil's face must have been evident, because after a brief pause, the C.O. looked back up at Phil and sighed.

"Alright, Lieutenant Barkley, if you will report back to me at thirteen hundred hours tomorrow, I will review your personnel file and see if I can come up with anything else for you to do. Dismissed!"

"Yes, sir, I'll be here sir."

Phil saluted the Colonel and went to the Bachelor Officers Quarters where he was assigned to a small room in one of the buildings. His room consisted of a bunk bed and a chest of drawers. The former occupant had left a mirror over the chest of drawers and a large pinup poster of Betty Grable on the wall. He looked at the picture for a minute and decided to let it stay. She was a beautiful and shapely movie star, and besides it gave him a feeling of not being so lonely. Also, she kind of reminded him of Linda.

As he continued to unpack his things and tidy up his room, he could not help from worrying about his status. He tried to think of what the Colonel would find for him to do. He surely did not want to be an instructor. That was too boring and was also very dangerous.

The next day, Phil reported back to the C.O. at thirteen hundred hours. The Colonel put him at ease and told him to have a seat. "Lieutenant Barkley, I have reviewed your records and I believe I've come up with something in which you may be interested. That is, your records show that you are well qualified for it."

Phil's face brightened with interest. "Yes sir?" he replied with sudden anticipation in his voice.

"Lieutenant, how would you like to join our test fight maintenance unit?"

Phil's mouth dropped open. "Ah, do you mean, ah, I'd be a test pilot, sir?"

"That's exactly what I mean, Lieutenant."

"Well, sure. Sure I would." Phil tried to hold back his excitement. He could hardly, believe what he was hearing.

"Lieutenant, you realize that its a very hazardous job and you will have to be very careful. It takes luck, talent, and quick thinking, to be able to come out of some of the situations that will occur while testing airplanes. I have reviewed your records along with Colonel Doakes, the C.O. of the Test Flight Maintenance Unit, and we concluded that you posses the qualities to be in the Test Flight Unit.

"But I must warn you Lieutenant, you will be testing some pretty ragged airplanes at times. You see, here at Frederick we test planes returning from overseas duty. These are planes that have flown their assigned number of missions and are sent back here to be used in training. They have to be tested first in order to see what is wrong with them and what modifications may be needed to prepare them for training purposes. Right now we are getting back B-25's and B-26's medium bombers, and occasionally some fighters. We don't test any larger aircraft at this base. But we also test new aircraft from the manufacturer, mostly the new A-26 Invaders. And, we have to test any plane that goes to the shops for repair or modification. We are not allowed to place any aircraft back in service until it has been thoroughly tested by the Test Flight Maintenance Unit."

"Excuse me, sir, but do you test single engine fighter planes here:" Phil was thinking how he missed flying in a single engine plane and doing aerobatics.

"Oh no, Lieutenant. That is mostly done at fighter bases. But we do have three P-51 Mustangs here that are used for our ground duty pilots to get their flying time in and to bone up on their aerobatics. Occasionally we have to test them when there has been some repairs accomplished on them."

"Oh, I see sir." Phil was not ready to give up yet on getting at one of those Mustangs. He'd find a way.

"Well then, Lieutenant, I'll have your assignment orders cut this afternoon and you can report to Colonel Doakes at the Flight Test Maintenance Unit in the morning at o-eight-hundred hours. You are dismissed "

"Thank you, sir!" Phil saluted as he snapped to attention. He almost skipped back to his quarters. He was very excited about being assigned to the Test Flight Unit. He could hardly wait to write and tell Linda of his good news. He also dropped off a note to home and to George.

The next morning Phil reported to the Test Flight Unit right on time. The secretary told him that he would have to wait a while since the Colonel was busy giving out the days assignments to the pilots. Phil sat down to wait. Time seemed to drag by to Phil but after about thirty minutes the buzzer on the secretary's desk sounded and she told him that he could go on in. Phil entered the office and saluted the Colonel.

"Lieutenant Philip Barkley reporting as ordered, sir." He noted that the Colonel sitting behind the desk was a tall, but stocky looking man. He looked as if he could lift a B-26 by himself. He had red hair and blue eyes with a ruddy complexion on his face that was sprinkled with a few freckles. The expression on his face appeared to Phil as if he was about to laugh. It seemed to him that this was a happy man.

"At ease, Lieutenant, and welcome. Please have a seat. I am Colonel G. F. Doakes and I want to welcome you to our unit. Say, what do they call you, besides Lieutenant, I mean?"

"My friends call me Phil, sir."

"Well Phil, here we call each other by our first names. We're kind of like a family. We are a pretty close knit unit. If we have problems either personal or with flying, we let them out and try to handle them ourselves. We do not keep secrets. It seems that everything works better that way. How do you feel about that?"

"Sounds great, sir! That's the way I like to do things too."

"Great!" the Colonel's voice boomed across his desk. "Well Phil, beginning tomorrow, you will fly as co-pilot with Captain Cooper and his crew. After one week of training with them, you'll learn our testing procedures for medium bombers. When you finish that, I will have a creW assigned to you. You see, here we have the same people assigned to a crew. It works better that way. You will have a co-pilot, a crew chief to test the mechanical equipment, and a radio operator to check the radio equipment. These men will remain with you and be your regular crew. It Will be up to you to make them into a top notch flight test crew. I expect top quality work from my crews. They have to be top quality to keep my accident ratio down and right now, my unit is rated near the top in the Air Corps." The Colonel leaned back in his desk chair. "What do you think, son? Do you think you can fit in here?"

"No doubt about it, sir. I am looking forward to serving in your unit and I will try my best to meet your qualifications."

The Colonel looked Phil right in the eyes, smiled and shook his hand. "Welcome to our unit, Phil. Report back here in the morning at eight-hundred hours and I will introduce you to Captain Cooper and you can get started."

After lunch, Phil decided to check in at the war orientation room. The battle of the bulge in France had been going on hot and heavy and he learned that the Allies had repulsed the Germans who were in hot retreat. He felt a little better about the war since it seemed to be turning more and more in the Allies favor.

Phil completed his training with Captain Cooper in test flight procedures and reported back to Colonel Doakes on Monday morning. As he entered the office he noticed that there were three other Air Corps men in the office. Phil walked up to the Colonel's desk and saluted. "Lieutenant Barkley reporting as ordered, sir."

The Colonel flipped a quick return salute. "At ease, gentlemen. Phil, I want you to meet your crew. This is Lieutenant Dan Holmer. He will be your co-pilot."

Phil shook the young man's hand. He guessed they were about the same age, maybe a year apart. They were about his height. Dan had shortly cropped dark hair. He was a clean, sharp looking young man who Phil suspected had just graduated from pilot school.

"This is Linwood Petit," the Colonel continued. "We call him 'Gabby'. After you get to know him, you'll know why," the Colonel laughed.

Gabby reached out to shake Phil's hand. Phil caught the mischievous look in the man's eyes. He appeared to be a few years older than the other two crew members. He was tall and slender with a sharply pointed nose. But his most striking feature was a grin that was bigger than any Phil had ever seen before.

"Gabby has been with us for quite some time and has decided that he might like to fly a little. I think he will make you a good radio operator because he already knows how to check them out," stated Colonel Doakes. "Finally," he continued, "meet Johnny Carlton, your crew chief."

"Glad to meet you, Johnny," Phil said as they shook hands.

The Colonel kept talking. "Johnny here does a great job. He never fails to come when he's called, especially at meal times."

Johnny grinned back at the Colonel and patted his belly. He knew why the Colonel was kidding him, for he was rather short and it was obvious that he liked to eat.

In a few days, Phil and his crew settled into testing planes. It didn't take long for them to become good friends. Phil quickly became confident in them. He was pleased with his crew.

One day they were testing a B-26. He had gone through all his test maneuvers and was flying along straight and level, headed back toward the base. He was sitting back in his seat relaxed and humming a tune. Suddenly, the right engine sped up real fast like it was running away. Phil quickly ran through the single engine procedures as he had been taught in training. The quicker you can get the engine killed, the propeller feathered, and the plane trimmed, the better it is and the longer you can stay in the air. Phil quickly observed that all the gauges and instruments were okay and that the engine seemed to run smoothly even with the propeller feathered. With the propeller feathered, the blades were turned straight to the wind and the engine would not turn over unless it was running.

Phil looked at Dan sitting in the co-pilot's seat. He had a smile on his face and was nodding his head towards the rear of the plane. He looked around into the bombay compartment. There stood Gabby Petit in the bombay with his right hand above his head. He was holding onto the cable that controls the propeller pitch for the right engine. He was bursting with laughter. Phil realized then that he had been tricked. He quickly brought the right engine back into synchronization with the other engine. He glanced back at Gabby and shook his finger at him. They all laughed. Phil cracked a smile. He also realized that the prank was good training for him.

A few days later Colonel Doakes checked Phil out in a B-25 Mitchell Twin engine bomber. He found that he loved the B-25 better than the B-26. It was not as fast as the B-26 but it handled better and unlike the B-26, it would maintain its altitude on one engine. The B-26 will not fly with only one engine. While flying the B-25, Phil found that Colonel Doakes was a jovial type person. He enjoyed telling jokes and kept Phil laughing during most of the flight. He liked Colonel Doakes and got to tell him a few of his jokes also.

The next day, Colonel Doakes asked Phil if he would like to fly a P-51 some. He laughed after looking at the excitement on Phil's face. "Okay, Phil, go get your parachute. And bring mine as well. I'll go get you checked you out."

The next day Phil hurried through his assigned test flights on the B-26 planes and went into the Test Flight Operations Office. He wanted to see if Col. Doakes would let him take a P-51 up for a spin. He had never flown aerobatics in a plane like the P-51 and he was anxious to try it out.

He walked into Col. Doakes office. "Sir, I have finished testing the B-26 plane that you assigned me this morning. Do you have anything else for me to do today?"

The Colonel looked at Phil in amazement. "You mean, you are through already?"

"Yes, sir. I had no problems, sir."

"That's fine Phil. You may be excused for the rest of the day."

"Ah, sir, I was just wondering. Would it be possible for me to take one of the P-51 planes up for a spin?"

The Colonel looked at Phil with a twinkle in his eye and grinned. "Well, I didn't think it would be long before you would be wanting to wing it out. I could tell yesterday that you were just itching for a chance."

"Yes, sir. I do need to bone up on my acrobatics."

"What for, Lieutenant? You are a bomber pilot."

"But sir, I feel that flying acrobatics helps keep my flying senses in touch with a sharp edge."

Colonel Doakes laughed. He was enjoying seeing Phil squirm and trying to make up excuses. "Now Phil, you know that you have to have a valid reason to take up a plane. You know you can't just go take a joy ride, don't you?" The expression on Phil's face quickly changed into one of disappointment. "No, sir. I didn't realize that."

"Well, let me check the roster here and see if I can find anything." The Colonel pulled out the maintenance roster and fingered through it. "Let me see here, there is a P-51 that's in the shop now for a 300 hour inspection. Let me call and check on its status." Phil's face brightened as the Colonel talked on the telephone.

"Well Phil, you're in luck. They have finished with the inspection but just hadn't had time to release it to us yet. You can test hop it if you want to."

"That's great, sir!" blurted out Phil at the news. He almost tripped over his feet in his haste to leave the office.

"Oh Lieutenant, take it easy . . . and be careful," The Colonel called to him as he left.

Phil was soon streaking down the runway and took off quickly climbing up into the clear blue heavens above him. He pushed the throttle farther and the plane responded by quickly climbing faster. Phil felt the powerful surge of the in-line Allison engine that powered the P-51. It was a thrilling feeling to him to be flying such a powerful plane.

He quickly reached 10,000 feet altitude and started his test flight procedures. He eased the plane into slight turns, low speed climbs and dives. The plane responded excellently. As he urged the plane into high speed turns and dives, he realized the quick response and excellent flying characteristics of the P-51. He felt the excitement creep through his body as he anticipated doing the aerobatics. He put the plane into lazy eights, barrel rolls, slow rolls, snap rolls, loops and high speed turns. He then put the P-51 into a power dive and quickly reached 400 miles per hour.

"Wow!" he said aloud to himself. "This is fast!"

He pulled the plane out of the dive and almost blacked out. He pushed the throttle all the way and headed the plane straight up into the sky. As he was streaking straight up, he looked into the blue space above. It was an eery but a exciting feeling that came over him as he seemed to be heading straight into space. He thought back when he was at home lying on the front porch in the sun and reading about Buck Rogers. It must have been this feeling that he was now experiencing that Buck Rogers had while flying out in space. But then, Buck Rogers had Wilma Deering beside him. There is no one else with him here. Just he and the P-51 heading for space. It was a lonely, unearthly feeling that had come over Phil.

Phil let the plane bleed off until it was just hanging on its propeller in the air. He was no longer climbing but was just mushing along in the air. He cut the throttle and the plane slid back into a slight stall, then it fell over into a tight spin. As the plane spun, Phil watched the ground and horizon turn around and around. It was a funny looking world that was spinning around before him. He eased the plane out of the spin and put it into a power drive to loose some altitude. Soon the plane was reaching 400 miles per hour. This was the fastest that he had every flown in anything. As he neared the ground, he noticed the Red River lazily flowing along under him. It was away out in the country where there were few houses. The river bed was fairly wide with long bends in it. Phil decided that it would be a good place to do some low level flying along its banks so he dived the plane down to it.

As he guided the streaking plane along the river, he noticed how fast the trees and houses seemed to hurtle by. At times he had to pull the speeding plane up quickly to miss hitting tree tops along the banks. It was a great thrill to Phil for being able to guide the plane so close to the ground and to hop over tree tops with ease, just missing them. His mind went back home again, to when he was working in the tobacco fields with Daddy Barkley and the hands. He remembered how the P-47 pilots from Goldsboro came swooping down in the tobacco field just over their heads, scaring them near to death. He knew now how they must have felt.

The next day Colonel Doakes called Phil into his office. As he entered, he was wondering, did someone complain about him flying too low the day before? Had he done something wrong? He had a puzzled look on his face as he saluted the Colonel.

"At ease, Phil. Have a seat." The Colonel noticed the puzzled look on Phil's face. "Is something wrong Lieutenant?"

"Uh, no sir, Colonel, not that I know of."

"Well, you looked like you had just found out that you had knocked up some girl," teased the Colonel.

"Oh! No, sir! Nothing like that."

210

The Colonel laughed and looked at Phil. "I am coming to dinner at the Officer's Club tonight and thought that you might like to join me."

"I'd be glad to sir. Lieutenant Homer is going out on a date and I was going to have to eat alone. What time should I be there?" He was very much relieved about not being reported for flying too low at the river.

As February came, Phil was testing the B-26, B-25, and P-51 airplanes. The base had recently received a used AT-10 and an AT-11 plane to use at the base. Since Phil was the only pilot on the base that had flown AT-10 and AT-11 type airplanes, Colonel Doakes put him in charge of checking out and testing these planes. A few days later, Colonel Doakes asked Phil to check him out in the AT-10 and AT-11. He was elated since this would give him a chance to do something for the Colonel. He had great respect for the Colonel. The Colonel had been very nice to him since he had been there. Phil enjoyed the joking and kidding that they engaged in from time to time.

The next day was February 4, 1945. After Phil had completed his test hops for the day, he went to the war orientation room to hear the latest news from Intelligence. Ever since the Allies had Hitler on the run, he went to the War Orientation Room each day. The news reports were just coming in announcing that Roosevelt, Stalin, and Churchill had just met at Yalta and had signed an agreement for an unconditional surrender of the Axis Powers. Phil was elated and went to his bachelor officers quarters to write a letter to Linda.

A few days later, Phil was standing on the steps in front of the Test Flight Operations office which overlooked the airport parking deck and the runways. He was watching a B-26 take off down the runway. Soon after the B-26 had lifted off the runway, he heard one of the engines start misfiring. Then the plane seemed to shudder and then it plunged nose down straight ahead. It plunged into a forest of trees a short distance from the runway and exploded.

Phil ran into Colonel Doakes' office. "Colonel, did you know a plane just went down?"

"Yes, Phil. I just happened to be looking out the window and saw it start to fall. Did it explode?"

"Yes, sir. A good distance off the end of the runway. It hit some trees and blew up. Was it one of our test planes sir?"

"No, Phil. All of our pilots are here. I'll call and see who it was." Phil learned later that it was a couple of the French student pilots that had just soloed in the B-26. He felt sorry for their families. The crash of the B-26 on take off began to worry Phil. He knew that he had been taught that if something happened after the B-26 left the ground on take off that he should try to land the plane straight ahead since it would not

211

maintain its altitude on only one engine. But he had been thinking of something different.

The next day, Phil decided that he would try his idea on take off with the B-26. He had been thinking that since the B-26 had a final approach speed of 160 miles per hour and a stalling speed of approximately 140 miles per hour, that maybe it would be better to hold the plane down on the runway on take off until it reached 160 miles per hour. Then lift it off quickly instead of letting the plane lift off by itself at just above stalling speed and then gaining the 160 miles per hour while climbing.

He held the B-26 down on the runway until his air speed read 160 miles per hour. Then he quickly pulled back on the control wheel causing the plane to hop into the air. He quickly leveled off and found that he still had 160 miles per hour and over 100 feet in altitude. It had worked! It certainly seemed to be a better way to take off a B-26. By doing it like that, if anything happened to the plane before he got the 160 miles per hour on the runway, he could then slide off the end of the runway if necessary. Then if anything happened after he took off, he would have at least 100 feet of altitude and approximately 160 miles an hour air speed, which would be better than being just above stalling speed. He decided that he would practice this on all his take offs on the B-26 and not say anything about it just yet.

It was the last part of February when Phil got the urge to go see Jim and Strawberry in Wichita. He was enjoying flying with his crew and testing airplanes but getting lonely. The war was going along well. The Allies here now in an all out drive on the Rhine Valley and MacArthur had recaptured Manila. It just seem a good time to take a long trip to Wichita. It had been weeks since he had been to Wichita so he had some gas coupons saved up.

Phil was in a good mood as he left Frederick early on Saturday morning. The sun was just beginning to peek over the tree tops in the East and it was shooting some golden rays up into the sky through some thin clouds that were lingering on the horizon. It looked like it was going to be a nice weekend. As he drove along the highway, his thought drifted to Jim and Strawberry. They seemed so happy together. She would talk to Phil about her job as secretary at the aircraft assembly plant but mostly she liked to tell him about cooking and fixing up their apartment and about going out dancing with Jim. Phil felt a little tug of jealousy pull at his heart. A moment later, a picture of Jean flashed into his mind. The tug of jealousy melted away. She was so enchanting and vivacious, so different from Linda. She was very intriguing. He wondered if she would be busy this weekend.

Phil was getting near Wichita when he glanced down at the

gasoline gauge. It was nearly empty. He decided that he would detour a little and go by his old friend that owned the gasoline station. He could use some extra gasoline if he had any. The gasoline station owner was glad to see Phil. He filled Phil's gas tank and Phil gave him several packs of Lucky Strikes. Soon Phil pulled into the parking lot at Jim and Strawberry's apartment.

They were glad to see Phil and welcomed him into their apartment. Phil put his B-4 bag into a closet close to the sofa in the living room. He always slept on the sofa since it was only a one bedroom apartment. After lunch Phil went down the hall to see if Jean was in. He knocked and she came to the door. She hugged him and gave him an eager kiss. He hugged her back and kissed her affectionately.

"Hey beautiful, are you going to be busy tonight?"

"No, Phil. I've just been waiting for you, silly. I canceled all my other dates." They both laughed at each other.

"Well, how about going out to the club with Strawberry, Jim and me?"

"That sounds good. What time?"

"Oh, how about six o'clock, okay?"

"That's fine," replied Jean.

On the way to the club Lido, Phil and Jim were cracking jokes and being funny. Phil noticed that Jean was not laughing very much and was quieter than usual. After dinner, she and Phil began to dance some waltzes. Jean began to get into a better mood. Later Phil went up to the band leader and had him to play and sing "Rum and Coca Cola." Everyone joined in and were having a good time singing, except Jean. Phil looked across the table at her and noticed that she had become quiet and passive looking. He took hold of her hand.

"Is there something wrong, beautiful?" She looked up at Phil and shook her head.

Chapter Thirty-two

The Colonel kept Phil real busy testing B-26 planes. It seemed to him that he was having to test nearly all the B-26 planes that needed testing. One day, Phil and his crew were taking off on a B-26 to test it, as usual, he held the brakes on the plane at the start of the runway until he had the engines revved up to full power. He then let off the brakes and the B-26 surged ahead down the runway. He held the plane on the runway until he reached 160 miles per hour. Then he suddenly pulled back on the control wheel. The plane leaped into the air, Phil quickly started leveling the plane off. Suddenly the right engine started backfiring and quit. He quickly went through a single engine procedure and abruptly had the engine stopped and the prop feathered. With the propeller knifing through the air, it cut down on the drag on the airplane and would allow the airplane to stay in the air longer.

He quickly glanced at the gauges. One hundred twenty feet altitude, air speed at 155 miles per hour. He called the control tower for emergency landing on the nearest runway which was to his right. He was already turning towards it.

"Frederick control tower! Frederick control tower!" Phil yelled into the microphone. "Emergency! Emergency! This is Air Force 236. I've lost my right engine on take off. Get all the dogs and cats off the runway. I'm coming in on runway two-eight-o."

The control tower quickly came back. "Roger 236, you have the airport. Good luck, boys."

Turning to the right made it necessary to turn into the side with the dead engine. That was very dangerous and was usually not done, but it was the only choice Phil had. He knew it would be close if they could get back to the runway at all but he didn't want to crash land straight ahead. That would surely be disastrous. He glanced over at Dan who was busy checking the instruments and trying to keep the one good engine at maximum power. He had a very worried look on his face. Phil kept turning the plane towards the end of the concrete runway. He was losing altitude and getting closer and closer to the ground. He pulled back further on the control wheel in the attempt to reach the runway. He was almost stalling the plane.

As he watched the end of the runway, he saw that the ambulances and fire trucks had taken up positions just off to the side of the runway. He could see the firemen on the side and on top of the fire trucks. They were prepared in case he crashed the plane. Phil saw that he could not reach the runway but would hit the ground off the end of the concrete. He also saw that he would still be in a turning position as he reached the level grassy area off the end of the runway. He quickly leveled the wings, kicked hard left rudder and pulled back hard on the control stick. The plane stalled as it hit the ground. The plane's wheels hit the ground together but with the force of the plane still going to the side and not straight with the runway, it caused the plane to veer straight towards the ambulance and the fire trucks. The crash crew took off and ran to get out of the planes way.

Phil hit the right rudder and brake as hard as he could with his right foot. He kept full throttle on the left engine. The plane started turning back towards the runway just missing the crash vehicles. The plane just made it back to the runway without getting stuck in the dirt alongside the runway. Phil kept the lone engine running fast enough to taxi the B-26 down the runway to the parking deck. It was then that he relaxed in his seat and breathed a sigh of relief. Dan and the rest of the crew were very relieved also. As he parked the plane and shut down the good engine he noticed Colonel Doakes drive up in a jeep.

"Hey, Phil!" the Colonel shouted from his seat down in the jeep. Phil struck his head out the cockpit window. "Yes, sir?"

"That was one helluva landing, Lieutenant! But you made it. What went wrong?"

"That, sir!" Phil pointed to the engine with the feathered propeller. "It started backfiring and quit on take off."

"Well you boys get down and I'll take you back to the office."

The crew got out of the plane and started getting into the jeep. Phil was the last to climb down and start to the jeep. Suddenly his legs seemed to buckle under him. Gabby saw him and grabbed him before he fell.

"What's wrong? You sick, Phil?"

"It's nothing, I, I just stumbled." Phil realized that the tension and excitement had caught up with him since he had relaxed and the emergency was over. Gabby knew better and still helped him into the jeep.

"Boys, you all did a great job saving that plane, and yourselves. I think you all need a couple days off to settle your nerves."

"Yes, sir, Colonel. We sure do," retorted Gabby, trying to influence the Colonel's remark more by using a shaky voice.

Colonel Doakes peered over at Gabby from the corner of his eyes and grinned. "Okay, you boys can have the rest of the week off. Just be sure to be here Monday morning, and in good shape too." He turned around and looked Gabby and Johnny straight in the eye. He knew that if the chance presented itself, they could pull some pretty big parties.

"Oh, yes sir, yes sir!" they both replied in unison. The jeep continued on to the Test Flight office. Dan looked at Phil. "Pal, that was a fast single engine procedure you did on that engine. It

215

helped save us this time."

"Thanks Dan. But you know what really helped? If it hadn't been for Gabby pulling that prank on me with the prop pitch controls awhile back, I don't think I would have been that fast. It was almost automatic for me today."

The Colonel was listening intently. "What pranks? You boys are not playing around with these planes are you?"

Phil quickly replied, "Oh, no sir. What I mean to say was that Gabby has been giving me some extra practice on single engine procedures by pulling the prop pitch control wires. It sure paid off today!"

"Well, you boys better be careful up there." The Colonel threw a wry grin at Phil as they pulled up to the office.

By this time, Phil's crew had gotten over their jitters and were getting excited over the open post. They quickly entered the office, took off their flying uniforms and checked out on the roster. Phil went to his quarters to rest awhile and think. It was Thursday and he had off till Monday to do as he pleased. He decided to write a letter to Linda. He told her about how much he liked his crew and about Gabby pulling pranks on him. He described a prank that he had once pulled on Gabby also. He told her that one day they had completed their mission in a B-26 and were just flying along back to the base. Gabby was in the bombardiers compartment in the nose of the plane when Phil saw a small town below them. He decided that he would play like he was dive bombing and strafing the town. He pushed forward on the control wheel and the plane went into a power drive. Suddenly he started shaking the control wheel with his hands. This made the plane vibrate as if machine guns were being fired, but then there were no machine guns on the plane. Gabby whirled around and looked up at Phil from the Bombardiers compartment. He had a pale and frightened look on his face. Phil quit shaking the control wheel and leveled the plane off. He laughed at Gabby all the way back to the field. Gabby knew he had been paid back for pulling pranks on Phil.

He finished the letter to Linda letting her know how much he was enjoying testing airplanes but he did not tell her about the emergency that just happened on take off that day. Phil decided that he would leave early the next morning and go spend the long weekend with Jim and Strawberry, and maybe date Jean.

As the long weekend was coming to an end, Phil reflected on what fun it had been. They had gone bowling, played cards, and also played some tennis together. He found that Jean was a real good tennis player. She had beaten him every game but one and he felt that she was just being nice on that one. Anyway, it was Sunday afternoon and it was almost time for Phil to leave to return to the base. Jean had invited Phil into her apartment for a

216

light snack before he had to go.

As they sat on the sofa warming their feet by the warmth of the fireplace, Phil noticed that Jean had gotten real close to him. He also realized that she had been staying closer to him the whole weekend. He had noticed that she had returned to being her old vivacious and fiery self. He felt good that his friend was again happy and he put his arm around her. She snuggled closer to his side. He looked down at her and smiled. He thought she looked lovelier than ever, and those greenish blue eyes were very beautiful. She pulled his face down to hers and kissed him gently. He knew he was enjoying this but it was time for him to leave. He gently got up off the sofa and put on his "Ike" jacket to leave.

"I wish you wouldn't leave, Phil. Can't you stay a little while longer?"

Phil wanted to stay longer but knew what the consequences would be.

"Beautiful, I would love to stay but I really have to go now."

"Okay, but I wish you could stay. I'll miss you!" She grabbed Phil and kissed him passionately. He held her close and kissed her also.

As he drove back to the base that night, he could not get his mind off Jean. He felt she was beginning to like him a great deal, and somehow he liked it that way. The next week, Phil's crew was in good spirits. They told him that they had spent their long weekends in Oklahoma City and that they had a real good time. Dan told him that he had met a girl friend there and that he would like to go back and see her again sometime. Phil told him that he occasionally went to Wichita, Kansas and he would be glad to drop him off at Oklahoma City if he wished. Dan was glad to get the ride and thanked him.

The next week, Phil and his crew were again taking off on a B-26 on a test flight mission when another engine quit on take off. It was just like the other engine that quit on take off except this time he did not have quite as much altitude. He just had 100 feet. It was the right engine again and with the nearest runway to his right, he again had to turn into the dead engine. Phil knew that it was going to be even harder to get back to the runway this time than it was the last. He and Dan had the plane at its maximum power settings. He tried to turn the plane tighter but felt it shudder and knew it was almost in a stall. He looked down and saw the drainage ditch that circled the airport off the end of the runway. Then he realized that the plane was going to hit the ground in the ditch. He knew that if he tried to pull the nose of the plane up anymore to try to land on the other side of the wide ditch, he would stall and crash. If he did not do anything he would hit the ditch and crash.

Suddenly, he shoved the nose of the plane down and at the

last minute before hitting the ground, he pulled back hard on the control wheel pulling the nose of the plane back up. The downward motion of the plane caused the main landing wheels to hit down hard on the bank of the drainage ditch. This caused the plane to bounce high enough to carry it over the drainage ditch to the other side. As the plane cleared the drainage ditch and hit the ground, the wheels started sinking into the soft dirt causing it to start veering to the right. Phil kicked the rudder and left brake to try to straighten the plane towards the runway. He kept full power on the engine, trying to reach the concrete runway and almost made it. The dirt was too soft and with only one engine, it finally mired down just off the side of the runway

As the plane stopped, the fire trucks and crash crew came roaring up beside it just in case a fire broke out. Phil and the crew started getting out of the plane as Colonel Doakes rushed up on his jeep. He yelled at Phil as he hit the ground.

"Lieutenant, what went wrong this time?"

"Same thing as before, sir. The right engine quit on take off!" Phil moved towards the jeep and glanced back at his crew. "Come on boys, lets get back to the office. We can talk there." Colonel Doakes could see that the crew was nervous and he noticed that Phil's voice was a little shaky. Phil had reached the jeep and started to get into it when the tension caught up with him. He almost fell getting into the jeep but the Colonel caught hold of his arm and helped him.

"Take it easy Phil. Are you okay?" The Colonel asked as he glanced over at him. He noted that his face was pale and his knees were visibly shaking.

"Yes, sir, I think so. But that one was too damned close for comfort." Phil was trying to keep his voice steady and his knees from knocking. He looked up at the sky and smiled. He then looked over at Dan who was also gazing at him and said, "He helped me today." The questioning look on Dan's face changed to a smile. He nodded his head affirmatively at Phil. The Colonel's voice came back.

"Well, you boys got back and with no damage and that is remarkable. In fact its unbelievable. This is the second time that you have had an engine go out on take off. You had to turn into a dead engine in order to get back to the nearest runway both times and I just saw you bounce that plane across that drainage ditch. That was quick thinking Lieutenant."

"I had to do something. That's my ass and my crew's that was on the line."

The Colonel grinned and glanced at Phil. "I've been thinking, boys. I don't recall having heard of a crew that safely landed a B-26 that had an engine go out on take off. This makes the second time that you have gotten back safely, and you did it turning into the dead engine! What are you doing differently?"

218

"Phil developed a new take off procedure," Dan blurted out.

"Is that true, Phil?" the Colonel asked.

"Yes, sir. I credit that to making it possible for me to at least get back to the air field." He related his new procedure to the Colonel, who seemed pleased with the idea and assured Phil that it would be studied and tried out by a review board.

Phil and the crew were allowed a couple days off before reporting back for duty. He and Dan relaxed at the Officers Club, playing cards and tennis for the two days. On Thursday morning Phil and his crew reported back to Colonel Doakes.

"Phil how would you like to fly up to Dayton, Ohio for the night?" the Colonel asked.

"Fine, sir," he replied with a questioning look. "What's going on?"

"Well, Lieutenant, you have had two engines go out on take off and we've had three other engines quit in the air in the past few days. We can't seem to find the cause. It could be the gasoline, but we're not sure. I need a crew to fly to Wright Patterson field in Dayton and have the gasoline tested."

"Sir, we would be glad to go." Phil jumped at the chance to go on a cross country trip. He knew that his crew would be excited also.

"Then get you crew ready. By the time you return to the office, I'll have the gasoline samples ready for you to take. You can take my personal B-25 for the trip."

"Yes, sir!"

The Colonel looked at Phil and winked. "And bring me back a good telephone number." They both laughed as Phil left the room.

The crew was elated when Phil told them of the chance to go to Dayton. They hurried to their quarters to pack overnight bags for the trip. Phil and the crew quickly returned to the Test Flight operations office, picked up the gasoline samples and went to the Colonel's B-25 plane, which was parked near the office. They entered the B-25 and marveled at the Colonel's private plane. It looked almost new compared to the planes that they had been flying, even though it had been overseas and back. There had been extra navigation and radio equipment installed. Phil was tickled to get to fly this nice airplane.

It was an uneventful flight from Frederick to Dayton. The weather was clear and the crew were enjoying the scenery, especially when they crossed the Mississippi River. It did resemble a huge winding snake along the countryside. It was late in the afternoon when they landed at Wright Patterson Airfield. Phil had to hurry to get the gasoline samples to the laboratory before they closed for the day. They told him that they would try to have the results from the test on the samples by eleven hundred hours the next day. Phil and the crew were assigned quarters in the visitors quarters on the base. After they cleaned up and changed clothes, they all left for downtown on the base commuter bus.

Dan and Phil decided to ride the city bus around town so they could get to see some of it. On one of the bus routes, they came to a seafood restaurant. Dan looked at Phil, "Hey pal, are you hungry?"

"Yes, I am, and I like seafood too."

"Great! I like to see food and eat it too."

Phil laughed at Dan's pun. Moments later, they entered the restaurant and seated themselves at a table. Soon the waitress brought them a menu.

"What are you going to order Dan?"

"Catfish," replied Dan unhesitatingly. "Huh? I don't think I'll join you," Phil said, shaking his head with disgust. "How can you stand them?"

Dan looked over with a twinkle in his eye. "Say Pal, have you ever eaten catfish in this part of the country?"

"Nope. I've never been in this part of the country before, except I did pass through here once last year. Got weathered in a few hours. No catfish then either."

"Well then, you've never eaten any Channel catfish. I reckon you're just used to those old mud cats in the South. I may be from Chicago but I think I know catfish, especially Channel catfish. The meat is so flaky and white. Better than chicken."

"Okay, okay, buddy. You've sold me. I'll try them."

When they finished their dinner, Phil and Dan returned downtown and spent the rest of the evening sipping a few beers at a lounge at the hotel. Then they returned to the base guest quarters.

The next morning the crew had a few hours to wait until eleven hundred hours. They all decided to ride the base tram around and take a view of the base. They came upon an area where they saw what looked like some damaged fighter aircraft had been parked. The crew got off the tram and decided to take a look at them since they were strange looking aircraft. As they approached the aircraft Phil recognized one of the aircraft. It was a German Messerschmitd ME-109 lying on its belly. On the other side of the ME-109 was a Stuka dive bomber. He remembered from the war orientation films that this was the German dive bomber that made an awful, eerie sound when in a dive. It was intended to scare the population and usually did. Phil realized that these were captured enemy planes that had been sent from overseas to be studied and examined. He went over to the ME-109 so that he could examine it more closely since it was one of the most famous German fighter planes. To him, it resembled a P-51 with a square cornered plexiglass canopy over the cockpit.

Phil and his crew were so interested in looking at the

captured airplanes that they were almost late getting back to the laboratory to get the results of the test. As he entered the laboratory office, the technician told him that the tests on the gasoline samples were all negative. The gasoline samples had no foreign ingredients in them. This meant that there had not been any attempt to sabotage the gasoline supply tanks back at Frederick Air Base as had been suspected by colonel Doakes. As soon as he heard the report, Phil hurried to the phone to call colonel Doakes. He knew that the colonel had grounded all flights at the base pending the outcome of the tests and would need the information in order to lift the ban. The colonel thanked Phil and ordered him to return to the base immediately. There was a lot of work for them to do.

A couple of weeks later, Phil went to see colonel Doakes. He had noticed a couple of A-26 twin engine bombers sitting on the parking ramp and wanted to ask the Colonel about them. It was April 12, 1945, a date that Phil would always remember. He entered the Colonel's office and saw that he was on the telephone. He had a very somber look on his face. He looked straight at Phil as he hung up the phone.

"That was Headquarters, Lieutenant. President Roosevelt has just died."

"Oh, no! Sir, I'm very sorry . . . It just can't be true!" Phil sat down heavily, almost in shock.

As the Colonel reached for the telephone he told Phil, "Lieutenant, I am closing all operations for the rest of the day. Everyone is now excused from duty."

"Yes sir," Phil replied as he stood up to leave.

The rest of that day Phil spent at the Officer's Club talking to Dan and some of the other pilots. They tried to play cards but no one seemed interested. Everybody was in a downcast mood. Phil had to wait a few more days before going to see the Colonel. He was still itching to fly one of the A-26 Invaders.

Chapter Thirty-three

It was the last of April 1945. The Italians had captured Mussolini and hanged him. Phil thought, as he viewed the pictures in the news release it was a gruesome sight. Hitler had been almost defeated. The Americans are nearing Berlin from the East and the Russians were near on the West. There were also reports that the Germans now have jet airplanes.

Phil and his crew had been having it pretty easy testing airplanes. They only had one emergency since the engines went out on takeoff except for a rudder that came loose on a B-26 in a tight turn. It was exciting but Phil managed to stop the plane from shaking when it came loose by slow flying the B-26 back to the base. It was closer than Phil had thought. They found that only one bolt was still holding the rudder to the plane when they landed. If it had come out, the crew would most surely have had to bail out.

The weather had cleared up and the weekend was supposed to be nice. Phil decided that he had enough gas stamps to take him to Wichita so he could go and visit Jim, Strawberry, and Jean. Dan wanted to go along and stop at Oklahoma City.

Early Saturday morning the two left on the trip. Phil dropped Dan off at Oklahoma City and went on to Wichita. When he arrived at Jim's apartment, Strawberry had a big bunch of fried chicken ready. She knew that Phil loved fried chicken almost as good as he loved North Carolina barbecued pork.

Phil enjoyed the fried chicken and Strawberry's lunch immensely. During the meal, they all started talking about flying. He looked over at his two friends.

"Say, you guys, how would you both like to go flying?" He knew that Jim had been up in a small plane before but he did not think that Strawberry had.

"I'd like that," Jim retorted as he looked over at Strawberry.

"Well, I'm game too," she said, "if you won't pull any didos or what they call stunts. I have never been up in an airplane and I don't know whether or not I will like it."

"Oh, I wouldn't do anything like that with you, Strawberry. I just would not try to scare you for anything in the world. I'll take it easy and I bet you'll love it."

"Maybe so. I know that Jean used to love to fly with her husband before he left for the Pacific."

Phil looked at Strawberry with a smile on his face and commented, "Say, maybe she would like to go too."

"Why don't you go ask her? She knows that you were supposed to come up this weekend."

"I think I will," he replied as he quickly left the table.

The door to Jean's apartment was not far down the hall from

Jim's apartment. When she answered Phil's knock on her door, she grabbed him around the neck and kissed him affectionately. He put his arms around her and patted her shoulder reassuringly.

"Phil, I am so glad to see you! Won't you come in?"

"Thanks babe. Glad to see you too. How ya doing?"

"Fine, fine. But I've been wondering when you would come up. You know I enjoy your visits so much. We do have a good time together, don't we Phil?"

Phil looked down into her greenish blue eyes which seemed to glow from her sharped featured face. Her dark wavy hair outlined the pink healthy radiance of her fair skinned face. He thought that she was more beautiful than ever. A little desire began to tug at his heart.

"Yes I enjoy being with you too, babe. You are lots of fun. Say, would you like to go flying this afternoon? There is a small airport just outside of town. They have some used Air Corps PT-13 primary trainer planes there that I could rent. Jim and Strawberry said that they would like to go up. How about it?"

"Oh Phil, I would just love to. I am crazy about flying and I have not been up in a plane since . . . well, in a long time." Jean stopped short of mentioning her dead husband.

"Okay, babe, I'll go get Jim and Strawberry and pick you up on the way out. Say, you had better take along a scarf or something to tie around your head. The plane we'll be flying has an open cockpit. We will be wearing goggles but you'll need something to tie your hair back with, okay?"

"Okay fly boy. I've flown in open cockpits before." They laughed together.

A while later, they reached the little airport outside of town. Phil rented the PT-13 for an hour and some flying goggles and two parachutes.

He took Jim up first. He showed him some aerobatics stunts and after a while, they returned to the airport and landed.

Jim got out of the plane and let out a huge gasp of air.

"Boy, that was exciting! I loved it, Phil!"

Phil laughed back at Him. "How did you like that loop, pal?"

"Say, that one almost took my breath. I think that I almost blacked out." He looked at Phil and grinned.

Strawberry started backing away from where they were standing near the plane. "I'm not going up with you if you're going to do that!" She looked at Phil, who was still seated in the rear cockpit of the plane. He noticed the fright on her face.

"Aw, Strawberry, I am not going to do that with you. I would not do anything like that to someone who has not been up before. Jim has been up before. Come on Strawberry, I'll be easy. You'll love it. I won't scare you. You'll see."

He tried his nicest and sweetest voice to calm Strawberry's

fears. After some more urging from Jim she finally got into the cockpit of the plane. Jim adjusted the goggles, safety belt, and parachute for her and Phil took off into the sky.

Phil decided that since it was Strawberry's first time up, that he would not stay long. He flew over the town and showed her the apartment building that they lived in. Then he came back to the airport and landed.

Strawberry looked up at Phil after she got out of the plane. "That was nice, Phil. I did enjoy it. The cars and people looked like little ants crawling around on the ground. Thanks for the ride."

"All right, Jean, you're next," Phil shouted from the rear cockpit.

"I'm coming," she replied, still trying to strap on the parachute Strawberry had removed. She climbed up on the wing of the PT-13 and stepped down into the open cockpit. She settled down into the seat and adjusted her goggles.

"Have you fastened your seat belt?" Phil shouted into the megaphone.

"Check," she yelled back. Jim came up and double checked her seat belt. He then gave Phil the okay sign with his fingers.

Phil revved the engine and they moved down the runway in a cloud of dust and noise. Soon he and Jean were climbing into the sky. They flew around a while doing turns and lazy eights. He noticed Jean in the rear view mirror. She seemed to be enjoying the ride but then she yelled into the megaphone. "How about doing a loop, Phil?"

"You're not scared?" he blurted back.

"Are you?" she retorted.

"Okay, you'd better hold on." He shoved the throttle forward to gain enough altitude to safely perform the loop. He then shoved the nose of the plane sharply down and did a tight loop. As he leveled the plane off, he looked back at Jean. She was laughing.

"Hey how about a spin?" she yelled at him.

He grinned back at her and pulled the plane up into a stall. It fell over into a tight tail spin. Phil did not want Jean to get air sick so he quickly pulled the plane back out of the spin.

"You okay?" he shouted back to Jean against the roar of the engine. "Sure, how about you?" she replied laughing.

Phil looked back and pointed his finger at her. She laughed back at him.

"Can you do a snap roll Phil?"

He now realized that she loved aerobatics and was not frightened. He put the plane through snap rolls, slow rolls, and barrel rolls. He glanced back at her in the mirror. She was laughing and enjoying it. She gave him two thumbs up signals.

"More, more!" she yelled to him.

"Okay. Hold on love." He put the plane into some high speed tight turns and then finished by flying the plane upside down in a long glide. He landed the plane and soon as he parked it. He quickly got out of the cockpit and hurried to help Jean get out. She was out almost as quickly as he was.

She grabbed Phil around the neck. "That was exciting, Phil, lets do it again sometime."

Phil was elated that Jean loved flying. "Hey love, I didn't know you loved flying that much!"

"Oh, I used to love to fly but I had never flown aerobatics before. Its so thrilling. I love it!"

It was early that night as they arrived at Club Lido. They decided they would all have steaks, enjoy a leisurely meal, and dance later. As the evening wore on, they became tired and were sitting around their table chatting. Jim arose and went up to the orchestra leader and requested a song. The soloist began singing Vaughn Monroe's "There, I've Said It Again," as Jim sat down beside Strawberry. Jim took Strawberry's hand as the words began.

Strawberry beamed at Jim. "Honey, that was so sweet of you. Thanks."

Phil glanced at Jean and smiled. He knew that she had been looking at him throughout most of the song.

Jean smiled back at Phil. It was then that she realized that she is falling in love with him. She began to think. He already has his Peaches back home. Then a question comes to her mind. Does he really love her? How much? He seems so fond of me. Maybe if, maybe I could. Suddenly a great desire for Phil settled in her heart.

Jean's thoughts were suddenly interrupted. "Love, would you like to dance?" Phil had noticed that she was deep in thought.

"I would love to," she replied, getting up quickly.

"A penny for your thought back there?" Phil whispered into her ear as he pulled her close to him.

"Oh, I was thinking about how nice a couple Jim and Strawberry are, and how nice and sweet you are."

"Gee, thanks love. Its easy to be nice to someone like you."

She laid her head against his shoulder contentedly for the rest of the dance. It was past midnight when they left the club and entered the apartment building.

"See you guys in a few minutes," Phil said to Jim and Strawberry as he continued on down the hall to Jean's door.

As she opened the door, she turned to Phil. "Please come in Honey."

"I'd better not love, its getting late."

She grabbed him. "Oh Phil, you are so sweet." She pulled his lips to hers and kissed him passionately.

The sudden expressions of affection startled Phil at first but he found himself liking it. He held her close and returned her kiss affectionately. He thanked her for a nice day and reluctantly parted from her.

"I really have to go, love. See you tomorrow."

The next afternoon Phil went down the hallway and knocked on Jean's door.

"Come in Phil and have a seat." Phil just stood in the doorway for a moment looking at Jean. She was dressed in a low cut, tight fitting pink dress. She had put a small pink bow in her wavy black hair. The little white ear rings set off the white lace around the shoulders. She looked so voluptuous that Phil was almost stunned for a moment. "You like?" she teased him.

"I'll say! You are just beautiful in that outfit."

"Thank you Phil. I was hoping that you would like it. Its been a long time since I've worn it."

"Where would you like to go this afternoon, love?"

Jean guided Phil to the sofa and started over to the record player.

"Honey, why don't we stay in this afternoon, sit on the couch and listen to some records and just relax."

"Sounds good to me," Phil caught himself not really wanting to go anywhere anyway.

The afternoon was almost gone and it would soon be time for Phil to leave to go back to the base. They settled back on the sofa with Jean leaning contentedly on his chest. She looked up at Phil's brown eyes. She thought how beautiful and intriguing they were to her. He looked down at her. The greenish blue eyes seemed to have a bewitching glint in them that fascinated him.

She pulled him down on the sofa and kissed him passionately. He felt her sexy shaped lips close on his. Suddenly he felt a tingling feeling surge through his body. He wanted to make love to her as she writhed her body closer to him. She felt him pull his pants down and started pulling her's down. He started helping her. She shuddered with passion as he pulled her hips closer to him. Suddenly they were both pulling and clinging to each other in a frenzy of passionate bliss.

It was way past time for Phil to leave when he finally arose from the sofa. Jean reached and clung to him.

"Please don't leave me, honey." she whispered.

He looked down at her. He wished that he didn't have to go either. "I have to, beautiful. Do you realize that it will be past midnight when I get back to Frederick? Technically that would make me A.W.O.L."

"I know," she said, pouting. "I wish you didn't have to. I'll miss you," she continued in a deep, sultry voice. Phil smiled at her understandingly.

Phil headed the car out of Wichita and on the road to Oklahoma City. He knew that Dan would be worried about him being so late in picking him up.

As he drove along the dark highway, he kept thinking of Linda. He knew that he liked Jean a lot but it wasn't the same as with Linda. The yearning pain in his heart was burning for Linda. He began to feel guilty.

One morning later, Phil did not have any test flights so Colonel Doakes let him off for the day. He decided to check by the war orientation room and see what was happening. A few days before, he had learned that Hitler had killed himself. It was May 7, 1945 and the news was coming in that Germany was surrendering. He was elated and rushed back to his quarters to write to Linda. When he arrived at his quarters he found that he had received a letter from Linda. He quickly opened it. She told him in the letter that she and a girlfriend had found a two bedroom apartment and had rented it. She was very happy about it.

Phil read the letter eagerly and wrote her a return. He told her about his happiness that she had the apartment but the large part of his letter was about the end of the war in Germany, and about flying. He told her about testing a new A-26 and doing over 450 miles per hour in a dive. This was the fastest that he had ever been. He did not tell her about their wings beginning to shake and flap before he pulled the plane out of the dive. This even scared him a little and he knew that it would upset her also.

He wanted to tell her about how nice Jim and Strawberry were getting along and about how happy they seemed to be in the hopes that she would change her mind about coming out and marrying him. However he realized now that she would not change her mind so he refrained from mentioning it. He remembered the last time that he talked to her on the phone that she had become irritated when he mentioned it, and now she had the apartment too.

Chapter Thirty-four

Phil was in the war orientation room on August 6th talking to some of his buddies about the war in the Philippines. MacArthur had recaptured the Philippines in July but there was still heavy fighting in some of the Islands nearby. Suddenly the officer in charge of the news called for everyone's attention. He then announced that the U.S. had dropped an atomic bomb on Nagasaki, Japan. It had been dropped by a B-29 called the Enola Gay and it had caused great destruction, almost destroying the whole city. For a moment, silence descended on the war orientation room. Everyone was astounded at first. Then exuberance exploded in the room. It was the best news that they had heard since Germany surrendered.

On August 9th, it was reported that another atomic bomb had been dropped on Hiroshima, Japan and that it also had almost been totally destroyed. Five days later, on August 14th, it was reported that Japan had surrendered. President Truman announced V-J Day.

Phil was overjoyed. It meant that World War II was over and that he could soon be home. He went to telephone Linda but realized that she would probably not be at home. He decided to wait until that night to call her. Suddenly he heard a lot of noise outside of the Officers Club so he went outside to see. Everyone was out running around and shouting, "The war is over." There was jubilation everywhere. Dan ran up to Phil and shouted, "Let's go to town and celebrate!"

"I'll race you to my car," Phil replied.

Phil and Dan and all their buddies that the '38 Chevy would hold headed for the town which was only a few miles from the air base. There were other automobiles already going into town with the occupants sticking out the windows shouting the good news. They reached main street and joined a large line of other cars going up and down the street. People were dancing, shouting and celebrating all over the place. Phil and the other drivers were honking their horns. Phil spotted a parking place, so they parked the car and joined the crowd in the streets celebrating. Late that afternoon, the celebration was still going full speed. Phil found Dan in the crowd and said, "Listen pal, I'm going back to the base to call my sweetie tonight. Do you want to go back too?

"Sure, Phil. I need to make a call too. Hey, we can eat at the Officer's Club and make our calls from there."

When they arrived at the club and started to get out of the automobile, Phil noticed his wallet was missing. "Hey, Dan. I can't find my billfold. Let's search the car."

They searched every nook and cranny of the car, but found nothing. Phil began to worry. "It had my driver's license, my pictures, and just over a hundred dollars in cash."

"Don't worry, buddy," Dan offered. "I'll loan you enough to last until payday."

"Thanks, Dan. I appreciate that. Damn! I just can't imagine where I could have lost it!"

"I expect that it was in that crowd," retorted Dan. "But you'll never find it there. You're only hope is that some honest fellah finds it and returns it to the base. But if I were you, I'd just count it as gone."

They finished supper and Phil went to the phone that was located in the Officer's Lounge. "Hey, Sweet Peaches, it's me!"

"Oh Phil, it's so good to hear your voice."

"Me too, Peaches. Have you heard the news?"

"Yes, honey, I heard it at the office this afternoon. They let us go home early today in celebration. When do you think you'll be discharged?"

"Oh, it's too early to tell. Maybe in a couple of months or so."

"I hope it is sooner than that, Phil. Maybe you can start college here in the Spring session." She paused. "You are going to college, aren't you?"

"Sure, sweetheart. But I've been thinking too. What if I could get on as a commercial pilot. They pay lots of money."

"What?" she exclaimed. "What do you mean that you want to fly? What about college?" Phil sensed that her voice was beginning to shake and he knew that he was upsetting her.

"Sweetheart, I, I just thought that maybe I could fly part-time and go to college too, under the GI Bill," he said, trying to reassure her.

"Don't be silly, Phil. You know you can't do that. If we get married you will have a small part-time job here in Raleigh in order just to live and go to college. I just don't think that you can go to college and fly for a commercial airline also. Besides, you'll have so much studying to do."

"Oh, Peaches, just forget I even mentioned it, sweetie. It was just something I had been thinking about looking into. Of course college is more important." As they continued talking, Phil noticed that Linda's voice seemed to become more calm.

A few days later, the government abolished gas rationing Phil was elated. He would be able to drive his car home when he got out of the Air Corps. Also, since gasoline was no longer a problem, he decided to go visit Jim, Strawberry and Jean.

It was a nice weekend in Wichita. Jim, Strawberry and Jean were very happy that the war was over. Jean was looking really vivacious to Phil. She clung to him at every chance and especially when Jim and Strawberry were not near. Phil enjoyed this very much but then he would bring up home occasionally in their conversation. Jean tried to steer the conversation away from home in an effort to keep Phil's mind off Linda. She was thinking that maybe she had a chance with Phil if she tried hard enough. Phil had also noticed that Jean had become more attentive to him.

It was early in October. Most of the training and testing programs of the base had been suspended. All of the French pilots that were being trained under the lend-lease program had left and gone back to France. Phil did not have much to do. If there was not any planes to test, Phil returned to his quarters or went to the Officer's Club to play cards or billiards.

One day Colonel Doakes called Phil into his office. "Phil, I don't know whether or not you have heard, but they are going to close down this base."

"Yes, sir, Colonel. I had heard that rumor. I just didn't know when."

"Well, its going to be right away Phil. I've just got orders to fly all the planes from here and store them up at Altus, Oklahoma. That's what I want you and the other boys to start doing tomorrow. Do you know where Altus is?"

"Yes, sir. It's not far from here."

"But Phil, I have something else I want to discuss with you."

"Sir?"

"Lieutenant, I guess you realize that you will be offered a discharge before long. May I ask you what you plan to do when you get out?"

"Yes Colonel, I do have some plans. I plan to go back to North Carolina, marry my fiancee and get a college education."

"Oh, so you do have plans. That's commendable, son. Everyone should have a college education. But Phil, I have something else in which you may be interested, and you can still get your college education."

"What's that, sir?"

"Well, I've just received orders today that as soon as I have completed the transfer of all the planes from this base, that I'm to report to Minter Field in California. I'm to start up a jet testing base out there. You do know that we are building jets now, don't you?"

"Yes, Colonel Doakes, I have been keeping up with that in the war orientation room. I believe that they have modified a P-63 King Cobra to accept a jet engine and they call it a T-33,"

"That's right, Phil. I know that you don't know this but they have a German rocket scientist out there also. They are talking of rocket ships and rocket planes, maybe even breaking the sound barrier. It's going to need some of the best test pilots we have to implement the program."

"It sounds like you'll have a great time, sir."

"Yes Phil, flying will be a most exciting field in the future. That's why I mentioned this to you. I was wondering if you might like to join me out there?"

"What?," Phil gasped. "You'd like me to be a test pilot for rocket planes?" He could barely believe what he was hearing. All his life he had read about and even dreamed of flying rockets. Now, there was a chance that those dreams might someday come true.

The Colonel continued, "My boy, I could arrange for you to go to college and fly for me also. I know that you have the talent. I have to say it, you are the best all around test pilot in my unit."

"Thank you, sir. You're very kind to say that. But this is very sudden. Can I have a few days to think this over?"

The Colonel smiled at him, knowing that the news had shocked Phil. "Sure son, take a few days and think it over good. I could sure use you out there."

As Phil returned to the Officer's Club, his mind was in a fog. He couldn't help from dreaming of flying jets and rocket planes. It almost scared him now that it might come true. He could hardly wait to call Linda. It would be seventeen hundred hours when Linda would be home from work so he had to wait an hour. It was one of the longest hours of his life.

"Hey there, Peaches. It's me, Phil."

"Hi, sweetheart. What are you so excited about?"

"What do you mean?" he asked, surprised.

"Phil, I can tell by your voice that you are excited about something. Are you coming home early?"

"Oh no, sweet Peaches, nothing like that. But that won't be long now because they are closing this air base. Actually, I have some better news."

"What could it be, Phil?"

"Sweetheart, Colonel Doakes has asked me to go to California with him. He wants me to help him start up a program at a new air base where they will be testing experimental jet aircraft He guaranteed me I can be in the program and go to college too. What do you think?"

Phil was completely surprised to hear Linda suddenly burst into tears.

"I can't, Phil," she said between sobs. "I just can't. I can't leave my new job. I can't leave my parents that far behind. And I don't want to lose you in a plane crash."

Phil could tell that she was very upset and that upset him. He had to do something quickly, because he had not intended for this to happen. "Sweet Peaches, I, I am so sorry to upset you like that. I didn't mean that I was going. I was just thinking about it. I am not going, sweetheart. Honest."

Soon Linda stopped crying and replied between sobs, "Phil, I thought that we had agreed that you would come back here and go to college. We are supposed to get married."

"We can, sweetheart. We can. It was foolish of me to consider it. Its just that it was such a generous offer, it didn't seem right to just tell the Colonel right off the bat that I wouldn't do it. But you mean more to me than anything in the world. Just please stop crying. I am so sorry that I mentioned it. In fact, let's just forget I ever mentioned it, okay?" He heard a sigh of relief in the phone. A moment later, Linda whispered, "Okay, honey. I'm sorry I got so upset. I love you. Call me again soon."

Phil felt dejected as he hung up the phone. Suddenly, he realized that he was going to have to make a choice. He could either stay in the Air Corps and have a dream job of flying rockets, or he could go home and marry Linda. He quickly decided to put his dream on hold.

Colonel Doakes kept Phil and the rest of the test flight pilots very busy transferring and storing the airplanes from Frederick to Altus, Oklahoma. They were almost through dismantling the air base when one day in late November Colonel Doakes called Phil into his office. "Phil, your orders are to report to the Seymour Johnson Air Base at Goldsboro, North Carolina. You will be mustered out and discharged there, that is, unless you have changed your mind about accompanying me to California."

"Thank you, Colonel. But I have not changed my mind. I still want to get out. Ah, I think you understand."

Colonel Doakes looked straight at Phil. One corner of his mouth turned upward into part of a smile. "I think I do, Lieutenant. But I could sure use you out in California." He stood from behind his desk and offered his hand to Phil. "Good luck, son." Phil shook the older man's hand firmly. "Thank you, sir." He knew he would miss Colonel Doakes a great deal. Phil returned to his quarters and began packing for the trip back home.

Chapter Thirty-five

It was the last of November when Phil left Frederick, Oklahoma for the last time. It was early Saturday morning when he started warming up the car for the trip. It had frosted on the windows and it took some scraping to get it off. Since he had called and told Jim and Jean the night before that he would go by and see them, he wanted to get as early a start as possible. It was almost noon when Phil arrived in Wichita. Strawberry had a large plate of fried chicken and biscuits ready. She had also invited Jean over for lunch. During the lunch Jim, Strawberry and Phil talked about North Carolina, being able to go home and about going to college. Jean hardly said a word. She remained very quiet. She had begun to realize recently that she could not get Phil. Now, she knew for sure. Jim told Phil that he though it would not be long before he would be following him back home. He wanted to get out and go to college in Raleigh maybe in Mechanical Engineering.

Phil thanked Strawberry for the great lunch and told Jim that he would be looking forward for them in Raleigh. He shook Jim's hand, walked over to Strawberry, hugged and kissed her on the cheek. He then took hold of Jean's waist. "Beautiful, I want you to know that its been wonderful knowing you. I have enjoyed every minute when we were together. You are a most wonderful person, and one day you will make someone a very happy man. I wish you all the happiness in the world." He hugged her closely and kissed her tenderly on the cheek. As he turned to leave, he noticed tears start to roll down her cheeks. His heart went out to her and he wanted to hold her close, but knew he could not.

"Good luck, Phil. I'll miss you!" she said as he opened the door to leave. The words kept coming back to him as he drove towards North Carolina.

It was late Monday afternoon when Phil drove into Raleigh, North Carolina. He soon found Linda's apartment and knocked on the door. No one answered. He glanced at his watch and saw that it was not quite time for them to be home from work yet, so he decided that he would go downtown and see what changes had taken place since he had left. When he arrived on the main street, which was Fayetteville Street, he found that it was still much the same as when he was there last. There were the Boone-Iseley and Eckerd Drug Stores where all the teenagers and college kids usually hung out. There was the Ambassador Theater. At the dead end of Fayetteville Street was the Capitol building and at the other end was Memorial Auditorium. It looked as nothing had changed.

It was time for Linda to be off from work so he went back

to the apartment. He knocked on the door. It opened and Linda screamed out, "Phil!" He grabbed her around the waist and picked her up. He swung her around and around while they kissed each other happily. "You look wonderful, Sweet Peaches." He stood her back on her feet and kissed her passionately. They clung to each other for several minutes, feeling so wonderful at finally being together.

"Phil, honey, you look so wonderful! I have never seen you in your officer's winter uniform before. It looks so nice on you."

"Thanks, Peaches, but you are the one that's beautiful. What have you done to your hair?"

"Oh, nothing much. I just reshaped it a little. Trying to stay in style. Don't you like it?"

"Sweet, I just think it is beautiful. I like the way it starts in waves and ends in the buoyant curls over the ears. And the color is more blonde than ever!"

"Yep," she replied. "And you know they say, blondes have more fun." She laughed at Phil and stuck up her nose at him.

"Yeah, with me!" he retorted, grabbing her and kissing her. Just then, the door opened and Linda's roommate came into the room.

"Phil, honey, I want you to meet my friend Lue. Lue, this is Phil."

"I would have never guessed," she laughed. "I'm pleased to meet you Phil. I have heard lots and lots about you."

"I'm sure it was all good," Phil teased as he shook her hand.

Linda took Phil for a quick tour of the apartment. It had two bedrooms with a small living room, a bath and a small kitchen. "How do you like it?" she asked.

"I think it is neat, sweetheart. I like it. It's a little small, but everything is very convenient," he smiled back.

"We love it, and its so close to downtown. I can even walk to work," she cooed as she took his hand.

They sat down on the sofa and hugged each other, very happy to be in each other's arms again. Soon Linda stopped kissing Phil and asked, "Honey, when are you supposed to report to Seymour Johnson Field? Are they going to discharge you?"

"Well, they are going to muster me out there, after my physical examination and all of my papers are straight. I have to report there Wednesday. I was just wondering, maybe I could spend the night here, go home tomorrow to visit my folks, and then report to Goldsboro the next day."

"Oh, Phil, that would be wonderful! I was hoping that you could spend the night here with us. You can sleep on the couch."

"Sure. That couch will sleep ten times better than those old cots I slept on in boot camp. That will be nice."

"After you muster out, when can you come back to Raleigh?" she asked.

Phil straightened up and with a soft voice replied, "I am hoping that they'll be through discharging me by Friday. Then I can come back and look for a room up here. Anyway, I'll be back here by Friday night."

It was almost time for supper when Lue appeared in the living room doorway. "Linda, would you and Phil like to have supper here? I know that Phil likes fried chicken and we have some in the refrigerator."

"That's nice of you Lue, but we could go out," Phil offered. His mouth was watering for some good Southern-cooked fried chicken but he did not want to impose on the girls.

"Lets do eat here. I'll help you cook, Lue," Linda said getting up from the sofa. "Okay, Phil?"

"Well, if you all insist. What can I do?"

"Nothing," replied Lue. "I know you are tired from all that driving so you just sit back and rest awhile."

As the girls prepared supper, Phil reclined on the sofa. Since the kitchen had an open bar between it and the living room, Phil could watch and carry on a conversation with the girls. He noticed that Lue was doing most of the cooking. He knew that Linda had never done much cooking before he left. He guessed that she still probably did not know much about cooking. Her mother never wanted her to cook. After supper, Phil praised both the girls for a wonderful meal. He thought, it was really the best fried chicken that he had tasted since Granny Barkley's cooking before he left home. Strawberry's fried chicken was good but Lue's was better.

Before long, it grew late. Lue went to her room saying that she had to work the next day and was retiring. Linda and Phil snuggled down on the sofa and relaxed. Linda turned the radio to a station that was playing some of Glen Miller's records. After a while, Phil got up off the couch and went to the telephone. He called the disk jockey at the radio station and asked him to play a song and dedicate it to Linda, his fiancee.

As he sat back down on the couch Linda asked, "Honey who was that you were calling?"

"Oh it was just a friend, Sweet Peaches. You will see."

He turned the volume dial up a little and settled back on the sofa. At the end of a song the radio disk jockey started talking. "I have a special request. The next song is dedicated to Linda by Phil." The words and music to "Have I Told You Lately That I Love You" started coming over the radio.

She looked into Phil's eyes, "Oh Phil that's so sweet. Thank you." She pulled him down on the couch and whispered into his ear. "I love you."

He slipped his hand around her waist and pulled her closer to him. "I love you too, sweet Peaches." He kissed her lips her cheek and tenderly kissed her ear and neck.

235

She felt a deep urge to love him back, an urge that she had felt before, only this time she did not feel afraid. She pulled him closer. He responded with a deep passion to love her as he slid her panties down. She felt a glowing sensation come over her as he started loving her. Suddenly, they both pulled and tugged at each other trying to get closer. She felt a wondrous sensation. It was a sensation she had been yearning for since that night with Phil at Holt's Lake. It was the night that Phil had asked her to marry him in the parking overlook on the lake. She pulled him to her tighter.

Phil was so filled with his passion for her that he did not feel her fingernails as they dug into his back. Both their bodies trembled and then they relaxed as if in a trance. They were both in each other's arms when Linda awakened and kissed Phil. He tried to kiss her but she pushed him away and started to arise off the sofa.

"Shhh, honey. I have to go to my room. You know that Lue will be getting up soon."

"Aw craps, that's a long time away!"

She slapped her hand over his mouth and whispered, "Hush, Phil. You might awaken her."

"I don't care," he whispered back. "I want you."

"Later," she whispered, and kissed him lightly on the cheek. She gently pushed him back down on the sofa and went to her room. She knew that she did not want to be in the living room when Lue would be getting up to go to work. As they were getting breakfast ready, Phil tried to help. When he burned the toast he threw up his hands.

"I quit. I quit. I'm just no good at cooking." Lue looked at him with a grin. "Sit down and relax, Phil. Linda and I are doing alright." She and Linda glanced at each other and laughed. After breakfast he hugged Lue, kissed her on the cheek, and thanked her for the breakfast

He pulled Linda to him and kissed her warmly. "Sweet Peaches, I'll see you Friday night."

Later, as Phil turned the '38 Chevrolet into the lane leading from the main road up to the Barkley farm house, a large lump came into his throat. The sight of the large white house with the porch around the front, the now barren crepe myrtle trees down the sides of the lane, the white painted wooden fence that ran down the sides of the lane and along the fields on the main road, and the brown colored fields dotted with hay stacks and cows grazing nearby, all brought back the memories of his teenage years at home. He thought about how good it seemed to be home and how great home looked to him. Even though it was winter time and the trees and fields were now brown and bare, it was a beautiful sight to Phil.

The car moved slowly up the lane. Phil could not see any

movement around the house nor in the fields, with the exception of the cattle. He knew that the twins were in school, and that Leah and Anita had started taking a nursing course in Wilson and they would not be at home. He pulled up in front of the house and tried the front door. It was not locked. He opened the door and went down the hall to the kitchen which was located at the farthest end of the hallway. As he peered through the doorway into the kitchen he saw Granny Barkley making biscuits at the kitchen table. He sneaked up behind her and jerked on her apron string causing her apron to fall to the floor. She whirled around striking Phil on the arm with her flour-covered hand.

"Who in blazes?" She suddenly recovered from her surprise as she recognized Phil. "Philip Barkley, my God!" She grabbed him, hugging him tightly, unaware that the flour on her hands was getting all over his uniform. "Let me look at you, son. Oh, you look so good in that uniform. Why it looks like you have grown two inches. How are you, my boy?"

"I'm fine Granny, and I'm so glad to be home again."

"Yes son, we have really missed you!"

"Uh, where is Daddy?"

"Oh, he's probably in the front room, nodding to sleep with his feet stuck up toward the fireplace."

"I'll go see," replied Phil getting anxious to see his father. Phil went into the front room and sure enough, there was his father sitting by the fire. His father heard him enter the room and turned to see who it was.

"Phil, my boy!" His father instantly recognized him and stood up quickly. "Welcome home son!" It was very evident that he was very pleased to see his son. He hugged Phil and told him to sit down so that they could talk.

Friday came and it was late in the afternoon when Phil left Seymour Johnson Air Base in Goldsboro. Things had worked out well for him and he had received his discharge papers. He went by the Barkley home and picked up the rest of his clothes and things. Granny Barkley had washed and ironed all his clothes and had them neatly packed in his suitcase. He thanked her, hugged her, shook his father's hand and headed the '38 Chevrolet back toward Raleigh. Daddy Barkley and Granny Barkley knew that there was no use trying to get Phil to stay with them longer. They knew that he was longing to get back to Linda for it showed in his actions.

It was almost dark when Phil arrived in Raleigh and knocked on Linda's door. As she opened the door, she grabbed him and kissed him lightly on the lips. He held her close, looking down into her soft, kind blue eyes. "Sweet Peaches, I can't stand it away from you."

"Me too, honey," she replied as she again kissed him tenderly. He tried to make the kiss linger but she gently pulled away. "Supper was ready a while ago. It's probably cold by now."

"Peaches, you didn't cook did you?"

"Sure, honey. I wanted to cook tonight. Lue has gone to visit her friends in Fayetteville this weekend. I got off a little early so I could make a good supper for you."

"Oh, sweetheart. You shouldn't have. You are so sweet. Come here, I want to kiss you." They embraced each other, then sat down to supper. Phil praised Linda almost after each bite, even though it was difficult to chew the over-done fried pork chops that she had prepared for him. He was very careful not to let her see him having any difficulty with her food.

That night Linda wanted to talk about Phil going to college but Phil tried to talk of his flying experiences. She continued to press on him to go to college and getting a degree in mechanical engineering at N.C. State College in Raleigh but he started talking about when they could get married. She stopped him about getting married by telling him that they will have to get more settled and decide on whether he will have to get a part time job or not when he enters college. He assured her that he wanted a college degree but wanted it in aeronautical engineering.

Phil felt downhearted for he was expecting for them to be married real soon. Linda was also beginning to feel apprehensive about Phil's career. She had thought that he would leave flying out of his career but now she was not sure. He reached over and pulled her close to him. "Sweet Peaches, I want to do what will make you happy. I love you so much."

"I know, Phil. I love you too, but we must do what will make us both happy."

"You are sweet, Peaches. I think that it will be best if I get a room close by and get a job to last until the next semester which starts after the first of the year. Maybe we can be able to get married then, okay?"

"I, I guess so. Maybe," she replied.

That night Linda arose off the sofa and went towards her bedroom. Phil followed her. As she opened the door to her bedroom, she stopped, turned to Phil and kissed him affectionately. "Honey, I think it is better that you sleep in the other bedroom tonight."

Phil was taken aback and stammered, "I, I, is something wrong?"

"No, Phil. It's just that I don't feel right. I'm scared that something might happen. We should wait until we get married. I want you so much too, honey. But can't we wait?"

Phil was so surprised that he stuttered, "Ah, ah, sure sweetheart."

She kissed him again lightly and closed the door. "Good

238

night."

Phil paused at the door, dismayed. He finally turned and went to bed. Sleep finally came but only after he decided that Linda was right. They should wait.

The next day Phil and Linda went looking for a room for Phil. They found one in a boarding house not far from Linda's apartment building. Phil moved into his room on Saturday afternoon but still stayed at Linda's apartment until Sunday afternoon. They looked into the newspapers for some jobs for Phil to apply for. He picked out some jobs at a couple of service stations and decided to go apply for them on Monday. They enjoyed the weekend together but Linda still did not want Phil to make love to her. He accepted this reluctantly.

Phil spent Sunday night in his room at the rooming house getting his clothes put into the chest of drawers and into the closets. His room was located on the third floor of the rooming house and was close enough to the downtown area that he could get a good view of the skyline from his window. The next morning he went to one of the service stations that had advertised for help in the newspaper. The owner interviewed Phil and since he had prior experiences in the service station business while going to high school, he hired him on the spot. Phil was tickled since the station was located near Linda's apartment. He would be working daylight hours each day except Sunday. Sunday would be his day off.

Chapter Thirty-six

In the weeks that followed, Phil and Linda went out together almost every night. On Sundays they usually went home to visit their families. One Sunday, however, it was warm and the sun was shining brightly. It was such a pretty day that they decided to stay in Raleigh and walk downtown and be with some of the gang at Eckerds Drug Store.

Linda wanted to walk around the Capitol building first since it was located at the dead end of Fayetteville Street. It was an old building, but well kept and beautiful. There was the faithful old peanut vendor on the walkway selling peanuts to the sightseers who would feed them to the squirrels and pigeons that called the grounds home. Phil bought Linda a large bag of peanuts and they had a ball feeding them to the squirrels and watching their antics. A couple of the squirrels were so friendly that they came up and took peanuts from Linda's hand. When the bag was empty, Phil and Linda continued walking down the sidewalk towards the drug store.

Such a pretty day had brought out a lot of college students who lived downtown. One could easily tell that many of the students were GI's that were taking advantage of the GI Bill which paid for their education.

As they neared Eckerds Drug Store, a young man walking towards them suddenly threw up his hand and said hi as he passed by. Phil suddenly recognized the boy. It was Eddie Hart!

"Wasn't that Eddie?" he asked Linda.

"Yes it was, honey," she replied.

"Ah, ah, I wonder what he is doing up here?"

Linda smiled reassuringly. "Honey, he works up here. He's been up here for a couple of months now, working for Carolina Power and Light Company."

"Oh, well," Phil stammered. "I had no idea." He tried to regain his composure to avoid revealing the agitation he felt.

"I'm sorry, Phil. I thought I told you. I guess I forgot."

"That's okay, sweetie. Lets get a Coke." As they turned to enter Eckerds, he decided it was best to forget about Eddie.

The following Sunday, Phil and Linda went to their homes to visit. Daddy Barkley handed Phil a letter from Jim Kelford. It said that they would be coming home and that they would be in Raleigh on December 15th. He also mentioned that he would probably be going to college at North Carolina State College.

December 15th came on a Saturday. Phil had asked off from his job so that he could be with his friends and Linda that afternoon. He had just arrived at Linda's apartment at noon and had gone inside when a knock came on the door. Linda opened it and a familiar voice yelled out.

"Hi, gang!" said Strawberry as she rushed in and hugged Linda and Phil. Jim quickly followed, kissing Linda on the cheek and hugging his old buddy tightly.

"Hi there, pal," he said. "Boy, I really missed you."

"Welcome to Raleigh," Linda exclaimed. "You know, its been over three years since I last saw you two!"

"It sure has," remarked Strawberry. "It just doesn't seem that long."

They all sat down at the kitchen table and Linda served pizza, which Phil had picked up on his way over to her apartment. After lunch, Phil produced a newspaper. He and Jim searched the want ads for an apartment.

"Well, we've decided it best that I try to go to North Carolina State College and get a degree in mechanical engineering. I know that it will be tough and we'll never make it on the $75 per month that the government will pay me to go to school. So, I want to find a small efficiency apartment, then get a part-time job. Maybe Strawberry can find a secretarial job too. If we can do that, I'm sure I'll get my degree. Say, how about you two? What are your plans, Phil?"

"Oh, Linda and I have been talking lately about me getting into the mechanical engineering program at State College."

"You don't sound too sure about it," Jim remarked.

"Well, truthfully, I'd like to stay connected with flying, so I am leaning towards the aeronautical engineering program. You know how I love flying. Maybe someday I'll get on with a commercial airline. Anyway, for now I guess we've decided that I'll go into mechanical engineering. Hey, maybe we'll have some classes together!"

"That would be great," said Jim.

Soon, Jim found some efficiency apartments in the paper so they all piled into Phil's Chevrolet to go apartment hunting.

"I'll drive since I know more about town and it will be safer," Phil grinned as he took the wheel.

"I doubt that, kiddo. I've never had a wreck or crash landing," Jim chuckled.

They finally found a nice one-bedroom efficiency apartment on the ground floor of an apartment building that was located about halfway between downtown and the college. The next week, Jim found a part-time job in a downtown department store. Strawberry got a secretarial job in the state legislature building. Phil was happy that things were working out well for his friends. Early in January, he and Jim went to the admissions office at the college. Both were admitted to the engineering program and they were to begin classes on January 14th.

The following Sunday was sunny and warm. Phil had been itching to go flying ever since he had heard there was a PT-13 at the Raleigh airport. A co-worker at the service station, who also worked out at the airport, told him they rented planes like the PT-13 and Piper Cubs for three dollars an hour. He had called Jim and Strawberry the night before and asked them if they would like to go out to the airport and watch him do some stunt flying, knowing that if they said yes, Linda would go along. He had been wanting to fly anything lately, and to luck into a chance to fly a PT-13 was too good to pass up. After lunch, they headed for the airport.

Phil parked his car in front of the hanger and they all got out of the car and went into the office. The manager gave Phil a parachute and a set of goggles. "The plane is outside and all set to go, Mr. Barkley."

"Thank you sir," Phil replied. "Hey," he said to his friends. "You all can watch me from the apron where they park the planes. I have permission to do the aerobatics over the airport and you can see really well from the parking apron, especially if you get near the runway."

"Lets go," Jim said as he took Strawberry and Linda arm-in-arm.

Linda looked at Phil anxiously. "Phil, please be careful."

"Oh, I will sweet Peaches. I can do stunts blindfolded. You'll love it! Its almost as exciting to watch as it is to do!

When they reached the parking apron, the PT-13 was standing ready with the engine idling and the propeller spinning lazily around. Phil patted Linda gently on the back and ran over to the plane, climbing into the back seat.

"Why is he getting into the back seat?" Linda asked Jim.

"It's called flying by the seat of your pants," Jim shouted over the noise of the plane's engine. "Pilots can feel the movement and attitude of the plane better from that position while they are flying."

Phil adjusted his goggles, then waved at Jim and Strawberry and threw a kiss at Linda. Then, he revved the engine and roared off down the runway. Once the plane was a couple hundred feet into the air, he put it into a quick snap roll. He wished he could be on the ground to hear Strawberry and Linda gasp. He continued the aerobatics with a few "Lazy Eights" and barrel rolls over the airport. Slowly, he climbed the plane higher, doing more snap rolls and slow rolls as he went. He pulled the plane almost straight up and put it in a slow flying position. This made it look like it was stopped in mid-air to people on the ground. He then cut the engine and let the plane fall into a tail spin. He quickly recovered from the tail spin and then nosed the plane down into a dive. He guided the plane down close to the ground where they were standing and then pulled it up sharply into a tight loop. When the plane reached the top of the loop in an inverted position, something fell out of it!

"It's Phil!" Linda screamed in horror. "He's fallen out of the plane!" She clutched Jim's arm tightly as they all looked skyward in amazement. Suddenly a parachute opened and began floating down toward the airport. Everyone breathed a sigh of relief. As the parachute floated underneath, the plane slowly righted itself and acted like a falling leaf. It came down and disappeared behind some trees off from the airport.

Jim looked at Strawberry and said, "I think that the wind will carry Phil down to the other end of the airfield. I'll get the car and we'll go out to pick him up."

"Oh, lets do!" Linda exclaimed anxiously. "Lets do!"

As Jim turned to get the car, they all heard the noise of an airplane engine. Looking out across the field. they saw the PT-13 suddenly appear over the tree tops. Moments later, it had landed on the runway. It quickly taxied up and stopped just in front of them. When the pilot jumped out and pulled off his goggles, they discovered it was Phil!

Linda shouted and ran towards him. She grabbed and hugged him.

"What in the hell!" exclaimed Jim. "You tricked us, didn't you? Why you bum!"

Phil was laughing. Jim and Strawberry were smiling. Linda had begun to frown.

"Who was the guy in the parachute?" asked Jim.

"He works with me at the service station part-time. He also works out here at the airport. We thought that it would be a neat trick so we went for it."

"I don't think it was so neat!" Linda scolded. Her relief over Phil's safety had quickly given way to hot anger. "You nearly scared the life out of me, Phil Barkley!" She pushed him aside and stormed back to the car.

Suddenly Phil's knees felt weak. He realized that it had been a juvenile prank and he should not have done it to her. Just then he wanted to take it all back, but it was too late. He began running after her, trying to make amends.

"Oh, honey. I, I didn't mean to scare you. I, I'm sorry! I thought that it would be exciting."

"Exciting? Exciting for you, maybe, but not for me!" she retorted hotly.

Jim and Strawberry said nothing as they climbed into the back seat. The ride home was long and silent. Phil dropped off Jim and Strawberry at their apartment and went on to Linda's apartment. It was almost supper time before she said anything to him except curtly replying yes or no.

Phil used his best manners and affection to try to soothe her feelings as they made sandwiches for a snack. By the time he left that night, he felt that she had began to warm up to him again. They had held each other on the sofa and they kissed each other a few times. She seemed to relax and even smiled when he said goodnight at her door. But as he left there was still a nagging feeling deep inside that he had really messed up that day.

Chapter Thirty-seven

During the following week, Phil took Linda out almost every night. They spent their weekends and Christmas holidays at their families' homes. On January fourteenth, Phil and Jim entered State College in the Mechanical Engineering curriculum. Phil had quit working full-time at the service station, but still worked some afternoons and on Saturdays. He had not mentioned flying around Linda since the day he went up stunt flying, but he soon began to feel the urge to fly again. One Saturday, he asked Jim if he would like to go up with him in the PT-13.

"Sure, buddy. I haven't been up with you since Wichita. It'll be great!"

"Well, tomorrow looks like a good day. I'll see if the girls want to go with us." Phil found Linda and Strawberry in the kitchen cooking supper.

"Hey girls! Jim and I want to go out flying tomorrow," Phil exclaimed. "Wouldn't you like to come with us?"

Linda shot a quick glance at Phil. "Not me," she said curtly. "I think I'll go to a movie. I think there's a good one playing at the Ambassador." She quickly turned back to her cooking. "You can go if you want Strawberry."

"Ah, I believe I'll go with Linda to see the movie. you boys can have an afternoon out on your own, okay Phil?"

"Sure, that's okay with me. You're sure you don't want to go?"

Linda turned and frowned at Phil. "We're sure. We're sure."

He smiled at her as he turned to go, but he knew that she still hadn't forgiven him about the prank he pulled on her.

A few weeks later, Linda invited Phil over to her apartment for a fried chicken dinner. She had learned from Strawberry how to fry it the way Phil liked it. When he came into her apartment, Phil grabbed her around her waist and kissed the back of her neck. "I love you, sweet Peaches."

"Honey, I love you too, but I have cooking to do!" She gently pushed him away and continued preparing the meal.

Phil walked into the living room and put on a record to play.

He danced back into the kitchen and tugged at her apron strings.

"Phil Barkley, what are you doing?" she exclaimed. "Why are you so happy tonight?" She grabbed her apron before it fell to the floor and looked at him. A slight smile began to escape her lips.

Phil grinned. "Oh, nothing. Its just such a pretty day and I feel great! And besides, I have you, sweet Peaches." He placed his hands on her hips and danced a little two-step around the kitchen. He kissed her on the cheek and moved back out into the living room, humming along with the song.

When they were halfway through the meal, Linda finally asked the question she'd been holding back for an hour. "Honey, just what happened to day to make you so happy. Something did because it shows all over your face."

Phil almost choked on a mouthful of fried chicken. "Well, sweetheart," he began. "Guess what?" He paused a minute to see if she would play along. She simply stared back, waiting for his answer. "I received a letter from Colonel Doakes today!" he continued. "He said the weather is very nice out in California. The sun shines all the time and it is warm and the countryside is very beautiful. He likes it very much."

"Is that all he said, Phil?"

Phil thought she sounded a bit impatient. "Well," he answered. "He did mention that a local college had a great course in aeronautical engineering." He saw a puzzled look come over her face.

"I wonder why he would say that?" she quipped.

"Well, sweetheart, when I was stationed at Frederick we talked about me taking aeronautical engineering out there. I guess he thinks that I am still interested."

"Well, are you?"

Phil saw the anxious glare in her eyes. He pulled his chair up close to hers and put his arm around her neck. "Sweet Peaches, I think that it would be exciting in California." He paused. "I know you would love it, but I am enrolled in mechanical engineering here. North Carolina is a wonderful place too, and as long as I have you, I am the happiest person around." He kissed her gently, with real affection, and felt her relax in his arms.

"I hope so, honey," she replied.

Later that evening, they sat on the sofa listening to soft music by Guy Lombardo. "Sweetheart," Phil wondered aloud. "Isn't it time for us to set our wedding date?"

Linda hesitated before answering. "Oh honey, we don't have to think about that now do we? I don't think we could make it very well just yet. I'd like for us to do some more planning, okay?"

"Ah, if you say so," Phil replied sadly.

Chapter Thirty-eight

By the end of February, 1946, Phil was thoroughly ready for winter to end. Going to school, studying, and working took up most of his time, but he did get to see Linda almost every night. There had been several heavy snows which had made working at the service station even more difficult. But he kept at it, trying to work as many hours as possible to save up enough money to get married. He figured the more money he saved, the quicker Linda would set a date for their wedding.

At times, he would bring up the wedding date in their conversations, but she always seemed to change the conversation to something about Phil's studies. He told her that mechanical engineering was very difficult and he was having trouble with the homework at times. He didn't tell her that it was mainly because he was not interested in it. When he occasionally mentioned aeronautic engineering, she would quickly change the subject. He never pressed it, but he felt sure that she would change her mind if he kept bringing it up. He was beginning to miss flying and dreamed of going to California.

One night, Phil knocked on Linda's door. "Come in, Phil. you must have finished early tonight. Can I fix you some supper?"

"No thanks, sweet Peaches. I have already eaten." He grabbed her and kissed her passionately.

"You are awfully cheerful today. What's the good news?"

"Sweet Peaches, I do have some good news and I want us to talk about it, so let's sit down. I believe you will be interested."

"What is it, Phil?"

"Sweetheart, I've just received a letter from Colonel Doakes. He is offering a Captain's rating for me and a job for you if . . ."

"What?" she exclaimed. "You mean you want to go to California?"

"Yes, honey. Doesn't it sound great?"

Her voice quivered. "I, I thought we had settled this, Phil. You are s-studying mechanical engineering here. We aren't g-going to California."

"But Linda, just think of the wonderful opportunity it will be for us both. You will love California." He saw that she was not giving in, but felt he had too much at stake to give up just then.

"W-will you be flying?" she asked.

"Well, yes. When I'm not in school, I would be flying. The Colonel said that I would be flying some of the experimental jets for him. He said they have a former German rocket scientist and there is more talk of building rockets and rocket planes. There is even talk of breaking the sound barrier and of rockets to outer space. He said there is a great future out there for me. Doesn't it sound thrilling?"

Linda put her hands over her face. "Maybe to you, Phil," she said as her voice rose. "But I don't like it!"

Her last remark had virtually been a scream. Phil realized she was becoming very upset. He tried to pull her close to give her a reassuring hug, but she resisted firmly. "Sweetheart," he continued. "At least think about it awhile." He felt that she would change her mind later if she could just think about it rationally.

"No Phil," she said loudly. "I won't leave my friends or my family or my job!"

"Sweet Peaches, you can come back anytime you want to see your family. You can even fly back here. Air Corps personnel get cheaper rates and I could afford it."

"But it won't be the same," she blurted out as tears sprang from her eyes and flooded her cheeks.

Phil realized that things were only getting worse. He began to become upset as well. His gut feeling was that her mother did not want her to leave. He decided it was best to leave so that she wouldn't discover that he was upset too. He pulled her chin up and looked into her teary eyes. "Don't worry, Peaches. Let's forget it. The most important thing is that I love you." He gently kissed her tear-stained face, but she didn't respond. An idea suddenly flashed into his mind. Maybe if they went to Holt's Lake it might bring back old memories and she would feel better towards him. "Sweetheart," he said, looking into her deep blue eyes. "Would you like to go down to Holt's Lake Saturday night? Maybe we can see some of the old gang there."

Her face brightened. "Oh, Phil. I would love that!" She kissed him gently on the lips. "But right now, I think you'd better leave, okay?"

"I understand," he replied. "Goodnight, Peaches."

The next day, Phil asked Jim and Strawberry to come along to Holt's Lake. When Saturday night arrived, they all climbed into Phil's car and headed for Smithfield. They arrived just after dark and quickly discovered there had been no changes in the place since they had left for military service. It seemed like ages since they walked through the front doors of the dance pavilion

There was a large group of young people there but hardly anyone they knew. After they had ordered some hamburgers, they sat down at one of the tables in the dining area of the dance hall. They were almost through eating when someone slapped Phil on the back. He turned and looked up. It was one of Phil and Jim's old buddies that played on the football team at Kenly.

"Hey guys! Remember me?" Phil and Jim jumped up and grabbed their old friend and hugged him.

248

"Hey, sit down here and join us old pal," Phil said happily. He noticed his old buddy had a slight limp as he came around the table to sit down.

"Where have you been?" Jim asked. "You just get out of the military?"

"Yep," replied his buddy. "I was in the Air Corps. Aerial gunner on a B-24. Took a piece of flak from an anti-aircraft shell in the right leg, but I'm okay now."

"Hey, we're Air Corps too," Phil said. They spent the next half-hour sharing their war experiences. Soon their old buddy left and they began dancing to Guy Lombardo's music. Phil and Linda danced the jitterbug dance a few times and Linda began to appear more cheerful. Jim and Strawberry had noticed that she was in a pensive mood since they left Raleigh.

During the following week, Phil saw Linda every night. She seemed happy again. Soon, Phil felt that everything was alright again between them. One night, as they sat on the sofa, Phil picked up the newspaper and glanced through it. "Hey, sweetheart. It says here that the weather is beautiful in California."

"Would you like to be there Phil?"

"Sure, sweetheart. You would too if you knew how nice it would be. It would be great for us."

She quickly arose from the sofa and went to the kitchen. Phil realized that she did not like what he had said. He became downhearted and soon left. He called her on Friday and asked her for a date. She refused and told him that she wasn't feeling good.

Chapter Thirty-nine

A couple of weeks passed in which Linda would only date Phil on the weekends. She told him that she was so busy at work that she had to bring some work home with her. He reluctantly accepted her excuse but wondered about it since she still acted cool towards him on their dates. He wanted to try to cheer her up so he invited her to go to see "Gone with the Wind" at the theater on Sunday afternoon.

"I would love to Phil. Could we invite Strawberry and Jim?"

"Oh sure, that would be fine with me." Phil replied with a little hesitation in his voice. He was hoping that they could go alone since he wanted to improve his relations with her.

Saturday afternoon was a nice sunny afternoon. It was March and the weather had warmed up nicely. Phil asked his boss at the service station if he could be off. He said yes. He went to see Linda.

"Sweet Peaches, would you like to go for a ride?" She looked at Phil and felt a little tug at her heart. She wanted to think that he was changing his mind since he hadn't mentioned anything about flying or California lately.

"Oh, its so nice outside. That would be nice Phil. I would love to. I'll go get my jacket." This made Phil feel good. He thought, maybe she has reconsidered and is not angry with him anymore. They went out to the park and Phil teased the monkeys a little but they wouldn't pay him much attention.

"Hey Sweet, lets ride out to the country, okay?"

"Sure, I'd like that," Linda replied happily.

He headed the car out of town and soon came to the airport. As they started by it, Phil suddenly turned into the airport driveway.

"What are you doing Phil? I thought we were going to the country."

"Oh I see my buddy's car, you know, the one that works at the service station and also works out here."

"Yes, I remember! I well remember!" A slight look of dejection comes over her face as she glances at Phil. "I thought that we were going to the country."

"We are, we are!" replied Phil quickly. "I just wanted to stop by and say hello to my friend.

As Phil drove up to the side of the hanger, he noticed his buddy coming from the aircraft parking area. "Hey, Kent!" Phil blew on his horn and yelled at his friend. "Over here." His friend heard his call and came jogging over to the car

"Hi Phil. Hi Linda. What are you guys up to?"

"Oh we're just riding around and I thought I'd stop and say hello."

"Say, I'm glad you did Phil. I've got something I think you will be interested in."

"Hey, what's that?" Phil was looking over at Linda but suddenly turned his attention to his buddy.

"The airport owner bought a nice PT-19 the other day. Didn't you tell me that you used to fly them in the Air Corps?"

Phil's face brightened and his voice became excited. "I sure did. Where is it?"

"Over there on the parking apron," Kent pointed his finger in its direction. "Would you like to take it up?"

"Would I? You bet I would."

"Well okay. Go get you a parachute and goggles. I'll crank it for you."

Phil looked over at Linda and noticed the look of dejection on her face. "Sweetheart, don't worry. I'll be alright. I won't be gone but just a few minutes. You don't mind do you?" Before she could nod her head, Phil was getting out of the car. She felt resentment building up inside her.

Phil flew the PT-19 around the airport area a couple of times and then returned. As he got back into the car where Linda was waiting he noticed the solemn look on Linda's face. He put his arm around her and tried to cheer her up.

"Now, that wasn't long, was it? I just couldn't stay away from my sweet Peaches for very long. No way!"

She tried to smile at him but couldn't. She told Phil that she didn't feel good and wanted to go back home. The apartment was cold when they returned to it so Phil turned up the thermostat. Linda sat down on the sofa and Phil got a blanket and put over her lap. "There. Feel better?" She nodded her head. "I'll go get us some hamburgers for supper if you want," he continued. "Okay? She nodded her head again, but did not smile at him. He soon returned with the hamburgers and they sat quietly at the table eating them. Linda was not talking much so Phil figured that she was not feeling any better. He decided it best that he leave. "Sweetheart, I had better go. Maybe you'll feel better tomorrow. I hope so. I'll call you in the morning."

He kissed her gently and went to his room in the rooming house. He did not go to sleep easily that night for he felt rejected and a little resentful. He could not understand why Linda became upset when he flew the PT-19. After all, he had not flown any recently. After Phil left, Linda went to bed but could not go to sleep. She tossed and turned nearly all night thinking and worrying about Phil. He didn't seem to be forgetting about going to California and flying.

The next morning, Phil called her. He had waited till mid-morning to call so as not to wake her if she was sleeping late.

"Peaches, this is Phil. How are you Sweetheart?"

"I'm okay, Phil," she retorted sharply. "What time does the

movie start?" She wanted to tell Phil that she couldn't go with him but she thought of Jim and Strawberry. She didn't want to disappoint them and it was supposed to be a real good movie.

"It starts at one o'clock, sweet Peaches."

"I'll be ready Phil." She hung up quickly.

Phil could tell by the tone of her voice that she was still peeved at him. He hoped that going to the movie would soothe her and things would be better. Phil picked up Jim and Strawberry first and then went and picked up Linda before going to the movie. Jim and Strawberry noticed that Linda was acting coolly towards Phil. "Gone With The Wind" was a long movie and it was almost sunset before it was over. As they came out of the movie, Phil noticed that there were not many people on Fayetteville Street. Phil thought since it was a warm and tranquil time of day that it would be nice to walk down the street and around Capitol Square.

"Hey guys, would you all like to walk a little, maybe around Capitol Square?"

"Yes, let's do," replied Strawberry. "Its a good time to walk and with the setting sun its beautiful."

"How about it, Peaches? Would you like to walk?"

Linda had been very quiet all during the movie. Everyone could tell that she was upset with Phil by the way she was treating him. Phil and Linda started down Fayetteville Street toward the Capitol. Jim and Strawberry followed a ways behind them. As they neared the Capitol Building, Phil started walking closer to Linda and tried to put his arm around her waist. She quickly pushed it away and stopped walking close to him. Jim noticed this and remarked to Strawberry.

"Is there something wrong with those two?"

She looked back at Jim with a worried look. "I think so Honey, and I'm worried about them. You know how Phil is about flying and going to California."

"Yes, I know he is still yearning to fly and is excited about Colonel Doakes' offer. He talks about it a lot, but he is worried about Linda. He wants her to marry him and them go to California."

Strawberry looked up at Jim. "Well Honey, I don't think that Linda is going to play second fiddle for Phil!"

"What do you mean?"

"She won't take second place to his love of flying."

"Well, I don't think he can give it up that easily. It has to be a hard choice for him. I think a lot of them both, and I hope they can work it out."

"Me too," replied Strawberry as she looked at the couple walking ahead of them. She noted that they were still walking separately.

That night, Phil used all his best manners and persuasion to make Linda feel better. He tried to convince her that everything would be fine and that they would be happy no matter where they were at. She felt better by the time he left and kissed him goodnight. The next few days Phil spent most of his time thinking about Colonel Doakes' offer. He could not get it out of his mind. He knew that he didn't want to quit flying. It was tugging at his heart and he was missing it terribly. The chance that Colonel Doakes was offering him was too good to be true. He had to make a decision. Take up Colonel Doakes' offer or forget it. He decided, maybe if he took up Colonel Doakes' offer, Linda would come with him anyway.

The next night, Phil called Linda and told her that he was going to the Air Force Recruiting Office to see about re-enlisting. She shouted back to him over the phone. "Is that what you really want Phil?"

"Its the best thing for us Peaches. We could be happy. You've always told me we can get married when things are more secure. Well, his offer can make us secure . . ." She hung up before he could finish. Phil was astonished, but then he thought to himself that she hadn't really said "no".

The next morning Phil skipped class and went down to the recruiting office and applied for a permanent commission as pilot, U. S. Army Air Corps. He called Linda and asked to come over to her apartment. He wanted to talk to her. When she answered the phone, her voice was anxious. "Phil, did you enlist today?"

"No, sweet Peaches, I just filled out some papers. I've have to go to Fort Bragg tomorrow and take examinations to get back in on a commission. It will take two or three days."

"Please don't go Phil, I don't want you to go back in!"

"But Sweetheart, we will miss a great opportunity. Can't I come over and talk about it?"

"Are you going to Fort Bragg tomorrow?"

"Well Sweet I'd like to go try. I might not pass." He felt the tension in her voice.

"Well, you can't come over. I don't feel good tonight. Goodbye."

Phil stood holding the phone for a few seconds. He realized that she was not giving in yet. That night Phil wrote Colonel Doakes a letter and notified him that he was taking examinations for a commission. The next morning, he left early for Fort Bragg. The next three days Phil spent taking mental and physical test. He tried not to worry about Linda but could not help it. He tried to get it out of his mind by thinking, surely she would change her mind and go with him to California. The final day came and Phil went before the review board for an interview. After it was over, he was asked to come back after lunch. Phil went to lunch but could not eat. He just sat and chewed on his fingernails. By the time he was to report back to the review board, he was in a cold sweat. The worry and apprehension about whether he had passed or not was getting to him. He thought, what if I don't pass? What if I don't pass? Linda will be happy, but I won't!

Finally it was time for phil to report back to the review board office. The officer in charge asked Phil to have a seat. He was so nervous and excited that he almost missed the seat when he sat down. The officer in charge began by sticking out his hand towards Phil. "Mr. Barkley, congratulations, you have passed all the examinations."

Phil let out a big gasp of breath. "Thank you, sir. Thank you, sir. When will I have to report for duty?"

"Well, Mr. Barkley, your appointment for a commission will come from Washington and I have been notified that your orders will come from there also. You won't know until then."

Phil was so excited that he rushed back to Raleigh, He called Linda and asked if he could come over. He tried not to appear very excited on the phone so as not to upset her. He wanted to be close to her when he told her the news. Maybe he could soothe her and things would be alright. She agreed to see him after supper that night. On the way to her apartment, Phil decided to carry a little assurance with him so he stopped at the florist and bought a dozen red roses for her. When he knocked on her door, Linda opened it quickly for she was beginning to miss Phil and she was eager to hear about the examination. Her heart was hoping that he had failed.

Phil held the roses up to her. "For you, my beautiful Peaches, with all my love." She took the roses and held them close to her chest.

"Phil, you shouldn't have. They are so beautiful."

"Its a match," replied Phil laughing.

Linda noticed that he was in a happy mood. She began to get uneasy. "Sit down Phil, and tell me about your trip."

Phil sat down on the sofa and pulled her close to him. "Sweet Peaches, it was a hard three days but I never let you out of my mind."

"But did you pass?" She looked straight into his face with a determined look. He knew he could not put it off any longer.

"Yes, I did Sweet."

With astonishment in her voice, she angrily asked, "Then you are going back in?"

"Yes," he began. "But sweet . . ."

She cut him off by suddenly pushing him away. She put her hands over her face and burst out crying. Phil tried to put his hand around her shoulder and soothe her. "We, we can be happy, sweetheart. I love you!"

She shuddered and jerked her shoulders away from him. "I

can't. I can't! I can't!" her voice suddenly became shrill. "Here. You can have this back!" She took off her engagement ring and flung it at him in anger.

Phil was astonished! He tried to put the ring back on her finger. "But Peaches, you don't mean it. I love you!"

She jerked her hand away. "Please go. Just go now!" she cried with tears rolling down her cheeks.

Phil had never seen her so ill and tried to soothe her further by kissing her cheek. She jerked away from him. "Get out of here!" her voice was filled with anger.

He reluctantly arose and left, slowly closing the door behind him. He heard her sobbing wildly when he closed the door. His heart was breaking as he walked down the walk. Linda locked the door and ran into her bedroom. She fell into the bed and cried. She felt that her life had been devastated. A few minutes later, she quickly arose and went to the telephone. She had to call her mother. Her mother had always made her feel good when she had problems. After a few rings, her mother came on the phone.

"Mother! Mother!" Linda sobbed into the phone.

"What is it? What is it my dear? What are you crying about?"

"It's Phil, Mother! It's Phil! He has re-enlisted in the Air Corps and will be going to California in June."

"And what about you?" her mother's voice sounded anxious.

"I don't want to go. I don't want to leave my job, my home, and I love my friends." she sobbed loudly

"You don't have to go my dear. You don't have to. We all love you and want you here. I hope you don't go. As you have probably realized, I have always felt that Phil was not right for you. You know there are friends here that you can be happy with and they are reliable."

Linda knew that her mother was referring to Eddie since she had always favored him over Phil. Linda finally hung up the phone. It rang almost immediately. It was Phil.

"Peaches, sweetheart . . ."

She slammed the phone up on the hook. He called back every night for the next week. He wanted to come over to talk to her. She told him that he could if he would cancel his re-enlistment. She hung up when he tried to evade giving her a definite yes.

Phil was getting very lonesome and was missing Linda a lot. He spent a lot of nights after school visiting with Jim and Strawberry. Since Linda refused to date him and would not talk to him on the telephone, it was on these visits that he was able to get bits of news about Linda. Strawberry and Linda sometimes ate lunch together at Eckerds Drug Store and it was at these occasions that they confided in each other. Phil got very disturbed one night at dinner when Strawberry told him that

Linda had started dating Eddie again. He was so disturbed that he arose from the dinner table and excused himself and went back to his room at the boarding house. As soon as he arrived at his room, he called Linda. When she heard his voice, she promptly hung up the phone. Phil decided to write her a letter. He pleaded with her to forgive him and tried to impress on her his love of her. Another week went by and she did not answer his letter.

It was Saturday night when Phil had returned to his room from working at the service station. He picked up his mail and saw a manila envelope from the Army Air Corps in it. He quickly opened it and there was his appointment as a Second Lieutenant in the regular U.S. Army Air Corps. He quickly opened the orders that were attached to it. It instructed him to report for duty to Minter Field, California in June. Phil was so elated that he jumped into his car and hurried over to Jim's apartment. He knocked on the door and Strawberry answered it. He grabbed her around the waist and tried to dance with her.

"Hey Phil, wait a minute. What's up?"

"Strawberry, I've got my commission and I'm going to California."

"That's nice Phil. When are you going?"

"In June," replied Phil jubilantly.

Is that what you want Phil?" asked Strawberry, thinking about how upset Linda was with Phil.

"Yes, I do Strawberry, I can't think of not taking advantage of this. Its what I've always wanted."

"What about Linda?"

"Well, that's what has got me worried. I think we would be very happy, once we were in California. I believe she will reconsider. I hope so because I love her so much."

"I hope so too Phil, but I don't know."

Phil tried for two days to call Linda but each time, she hung up on him. Finally the third night, she consented to listen to him when he called her. He pleaded with her and she began to talk with him. Finally he mustered enough nerve to tell her about getting his appointment and would probably be going to California in June.

She screamed, "You haven't changed! You haven't changed!" at him and slammed the phone up on the hook. This worried Phil so much that he could hardly go to sleep that night. He tried to call her every night for the next several days but she would not answer the phone. Lue would answer occasionally and say that Linda was not there. He tried writing her a letter but she did not answer.

One night Jim called Phil and told him that Strawberry had found out from some of Linda's girlfriends that Linda had become engaged to Eddie. This news shocked Phil and he became distraught. He started drinking at a local bar. This became heavier each night and at times he did not report for work at the service station.

Chapter Forty

Over the next few weeks, Phil became so despondent that Jim and Strawberry began to worry about him. He had dropped out of college and was working at the service station full-time. He didn't eat regularly and began to drink. Even the spring weather didn't seem to lift his spirits. April had arrived with its warmer days and blooming flowers. Phil even refused an offer from Jim that they go flying one weekend.

One night, Jim called Phil and invited him over for hamburgers. "I have some news for you, buddy. I think you'll like it."

That evening, as they sat in Strawberry's kitchen eating the hamburgers, Jim told Phil that he had received a letter from Jean Collier. "She asked about you, Phil."

Phil's expression suddenly brightened. "Really? What did she say about me?"

"Oh, not much. Just that she missed old times and wanted to know how we were all getting along. She asked how you and Linda were doing. She wanted to know if you were married yet."

Phil's voice became anxious. "Did she say anything about herself?"

"Well, just that things were about the same with her. She said that she seldom went out and that it was just not the same world with us three gone."

"Hey, that's the first smile I've seen on your old ugly puss in weeks, Phil," Jim said. Phil blushed. He was unaware that he had been smiling.

"Maybe you should call her, Phil," Strawberry suggested. "It sounds as if she needs cheering up again."

"Yeah," Phil said distantly, suddenly lost in happy memories of the times he had with Jean in Wichita. "Maybe I will."

Shortly after supper, Phil made the excuse that he was tired and didn't want to stay up too late. "Besides, I don't want to get in the way of Jim's studying," he said. He went straight back to his room and dialed the operator in Wichita. Soon, the phone was ringing in Jean Collier's apartment.

"Hi there, beautiful," he said as she answered. "How's tricks?"

There was a pause at the other end. "Phil? Is that you, Phil?"

"Yes love, it's me. How are things in Wichita?"

"Oh, Phil, you surprised me," she exclaimed happily. "But I'm so glad to hear from you! Everything is about the same here How are things in North Carolina?"

"Fine, love. Just fine. The weather is getting nicer every day. Jim and Strawberry are doing okay. I just got home from their apartment. We had hamburgers for supper."

"What are they up to?"

"Well, Strawberry is working and Jim is still going to college. He works part-time too."

"Are you still going to school?"

"I dropped school and now I'm just working at the service station full-time. I got a good offer from the Air Corps so I re-enlisted. I am supposed to report for duty in California this June."

"That's just great, Phil! I know how much you like to fly. I am so happy for you. I'm sure Linda will love California."

"Uh, yeah," he stammered. "I guess so." He continued to talk to Jean, but never mentioned that he and Linda were having problems.

Later that week, Jim and Strawberry invited Phil for supper again. Even in a slightly depressed state, Phil wouldn't turn down Strawberry's fried chicken.

During the meal his friends laughed and joked with Phil. He told them about his conversation with Jean and they talked about old times in Wichita. As they finished eating, Strawberry turned to Phil with a serious expression on her face.

"Phil, I have to tell you something that I'm sure you are unaware of."

"What's that, Strawberry?"

"Linda and Eddie are getting married Sunday."

"Ah, ah, are you sure?" Phil stammered, suddenly in shock.

"I'm sorry to have to be the one to tell you, Phil. She told me herself today." Strawberry put her hand on Phil's wrist to reassure him.

"She can't!" he exclaimed. "She just can't marry that . . ." He stopped short of calling Eddie a weakling. "I thought she'd change her mind . . ." his voice trailed off. His face suddenly paled and he stood from the table. "I've got to go." he said and quickly turned so his friends wouldn't see the tears stream down his cheeks.

Phil tried again and again to call Linda before Sunday, but she wouldn't talk to him. Her roommate, Lue, would answer the phone and make excuses for Linda. It was a very agonizing weekend for Phil. He was so despondent that his boss noticed and told him to take a few days off from the service station. He called Jean and told her about Linda and him breaking up. He decided to go out to Wichita and see her. He thought to himself that she had always made him feel good when they were together and he needed that more than ever.

He only had a few days off so he decided to fly to Wichita on a passenger plane. Jim and Strawberry took him out to the Raleigh airport. As Phil entered the four-engine constellation airliner, he marvelled at its huge size. It was the largest airplane that he had ever been in. He waved goodbye to Jim and Strawberry from his seat beside the window. The large plane took off down the runway and as it lifted up into the sky, Phil felt that familiar exhilaration of flying coursing through his body. Suddenly, it was as if his spirits were rising with the airplane as it lifted off the ground. In that instant, he forgot Linda and realized that he could hardly wait to arrive in Wichita!

Jean was waiting to greet him. As he approached her at the gate, he suddenly realized just how beautiful she really was. Her figure was still trim and more shapely than ever. She had on the prettiest pink outfit with a white, knit sweater to ward off the coolness of the day. Her dark, wavy hair set off her smooth, pink complexion. In her hair she wore a small red ribbon to compliment her dress.

Phil hurried through the gate and grabbed her. Jean pulled him close and they kissed each other happily. He looked down into her beautiful greenish blue eyes, noticing that the mysterious glint was still there. It had always intrigued him. The smile on her face still had a glimmer of merriment in it. He realized that he was feeling better that he had felt in a long time.

The next two nights, Phil and Jean went to the Club Lido. Phil had always enjoyed dancing with Jean and Guy Lombardo's music made it even more enjoyable. They even tried to Jitterbug during one tune. Jean stumbled and almost fell, but they both laughed it off.

Saturday night, they sat on the sofa in Jean's apartment. They had been to the zoo that day and then to dinner at the Club Lido. Phil was suddenly sad that he had to return to Raleigh on a flight that left early the next morning. He gazed down into her soft face. Their eyes met and they drank each other in deeply for a few seconds. They kissed each other hungrily for an hour, but neither wanted to press further for fear of ruining the whole weekend. Phil didn't sleep much that evening, but he felt more content than he had in months.

The next morning Phil sat at the window of the Constellation looking out at the landscape that was sliding along under the plane. He could see the patchwork of green and brown fields below him. It looked like a quilt made of square patches with some large green squares of forest. As he looked straight down he could see a highway snaking along the country side. The auto that was traveling on the highway looked as small as a flea crawling along the road. He looked towards the front of the plane and saw something on the horizon that looked like a crooked white line marked along on the ground from North to South. It was the mighty Mississippi River coming into view. The early morning rays of the sun could be seen glimmering on the water.

Phil leaned back in his seat to enjoy the peace and comfort

of the airplane. He felt relaxed and almost nodded off to sleep listening to the steady drone of the airplane engines. He thought to himself that he had not been this relaxed and happy in a long time. Jean had made him forget Linda for two wonderful days. The more he thought about it, the more he realized that she had always made him feel happy when they were together. He felt sure that he was falling in love with Jean. Then again, maybe he had always been in love with her.

Chapter Forty-one

After returning from Wichita, Phil spent the next couple of weeks working all he could at the service station. He became lonesome again now that he had lost Linda. Jim and Strawberry tried to entertain him as much as they could by having him over for meals and going to the movies. Occasionally, they would talk about when they were in Wichita during the war and Phil would become more cheerful.

One night Phil lay in bed thinking about his trip to Wichita and being with Jean. Lately, each time he thought of her he felt a tug in his heart for her. The more he thought of her, the more he yearned for her. He wanted to go back to see her so he decided to call her. She answered after a few rings.

"Hello."

"Jean? Is this Jean?" Phil asked hesitantly. He thought the voice did not sound like Jean.

"Yes, this is Jean Collier. Uh, is that you Phil?"

"Yes beautiful, this is me. What has happened to your voice? I didn't think it was you answering."

"I have a slight cold Phil and I'm a little hoarse, but I'm okay. It's so nice to hear from you! Are you doing alright?"

"Yes love, I'm okay. I just kept thinking of you. I miss you a lot."

"I've been missing you too, Phil. We had a wonderful couple of days together, didn't we?"

"Yes love, I remember. I remember a lot of days we had together. I want to see you again."

"Oh Phil, I want to see you again too!"

"Listen, how about if I get off a few days and come to see you in Kansas?"

"That would be wonderful, Phil. When can you come?"

"I think my boss will let me off for a week. I'll have to drive out, so it will take a couple of days. Tell you what, I'll see you on Monday or I'll call and let you know why I couldn't come. How about it?"

Saturday morning Phil left Raleigh and headed west on Highway 70. It was almost lunch time Monday when he pulled up to the apartment building where Jean lived. He thought of the many times he had been there and how every one had been pleasant. It seemed as if Strawberry and Jim would be coming out the front door anytime.

He went up the stairs to the second floor and knocked on Jean's door. She was supposed to be at home since she said that her father would let her off from the photo shop for a few days. Seconds later, she opened the door.

"Hello, beautiful!" he said, grabbing her tightly around the waist and kissing her on the cheek.

She turned her face and kissed him full on the lips. "Phil I missed you so much," she whispered into his ear. "I love you!"

"I love you too, beautiful," he whispered back. A happy chill ran up his spine at the sound of her words. They were sweet music to his ears.

"Aren't you hungry?" she asked momentarily. "I fixed some chicken for you!"

"Oh, you shouldn't have!" he replied, almost passing her going through the front door. "But you won't hear me complain."

That night they went to supper and then to a movie. After returning to Jean's apartment, they sat on the sofa listening to records. The soft, soothing tones of Glen Miller's clarinet made them both feel romantic. Before long, Phil pulled Jean close and they kissed each other passionately. Phil gazed into her greenish-blue eyes. They still had that bewitching glint that seemed to hold him like some sort of charm.

"Love, I have something to ask you," he said. Jean looked up into his brown eyes.

"Honey, what is it?" she whispered sweetly.

"Will you marry me?"

Jean looked deeply into his eyes, then pulled him to her tightly. "Oh, Phil. I've waited so long for this day. I think I've loved you since the first time we met. Of course I'll marry you."

The next three nights they went to the Club Lido. They ate, danced, and had a great time together. Phil discovered a new song that he dedicated to Jean each night. It was "I've got the sun in the morning and the moon at night."

On the last day of Phil's visit, Jean asked him to take her flying. He jumped at the suggestion. He had not felt like flying in a long time but her request suddenly exhilarated him. They went to the little airport on the outskirts of town where they used to rent a PT-19. Jean laughed and enjoyed the flight immensely. Phil was overjoyed at the feeling coursing through his body again. It was even better than it had ever been. He loved flying so much, and now that he had someone to love who shared that enjoyment, he didn't think life could get much better.

Phil had promised his boss that he would be back in time to work at the service station on Saturday. He didn't want to leave Jean, but felt that he should keep his word and return. She would need some time to prepare for their wedding anyway. They had set June 1st as their wedding day. Phil knew that he was supposed to report to California in mid-June, so they decided to get married when he came through Wichita on his way to his new duty.

Phil rolled down the window of the car as he headed east out of town towards Raleigh. The cool fresh morning air felt good as he left the city behind and entered the courntryside. He felt happier than he had been in years. He had to drive hard in order to get back to Raleigh on Friday night. He stopped at a motel only once and spent a few hours asleep in the car the next night. Then drove straight until he reached Raleigh. He arrived before bedtime so he called Jim to say that he was back in town safely.

Over the next few weeks, Phil called Jean almost every night. One night near the middle of May they were talking about being apart when Jean suddenly said, "Honey, I think I'll fly to Raleigh next weekend. I want to see you so badly! Besides, it would be nice to see Jim and Strawberry again."

"Hey love, that would be great!" Phil replied.

"Well, please ask Strawberry if I can stay a night with them, okay?"

"Oh, they would love for you to come. They'll be so happy to hear that you are coming. I know they are planning to be home this weekend. Just plan to come anyway. I know it will be okay."

"Well, if you're sure."

"Oh, I'm sure about that," he replied.

"Alright. I'll see you on Saturday morning. I love you, Phil."

"I love you too, Jean. I can hardly wait to see you!"

Of course Jim and Strawberry were happy to hear that Jean was coming to see them. On Saturday morning, they all piled into Phil's car and headed for the airport to pick up Jean. It was almost noon when her plane landed. When she came down the ramp of the plane, Phil ran out to greet her. They hugged and kissed each other happily. By the time they released each other, Jim and Strawberry had come up behind them. Jean hugged them both affectionately.

"Boy, Jim, I almost didn't recognize you without your uniform. But you are looking more handsome than ever."

"Hey, watch it," chided Strawberry. "That's my man," she giggled as they turned arm-in-arm toward the terminal. "Now tell me all about this wedding," Jean began as they walked away.

Moments later, Phil eased his '38 Chevy into low gear and pulled onto the highway for the twelve-mile trip back to Raleigh. Jean listened to Strawberry chatter in the back seat about what she and Jim had been doing since leaving Wichita. Occasionally, she glanced out the window of the car at the rolling hills, covered with oak and pine trees and thousands of flowers.

During a lull in Stawberry's conversation, Jean said, "Oh Phil, it is so beautiful here. These trees are so huge and everything is so green! But what are those lovely little trees with the white flowers all over them?"

"Those are Carolina Dogwoods, sweetheart."

"Well they are absolutely gorgeous," she exclaimed.

"Wait until you get closer to Raleigh. There are thousands of them there. We even have pink ones and red ones."

After they arrived at the Kelford's apartment, everyone freshened up and then they left for a place called The Chicken Shack for dinner and dancing. Phil liked to eat fried chicken there and dance to the music on the jukebox. It sort of reminded him of going to Cash Corner when he was a teenager.

As they sat at the table finishing their fried chicken, Jean remarked, "Phil, I believe this is better fried chicken than I make."

"Oh, I wouldn't say that," Phil replied. "But I do think they stole Strawberry's recipe," He winked at Strawberry, who giggled at his compliment. "Hey, let's dance," Phil said, grabbing Jean's hand.

"Pick out a good Glen Miller tune, Phil," she replied.

When the number ended, Jean turned to go toward their table, but Phil held her back for a moment. Suddenly, the song "Music, Music, Music" blared from the speakers. Phil had put two coins in the jukebox without telling Jean. He smiled at the questioning look on her face as the words rang out over the dance floor. "Put another nickel in, in the Nickelodeon. All I want is music, music, music!" he sang along with the song. "Hey beautiful," he said. "Let's jitterbug."

"Oh, Phil. You know I can't do that very well."

"Oh, yes you can."

He grabbed her hand and swung her around. Soon they had an open space to themselves in the middle of the dance floor. A lot of the other dancers, especially younger people, stopped to watch them dance. When they finished, the crowd applauded. Jean hurried back to their table and plopped down into her chair.

"Phil Barkley," she gasped. "Don't ever do that again. I am pooped!"

"Sweetheart," he grinned. "You were great. They loved you."

"But I'm not used to that kind of exercise."

Phil looked lovingly at this beauty he was to marry, thinking what a lucky man he was. The weekend would pass too quickly for him, but at that moment, he was aware of nothing in the room but Jean Collier and her bewitching, greenish-blue eyes.

"I swear, I don't think I've ever seen two people as happy together as you two," Jim exclaimed. Jean and Phil both blushed.

Chapter Forty-two

On the Monday after Jean had returned to Wichita, Phil received his orders from the Air Corps. After reading them, he decided to call Colonel Doakes.

"Phil, how are you my boy?" the Colonel's voice boomed over the phone a few moments later.

"Just fine, sir."

"Did you get your orders yet?"

"Yes, sir. I'll be reporting for duty on June 24th."

"That's great, son. I'm really looking forward to seeing you again. This program is even better than I had described it to you before. I can't wait to see your face after your first flight in a rocket powered plane."

Phil's mind flashed back to one day when he was sixteen, sitting on his father's front porch, reading a Buck Rogers comic book.

"That's why I'm calling, sir. I want to thank you for everything you've done for me. I really mean it when I say that getting into this program is a dream come true."

"Well, don't come out here thinking that I did you a great big favor, son. I wanted you here because you're one of the best young pilots I've ever known. By getting you into this program I'm doing myself a favor."

"Still," answered Phil, "I appreciate your help. By the way, I may need a bit more help for something else."

"What's that, my boy?"

"Do you think you could reserve one of those housing units that are just outside the base for me, sir?"

"You mean the ones for married Personnel, Phil?"

"Yes, sir."

"Well, congratulations you young son of a gun! I guess you finally convinced that 'Peaches' of yours to come along."

"Uh, not exactly, sir. This is the girl you met once at the Club Lido in Wichita. Her name is Jean Collier. I'll explain about 'Peaches' later."

"I see. Well, as I remember this girl from Wichita, she's a very Pretty girl. I wish you both the best, son. When is the wedding?"

"We're to be married on June first. Then we plan to spend our honeymoon in and around San Francisco."

"Sounds like a good plan, son. You relax a bit and see some of this great California countryside with the little lady, and leave the rest to me. I'll get you one of those nice officers' apartments and you can move right in as soon as you arrive how's that?"

"Great, sir! I know Jean will be happy to hear it."

The two men chatted a few more moments about some old

acquaintances before saying goodbye. That evening at six-thirty, Phil called Jean to tell her the good news about their housing arrangements. Then she told him how well their wedding plans were progressing.

"Mother has reserved the church for that Saturday, and we can use the fellowship hall downstairs for our reception afterwards," she explained. "By the way, while I was in Raleigh, I completely forgot to ask Jim and Strawberry if they could come to our wedding! Do you think they could?"

"Sure, honey," Phil replied. "I'll ask them today. As a matter of fact, I was thinking they could ride out with me, come to the wedding, then drive my car back to Raleigh. Jim could sell it and send us the money when we get to the air base. That '38 Chevy should bring at least a few hundred dollars."

"That's a good idea, Phil. I'm sure we will be able to use the money after we get settled in. You know, to buy curtains and things?"

"Uh, okay love. You may be right." The sound of excitement in her voice was so good to his ears, Phil couldn't bring himself to tell her that he had planned to use the money to buy another car once they reached California. He pictured his bride-to-be, standing in her apartment, talking to him on the phone. An almost overwhelming desire came over him to be there with her right at that moment. A second later, he said, "I miss you, Jean."

"I miss you too, Phil. Oh darling, I can hardly wait for June first to get here. I wish it was today!"

"Me too, love. Me too."

After saying goodbye, Phil decided to pay a visit to his old friends. When he arrived, Tim and strawberry were just finishing supper. Phil noticed a plate in the middle of their kitchen table in which pieces of ham peeked out from the sides of the few biscuits that remained.

"Go on, Phil," strawberry laughed as she caught him eyeing the food. "You know you're welcome to eat as many of those ham biscuits as you can hold. How about a Coke to wash them down?"

"Thanks," Phil replied with a grin as he sat down beside Jim. "How would you two like to come with me to Wichita for the wedding?" he got right to the point.

"That would be great!" Jim replied without hesitating. "But I'm afraid we can't afford the plane fare."

"Don't worry about that," Phil said just before biting into his treat.

"Does that mean you are going to pay for the tickets?"

"Not exactly," Phil muttered between bites.

"I'm afraid I don't understand," Jim said.

"We could drive out there," Phil began to explain. "Then

you and strawberry can drive my '38 Chevy back here. You could sell it for me and send the money to us in California."

Jim looked at his wife. "Sounds okay to me. I'll be on summer break from college. If strawberry could take off a few days from work, I don't see why we couldn't go. What do you think, honey?"

Strawberry couldn't hide the excitement in her voice as she said, "I'm sure I can get away for at least a week. Oh, Jim, I'd love to go to the wedding."

"Well, its settled," said Phil as he popped the last bite of the ham biscuit into his mouth.

"How much commission do I get from selling your car?" Jim asked jokingly.

"That depends," Phil replied. "On how much you sell it for, old boy. The higher the price, the higher your commission."

"Well, you can just start planning your retirement right now, buddy."

Phil let out a big laugh as Strawberry chimed in, "If Jim sells it, you'll be lucky to get cab fare, Phil."

"Wait and see," Jim retorted. "Wait and see."

During the next week, Phil spent his time saying his goodbyes to fellow workers and friends he'd come to know in the neighborhood. He cleaned his car so it shone like new money. He even made a trip out to say goodbye to Kent, his buddy who ran the airport. By Monday morning, May twenty-seventh, Phil had all his affairs settled, his bags packed, and his farewells complete. He closed up the apartment and left they key in his landlord's mailbox. When he arrived at Jim and Strawberry's place, he found them waiting in their living room with bags packed.

"I thought you were eager to get an early start, pal." Jim joked as they loaded the bags into the trunk of the Chevy.

"I would have been here earlier if I had known you were going to get you up before daylight. What did she use to get you out of bed, a stick of dynamite?"

"Actually, I got up first, old buddy. The trick was to allow her only ten minutes in front of the mirror."

Strawberry laughed and climbed into the back seat. "When you're married to someone as good looking as me, that's no trick at all, darling."

Phil and Jim looked at each other and laughed. "What have got to say to that?" Phil asked.

"What can I say," Jim replied. "I have to agree with her."

A moment later, the Chevy was moving westward, carrying three happy people, whose joking and easy laughter were borne out of a friendship that seemed to be years older than it really was, toward a new beginning.

They arrived in Wichita late Thursday afternoon as the sun

settled itself behind the flat horizon in a pink and purple blaze of color. Jean had moved out of her apartment during the previous week, so Phil drove straight to her parents' house. As he parked the car in their driveway, the porch light came on and it seemed that Jean was suddenly beside the car. She could hardly wait for Phil to get the door open before smothering him with hugs and kisses.

"Hey, save one of those for me," Jim said as he stretched his ride weary body and opened the car door for his wife.

Phil tossed the car keys to Jim. "You can have your hug after the bags are unpacked." They all laughed at Phil, whose face was covered with red lipstick smudges.

"Yes, master," Jim replied, bowing low and making a sweeping gesture with his hand.

Ten minutes later, they were all seated in the Collier's living room, sipping piping hot coffee and talking about their trip from Raleigh. An hour after that, Jean's mother was feeding them all a huge meal of roast beef, potatoes, and all the trimmings. By ten thirty, Jean's father was snoring softly upstairs, Jim and Strawberry were fast asleep in the guest bedroom, and Phil was snuggled under a blanket on the living room sofa. Jean and her mother, who were both too excited about the next two days to close their eyes before midnight, were quietly going over last minute wedding plans at the kitchen table.

Phil was very impressed as he walked with Jean through the church and fellowship hall the next morning. Mrs. Collier had decorated the church as well as any professional wedding director would have done. Jean didn't tell Phil how many issues of The Saturday Evening Post, McCall's, Look, and Life magazines she and her mother had examined at the public library, searching for ideas from photographs of other people's weddings and receptions.

"Mrs. Collier, this is just beautiful," Phil exclaimed. "I sure am lucky to have picked you for a mother-in-law."

Jean's mother blushed slightly. "Why thank you, Phil."

Early that evening, the two young couples piled in Phil's car and headed toward the Club Lido for a "last" evening of dining and dancing. Even though he knew it was going out of style, Phil was looking and hoping he would get to dance the Jitterbug one more time.

"Hey Phil, let's drive past our old apartment building," Jim suggested.

"Yeah," Strawberry chimed in. "That's a great idea!"

Moments later, as they sat in front of the familiar building, Phil began to remember the first time he came to Wichita. He would never forget how Jean's bewitching eyes and dark hair had captivated him. He glanced at her and smiled.

"What are you thinking about, Phil?" Jean asked.

"About how you cast a magic spell over me the first time we met, hon."

"Come on, you two. You're not going to get all mushy on us are you?" Jim teased.

"Did you hear a noise in the back seat, darling?" Phil teased back. The girls laughed.

A few moments later, as they continued toward the nightclub, Phil's memories returned to that first night he met Jean. He would never forget the feeling he had as he lay on Jim's sofa, trying to think of Linda, but not able to forget Jean.

At nine o'clock the next morning, they all sat down to a sumptuous breakfast of hotcakes, bacon, eggs, biscuits, coffee, and strawberry preserves. Jean's mother told them to eat hardy because they would get no lunch, since the wedding was at one o'clock that afternoon.

As they were finishing the meal, Jean's father pushed his chair slightly away from the table and leaned back. "Phil, you ought to get married more often," he joked. "I haven't eaten like this in years."

"Listen to you," Mrs. Collier teasingly chided her husband. "You'd be as big as a house if I fed you any more than you already eat."

Mr. Collier threw her a kiss across the table. "Phil, if Jean turns out to be half as good as her mother, you'll be a happy man like me." Jean's mother blushed.

"Well, Mr. Collier," Phil replied, "I've always heard the fruit doesn't fall far from the tree."

"Well," Jim chimed in, "it has taken me a couple of years to train my wife, but I think she turned out okay too." He ducked as Strawberry swiped at him with her napkin.

"Okay, boys," Mrs. Collier scolded. "That's enough buttering up the women. You three need to go upstairs and start getting ready. We have to be at the church by quarter past twelve." She rose from her seat. "Girls, let's just stack these dishes over next to the sink. I'll wash them tonight."

As they climbed the stairs, Jim put his arm over Phil's shoulder. "You getting nervous, pal?"

"Well, it is my first wedding," Phil replied.

"You'll get over it," Jim chuckled. "It's kind of like flying. No matter how many times you go up, you never forget your solo. But each day after that, it gets easier."

They stopped near the bathroom door. Jim noticed a tear welling up in Phil's right eye and knew he was thinking about Linda. He suddenly grabbed Phil and hugged him hard.

"Hey buddy. Everything's going to be okay." He leaned back a moment later, holding Phil by the shoulders. "You got the right girl, Phil. Do you understand? You made the right decision."

Phil wiped the tear from his eye. "Yeah, pal. I know you're

right. I've thought about it a lot over the past month. I loved her so much and I thought she loved me. But she didn't love all of me like Jean does. She never could love the part of me that has to fly. I just could never understand why."

"Well, it's time to let it pass," Jim said. "There's a pretty little girl downstairs who loves every ounce of you, even the part that has to fly." He patted Phil on the shoulder. "Now, if you don't get in that bathroom and get ready, I'm going to get in there first and use up all the hot water."

Phil laughed, then took a deep breath. "Thanks, Jim. I'm not sure what I would have done if it hadn't been for you and Strawberry sticking with me through everything."

"Do you remember the first time I threw a football at you?" Jim asked.

"Yeah, sure," Phil answered with a puzzled look. "It hit me in the head because I wasn't paying attention."

Jim smiled. "I knew we were going to be best friends from that minute," he said. "Anyone who could take a shot like that and get right back in the game, had to be okay."

They chuckled together over the memory and then Phil went into the bathroom to shave.

When Phil, Jim, and Strawberry arrived at the church, there was already a large crowd of people gathering by the front door. Phil had become so nervous that he stumbled a few times as they went up the steps.

"Hey, old man," Jim teased. "You need some help?"

"Cut it out," Phil replied. "I'll be okay."

"Yeah, but will it be today?" said Jim.

"Leave him alone, Jim," Strawberry scolded as they reached the top of the steps. When they were inside the church, she grabbed Phil and stood him in front of her.

"You look so handsome, Phil," she said while straightening his tie. "There's nothing like a military dress uniform to make a man look like a million bucks!"

It seemed like only a few minutes later when Phil realized he and Jim were at the front of the church, with the minister nearby, waiting for the wedding march to begin. Suddenly, the familiar music began and everyone in the audience stood, turned, and looked down the aisle expectantly.

Phil's heart leaped as Jean and her father stepped into the doorway at the other end of the aisle. She was more beautiful than she had ever seemed before. The white wedding gown and the long train that flowed behind were punctuated with the small bouquet of pink roses Jean held in her hands. She simply dazzled everyone, including Phil. But he could think of nothing but Jean's eyes and how they sparkled. Her smile told him that this was the happiest day of her life and that she was so proud to be marrying him. He took a deep breath to get rid of the lump in his throat. In his mind, Phil practiced saying "I do."

Two hours later, the happy couple ran down the front steps through a shower of rice and jumped into the back seat of Phil's car, where Jim and Strawberry were waiting to take them to the Wichita airport.

"Does this cab go to the airport?" Phil joked.

"How much money do you have, sir?" Jim played along.

"Do you mean to tell me my wife's good looks aren't enough?" said Phil. "All I have besides that is about a hundred pounds of rice in my shorts."

They all burst out laughing as Jim sped away from the church amidst the clanking noise of the tin cans that were tied to the rear bumper. Phil glanced at Jean to find her staring at him with a strange look in her eyes.

"What is it, sweetie?" he asked.

"Oh, Phil. I love you so much," she replied and threw her arms around his neck and smothered his lips with passion. They were still kissing when Jim stopped the car at the airport.

"All ashore that's going ashore," Jim said loudly.

"Do we have to?" Phil said as he broke his embrace with Jean.

"Why, not at all, pal. Strawberry and I would be glad to take over here. We could use a honeymoon trip to California."

Fifteen minutes later, Phil and Jean were standing at the gate, saying their goodbyes to Jim and Strawberry.

"Thanks for everything, buddy," Phil said as he shook Jim's hand. "Come out to see us sometime."

"We plan to," Jim replied. "Call us when you get settled in at the base."

"Okay, girls," Phil teased. "It's time to dry the tears and put away the hankies." Phil hugged Strawberry, then put his arm around Jean's shoulder and they walked toward the plane.

As their friends were climbing the ladder, Strawberry took Jim's hand and said, "Honey, I think Phil has finally found his second fiddle."

"I think you're right, love," Jim replied, thinking about the scene in front of the bathroom door that morning. "I never saw either of them any happier. Now I'm satisfied that Phil's dreams will come true."

Seeing Jean's face through one of the plane's windows, Strawberry waved a final goodbye. "I think they already have, Jim."

About the Author

Lester Mitchell was born in Johnston County, North Carolina near Kenly. He served in the U.S. Army Air Corps as a test pilot during World War II. He retired from the U.S. Postal Services in 1984 in which he covered the North and South Carolina territory for the Engineering Department. Since his retirement, writing is one of his hobbies. He now lives in Raleigh, North Carolina.